Dreamer's Folly

Book One of The Wayward Light Saga
A. Samuel Bales

Cassian Press

ISBN: 979-8-9884875-1-7 (paperback)

ISBN: 979-8-9884875-2-4 (hardcover)

ISBN: 979-8-9884875-0-0 (ebook)

Library of Congress Control Number: 2023911189

Book Cover by Alejandro Colucci

First edition 2024

Published by Cassian Press

www.asamuelbales.com

To skeptics, who improve our world simply by questioning it. To my wife, who, on the other hand, never doubted. To my mom, dad, and brother who are always there for me. And to my children, Finny and Cassidy, who taught me the meaning of life.

When the last flame dies and the frigid cold of a winter night tightens its grip beyond the very bones... when even the most tenacious have succumbed and by all logic our only hope should be for a swift end, faith draws yet another breath.

But how many faithful lie frozen in the snows? And why—because robed men the world over preach their tales with illogical conviction? Should not this deceit earn our rebuke? Yet, if faith helps but one survive the night, was it not just? Need not the human soul a beacon to guide it? Is it not just as vile to hold decency and peace in one's hand, yet not administer it?

—Vincet Ellemere

CHAPTER ONE

"Traveler's trousers!" Jeld panted as he slowed from a sprint at the crest of a hill.

Beyond a stretch of verdant fields below, the city of Tovar sprawled almost endlessly in either direction. To the east, the River Kline swept past to spill into the glimmering ocean pressed against the city's backside. Even the great ocean seemed dwarfed by Tovar. But before it all, the jagged beginnings of a tower of black stone marred the pristine countryside.

The boy collapsed onto his rear, sucking in heavy breaths. He was small of stature, his dark hair never neat, and his blue eyes quick and curious, as if the secrets of the world might escape should he move too slowly. Not but a blink after he sat, the sound of rapid footfalls filled the air and his sister called out from behind.

"I almost had you this time!" Niya said.

"I should hope so, your legs grew nearly a leap since last year."

Even three years Jeld's junior, Niya was almost as tall now. The chill fall breeze tousled her hair. It was short as girls' hair went, its length just beyond the width of her father's fist, the meager excess marking the time since last she'd earned a hacking with his long knife.

"A leap? I don't know about—*Idols*, is that the new prison?"

"Thinkin' so," Jeld said. "Not exactly welcoming."

"*Prince's Prison*, didn't that fellow call it?"

Jeld eyed the elaborate spired keep overlooking the rest of the city from atop the western cliffs, then looked back to the prison.

"Yeah. Welcome to you too, Prince Dralor."

Niya collapsed at his side and they both fell silent.

"Do you think we'll stay long this time?" she asked after a while.

"Depends on the winter, I suppose. 'Wagoners don't get paid for leavin' shit where it's at,'" Jeld mocked in his father's low growl.

Jeld felt Niya tense beside him. Not knowing how to respond, he stayed silent and let his eyes trace the city wall. The wall might be called modest were it surrounding a smaller city, but around the vast Tovar it was called a marvel. His gaze followed the wall past the grand northern gate to a less extravagant one the traders called Kingsfinger Gap, where taxmen would soon dip the king's greedy fingers into his father's purse.

Niya's unease tugged again at Jeld's awareness and he tore his attention from the city to ponder how to cheer her up. His eyes settled by chance upon her battered and muddied boots and an idea struck him.

"Oh, someone isn't going to like that one bit."

Niya's eyes widened.

Jeld winced. "Er, not Quintem. *Him.*"

Niya followed Jeld's gaze to her filthy boots and a huge grin stretched wide as Tovar across her face.

"Cobb!" she said, jumping to her feet. "I wonder if he sold his prized boots yet. Or broke down and wore them?"

Jeld laughed. "Not a chance. Every traveler too dirty, every king too clean, and—"

"'And every cobbler too poor!'"

Jeld stood as Niya joined in his laughter. He was equally fond of the old cobbler, his thoughts already drifting back over the years to their first wintering with him, back even before the dear man had built their little sleeping roosts across the attic joists. He smiled wider.

"Hya! Hya!" came their father's distant bark.

Their smiles melted away. Certain Quintem wasn't just barking to the horses, Jeld walked over the crest of the hill and looked about. On the road below, their father sat at the front of his wagon cracking the reins at his team. Behind him, encouraged by a taut rope, another team of horses followed with a second wagon. Quintem didn't look back as he rounded the final bend toward Tovar, and Jeld wasn't sure he would at all before disappearing into the city without Niya and him.

"He's up ahead already," Jeld called over his shoulder. "I imagine he'll remember us when he gets to wrestling our wagon through the city, and not fondly."

Jeld set off down the hill at a jog. Niya followed close behind, all traces of the happiness she'd found left upon the hilltop behind her.

"Hello, Da!" she called, running ahead toward Quintem's wagon.

Jeld studied his sister as he approached the rear wagon. Her smile was almost as wide as the one she'd worn on the hill, but it didn't touch her eyes the way it had at his mention of Cobb. He could see the difference with little effort, a talent for which he had his father to thank. It was a skill not born of the blood but honed within it.

He patted his horses. "Hello Stalus. And hello Lionus."

Untying the tow rope, he climbed up onto his wagon and took the reins. Ahead, Niya crouched atop the back of Quintem's wagon and coiled in the rope dragging behind. She then scurried over the huge mound of goods and sat beside their father.

"Would you like me to drive so you can check the books and wares before the gap, Father?"

Jeld looked on as his father raised an eyebrow at Niya. Quintem would never see through her act, but that wouldn't stop him from suspecting foul play on pessimism alone, especially on a tax day. Jeld reached back and rested his hand upon a crate. It wouldn't be the first he'd broken to divert his father's ire.

Quintem squinted at her before grunting and handing her the reins. He pulled a hefty ledger from beneath his seat and began to pore over a page.

Jeld slowly returned his hand to the reins as they drove on, though his eyes lingered on Quintem and Niya beyond the bulging mound of goods packing their wagon. Their haul was always at its largest on the way to Tovar, traders loading up their livelihoods city after city. For all else, people knew his father as a man who would not be stopped by anything, and their confidence was not misplaced. The very wagon beneath Jeld was a testament to that, he considered. *Bandit*, he and Niya had dubbed it, compliments of the trio foolish enough to have attempted getting in their father's way.

His breath caught as bright red flashed in his memory—blood soaking across a white shirt, a glistening sword, a man's terror-stricken eyes...

Jeld shook the memory aside. Never mind all that. Things had been a whole lot better ever since that day. Bandit was so much more than a wagon, it was freedom. Their own space. Space away from Quintem. He smiled as he drove on toward Tovar. Wintering in the city was much the same—freedom.

When at last they reached Kingsfinger Gap, Niya rejoined Jeld and they stared through it with wide eyes. The road, which had turned from packed dirt to rough stone not long before, pierced through the gate as if into another world, quickly disappearing beneath the feet of a bustling crowd.

"If I wanted his fingers in my arse, I'd buy him a drink first, shiny tits!" Quintem barked up ahead.

A city guardsman outside the gap howled in laughter, his polished chest plate catching the sun with each chuckle.

"I've been waiting here an Idol's damn naptime to hear your next line. What was it last time? Somethin' about my sister pulling your wagon?"

Jeld shook his head. People often thought his father was a hoot, as if his foul slurs were merely in jest.

"It ain't the only thing she pulls," Quintem grumbled. "Arright, just be on to the market then."

The guardsman cackled. "Nice try. You know the drill, off to the tax line. On through, on through." He turned to the next traveler. "On up, on up!"

As they rode through the gap, a wave of activity nearly knocked Jeld from his wagon. His eyes flicked through the crowd from face to face, mind reeling as he unthinkingly searched for any of the thousand shades of dangerous he had learned to spot upon his father.

Following Quintem, Jeld pulled his wagon to a stop before a fancy building flying the king's colors—a white sword set against a deep crimson. A stout stone obelisk stood beside the entry walk, the likeness of an imposing fortress etched into it. *Havaral,* Jeld recognized from his single yet unforgettable visit there years back. Once the capital under the mad king's rule, the impenetrable stronghold remained the symbol of the kingdom's treasury, the purse of Avandria.

A bored-looking guard circling two other wagons ahead of them expanded his route to envelop their own. Quintem stood and craned his neck as if he might behold some surmountable obstacle to be bashed rather than merely the backside of a line, until at last an older gentleman approached. He walked at a prompt pace that Jeld had not forgotten, his every movement sharp despite his age.

"Good Quintem, welcome," the magistrate said. "Children. My, you've grown."

"Minol," Quintem grumbled.

He dismounted with his overgrown ledger in hand as the taxman circled their wagons like a general surveying a battlefield.

Porters soon approached and began unloading Quintem's wagon.

"Actually, good Quintem, let us do our business more comfortably inside. I trust I can draw my documents from your books just fine."

"That why you're tearing my wagons apart?"

Magistrate Minol smiled. "Shall we?"

He turned and started toward the office at his brisk pace. Quintem followed, as did Jeld, hopping down from his wagon and jogging after them. Just outside the door, Quintem turned and frowned down toward Jeld, who backtracked until a hand pressed to his back. Jeld spun to find Niya just behind.

"I need to learn the business, Da," she pleaded. "Then one day I'll be able to take care of myself. Wouldn't you like that?"

"'Tis a day sad but oh so proud when our little birds flit from the nest," the magistrate mused, all the philosopher. "And oh so freeing it is..."

"Huhng," Quintem grunted, all the ape.

Magistrate Minol nodded toward the vacant guard. "Our good guardsman Ginald is dedicated to securing your goods while we conduct business."

"That right? Not to keep us from driving on past before the king gets his fistful?"

The magistrate led them inside without another word, Quintem giving Niya a stern glare before following after. Bright wood paneling lined the walls of a large room within. Upon one wall hung a portrait of Tovados—warrior Idol, namesake of the city, and progenitor of the royal line. A desk spanned the length of the room before countless shelves packed with ledgers.

Magistrate Minol lifted a hinged expanse of the desk and passed through, catching it behind him at the last moment. He dragged a chair across from where Quintem had sat notably not opposite then delicately set his ledger upon the desk and flipped it open with aimless precision. As he had made no attempt to further navigate the ledger, it seemed either exactly the page he'd intended, or no page in particular. Jeld guessed the former.

"To business," the magistrate said. "Your books please, good Quintem."

"We *could* go a little easy," Quintem said, sliding his ledger toward the magistrate. "Our friend wouldn't miss the difference. Might be more in it for you, too."

"I'm certain he *would* miss it. I assure you, our *king* is quite content with our arrangement."

The magistrate pulled Quintem's ledger closer and peered down at it over his nose.

"More bearskins this year," he muttered, blindly scribbling notes as he read. "Last year it was cowhides, was it not? Well, fashions do change. And berry wine, fine polishes, leather swatches. Nails, ales, wool. Ashwood. Quite a journey. Must have been... Joggeton,

Wayvalley... Plemenol, Glendmill... Delvarad—my, you've been halfway across Avandria haven't you?"

"Trenton too," Niya blurted, earning a glare from her father. "We stopped there to buy iron. The nail makers in Plemenol give a steep discount if you trade iron."

"Ah, Trenton! Of course, my girl. Very efficient is your father."

The magistrate gave Niya a warm smile then went on murmuring about trade trends and scribbling notes until at last he made a final mark with a flourish and turned around two identical documents more fine than most paintings. Niya craned her neck as the magistrate passed one to Quintem.

"Er, it seems low," she said. "Aren't our books a bit—"

Quintem slapped the back of her head and snatched up his copy, slamming his ledger closed around it.

"Khapar's blazes, girl! You—"

A stern gaze from Minol stifled Quintem's curse.

"Are we done here?" Quintem asked.

The door creaked open. One of the young porters from outside entered and handed Minol a parchment.

"Sir, the tally."

"Thank you, Noel," Magistrate Minol replied.

The magistrate looked over the document then smiled through a disdain Jeld now realized had been there all along.

"Once again, your books speak the perfect truth. I drew my copy short one case of bear pelts for you, for raising such a promising young lady."

"Pleasure," Quintem said. He walked toward the door with steps that wordlessly beckoned his children.

"Thank you, Magistrate," Niya said, rubbing the back of her head. "It was a pleasure doing business with you."

Jeld nodded to the magistrate and followed after his father and sister.

"It is always a pleasure doing business with you as well," Magistrate Minol called after them.

"*Children,*" he added once Quintem had passed through the door.

***

Jeld gave a fresh board at the end of an otherwise faded wooden platform another stroke of his file and looked over to Cobb. Stripes of light from between the boards of the attic walls crossed the old cobbler's face.

"That should do," Cobb said. "Nicely done, you two."

Niya fanned a blanket over the newly extended platform and laid down, stretching out her legs.

"Ahhh," she sighed. "It's perfect."

"Good, good. I wish you would have told me sooner."

"I'm happy enough just not having to share Quintem's room, bed or no bed. To be honest, I was too tired to notice. I always forget how busy he keeps us the first few days."

"Perhaps not the best roommate, your father. Well I hope I didn't work you too hard today."

"Oh no," Jeld said. "Believe me, it was great to be at it again. Besides, have to earn our worth."

"Your father pays a fair boarding. But if you insist, Idols know I can use the help. And the company."

"As long as the day ends in a bowl of *sole stew*, you won't hear us complain."

Cobb smiled. "I'm glad my recipe hasn't lost its shine, but I think we'll try something different tomorrow."

"Let me guess," Niya said. "Sole *thick soup?*"

Cobb winked at her then grabbed a rafter overhead and pulled himself upright with a groan.

"I'm getting too old for crawling around in attics. I think you two might be on your own next time if you don't quit all that growing."

"We can manage," Jeld said. "You always see to that. Thanks Cobb."

"Oh, it's nothing personal. Just laziness, really. The more I teach you, the less work I have to do myself, you see?"

"Sure, whatever you say, Cobb," Niya said.

"And I say plenty, don't I? Enough for one day, anyway. You two rest up. Plenty of feet to clothe tomorrow."

"Good night, Cobb."

"Looking forward to it," Jeld said.

Clinging to the rafters, Cobb crossed the attic and ducked out through a small opening.

Jeld crossed to his own platform and pulled off his boots. The lingering daylight was almost giddying, a sweet reminder of how much sleep he'd be getting tonight. His eyes fell closed the moment his back pressed against his bedroll.

"Do you think the taxman is in on it?" Niya asked.

Jeld groaned. "Huh?"

"Magistrate Minol. He only wrote down part of our haul."

Jeld rolled over to face her. "On about that paper again? Probably just Quintem underreporting."

"Well, he was. But the magistrate's numbers were even lower."

"Maybe Quintem moved more stuff into our smuggler's hold."

"He did that too, but it was lower *still.*"

"Maybe the magistrate messed up?"

"Minol?" Niya scoffed. "He's got to be in on it! In on something... but Quintem smuggles to keep money from the taxman. Why would the taxman help?"

"Quintem always says that everyone's in it for the same thing."

"Money."

"Yeah. But I think all I'm in it for right now is sleep. Goodnight, sis."

"Alright. Goodnight."

Jeld closed his eyes. He let out a deep breath and felt his body sink with a wonderful weight toward dreams.

"Play watchers?" Niya asked.

Jeld sat up. "Yup!"

He pulled on his boots and they both hurried up a ladder and through a trapdoor onto the roof. A bench sat just behind a low parapet.

"Looks like Cobb spruced it up again, yeah?" Jeld said, sitting upon the bench.

Niya sat beside him. "Definitely. Good as the day he built it."

Down below, a woman emerged from an alley and hurried down the street.

"Her," Jeld said.

"Something happened... she didn't even have time to put on the coat under her arm."

"I think that's an apron she's got. Just a server running late to work, I think?"

Niya nodded. As the woman turned toward a tavern, a man in a tattered black robe reached out toward her imploringly and called out.

"Drink fouls our hearts! The juice of chaos and anger! And sadness! How can *They* love what cannot love itself? Abstain! Repent! Rekindle the light between us, and They will return!"

"Idols!" Niya swore as the woman hurried into the tavern. "I'd hoped the Sayers would have run out of things to *say* since last winter."

The Sayer started slowly down the street, turning his attention to another passerby.

"Came together in dreams to lead us to salvation from the mad king, and how do we repay them? With sin! With death! With disorder! They have not risen to protect us, but have fled our wickedness! There *is* no great *Discord*, only the discord in our hearts!"

Niya's word of complaint but a distant whisper, Jeld's imagination drifted with the Sayer's words.

"How is it that Cobb isn't Idolic?" Niya asked.

"Hmm?" Jeld blinked his daydreams aside. "Oh. Er, Idolic *cobblers?* Don't you think the Idols' touch would just be for more... well, interesting talents? You know, like General Handan Tovaine melting through a battlefield, not... not someone making shoes?"

"But Cobb says anyone good enough at anything can be Idolic. He's as good as they come. How could that blacksmith down the street be Idolic but not Cobb?"

"Doesn't Cobb also say any craftsman below Hilltop with Deylus's hand by their door is either a total fraud or the most decent tradesman in Avandria?"

"So... maybe she's decent."

Jeld shook his head. "Fraud. Cobb's right. If that smith was Idolic she'd be selling weapons and armor on Hilltop, not making nails in Midtown."

"That one there," Niya said, pointing to a man walking below. "Just got off work at... at the docks. He's bringing that bread and flowers to his girlfriend. But he's... anxious? A first date! He's nervous for his date!"

Jeld nodded along. "Messy sun-bleached hair, dark tan... a dock worker alright. Taking bread and flowers to dinner, yeah. A date... but I think he's already bound."

"Nervous for a date with his own wife?"

"No, I think the date is with someone else."

"What! How do you figure?"

"He keeps fidgeting with that little tunic pocket," Jeld said. "He's hiding his binding rings in there."

"You're as bad as Quintem! You always see the worst of people."

"I'm not like him and you know it, but if there is anything he does right it's spotting wolves behind smiles."

"He doesn't *spot* wolves, he assumes *everyone* is a wolf!"

"But I'm not doing that! I see smiling sheep sometimes... I can't help it if there are a lot of wolves out there."

Niya looked him in the eye. "I *challenge.*"

"Challenge? Already? You won't get another until Hallsday if I'm right."

"You're not. Let's go chase that sheep!"

Niya ran toward the edge of the roof and leapt off, plunging from sight.

"Now who sounds like a wolf!" Jeld called.

Rubbing his eyes, he let out a breath of laughter and chased after his little sister.

CHAPTER TWO

N iya pressed her needle through a half-fastened toe patch and tugged her stitch tight. There was little else wrong with the boot by its owner's account, but as was Cobb's way she'd be hunched over her workbench sprucing it up for the better part of the next bell. Unlike the rest of the workshop tucked away in the back, the table at which she sat protruded into the showroom. A prime spot from which to demonstrate workmanship, Cobb would say, but more so to better jump to the aid of customers. And so he had.

"A woman's shoe," a young man said down his nose, his voice thick with a Topper-tongue accent.

Cobb replaced the shoe and beckoned the Hilltopper to another nearby display. He held up a pair with intricately etched leather and a pointed toe polished to a mirror.

"They are lined with sheepskin from the flocks of Glendmill," Cobb said. "I can tell you many things, but if you try them on, *they* will tell you so much more."

The man sneered at the shoe like a starving man considering a molded roll before sitting in a plush chair with a grimace and holding out his foot.

Niya scowled. It was her favorite chair. Her frown deepened as Cobb began servilely to work the buckles on the man's shoe.

She winced at the poke of a needle. Sucking her finger, she sighed at a meandering seam and set to work making corrections. She was halfway through mending the second boot when Cobb set two steaming bowls upon her workbench and sat beside her.

"Two more happy customers," he said.

Niya blinked. "Two? I only saw the snooty boy."

"Right."

Niya blinked again.

"And left," Cobb said with the slightest wink. "The two customers."

"Oh! I get it. How is it that you never run out of clever jokes?"

"Oh I think I ran out of the clever ones a long time ago. These are all I have left."

Niya smiled, but her face grew serious as she watched Cobb look over her work.

"You really love what you do, don't you, Cobb?" she asked after a while.

"You know that I do. There is nothing more important than being passionate about one's trade."

"What of servants like the ones that change that snoot's nappy? They can't love their trade."

Cobb frowned. "You're right, as usual. Maybe it isn't about trades. Perhaps we all just need something to live for, be it trade, family, hobby."

He tapped one of Niya's nails deeper. "What would you like to do someday?"

"I want to own a shop," Niya said at once.

"A noble dream! What manner of shop?"

"A food shop."

"Like a butcher or a baker? Or a fruit stand in the market? Or you mean a corner store with flour and nuts and whatnot?"

"All of that. Bread, meat, fruits and vegetables, flour, nuts. All of it, and even cooked meals! An *everything* store!"

"Hmm. Hmmhmm..."

Niya pursed her lips, her heart quickening with each thoughtful flicker of Cobb's eyes.

"Huhm," Cobb said at last. "I wonder why nobody has done this yet? It's quite brilliant, actually."

Niya beamed. "Patrons would need only visit one store. And the *meals*, well, I know from living on the road that not everyone has a—"

Niya froze as a shout carried in from outside. She couldn't make out the words, but she knew the voice – and the tone.

"Go to the back!" Cobb said.

Niya's eyes glazed over. A thousand horrific memories pressed in around her until there was nothing but despair.

Cobb's hand closed on her shoulder and she sucked in a breath, her wide eyes snapping to his.

"The back," Cobb said. "Now!"

She ran. The front door crashed open just as she disappeared into the workshop.

"Girl!" came Quintem's roar.

"Please, keep your voice down," she heard Cobb say. "The children are sleeping above."

Cobb's hammer tapped along with Niya's every footfall as she scoured the workshop for a place to hide.

"Where is she!" Quintem barked, his words slurred.

"I told you, sleeping above. Please, calm yourself—"

Niya jumped as a crashing cut off Cobb's words. She scrambled behind some crates and began burying herself in a pile of leathers.

"I ought to give you the message for her, you gutless old fool! Got a problem with me and you can't bring it to my face? You take it to the Mother-bleedin' law?"

"I said nothing of you, Quintem. I saw your books and I had to report that magistrate, but I didn't say a word about you, Quintem. Not a word."

"Save it! What do you care if I pocket a few pebs of your precious tax money? It was my purse or the king's. Who do you think needs it more?"

"Quintem, I—"

"Like ya haven't taken a shortcut to save a peb? You've bought cheap leather to save a nickel, I know it 'cause I shipped it for you! It's the same damned thing! Now where is she!"

"What's this got to do with Niya? This is business between us."

"Only she knew!"

"I told you, I saw your books. But I didn't report you. Are you in trouble with the law? I was very careful about—"

"The law? You naive old prick, the people you're pissin' with *own* the law! And now they own me."

"Quintem, please, I can help—"

"You don't know these bastards! You don't know what you stirred. I'm through thanks to you and that treacherous rat! Damn it, where is she!"

"Please, this is strictly between us. Let her sleep."

Niya flinched at the sound of something shattering.

"You forgot to hide her shitty stew! And books be damned. Smuggling be damned. This is about compromising a bought magistrate. *Rusrivon's* bought magistrate, damn it! Only the girl knew. Where is she!"

"Wait, you're right. You're right. I merely overheard her talking to her brother. She never betrayed you. Never. This is between—"

Cobb cried out behind the sound of a blow.

Niya curled herself tighter into a ball, fighting futilely to still her shaking.

"Stop this, you ape!" Cobb roared. "This will not solve anything! Get out of my shop! Get out! Out!"

"Where!"

"Gone! She's—"

Cobb cried out again.

"You've tormented these children enough! Out! Get out!"

Niya hugged her legs tight as Cobb's pained yet defiant screams assailed her, worse than any beating she'd endured. And it was all for her... to protect *her*. Eyes mad as she beat back the fear, her jaw set and she crawled from her hiding spot.

Running back toward Cobb, her legs brought her to a sudden stop despite her resolve as she spotted Quintem through the clutter of the shop. His face was twisted in madness, his forehead wet with sweat, eyes drunk with rage. Blood gleamed upon his knuckles.

Niya tried to move, tried to speak, but couldn't. Then her eyes fell upon Cobb. He lay spilled over his workbench, fighting to lift his battered face from the pair of boots she'd been working on in that distant, peaceful life. She steeled her nerves and stormed into the open.

"Father, please!"

"Niya, run away!" Cobb shouted.

"Girl! Get over here!" Quintem roared, his unsteady eyes shooting past Niya before turning back to lock onto her.

Niya unconsciously backpedaled. "I didn't tattle. I didn't tell anyone!"

Quintem stormed toward her. "Good girls don't hide!"

"Stop this, you fool!" Cobb called after him.

"I didn't tell anyone!" Niya pleaded. "I didn't! Please!"

Niya fought to keep from fleeing the beast. She had tried running once before, and never again. But then she met his eyes and knew today was different. Just as he closed on her, she turned and dashed back into the workshop, weaving between shelves and crates and workbenches.

Quintem shouted some terrible and unintelligible curse and crashed after her.

Where? Where! Wiseman show me!

Niya searched desperately for a place to hide as she ran, but quickly realized hiding was futile—escape was her only option, and that meant she had to circle past him.

"Da please!" she called to lure him aside then started toward the opposite wall.

She sped along a narrow row of supply shelves. Straight ahead, across the showroom, the door of the shop hung open. Her eyes fixed unblinkingly upon it as her arms pumped her flight ever faster.

Almost—

A hand shot out and bit down upon her wrist. She cried out as a horrible tearing pain erupted in her shoulder, and suddenly she was flying backward like a child's dolly in the terrible grip. She slammed into a workbench and screamed into her father's mad eyes as he wrenched her atop it. She could almost thank his fist when it rose to cover those horrible eyes, but then it fell. Pain exploded in her temple and her head slammed back into the tabletop.

Niya frantically bucked, pushed, pulled – fought with each and every muscle to break free, but it was futile. She screamed a horrible, agonized scream before another blow smashed against her forehead. Then another. And another. Soon she didn't feel the blows, only heard them, and somehow that was worse. Her screams turned to muffled sobs and she cursed her lingering consciousness.

***

Jeld's heart sank at the sound of a distant scream. He cracked the reins hard, driving Stalus and Lionus into a sprint. It was only a few short breaths before he could see the shop ahead, its door hanging open to the evening air.

"Treacherous bitch, you ruined me!" Quintem's voice roared over the clapping of hooves.

Jeld leapt from the wagon and ran toward the door.

"Stop this!" Cobb called. "Quintem, enou—" His words cut off in a pained grunt.

Jeld ran into the shop, his eyes wide and heart thumping as he dashed deeper toward a faint and horrible wailing. He took no notice of the carnage he passed, not even the remnants of a bowl of stew shattered against Cobb's prized display. Everything was a blur. There was only Niya's cries.

Suddenly he froze, his senses racing to catch up. Just ahead, Cobb was struggling feebly to his knees, his blood-soaked face a mask of agony and sheer determination. Beyond him Jeld spotted Quintem, mad eyed and wet with sweat and blood and spittle. On a table before him, Niya's face was a nightmarish mess of blood, her limbs limp and eyes shut. She was silent now.

Cobb collapsed and Jeld met his pained eyes before the old cobbler seemed to nod at something ahead. Jeld followed Cobb's gaze across the floor and understanding dawned on him. Creeping ahead, he grabbed the tack hammer just beyond Cobb's reach, tucked it into the back of his trousers, and stepped out into the open.

"Boy," Quintem said. "She's done it now. Sold us out. Tried to ruin us both. Cheated us!"

Quintem reached back for another blow.

"Wait!" Jeld yelled.

He ran to his father's side and looked down at the small, still form of his beaten, bloodied sister. Fighting to hold his rage and grief at bay, he put a hand upon Quintem's shoulder.

"It'll be okay," he said. "We survive, remember?"

Quintem turned and a breath of ale pressed against Jeld.

"No, boy. The bastards cut me out. Girl's done us in this time. Her and the cobbler both."

Quintem reached his clenched fist higher and swung. Jeld pulled the tack hammer from behind his back and brought it down with what little windup he could afford. It slammed with a ring like steel on rock against the back of his father's head and he fell to his elbows over Niya. His dazed and drunken eyes slowly taking in the wild fury upon Jeld's face, he scowled and reached out.

Jeld swung harder, this time to a wet crunch. Quintem collapsed atop Niya and the sight of him upon her set Jeld's blood boiling further still. With an inhuman roar Jeld pushed and pushed at Quintem until they both tumbled to the floor. Though Quintem lay motionless, his face pressed into the floor, Jeld swung again. Then again. Blood spattered across his face and still he swung and swung until the crunching turned to the rap of steel upon the wooden floor and the blows rattled up his arm.

He let the hammer fall from his grip and hurried to Niya's side. The world seemed to freeze as he stared helplessly at her still and battered form until suddenly he sucked in a breath and the world raced around him.

"Niya?"

His own pulse beat in his ear.

"Niya! Niya wake up!"

He lowered an ear to his sister's mouth and held his quavering breath. A terrible silence stretched on until at last her faint breath came.

Jeld loosed a breath of laughter, but panic wasted no time in consuming it.

Help her! But how? How! Ask Cobb. Of course, ask Cobb!

He spun around. Cobb lay still upon the ground where he'd been reaching for the hammer.

Hammer...

A barrage of images of the hammer sinking into his father's skull bombarded him. Jeld blinked them away and focused on Cobb. He had a large, bloody gash on his temple. His eyes were closed.

"Cobb? Cobb?"

Racing to Cobb's side, he reached out and shook the dear man gently but Cobb only limply resettled. Jeld felt the contents of his stomach start to rise up. He lowered his ear to Cobb's mouth like he had with Niya and waited. His own held breath spilled out and he held it again, but still no sound graced his ear nor any breath his cheek.

"Cobb... wake up! Cobb, you're okay, wake up!"

He laid his ear on Cobb's chest and listened, waited for the dear man's chest to rise against his cheek, but he knew then it would never come. His eyes fell upon Niya's arm dangling from the workbench. He wanted nothing more than to lie there with Cobb, to curl up into a ball against him and cry until he could escape into dreams. Even the most haunted dreams would do. But he could afford no time to grieve.

He jumped up and, stepping over the mutilated body of his father, ran to the side of the only person he had left.

CHAPTER THREE

J eld winced yet again as he made a final stitch through the last of Niya's seven gashes. When she did not so much as stir upon Cobb's bed, Jeld said a silent whisper to the Mother that the pain not manifest in Niya's dreams. Some said they still had power there, though it seemed to Jeld they'd done him no more favors there than in the real world.

He picked up his father's long knife and cut the thread then looked his sister over. Her head and face were crossed with strips of leather pressing white swatches of Cobb's finest wool against her wounds. Dark bruising was already creeping out over what few patches of skin remained uncovered by bandages. Her chest rose and fell slowly.

Jeld tipped a bottle of his father's potent brew over the gash on Niya's hand, but only a single drip trickled out. He pondered for but a moment before rising from the bed and hurrying downstairs to the workshop. On the periphery of his vision, Cobb's still form tugged at his eyes and he flexed his will to keep from looking. Even so, his mind bombarded him with memories of that which he denied his eyes.

He took a deep breath and the images faded. Hurrying onward, he focused instead on another still form, a deep bitterness rising up within him that he should find his father's mutilated corpse a welcome distraction. If he looked only below the neck, it seemed his father might merely be unconscious on the floor as he had been so many times before.

Jeld knelt and slowly reached into Quintem's shirt. Just as his hand closed on a flask inside, a knocking sounded at the door and he toppled onto his back.

"*Idols,*" he whispered, then called to the door. "Who is it!"

"Hmm? Ah... Tarey Sullin. I was told to check back—"

"Cobb is away right now, sorry."

"Cobb? Who—when will he return? My... Will's birthday is in three days."

"Uh, not sure. Family emergency. Could... could be a little while."

The door rattled. "Not sure? I need to get..."

Jeld plucked the flask from his father's pocket and hurried back to Niya's side, the customer's voice fading behind him. He rinsed the cut on her hand with the contents of his father's flask then tied a final bandage over it. His mind aching with fatigue as it began to peek out from its cocoon of shock, he sat watching her breathe. She seemed to wince and he cursed the Idols. How badly he wanted to lay by her side, if not to comfort her then to defer what must be done next.

With a silent whisper to the Warrior for strength, he stood and returned to the grisly scene poisoning his memories of the only peaceful constant he'd ever known. Something had to be done about the bodies.

***

Jeld cringed from a filthy iron grate even as he pulled at it with all his strength. He winced as it ground noisily along the stone floor, then craned an ear up to listen for any sound of alarm. Hearing only the roar of the raging river of refuse below, he jumped up and crossed the circular stone enclosure toward an opening leading back out into the dark city square.

Stinky Square, most called it. At its center, the stone privy offered meager privacy to those who might make use of its amenities. It was not by appearances unlike the many such public privies throughout the city, but what earned this square its name was the numerous man-made rivers of filth converging beneath it.

Jeld froze just before the exit as Stalus gave a nervous whinny from outside.

"I'd like to piss on whichever blue blood decided we needed to double our patrols," came a gruff voice.

"Not me, Frinny," a second man said. "I'd like to kiss him. Don't figure I had it in me to dig another hole or move another blazin' boulder. I needed this job. Thank that man for my sanity."

"People killin' each other for years and I get an easy schedule and leave days to boot, but them Hilltoppers' fancy shops start gettin' busted up and I'm on double duty. I tell ya, Ben."

Jeld pressed himself against the wall as a light danced across the threshold.

"Fine by me. Twice the money. Shoo along some mouthy dissidents, drag a drunk or two into the gutters. Oh, and establish a presence of authority *in the name of the king's law!* Or something like that."

"Easy for you to say. Give it twenty more years and tell me that money does a prince's bit for you when you're too busy and too tired and too damn old to do anything with it anyway."

Jeld's heart raced as the voices grew louder, his mind churning through options.

"If somehow you're still alive in twenty years, Frinny, I'll tell ya then what I tell ya now— I know just how I can have fun with that money. Unlike some of us, I intend to be in full working order still at that age."

Stalus whinnied again and in that very moment a plan solidified in Jeld's mind. As if on his horse's cue, he unfastened his pants and stepped out into the dark square playing at retying them.

"Easy, boy. Easy there," Jeld said without looking up.

"I hope he's talking to the horse," Ben japed.

Jeld pretended to start violently as he looked up and saw the watchmen. Both had swords at their sides and the younger of the two carried a long spear with a glowing lantern hanging from atop it.

Frinny fought back a smile, his younger partner loosing a cackle before catching an elbow in his side.

"What brings you out tonight, boy?" Frinny demanded, the trace of humor upon his lined face quickly disappearing.

Jeld let his mouth hang open as he eyed their spears. "Are you watchmen?"

"Yeah, lad," Ben said, "but you'd best answer Sergeant Frinald's questions before you go askin' your own. What're ya doin' out tonight?"

"Gotta take these polishes back to the clown that made 'em. At least, the cobbler said he's a clown, anyway. I like the guy well enough. Cobbler said they were soupy and the colors were all wrong."

Frinald continued to stare suspiciously as his partner turned his attention to the wagon.

"Nice wagon," Ben said.

"It's my father's. I have my own, but his was blocking it in. I first learned how to drive on this one though, so I don't mind."

Ben lifted a canvas cover at the rear of the wagon with his spear. He flinched back as a noxious odor wafted out to join that of a full shitcatch and the already overwhelming stink of the square.

"Idols!" Ben cursed and let the flap fall.

"Sorry. Polishes. They're always rank, but these soupy ones are worse still."

"Must be an urgent operation... this shoe polish business," Frinald said.

"Tellin' me. He said we got an order for a big customer—a royal or somethin'—that's supposed to be done by midday tomorrow, and these polishes weren't gonna cut it."

Frinald held his stare.

Jeld continued. "You ask me, I think it coulda waited but my guy is just trying to stick it to the polish maker for selling him rubbish. Wouldn't be the first time he made me work at this bleedin' hour. Pays me for it but what good is that if I'm always working?"

Ben groaned.

Frinald grinned and rapped his partner on the back.

"You hear that, Benny boy? That's a wise lad there. Don't let a peb convince ya that play time is work time. Boy, you could teach a thing or two to my young apprentice here."

A chorus of drunken barks sounded in the distance.

"Duty calls, my wise and extremely ancient master," Ben said.

Frinald grunted. "On ya go then, boy. Be careful, city's going to shit. And it weren't so nice before."

The watchmen turned and started off toward the commotion.

"And empty that damned shitcatch while you're here, kid!" Ben shouted over his shoulder.

"I will!" Jeld called after them.

Jeld let out a breath as the banter of the two watchmen faded with their lantern light. Soon there was only the creak of shop signs swaying in the gentle night breeze, and the occasional clatter of hooves clapping down a distant street over the hushed roar of sewage flowing beneath the starlit square. Jeld's mood fit the scene perfectly. It felt right that he should be walking amongst shadows.

Patting Stalus on the head, he tugged at a false board beneath the tailgate and froze as the smuggler's hold fell open. Images bombarded his every sense. Bright, glistening red. Cobb's final, knowing stare. Quintem's mad eyes. The crunching of skull. The taste of blood. Niya's battered body, her agonized screams, her soft sobs. Her silence.

Jeld blinked the memories clear. Just inside the hold, two pairs of boot soles looked out at him, their distinct states of repair telling stories like lines upon a face. He blinked again and they were just boots once more. Grabbing the worn pair, he pulled with all his strength. The body, just a blur in his censored vision, toppled unceremoniously to the ground. He dragged it the final few leaps to the drain he'd pulled open.

Letting down the mental defenses that had preserved his sanity, he looked down. Lying on his back in what faint light reached through the doorway, Quintem looked almost unharmed. On closer examination, Jeld could see red lines where blood had run from the huge wound on the back of his head, and an open wound on one cheek where the finely tipped hammer had met the floor beneath. Quintem's hands too were stained red with blood – blood that did not belong to him.

Jeld pushed. He wanted to think it was easy to watch Quintem fall into that foul torrent of filth, but it was not. Not because he felt sympathy or regret, but because all his father had robbed him of seemed with finality to fall as well. Worst of all, it meant everything that happened that night was real.

He took a deep breath and returned to the smuggler's hold. The second set of boots was spotlessly clean. Even in the dim light, a white shine gleamed upon their skyward toes. Jeld set his hands upon them.

His hand beginning to tremble, he let out a single anguished sob and pulled. Jeld's heart wrenched as Cobb's head hit the ground. He kneeled by the old shoemaker's side and looked down at his serene face.

"You could have kicked Quintem to the gutters long ago," Jeld said, his voice quavering. "It was all for us, wasn't it? For Niya and me. And look what it got you."

Jeld remembered his last glimpse of Cobb alive, looking to the tack hammer just out of reach. The gentlest man he had ever known, saying with his eyes, *do what must be done.* And so he had.

"Thank you, Cobb," Jeld whispered.

And so I will.

He pushed.

***

Jeld breathed in small, shallow breaths as if to take in less of the acrid remedies lining the dark aisles. His eyes glazed over as he scanned the small signs placed before each jar. Though he couldn't read, he knew that most words were not usually half as long as these, and he was fairly certain he'd never even seen some of the symbols before.

A floorboard creaked from behind.

"I thought I heard a little creature scuttling about back here," a kindly voice said.

Jeld tried and failed to assume a smile before turning. The man at the end of the aisle was not the hunched old mystic he had imagined encountering in such a place, but rather a middle-aged man with a well-trimmed mustache, a white apron, and the same penetrating rat-or-customer stare shared by all shopkeepers, Cobb included.

"Is there something I can help you find, my boy?"

"Ahh... yes, my..."

The next words would not come, as if left unsaid everything that happened might vanish like an untold dream forgotten. He closed his eyes and drew a breath.

"Yes, please. My sister was... mugged. She has deep cuts and bruises all over. Her face is all swollen. One of her arms may be broken. She was hit in the head and... and she hasn't yet woken. Can you help her, sir?"

Jeld watched the apothecary intently, hopeful for an optimistic smile and a gesture toward some miraculous pill, yet bracing himself for the worst.

"Unconscious... *Mother's touch*, that's serious, boy. Terrible, terrible. I'm very sorry. So many muggings of late, I don't know what it is."

Jeld's heart sank as the man continued.

"Well, you really should get help. Medicine can only do so much without proper care. She'll need her cuts stitched, it sounds. And cleaned. And her arm splinted."

"I've done all that."

"Ah, have you then. Very nice, very nice. Well, medicines *will* be an important part of her recovery..."

The shopkeeper set to rubbing his chin, his eyes flitting about the shop. Suddenly he sprung forward and Jeld jumped back against the shelves, staring after the shopkeeper as he disappeared into the shop.

A twinge of hope returning to Jeld's face, he hurried after the apothecarist. He peered down each aisle until he found the shopkeeper scooping some powder from a large jar into a vial. The shopkeeper stoppered the vial and resumed his brisk pace, making three other such stops before leading Jeld to the front and setting four vials atop the counter. He picked one up and grasped it between his thumb and forefinger.

"Alright. Pay close attention. Using a *medicine right* is as important as using the *right medicine*, do you understand?"

"Yes," Jeld replied quickly, his mind on Niya.

"This... is *Irra leaf*. It cleans the infection from wounds. You put a little bit in each cut, twice daily until reddening fades, then once daily."

He jotted down a note but stopped suddenly and looked up at Jeld.

"You read?"

Jeld frowned. Even in the best of times it was a sore subject, and now, as he stared at the vials on the countertop, all he could think about was how much time his ignorance would cost him if he must endure this dialogue for each. He had to get back to Niya soon, had to—

"Son!"

Jeld's mind snapped back to the present, his face reddening.

"Don't be ashamed, but I'm not talking for fun. I'm talking to make sure you properly tend to your sister."

"I'm sorry. I only want to help her."

"Then listen very carefully. Green, clean. Got it? What does green do?"

"Clean."

"Very good."

The apothecarist dropped the green vial into a sack and held another out before Jeld. They repeated the ritual for each vial, Jeld reading back each mnemonic in turn to chisel it deep into his memory.

"Now all together, son," the shopkeeper said after the last.

"Green, clean. Tea powder brown, bring fever down. Black pill swallow, sleep will follow. Pill white, will pain fight."

"Perfect!"

The shopkeeper began flipping through a thick ledger atop the counter.

"Twenty-two, that'll be," he said at last with a heavy sigh. "I'd help you for free if I could, but the shop wouldn't be here for the next person."

His eyes wide, Jeld started digging through his purse.

"Oh I suppose I could keep the doors open for a few more customers yet if I made it an even twenty," the shopkeeper added. "Perhaps she could also do without the—"

Jeld set two bricks and a peb on the counter. Even with the sixty some peb remaining from Cobb's drawer, it was a painful sum.

"Thank you, sir."

"Oh sure. Hard to be a good businessman when you care. And it's Len, by the way. Len Farins. *Sir* was my father's name."

With a wink, the apothecarist unlocked a cabinet upon the wall behind him then pulled it open and began stuffing Jeld's coins into a purse within. Vials lined the cabinet shelves.

"What are those ones?"

"Hmm? Oh. Specialty medicines, rare... remedies. Well, anything expensive, if I'm honest."

"Do they work?"

"Oh yes. Some. Others... ground crauul teeth, seahorse tails... perhaps not."

"Will the things you sold me work?"

"Ah. Well, yes. They'll serve their purposes."

"Will they save her?"

Len frowned. "They could. The next few days will be... telling. If her wounds fester deeper within, where Irra leaf can't reach, though..."

"What then?"

The apothecarist pursed his lips then pulled a vial from the cabinet and held it to the meager light. Green and brown flakes shifted within.

"Then you'd need Andlock. But let me be clear because I don't want to offer false hopes—the cost is... out of reach for many. Believe me, if I could give it for free I would, but—"

"How much is it?"

"Thirty pebs per dose. Ten doses would best serve her. But lad, Andlock is a mischievous drug. It often does more harm than good. It's best used only as a last resort."

"Three hundred pebs..."

"Give the others a try first, son?"

Jeld blinked. "I need to go. Thank you."

"Pleasure is all mine. Best of luck with your sister."

Jeld took the sack of medicines, gave the man a grave nod, and was off at a run toward Niya's side before even reaching the door.

CHAPTER FOUR

J eld sped through the shop toward the sound of violent coughing and burst into Cobb's bedroom. At the bedside he squeezed Niya's hand and cradled her head in his arm as the fit took its course.

"It's alright. You're alright. You'll be good as new soon."

Niya's breaths slowed and soon her eyelids twitched in dreams. Beads of sweat upon her brow gleamed bright against her bruised skin. She began to shiver violently despite the hot, sweaty hand within Jeld's grasp. Jeld managed to reach a damp cloth and set it upon her forehead. Cursing and thanking the Idols in turn as Niya cycled through waves of sweats and shivers and calm, Jeld stayed at her side until at last she slept soundly then eased himself free.

As Jeld plucked the lamp from the bedside table, his eyes fell upon four half empty vials of medicines. Cursing the Idols once again, his mind drifted back toward the vial of green and brown flakes within the apothecarist's locked cabinet.

Andlock.

Setting his jaw, Jeld made his way through the disorderly shop to the front door and pulled it open. He peered up at the stars, but finding dawn and any prospect of earning three hundred pebs a long way off yet, he returned inside and started back toward Niya's side.

Something caught his eye and he picked up a boot from a pile of wreckage. He thumbed the supple leather and his eyes grew distant before he took a breath and returned Cobb's prized boot to the top of a display beside its pair. Looking out over the filthy shop, he set his jaw again and set to cleaning.

***

Jeld looked back over his shoulder from atop his father's wagon. At the end of a tow rope, Stalus and Lionus plodded along before Bandit. The sight would ordinarily have brought a certain smile to Jeld's face, but today it brought only a tear to his eye.

When he turned back around, the invigorating ocean air suddenly welcomed him to Southern Tovar. The sea breeze had an odd way of pervading the senses all at once, like it had been sitting just out of reach. That cool, crisp, refreshing air that promised the freedom of the seas, the soft touch of sand beneath one's feet, the calming rhythm of the ocean's roar. In another of the sea's many wonders, the unabashed stench of salty, fishy rot accompanying its perfume of promises failed somehow to diminish its beckoning in the least.

Shaking his head clear of the ocean's promises, his mind fixed on Niya alone, Jeld corrected his course. Pulling a second team was easy enough on the open road, but it required constant supervision within the crowded and often narrow city streets. This was probably the only reason his father had kept him around, he considered.

A man in a tattered black robe stood in the street ahead, madly yelling the usual accusations.

"... kindled by our light to protect us! Born again in the place of our dreams, they liberated us from the mad king. But they are not Idols of war, but of peace! From the broken shards of war they forged a peace the likes of which has never been known!"

Jeld stared down at the man as he neared.

"And how have we repaid their deliverance? With open arms?" The man suddenly stabbed a finger up toward Jeld. "No! With *raised* arms! Rebellion! Chaos and war! *Murder!*"

Peeking over his shoulder as he passed, Jeld was relieved to see the Sayer quickly turn on a new target.

"The Mother's blood is on the hands of us all!" the Sayer's voice followed. "We are greed! We are filth! They have not *ascended* to wage war on Discord. There *is* no Discord! There is only the discord within us, the *sin* within us that dampens the light. Cleanse yourselves of your sins, your greed, your hate. Show love, love yourself, love Them, and only *then* will our light return Them to us!"

As Jeld drove his wagons ahead and the Sayer's words faded into the distance, he found himself wondering at the lunatic's tales. The Idols were real, that much everyone knew. Things didn't fall into the questionable realm of legend until at least a few generations past, but even Cobb had seen one of the Idols. And not just once, Cobb was wont to say, but many years amidst the weeklong *Fallstival* parades as the people celebrated the fall of King Caedis.

It was much the same across the kingdom, to hear it told, the other Idols each taking part from the city they ruled. The Mother at Havaral, the Wise One at Enniad, the Craftsman at Caerghallad. Only the Traveler had no city to call home, though it was said he often visited common folk at the crudest of drinking holes or even quiet roadside camps each Fallstival night. Even after the Vanishing, the ruins of Khapar could forever attest to the undeniable tangibility of Tovados the Warrior Idol.

Jeld welcomed the distraction as he rode fatefully onward, his eyes growing distant, hands driving the reins on habit alone. That the Idols disappeared was another point he knew for fact. *Where* they went, though, was the big question. Extinguished by man's sin? Ascended to dreams? Battling Discord? *Dead?* Whatever the case, they weren't doing Niya a blazin' bit of good.

"Come on in, come on down!" another voice called over the Sayer from somewhere ahead. "Gather up and gather 'round! Step right in to Temple Square and see our amazing Idolic duo!"

Jeld drove ahead as the narrow street opened into a square. Though lined with storefronts like the countless streets snaking through the city, the buildings kept a polite distance, offering a welcome reprieve from the captivity of Tovar. Two boisterous gatherings were formed across the square at the foot of the towering old Temple Theater. A man wearing a red suit with shiny gold buttons was waving passersby deeper into the square.

"You heard it right, we've got a duo. Yes sirs and yes ma'ams, that's not *one* Idolic, but *two!* We've got the amazing Alal—fastest man alive, touched with the Warrior's speed! And the impossible Yelana—with the Huntress's grace and the Warrior's power, see her leap the height of ten men and soar through the air like a bird!"

A dozen memories of Niya beaming upon entering Temple Square flashed before Jeld's eyes. He set his jaw and drove on.

From the center of the nearest gathering, a woman in a shining silver suit leapt into the air. She soared impossibly high then higher still, spinning and flipping every which way before diving gracefully toward the ground. Were it not for Jeld's high vantage he might have expected to see a circle of burly men waiting with a stretched blanket as he'd seen in any number of street parades, but as it were he saw clearly the empty cobblestones beneath her.

When it seemed she would crash head first into the ground, she landed with a roll, popping up into a low flip before coming to a final stop upon her feet, soft as a snowflake. The crowd boomed with applause. She bowed a deep, graceful bow and began a still impressive display of acrobatics far closer to the ground.

A roar issued from the other crowd and Jeld turned. At the center of the gathering, a shirtless, muscular man covered in a sheen of sweat from bald head to belt was juggling several balls in a high arc overhead. A girl perhaps Jeld's age picked up another ball from a pile at her feet and tossed it to the juggler. The crowd *oohed*, then *aahed* as the juggler snatched it into his whirlwind. The girl threw again and again until the torrent of balls stretched beyond all save the towering theater and sweat streamed down the juggler's body and the *oohs* and *aahs* rose like a heartbeat.

The girl threw the last ball. The juggler reached out and caught it, but Jeld could see at once that something went awry. A ball struck the ground and the crowd gasped and yelped. The juggler's stone face broke into panic. He tried frantically to recover but the whirlwind broke into chaos and he suddenly ducked behind upraised arms as a seemingly endless stream of balls rained down toward him.

When the last had fallen, the man emerged slowly from beneath his arms and looked down in astonishment at a perfect circle of balls surrounding him. Finally, he flashed a clever grin to the gaping crowd and the square erupted in thunderous cheers.

Realizing his own mouth was hanging open, Jeld closed it and pressed his team onward into the alley. He looked over his shoulder and found Stalus and Lionus just behind, the tow rope hanging loosely between the wagons. He smiled a sad smile.

"Good horses."

He continued through the alley, and just as the bustle of the crowded square began to fade, the sound of men at work filled its place, growing louder with each hoofbeat. A wagon passed by beyond the alley, no doubt heading to the same place just around the corner. The *theater's asshole*, his father liked to call the warehouse, ever fond of the shady empire that would be his undoing.

Just as he cleared the alley and readied to turn along the backside of the theater, a thought occurred to him and he turned the other way. *Show the goose before the swan,* Cobb's voice seemed to say as he dismounted and set to untying the tow rope. Jeld gave Stalus and Lionus a lingering pat then climbed aboard Bandit and circled about.

The back wall of the theater fell away beneath a line of broad arched columns, a vast warehouse within buzzing with activity. Massive shelves stacked high with crates ran inward from each column to form numerous distinct stalls. Perhaps two dozen men were fast at work loading and unloading wagons. Just inside, beneath the farthest columns, a man soft in shoulder and chin alike sat writing at a desk.

Jeld brought his wagon to a stop just before the desk and hopped to the ground. When the man behind the desk only stared at him beneath a raised eyebrow, Jeld cleared his throat to break the awkward silence. Still the man said nothing, merely tilting his head as if to a chicken at sea.

"Ah, excuse me, sir," Jeld said finally when it seemed the man's neck might break.

"Yes?"

"I would... I would like to sell this fine wagon."

"I see...."

"I couldn't bear to see it go to some dealer, only to be sold to another wagoner like you for twice its worth."

"Well, I—"

"You'll find no better wagon for the price. Any dealer will wring you out. Trust me, I've spoken to two. I'll give you a real deal."

The man shifted in his chair. "Yes, a fine wagon, but we haven't a need, and the—"

"Nice thing about owning a warehouse is you can buy it now for a real deal and you've plenty of room to store it until you need one. Save yourself a load of money in no time."

"I'm afraid I can't help you."

"This wagon would—"

"I'm sorry, but you need to leave!"

Jeld's eyes fell shut as all hope crumbled within him. He turned away without another word and climbed slowly back onto the wagon. His hands unthinkingly found the reins yet he sat there unmoving, only staring ahead at Niya shivering in her bed, his purse too light to treat her. Finally, he gave the reins a light flick and slowly turned the wagon about.

He had gone just a few leaps when Stalus's nervous whinny caught his attention and he looked up to find a man peering into the back of his father's wagon across the alley. Suddenly all traces of dismay were swept aside by a burning anger that the day might somehow assail him further. Well Idols be damned if the day would keep him from saving Niya. He straightened his posture, issued his team a loud *click*, and flicked the reins.

Seeming not to notice as Jeld neared, the man crouched beside a front wheel and peered beneath the wagon as if checking the axles. He was thick and wore a black suit; not fancy like a gentleman's, but a suit that somehow belonged on the streets – nice but not too nice, fitted but with plenty of space left over to throw a tooth-shattering punch without busting a seam.

A thug, Jeld considered as the man ignored his unmistakable approach, but not just any thug. He looked up at the high windows lining the back of the warehouse. He'd seen the man's sort before, each time his father did business with the very people who owned the theater—and its *asshole*.

As if on cue, the man turned. Meeting Jeld's glare, the corners of his mouth seemed ever so slightly to turn upward as the wagon came to a stop.

Even prepared for the sort, Jeld squirmed beneath the man's stare. Still, the tough-guy act set his blood boiling and he ignored the man completely as he climbed down and started refastening the tow rope. Passing by the man with feigned confidence, a hand drifting nonetheless closer to the long knife at his hip, Jeld climbed atop his father's wagon and raised the reins high.

"Nice wagon," the man said at last.

"Thanks."

"Was this one for sale next?"

Jeld squirmed further.

"Good on ya. That's just good business," the man added. "You seem like a smart kid. Why part with such fine wagons?"

"Money."

"Why not take up service here? We've just lost one of our independent wagoners."

The man's penetrating stare seemed to pierce suddenly deeper. Jeld's eyes widened and he coughed to obscure his reaction.

"Ah, thanks, but I need a lot of money. Actually I'd best be—"

"You know, his wagon looked quite like yours. Say... where did you say you came by this?"

Jeld stared back. Squirrelly wasn't going to get him anywhere with this fellow.

"It was Quintem's wagon, as you well know. My father's. And it's mine to sell. What do you want?"

"Ahh. With that attitude you could only be Quintem's. Just had to be sure you weren't some street kid running off with his wagons while he took a booze nap. We gotta look out for our wagoners, right? How is your father, these days?"

"He's dead."

The man's cold exterior wavered. "Sorry, kid. Did... ah... *somebody* do this? The boss doesn't take kindly to that kinda thing. Maybe we could set things right."

"He just... got hammered one time too many. Didn't wake up from his booze nap this time."

The burly man's shoulders sank a bit. Jeld was fairly certain it wasn't sorrow for the loss of Quintem, but rather disappointment that booze didn't have arms to rip off.

"Sorry, kid. Don't touch the stuff, alright? They say it runs in the family. When did that happen?"

The bastards cut me out, Quintem's voice replayed in Jeld's head. And whatever they did was why Niya lay crippled in Cobb's vacant bed.

"The night he last met with you people."

"Ah. Well, sorry again, kid. So, ah... you sure about givin' up wagoning? You know the business already, ya? Tricks of the trade? How our... little operation here works?"

Despite the man's discretion, Jeld knew what he was after. It all made sense now. Loose ends. This guy tied loose ends, and Jeld didn't like the sound of being tied.

"Sure I do," Jeld said. "Some wagoners are independent, others are all yours. We were independent, moved wares for some of your contracts. Had a few of our own, too. Yeah, I know the business as much as any wagoner."

"What do you know about our... cost cutting methods?"

Magistrate Minol's face flashed before Jeld's eyes.

"You mean like running that sweatshop back there?"

"Right... yeah, this business is all about the logistics. I don't suppose your father had any methods of his own that we could pass on to the crew?"

Jeld frowned. "No? I suppose he didn't include me on everything."

The man frowned. "You seem like a smart kid, but you've got at least two things to learn. One – the truth is in the eyes, or in your case it ain't. And two—lying to me is very, very unwise."

The man circled to the back of the wagon, flipped open the smuggler's hold, and raised an eyebrow up to Jeld at the reins.

"Smuggling?" Jeld asked. "Sure, but I figured you knew that already. Isn't that why you cut him out?"

The man again turned his piercing stare upon Jeld for a long, unnerving moment before at last seeming to shrug.

"I'm sorry about your father. You're better off without him, though."

"Ah... thanks," Jeld said, his stomach unclenching. "Well, I'd best be off."

"Not quite. How about thirty-two."

"Sorry?"

"Thirty-two. Bricks. For both. It's a fair deal, basically split what any dealer would take us for. Deal?"

Jeld's eyes flicked to Stalus and Lionus. He thumbed the reins before loosing a heavy sigh.

"Alright. Deal."

The man extended a hand. "*Ement*, by the way."

Jeld eyed the hand cautiously from atop the wagon before reaching down and giving it a firm shake.

"Jeld."

A twinkle seemed to light in Ement's eye, as if in reminder that he could now rip Jeld's arm off should he like, but he let go and produced a heavy coin purse from his jacket. He dug through it and held an open palm out to Jeld, three silver royals and two silver bricks gleaming upon it.

Fighting back tears of joy and sorrow alike, Jeld reached down and plucked up the princely sum as casually as possible.

"Thanks," he said.

"Keep that safe, kid. What do you need the money for anyway? I hope you're givin' up them wagons for a good reason."

Jeld's eyes fell to the ground before he opened his mouth to speak.

"Save it," Ement said. "Our business is done, and I don't need to know, so you can do us both a favor and hold your lying tongue."

"I'm sorry."

"Don't be, it's your business. I got mine too. Speaking of, I'd best get back to it."

Jeld nodded.

"So..." Ement added.

"Oh. Right."

Thumbing the reins one last time, Jeld gently set them down and hopped to the ground. He stared as Ement climbed aboard and grabbed them up.

"You seem like a good kid. Keep that money safe."

Jeld watched as Ement drove the wagons back toward the warehouse. Even Stalus didn't so much as look back before disappearing inside, and then they were gone and Jeld stood alone, on foot, in Southern Tovar. He glanced down at the fat purse in his hand. Despite holding more money than he'd ever seen, he felt empty and naked.

He tucked the purse into his shirt and walked back up the alley toward Cobb's. Crossing the bustling square, every little bump and squeeze was a painful reminder of his absent wagon. As he neared the far side of the square, the crowd grew thicker and he soon found himself weaving and pushing his way along, his path closing immediately behind him with each step. Still he pressed ahead until suddenly he stumbled into a clearing and crashed into someone's backside.

Jeld's eyes went wide as he looked up to find a watchman standing over him with a sword in hand. He scrambled back against the crowd.

"Who goes there! Who dares molest a hiney bound to service only the king!"

Laughter sounded all around as the watchman leveled his sword at the crowd, but the sword soon drooped flaccidly toward the ground.

"By the Idols, my sword's gone soft as King Loris's—er, backbone."

The crowd laughed again.

"Enough of that! I'm afraid there is no entertainment allowed at... the theater. New city ordinance, in the name... *of the king's law!*"

At the last, the watchman struck a fist to his chest and stomped his heel to a crisp attention. His overly large helmet fell over his face and the crowd laughed once more.

"Hey!" the comic shouted through his helmet and wandered off shouting more jokes.

Jeld let out a breath and, feeling smaller and ever emptier, ran toward the apothecary.

Chapter Five

J eld sat upon the edge of the small porch lining the front of Cobb's shop. Behind him, the shutters were boarded closed. His thoughts were lost in his own long shadow when something caught his eye and he looked up to find a man with a well-kept beard and dressed in dark wools standing before the door.

"Open?" the man asked.

Jeld looked to the boarded-over shutters and back to the man.

"Closed. Sorry."

"I see. Well, I'd like to check—"

"Shop's closed. For good. Done. Gone."

"That right? Shame, old man made the best watch boots in town."

Jeld swallowed.

"You his kid or somethin'?"

"Right. Ah, grandkid."

"Yeah? Where's your gramps?"

"He's sick," Jeld said, coming to his feet.

"Shame."

"Yeah, I'd best see to him, actually."

"Thinkin you'd best see to the seven pebs I paid for boots."

"Oh... sure. I'll be right back."

Jeld started through the door and made to shut it, but the man's hand closed upon it.

"Think I'll join you."

"Right. Sure. It's no trouble, I'll get your commission back."

Jeld hurried inside and set to digging through a drawer at Cobb's favorite worktable as the man paced the showroom.

"You know, you gotta be careful boarding a place up these days. Prince has us cleanin' up the city, and seizing defunct properties has more coin in it for watchmen than lockin' up drunks does."

"Ah. Right. Thanks. I'll have it all opened up again soon."

"Closed for good, didn't ya say?"

Jeld counted seven coins from the twenty odd pebs making up the whole of his worth and closed the drawer.

"I... I was just upset. Hard to watch my granda' like this."

"Mm. Sure. Maybe I'll have a look at him? I've seen to an old man or two in my days."

"That's... kind. But he just needs rest now, thanks. Here's your coin. Sorry about the boots."

"You sure? Thinkin' maybe I'd love those boots more than I'd love my pebs, if your granda' is on the mend."

Jeld crossed to the man and held out the pebs. "Who knows how long it'll be. Best take your money back for now."

The man eyed Jeld and the coin. "Thing is... I'm not so sure I buy your story. Maybe you just stuck the old cobbler and squatted in his shop, see? So, it wouldn't be right for me not to check. Now, back this way, is it?"

Jeld pursued the man toward Cobb's room. "Wait. Wait, please!"

The man ignored Jeld's pleas, pushing the door to Cobb's bedroom open.

"What the—"

"My sister, she—"

The man spun. "Naw. Had enough stories. I'll do ya this favor, I'll take my pebs and all the rest in that drawer of yours, and you got maybe two bells before I come back with a squad and seize this place."

Jeld scowled openly at the watchman even as he backed behind a work table. "I see. What's a couple lives when you could pocket some easy coin and snag some property for your mad prince, yeah?"

"*Mad prince,*" the man scoffed. "Only a street urchin would compare him to the mad king."

"What's a prince need a shoe shop for!" Jeld spat. "Or is it just a bone to keep his watch dogs happy?"

The man's nostrils flared before he forced a bitter smile and held out his hand.

"Let's have those pebs."

Jeld eyed the hand, his gaze flicking to a bead of sweat running down the man's temple. He slowly reached the coins out as his other hand inched toward the knife at his hip.

Suddenly a stoney grip closed around Jeld's wrist. Pain exploded at his shoulder and he found himself flying forward across the table. He drew his blade and lashed out, but the watchman caught that wrist too. As Jeld slammed into his attacker, he hooked the table with his toes and brought it down against the man's knees, sending him toppling backward with Jeld in tow.

The watchman landed hard upon his back with a pained grunt. Jeld let the momentum of the fall join all his strength behind the knife and drove it downward. The jarring impact turned the knife off target but still it plunged, biting into the man's collar. It had sunk no less than half its length when a wheezing scream escaped the man and Jeld felt the immense strength of his grip clamp down around his wrist. Jeld's fingers grew suddenly stiff and disobedient. His hand slipped away from the knife's hilt as the man pushed his arm back, leaving the knife protruding from the man's thick woolen jacket.

The watchman twisted Jeld's arms around and pinned them behind his back. A horrible pressure constricted Jeld like a giant snake. He cried out as pain shot through one of his ribs. The next breath wouldn't come as he strained at muscles that had ever before served him unthinkingly. A second rib seemed to snap and he screamed a silent, breathless scream.

Glittering spots danced before Jeld's eyes. His vision began to blur and he knew he had only seconds before he began sleeping through his own death. *And then this monster will see that Niya sleeps through hers.* His eyes went wild as he frantically sought a way out. He bit at the man's chest but his teeth closed only on dry wool.

Shadows encircled the edges of his vision. His head lolled onto its side against his killer's jacket. The coarse, black wool seemed a bed of blighted grass. His eyes screamed the horrors of dying in such an embrace, his stomach twisting in revulsion even in death. The shadows pressed inward until there was only a circle of light, his father's knife standing like a pillar at its center.

Jeld's eyes widened. He summoned his every remaining bit of strength and the light pushed back the encroaching shadows. He arched his back, raising his head high above his black embrace. His eyes skyward, he had no words for the Idols, only a last choked scream of defiance to his enemy. He threw his head down against the hilt with all he had left.

The watchman gave an agonized scream and his grip loosened slightly. A sweet taste of air seeped into Jeld's lungs. He pulled his head back and slammed it down again. The scream rising horribly in pitch was music to Jeld's ears as he ground the knife deeper until his bloodied face stood just above the black coat and none of the blade but the hilt remained.

The man's scream turned into a rewarding gurgle and air flooded Jeld's lungs as he suddenly found himself flying backward through the air. The back of his legs struck the downed table and Jeld's top half resumed its descent unaccompanied. He reached back his arms to catch himself but they struck the upended table legs. Pain exploded in his head and the dim shop above burst into a flash of blinding brightness for the briefest of moments before retreating down some long tunnel until there remained only darkness.

A sliver of light surprised Jeld with the news that he was not dead. The line grew and the darkness gave way to a spinning blur resembling the ceiling of the shop. He wondered at how much time had passed since... what was it that he'd been doing when he'd... when he'd what?

Jeld raised his head and the room spun terribly like some visualization of the pain that screamed within his head. He lowered his head back to the ground and put his hand to his forehead as if to stabilize the spinning room. He felt wetness on his fingers and moved his hand in front of the distorted scene beyond. Even in the dim light it gleamed red.

Like lightning strikes revealing an ominous storm, images like foggy memories flashed somewhere near the threshold of his subconscious. A hand closing about his wrist. The hilt of his knife against a dark blanket of shadow. And then the face of a man with a well-kept beard looking down at him. Only this last was blurry and spinning. *How odd that even a memory should spin...*

Somewhere deep within Jeld's subconscious, he was screaming. Screaming to stir himself from his stupor. The image of the bearded man was then covered by a large boot rising high above him. As the boot slowed near its apex, all of his memories came flooding back in a nightmarish instance, and when the boot began to plunge rapidly down, the screaming voice of his subconscious burst into clarity but all he could do was flinch.

Something wet splashed across Jeld's face and a booming, hollow *thud* sounded all around. Had the foot missed, some cruel twist of fate forcing him to endure another? Or had he been spared? For torture? For prison? For money?

He opened his eyes. The boot was gone, as was the face. But there was something else in the fuzzy torrent above. A blurry figure, much smaller than the watchman he swore he'd seen just a moment before. The figure slowed its nauseating revolution and assumed its true position standing over him. He blinked in disbelief as several of the indiscernible figures came together into the slender form of Niya.

A tack hammer slipped from her fingers and tumbled toward the floor. Her tired eyes met Jeld's and he saw the faintest smile touch her lips. The fleeting smile fell away and Niya's eyes rolled back. Jeld screamed at his own tired body to jump up and catch her but it only lay frozen. He watched in dreamlike slowness as her body fell toward the floor and disappeared behind a still ridgeline of dark wool.

When Jeld's body again responded to his commands, he crawled to Niya's side and cradled her head in his arms.

"Niya? Are you alright?"

Niya smiled, her eyes still shut. "I saved you."

"You did," Jeld laughed. "You saved me. And you're awake!"

"Still good... for something."

"Good for plenty. Come on, let's get you back to bed."

Jeld picked Niya up and started for Cobb's room, wincing as pain shot through his shoulder and ribs.

"Not Cobb's," Niya breathed.

"Hmm?"

"Our roost. Not Cobb's room."

"Ah... I think you'll be more comfortable in—"

"Please."

Jeld stopped and looked down to find his sister staring up at him. "Yeah. Yeah, okay."

He struggled up the stairs and across the attic, easing Niya gently onto her sleeping platform. She loosed a series of wet coughs and laid her head back down with a groan.

"Not fun, Brother. I don't recommend it."

Jeld beamed. "You have no idea how happy I am to hear your voice."

Niya managed a smile before her eyes grew distant.

"They're dead, aren't they?" she asked after a while.

Jeld only stared back.

"It's okay. I think I knew." Niya frowned bitterly but it was broken by a quivering lip. "Cobb didn't deserve this. He shouldn't have even taken us in—"

"Cobb knew what he was doing."

"If only he would have just left us—"

Her voice broke in a sob and she fell into another fit of coughing.

"He would do it all again," Jeld said. "I've got some medicine for you. It'll make you good as new. I'll be right back."

Jeld patted Niya's arm and hurried back downstairs. He filled a bowl from Cobb's cauldron, sprinkling a dash of Andlock on top before returning to Niya's side.

"Mmm... smells good."

"Sole stew for ya."

"Smells like sole *soup*," Niya said.

A broad smile pressed a tear from Jeld's eye. "Right you are. Totally different smell, ya know. Come on then, best eat up."

Niya took a deep breath then set her jaw and began fighting her way upright. Jeld set the bowls down and reached to help her.

"No," Niya groaned. "I've got it."

Jeld fought to keep from aiding her as she muttered a solid string of curses, but the struggle proved well worthwhile when at last his sister succeeded. His smile quickly faded though as Niya pressed a hand to her forehead.

"Head hurt? I've got some medicine for that."

"No. Thanks, I'm fine."

Jeld forced a smile and handed her one of the bowls. "Enjoy."

"How much does this stuff cost?"

"Going rate on carrots and potatoes isn't too bad. The rest is from Cobb's stores."

Niya stared back impatiently.

Jeld shrugged. "The medicine? Maybe three?"

"Just three? Wait—three *what?*"

Jeld sighed. "Bricks... per dose."

"Three bricks per—how many doses!"

Jeld sighed again. "Five? Maybe ten."

"*Dreams!* How can... how?"

"Cobb had some money saved."

Jeld took a bite of stew as casually as possible, but at once he felt Niya's prying eyes upon him. He sighed once more.

"I sold the wagons."

"You *what?* The wagons?"

Her shaky voice broke at the last and gave way to a fit of coughing. The coughs turned to gasping retches and again she held her hand out to keep Jeld from helping. When the fit subsided, she closed her eyes and spoke again in a delicate voice.

"What will we do?"

"All we need to do right now is get you well. After that we can do anything. Work the shop for a while? If it doesn't suit us we can get a wagon again. Or start that *everything store* you told me about."

Niya's eyes grew distant. "Thanks for taking care of me, Brother."

Jeld fed himself a spoonful of stew to hide his quivering lip.

"Eat up, this week's dinners might be the finest in the city. More expensively seasoned even than whatever slop's on the king's table up there on the hill."

Her eyes went wide above her spoon. "Idols!"

"That bad?"

"Are those... oh, he's not going to like that."

"What? Like what?"

Jeld followed her gaze to his boots and felt a stab of remorse for making her see Cobb's prized boots like this.

"What did you *do?*"

"Just... shortened them up a finger or two, added a few new straps to snug them up..."

"I can't believe you'd—couldn't you at least have—*why?*"

"I don't know, I just... they were so... optimistic? So *naive*."

"The boots were naive?"

"Not the boots, the whole... the whole idea. I don't know. I shouldn't have."

He looked at Niya expecting outrage but found her eyes already distant.

"That day on the hill seems so long ago, doesn't it?" she said.

"Hmm?"

"That's just what you said then, about my muddy boots. '*He isn't going to like that.*' Remember?"

"Oh, right." Jeld smiled. "And Cobb *didn't* like it, did he? I tried to warn you."

"I almost beat you to the top of the hill."

"You'll get me next year."

Niya smiled unconvincingly then looked down into her bowl.

"Eat up," Jeld said. "Need your energy."

Niya took a tiny bite. "My medicine, you mean."

"How's the soup? Good as Cobb's?"

"Stew's sitting okay."

They shared a laugh that warmed the attic. Beneath the joyous glee though lurked a sorrowful harmony. Jeld's was a laugh of regret, for loved ones not protected, for wolves left unchecked too long, for too many thoughts and deeds that so resembled those of his father. Niya's was a mournful laugh, mournful of better days and of a good man lost, of races never run, roads left unexplored, *everything stores* never opened, and missed adventures by a brother's side.

For bells they lay there beside one another upon Niya's makeshift roost, high above the world and its concerns, sharing stories of the youth they had so quickly left behind, until late in the night they lay with tears of times good and sad in their eyes, in dreams taken.

***

Jeld awoke with a start. He blinked in the darkness to be certain his eyes were indeed open. A faint memory of some massive, intricate door crashing closed played at the edge of his mind.

A dream. Woken by a dream.

Sinking back into his thin mattress, he tried to recall the rest of the dream, but already his conscious thoughts tainted the delicate memory and, like a caught snowflake, it melted away.

A crash echoed through the attic and Jeld jolted upright.

"City Watch!" came a booming voice from below. "Anybody home?"

Jeld found Niya's shoulder in the darkness and shook her gently.

"Niya!" he whispered.

"Looking for our friend," called the watchman. "Open up or I'll seize this place on grounds of being defunct alone!"

Jeld leaned through the darkness toward Niya's ear, flinching in surprise when his nose touched her cheek.

"Niya! Wake up, there's watchmen here!"

Jeld strained to listen for activity below. His quick breaths deafening, he held them and craned his ear toward the shop. When only silence greeted him, a recent memory flashed through his mind—a crisp sting of cold upon his nose. He pressed his nose again to Niya's cheek and the same icy chill pressed back. His stomach twisted violently. He pressed two fingers gently to her neck but felt no lively rhythm, only a deathly, cold stillness.

"Ni—Niya..."

Jeld cupped her cheek, jerking his hand back from her cold, tight skin before letting it settle again upon her. An anguished moan escaped Jeld's lips.

A raging wave of shock crashed against him. He flailed to stay above the surface, the darkness of the attic suddenly so bright and warm even in despair compared to the depths of emptiness beneath the roiling torrent. He felt it pulling him downward, and even as he craned his neck skyward for breath, he slipped below the surface with a silent scream.

His eyes opened sharply and the panic was gone, flailing stilled. It was silent, peaceful here beneath the surface, the pains and cares of the world just the faintest speck of light far above.

"This is your last warning!" came another voice from below.

Jeld pulled back from Niya and only faintly felt a muted pain stir deep within himself, the feeling foreign, distant. He stood and crept across the attic then ducked out into his father's old room. More shouts erupted through the cracked doorway atop the stairs as Jeld grabbed the old leather pack from Quintem's bed and darted about the room on silent feet, his hands mindlessly plucking up things of use.

There came a splintering crash from below and the voices came again clearer.

"Anyone home? Lookin' for our friend. Had some business here, I think. If ya help us, I'm sure we can work something out..."

"Don't mind if we don't, either," came the second voice.

Jeld tiptoed back into the roost, turning sharply along the wall and starting up a makeshift ladder. He stopped at the top before a small door and glanced through the darkness to where Niya lay still below. For a moment it seemed his emotions would surface and break him, but with a conscious effort, he let himself sink back into the empty depths then climbed through the doorway.

He emerged onto the roof of the shop. Stars shined bright in the clear sky, setting his breath aglow. The cold air felt good, a welcome, tangible, familiar assault upon his body. He jumped off onto the neighboring rooftop, climbed down to hang from a lower balcony, and dropped to the alley below as he had countless times before.

At the alley's end he started west, but quickly turned in the other direction. Then he stopped, spinning about. He found himself staring at the shop and through the depths that were the only thing keeping him from collapsing into a ball upon the ground, a rage sharp and white hot broke through the surface and set his blood boiling. Idols be damned if he'd see the memory of the shop taken from him – from Cobb, from Niya.

Peeking around a corner, he saw the shop's door hanging open to the night. Lantern light shone from somewhere within, swaying to the rhythm of a chorus of clatters and shouting. He dashed to the door, crouching behind it and peering inside. With a quick rummage through his pack, he opened a stout jar of leather polish and tucked it beneath a corner of the thick entry runner.

I'm sorry, Jeld thought. Not to the men within but to the very walls, the rooftop bench, the attic roost, the memories. Sorry to Cobb. Sorry to Niya.

He pulled his knife from the top of his boot and struck a flint. A stream of sparks fell onto the glistening polish and a dome of blue flame came alight atop it with a low whisper. Orange tendrils of fire soon passed through the dry old rug and crept deeper into the shop.

Jeld ran into an alley across the street to stand staring back at the shop. Alarmed shouts issued from within and the watchmen spilled from a side door. Soon, the flames within reached the ceiling and smoke surged from the door. The whole shop loosed a deep roar and the light of the flames began to lick through cracks in the walls and from windows. As the first flame kissed the night sky, Jeld stared past burning memories and blazing walls into the attic roost to a still form lying atop a small platform.

He tore his gaze away, turning his back on his sister for the first and last time, and drove himself deeper still into the depths. Without thought, his mind distant, eyes unseeing, and feet leading the way anywhere but back, he took his first aimless steps from the ashes of his life.

So fickle can the masses seem from high above, their problems so miniscule to the grand scale of civilization that patience and compassion do not come easy. But while the prosperity of society indeed exceeds the importance of the prosperity of only one, does a king stress more over feeding his kingdom than a mother over feeding her child?

—Vincet Ellemere

CHAPTER SIX

T he flames still dancing in Jeld's eyes did naught to warm him as he sat shivering in a dark alley. His legs had carried him west and south. He didn't remember much else of the last days, only that his small tunnel of perception had grown brighter and darker again several times, and then he was here.

He sat curled in a tight ball with his back pressed to the rear door of some shop. Just beyond his frozen toes and the reach of a narrow awning overhead, the cobblestones disappeared in a clean line beneath a thin blanket of snow. He stared blankly ahead as he shivered violently. The cold was piercing, but it was the silence and emptiness he could no longer bear, each shadowy span of snow or worn stone wall offering his mind an empty canvas that suppressed memories threatened to fill. When the familiar face of a young girl began to take shape upon the snow, he stood stiffly but suddenly, turned naturally in the direction he'd been walking – any way but behind—and resumed his retreat.

Looking about as he walked, he began to take in his surroundings for the first time since fleeing the unspeakable horrors he dared not remember. There were no stars overhead, only a fine sliver of moon peeking through a thick bank of black clouds. Most of the buildings were dark and silent, the people much the same as they appeared from the shadows, veering or often staggering aside before disappearing behind. He vaguely recalled a time when every set of eyes had told a story, but as always when his mind ventured to days past, he flinched from it like a gaze from the sun.

Suddenly, a pair of watchmen emerged from the darkness ahead. Jeld's knuckles turned white upon the hilt of his father's long knife. Forcing aside a flash of a memory threatening to explain his detestation, he turned abruptly down an alley before they could grow near enough to see his ragged clothing. He hurried through several twists and turns of the narrow city streets before letting out a breath.

As his pulse quieted in his ear, he heard boisterous shouts in the distance and turned slightly off course to follow them. Soon he came to a light spilling across the road from a side street. Stepping cautiously into the light he peered down the way, but the narrow street wound quickly out of sight, voices echoing out around the bend.

Even as a now familiar voice whispered warnings of wolves into his ear, another sensation drew him onward. Jeld sniffed at the air and a savory scent of roasting meat twisted his stomach. He turned onto the narrow street and walked cautiously past closed doors and dark windows toward the light and voices.

Just around a bend, the street came abruptly to life. Jeld squinted as he took in the scene, glowing windows and open doorways lighting the way bright as day. Dozens of people milled about and clustered around the many open doorways. Drunken songs and shouts and catcalls filled the air. Men clung to tankards and women underdressed for the cold to varying degrees.

Jeld walked deeper into the bustling strip. Through one of the windows he could see a particularly underdressed woman dancing and beckoning amongst silky red drapes. Jeld's face reddened, his eyes fleeing across the street only to land upon another dancer before at last settling on an innocuous pub. As he passed the entry an intoxicating scent of hot food far more enticing than any window woman beat against him amidst a chorus of music and laughter.

Cutting through a crowd outside the doorway, he passed beneath a worn wooden sign bearing a mule with a barrel upon its back and slipped inside. His breath caught and he paused in the doorway, looking nervously at the jovial crowd that might once have energized him. Still the enticing scent drew him inward toward a bar at the back of the establishment. He sat upon a stool before a polished bar top, beside the wall where wolves could only attack from one direction.

The barkeeper slapped a cup down in front of Jeld then resumed polishing the countertop in a cadence as natural as the drawing of breath.

"Welcome to the Drunken Ass. What's it to be?"

"Just water and a meal," Jeld said, his hoarse voice somehow distant.

The barkeeper's eyes flicked up to Jeld before he turned and walked down the bar. He returned a moment later, setting a bowl of stew in front of Jeld and filling his cup from a pitcher.

"Two peb," the barkeeper said, resuming his polishing after another suspicious look.

It was only at the mention of pebs that Jeld recalled the concept of money, and the fact that he hadn't any. A corked jar flashed in his memory, greenish flakes shifting within. Jeld flinched and shook the thought aside.

The barkeeper's rag froze, a sight as disturbing as the sea going still, and he captured Jeld's eyes in a piercing stare.

Jeld's gaze fell to his lap and landed upon his pack. Despite carrying—even coveting—the bag for days, he'd not dared open it on even the coldest of nights. The barkeeper's stare growing heavy, Jeld offered a reassuring grin and hesitantly reached into his pack. Feigning a search for coins, Jeld did his best to avoid touching anything as he racked his brain for a plan.

"Another for my friend here, eh Gil?" a man shouted from somewhere down the bar.

Peering up through his scraggly bangs, Jeld saw the barkeeper narrow his gaze before hurrying off toward the cup in need. Just then his hand brushed cold iron and suddenly he glimpsed a memory of a tack hammer. Then more memories, his father's face, mad eyed and wet with sweat and spittle. Jeld's own inhuman roar. A wet crunch and the spattering of blood against his face.

Jeld gritted his teeth and forced his mind clear. He peeked up again to find the barkeeper's back turned. In that moment a feral instinct, that primitive voice promising survival, whispered sharply a single word into his ear—*run*.

He snatched the bowl from the counter, spun off the stool, and dashed toward the door. As he wove through people, tables, and chairs alike, he heard the barkeeper call out. A wave of alarm rose up throughout the tavern, but by then he was closing already on the exit – his portal to safety and a full stomach. He passed through the doorway and landed his first footfall upon the snowy cobbles beneath a dark predawn sky, the cool taste of freedom filling his lungs.

Suddenly his pack strap bit into his shoulder, the jolt spinning him around and sending him tumbling to the ground. He landed hard on his back, a flash of pain erupting from his broken ribs. As he sucked at the air like a grounded fish, a broad-shouldered hulk of a man filled the doorway of the Drunken Ass, a familiar pack strap dangling from his boulder-sized fist. The man threw down the strap and charged, closing half the distance to Jeld in one huge, lumbering step.

His eyes widening, Jeld rolled onto his stomach and kicked off into a sprint. He staggered left and then right on unsteady legs before speed alone stabilized his flight and he was off before the giant closed the gap with a second monstrous bound.

Jeld grew the distance quickly without sparing another look back, a miraculously half-full bowl of stew in one hand and a threadbare pack in the other. At the main road he turned sharply west. Behind him, the path of his flight from the bruiser joined with that of his far more frightening pursuer; one which cannot be outrun, unseen, or forgotten—only faced, in time.

***

The sound of a coin dropping into Jeld's bowl roused him from his stupor. He snatched it from the dark wooden bowl and swept a glare about the snow-covered market before him. It was unusually crowded this afternoon, and people were smiling more today than was typical of any of the many markets he'd worked of late. It was his third day at this particular spot, a rare and luxurious tenure, typically having been shooed by a shopkeeper or beaten away by passing watchmen after mere bells.

When Jeld was confident that none of the market-goers were watching, he reached down the front of his ragged pants and pulled out a small purse he'd filched from a drunk weeks back. Behind the cover of his upraised knees, he inserted the coin into the purse, checked the knot securing it to his pant ties, and quickly stuffed it back into the front of his pants.

He set the bowl back on his knees, his thoughts drifting back to his foolhardy flight with it from that boisterous strip. *Love Alley*, he had since heard the place called. So too had he learned that calling a Tovarian woman *lovely* was thereby certain to earn a slap, if the same chatty drunk spoke true.

It had since proven invaluable, this bowl of his. It made a fine rain catch, a trough scoop on drier days, and a snow melter on colder ones. It held his food on the rare occasion when he possessed more than could fit in his mouth. Above all else though, it had come with a lesson. His bold thievery that night in Love Alley may have graced him with a fine meal, but he knew keeping up such behavior would net him only a cage, a lost hand, or a short rope. As such, most commonly Jeld put the bowl to use as a begging cup, turning only to cautious thievery in times of desperation.

Another coin clanked against Jeld's bowl, rousing him from a shivering daydream. He looked up to find a little girl staring at him with wide eyes. She wore a simple brown dress and her hair was clean and curly. Jeld stared back as she stood motionless above him.

"Come on now, away from there," said a man from behind the girl.

"But Da, I'm the Traveler today, remember? He gives to the poor."

"Well you'd best keep traveling, then. Come on now," her father said.

Jeld stared after the girl as her father led her away, their eyes meeting as she looked over her shoulder. How interesting he must be to her, Jeld wondered. A young man with no mother or father, no home nor rules, not a peb to his unknown name. And she with her loving parents, no doubt on her way back to a warm home with plentiful food and sisters and brothers, perhaps schooled in music and reading and writing and a trade.

The chime of the evening bell stirred Jeld from yet another departure and he found himself staring at an empty space where once the girl had been. He blinked and looked down to find a silver brick shining brightly up at him from the bottom of the dark bowl. Jeld stared down at the coin with his mouth agape before abruptly snatching it up and sweeping another suspicious glare about the square.

The market had become even more crowded. Three men wearing dark crimson cloaks passed in front of him, prompting him to notice dozens of others wearing such cloaks, all the crimson red of Tovados, The Warrior Idol. And with that he saw the other colors. White like the Craftsman's apron, the vibrant green of the Mother, black for the Wiseman, and brown like the dress of the little girl who had dropped a brick into his bowl, like the color of the open road—the color of the Traveler. Everywhere were the colors of the Idols. *Fallstival.*

The realization swept over Jeld, sending his thoughts tumbling back toward memories of days past, memories of a kindly man who oft told him Fallsday tales of old. Staring out at the jovial crowd, Jeld let himself sink back into that safe place deep within where such feelings could not penetrate. Soon the crowd was again just a flock of unsuspecting sheep, and with that a thought came to Jeld. There was one thing better than fat, dumb, and happy festival-goers, and that was fat, dumb, happy, *rich* festival-goers.

Jeld stuffed the silver brick into his purse, gathered up his pack and bowl, and hurried from the market. Staying mostly in alleyways, he cut a familiar path through the city. Soon a familiar clanging of metal arose amidst the city's voice, growing louder with his every step. Halfway along a block, he turned and began to climb up an old brick wall, the handholds coming quick and easy.

At the top he crawled onto the roof and set at once to packing his meager belongings, but his eyes flicked often across the rooftop to a broad chimney spewing white smoke. It wasn't long before he sighed and sat against the chimney. He let out a long breath as the heat of the bricks permeated his clothing and reached his cold bones. His eyes grew heavy to the steady beat of the smith's hammer echoing up the chimney.

Jeld forced his eyes wide and came to his feet. Gathering up the rest of his belongings, he walked to the edge and looked back over the rooftop. It wasn't much, and yet it was everything. His first stability, first safety, first warmth after weeks of complete transience. With a heavy sigh, he turned away and began his journey through the crowded, colorful streets toward deeper pockets.

CHAPTER SEVEN

T he winter sky was dark already despite the early hour, the cobblestones even and unbroken as they sloped ever upward beneath the feet of the parading Fallstival crowds. Crisp and cold air bore not a hint of the filth inescapable down the hill. Breaths glowed in the light of endless shops lining the streets.

Someone bumped into Jeld's backside and sent him careening into a woman with the same green hood adorning many in the crowd. Jeld gritted his teeth, pocketed the woman's coin purse, and pressed ahead. While he longed for a respite after three days in the bustling Fallstival masses, the concealment it offered was all that kept the numerous roving watchmen from taking notice of him. As such, begging had quickly proven impossible this far west, turning him toward less willing pockets amidst the Hillside crowds.

Another person knocked into him and a cold sweat beaded upon his brow. Watchmen or not, he pressed his way toward the bank of the ever flowing river of humanity. Spilling into a narrow alley, he nearly tripped over someone lying on the ground. The man's face was pressed against the cobblestones and seemed bonelessly to pool together with a puddle of vomit that lay beneath it. Jeld paused with his supple but ragged boots just beyond reach of the puddle's longest fingers and pursed his lips.

The man was so pathetically helpless it would be a vile crime, he considered, but... if the man had enough money to drink himself stupid then surely he had money to spare. For all he knew, he'd be helping the man out by taking his booze money away, Jeld told himself unconvincingly. Shaking his head, he stepped over the man and continued along only to pause after just a few steps.

Surely the poor sap would be picked over on short order, might not it just as well be him? Jeld backtracked and stared down at the man. With a sigh, he crouched and began rifling through the man's pockets. Finding them already empty, he cursed the world for making him compromise his values without gain. Loosing another sigh, he moved the man's hand beneath his cheek to keep him from drowning in his own vomit.

Suddenly a fanfare of horns echoed up the alley. Jeld peered out to find the crowds parting. Columns of mounted knights in gleaming armor began to file past, hooves clapping along the cobblestones. Behind them, a striking figure in a mixture of polished steel and black leather armor rode upon a beautiful white horse. A crimson cloak billowed behind him. Upon his black cuirass was emblazoned a large sword, symbol of House Tovados.

Jeld's fingers clutched the hilt of his knife. There were but three men in the city who would bear that crest—the king, the legendary Idolic warrior General Handan Tovaine, and the man parading by as if the people should praise him for building more prisons and cleaning up the city with the point of his sword. Prince Dralor. The Black Prince.

Whether by Fallstival spirit or Hillside privilege, the cheers nonetheless grew louder as the prince neared. Memories flashed in Jeld's mind—the prince's watchmen standing over him, Cobb's hammer slipping from Niya's fingertips, the terrible cold touch of Niya's lifeless cheek upon his nose.

Suddenly a hand closed on his shoulder.

"Easy," a woman's voice said.

Jeld sucked in a breath and found himself near the front of the crowd, his knife drawn at his side. The prince was nearing. Sheathing his knife and turning, Jeld found a woman standing behind him. Her thick curly gray hair was pulled back in a tail that did little to contain it. The lines upon her face were deep and her hands veined and boney, yet her grip was strong and she stood without the slightest stoop.

"Easy," the woman said again. "Come, come."

Jeld looked back over his shoulder to the prince as the woman ushered him through the crowd and onto a quieter side street.

"Right. What is it then, crown do ya wrong?"

Jeld stopped. "Who—"

"Because if every person the crown shit on just dove onto the prince's sword, I don't see how we'd be much better off. Keep moving now, tight schedule."

"But I—Who are you?"

"There's better ways. Not to kill the prince, mind you—well, even that, I suppose—but to make it known that we Riversiders and whatnot even exist. To make sure they know their sinning has consequences."

"You sound like a Sayer."

She smiled. "Just another victim of the crown who couldn't bear to see you split in half. *Raf*, by the way. You?"

"Uh, Jeld."

Raf led Jeld onto a pristine Hillsider street lined with stores. She moved with ease, as if her age were but a costume. The street was completely deserted, owing to the parade, Jeld presumed.

"*Better ways,*" Jeld said. "Let me guess, be a good citizen? Thank them kindly for their shit?"

"Throwing rocks."

"Throwing... rocks," Jeld echoed.

Brushing off a dusting of snow, she picked up a rare broken Hillside cobblestone and pitched it at a shop. It struck a hanging sign bearing a beautiful carving of a flowing dress, toppling it to the ground with a loud clatter.

Jeld glanced quickly about for any sign of the City Watch.

"They're busy."

A shout erupted from the dress shop and they ran around the next corner.

"So, *rocks*. Rocks are going to bring back my—" Jeld blinked aside memories best forgotten. "Going to change things, then?"

"No worse than jumping on the prince's sword will. But, no. There are many kinds of rocks. In fact... got quite a stone cooking up tonight. Perhaps you'll tag along? We could use your help."

"We?"

"Friends of mine. Like us. We'll not right all the world's wrongs, but I can promise we'll be heard."

"Heard? What's the point."

"Sometimes it's not about what the rock breaks, but about who else realizes they can pick one up."

Jeld's thoughts grew distant until soon the woman came to a stop before a small stables. She knocked and the doors came open at once. A man inside eyed Jeld.

"He's okay," Raf said.

Without a word, the man climbed aboard a hitched wagon and took up the reins. Climbing onto a bench upon the back of the wagon, Raf gestured for Jeld to join her.

Jeld eyed Raf, then turned his gaze to the wagon. Countless memories of days rolling along the countryside upon a wagon flooded his mind, days leaning back against a mountain of freight to behold the stars above, days with—

He gritted his teeth and sat beside Raf. The reins cracked and they were off, but with the first rock of the wagon came the unmistakable whine of a swine. Raf only grinned, and Jeld said not a word of the oddity, only wondering what sort of *rock* a swine could be made to be as the wagon made its way west.

The beautiful albeit narrow homes lining the streets widened with each block up the hill, and so too did the spaces between them until each was surrounded in an ornately manicured garden. Jeld again gritted his teeth. What use could any person have for a home of such size? How could anyone slave away at fruitless gardens when there were people starving down the hill?

They came to a low wall no more than two leaps in height and stopped before a gate flanked by a pair of guards. A mere bump compared to the city wall and the walls of the keep, Jeld wondered if this wall served any tactical purpose or merely helped keep the Toppers from glimpsing any disorderly bushes.

"A hog for the spit, by order of the lord governor, good guardsmen," the man driving the wagon said.

"A second this year?" said one of the guards. "Must be *some* Fallstival party. Go on."

The wagon passed through and the gate closed behind them.

"Easy enough," said Raf. "The hams love their ham."

"I was beginning to wonder what the pig was for."

"Oh the pig is more than just our ticket in."

They rode on in silence save for the clap of hooves and occasional squeal. Sprawling mansions and vast snowy gardens dwarfed the once impressive homes that had so irked Jeld but moments before. Any reservations as to his complicity in whatever it was they were doing vanished behind the same rage that had seen him blindly marching blade in hand toward the prince.

"We're almost to Demerious's mansion. We'll do our thing while my friend leads the wagon off. You and I will cut off the road on foot and run for the wall. There'll be ropes waiting for us."

Jeld's heart began to race. While joy was a distant memory, he felt something close to alive for the first time since he dared remember.

Just when it seemed the mansions could grow no bigger, the wagon pulled to a stop in the gardens before an absurdity of a new level. Taking a deep breath, Raf slid off the wagon to the snow covered ground and began unfastening the tailgate. Jeld followed suit, and sure enough when the gate fell open there was a pig inside.

Together they pulled at a rope fastened about the creature's neck and led it out. The wagon pulled away at once, leaving Jeld feeling every bit like he was standing before the lord governor's mansion with a pig. He stared up at the beautiful, disgustingly excessive monstrosity.

Movement caught Jeld's eye and he turned from the mansion just as Raf plunged a knife into the pig's neck. The hog shrieked and flailed about wildly, rolling about in the reddening snow. Soon it came to a stop on its side, legs still kicking.

"Come!" Raf said, tugging Jeld into flight.

Jeld stared over his shoulder as his legs followed after Raf, who once again surprised Jeld with her speed. Streams of glistening red reached out across the pristinely white snow toward the door of the lord governor's mansion. Still the pig's legs twitched.

"Jeld!"

Sucking in a breath, Jeld turned and jogged alongside Raf. A woman screamed from somewhere behind just as they pressed through a line of bushes. Without a word they both sped down the hill, weaving between more manicured shrubs and hedges.

"Through here," Raf huffed, veering between two rows of what looked to be grapevine.

They emerged behind another mansion, speeding past a gawking stableboy leading a horse before at last reaching the wall. A rope hung down from beyond it.

Raf waving him ahead, Jeld led the way up and over the wall. He dropped to his feet in an alley in the relative safety of Hillside and stared up at the rope anxiously. He let out a breath when finally a leg kicked over the wall and Raf emerged to work her way down the rope. They wordlessly worked their way back toward the safety of the crowds until the weight of Raf's gaze brought Jeld to a stop just before a bustling street.

"Well?" she panted with a grin. "Trust me, the statement we made will be heard long and far. And... doesn't feel too bad either, am I right?"

Jeld frowned before loosing a breath of something like laughter.

"I must be off," Raf said. "What do you say, throw some more rocks with me some time? I can't promise anything as dramatic as our pig, but—"

"Yes," Jeld answered quickly.

Raf smiled. "Stop by my shop any time and we'll give the Toppers something to think about."

Jeld spun as a loud crash sounded from behind. A woman in a red cape of Tovados staggered past, singing and banging a wooden sword against a pot before disappearing into the festive crowds.

"You have a shop?"

Raf nodded. "Candle shop. Just off Trumbley Market. You know the place?"

"Oh. Yeah. Really?"

"Didn't take me for the tradesman sort? Yeah, really. Not a bad setup, either. Even right next to the butcher, so I get my share of discounted tallow."

"Well, I'll see ya. And... thanks."

"Oh sure. You catch yourself wanting to single handedly off a prince again, just come find me and we'll stick it to them Toppers somehow."

Jeld flushed. "Right. Thanks."

Raf winked and disappeared into the crowd.

His thoughts heavy, Jeld didn't so much as pick a single pocket as he rejoined the crowd and let its currents whisk him away to his latest residence beneath the deck of the *Barking Crab.* There, he pressed himself into a corner where he hoped he might avoid the worst of night's bitter chill, but he would not escape the dark thoughts and visions of faces best unnamed that followed him always into dreams.

*****

A raging fire reached high into the night sky, blinding against the darkness surrounding it. The sight stirred emotions buried deep within Jeld, but all gave way to fear as the inferno's crackle grew into a menacing, monstrous snarl. Suddenly a sharp, deafening bark jolted Jeld from dreams. His eyes shot open but blinding firelight—real firelight—quickly forced them to narrow to a squint. The snarl and barking of dogs assailed his tired senses and set his sluggish heart pounding. As his eyes adjusted, the toothy maws of two hellish hounds began to take shape amidst the fire.

"City Watch! You've got ten blinks until I let Nose and Nuts at ya!" a nasally voice called. "Don't bother me none, neither. Less I have to feed them, and they *love* crab meat!"

The dogs went wild and Jeld scrambled away, but his backside only pressed futilely against the base of the Barking Crab. He pounded on the boards running overhead.

"Nose got his name for sniffin' out shits like you. Five more blinks and you'll find out how Nuts got hers!"

"Wait!" Jeld shrieked. "I'm coming out!"

"Best hurry, doesn't look like Corry boy here can hold that rope much longer."

Jeld pulled his purse out from the front of his pants and hacked it free with his knife. Stuffing both into his pack, he threw it into the corner and hurried toward the beasts. As he neared, one lunged and its sizable jaws snapped sharply closed just out of reach.

"I'm here! I'm here!"

"Back, ya brainless heaps!" a second, strained voice called.

The two hound heads slowly pulled away, disappearing behind the glare of the torch-light. Just before Jeld could duck through the opening, a torch stabbed through and he narrowly rolled aside, cringing back from its heat. A man's face emerged behind it, nose twitching above a sneer. Jeld was certain this was the owner of the nasally voice even before the man spoke.

"Ah, young one. Took a while though, didn't he, Corry boy?"

The watchman stabbed his torch toward the corner and the firelight fell upon Jeld's pack.

"*Hah!* See, Corry boy? They'll always pull a fast one on ya, don't you forget it. Now, boy, go fetch that bag of yours before I have Nuts try. Gets confused sometimes, dumb bitch."

Jeld looked over at his pack then back to the watchman.

"Oh *please* try somethin'."

"I'm going!"

Jeld hurried toward his pack.

"Don't ya dare dump nothin', neither!" called the watchman.

"I wouldn't! I'm coming!"

When Jeld returned with his pack, a hand closed on his shirt collar, dragging him out beneath the open skies. A menacing snarl sounded to Jeld's side and he scrambled to his feet even as the grip clamped down upon the back of his neck. Straining his eyes to their corners they fell upon the two huge hounds baring teeth and staring at him like a fresh piece of meat. A young watchman with eyes not yet jaded by duty struggled with a taut leash.

"Ay! Nuff!" barked the weaselly watchman.

The larger of the beasts fell silent, all traces of its fury disappearing in an instant. The smaller, meaner-looking hound kept up its tooth-baring snarl.

"Nuts! Quit!"

Nuts issued one more pointed bark at Jeld then circled several times and plopped to the ground panting.

The weasely watchman tossed Jeld's pack over to his young partner then spun Jeld west and rapped him between the shoulder blades.

"Arright, you. Move."

Jeld's mind raced through means of escape as he started ahead, but each scenario he considered seemed to end in dogs eating him.

"Ah... Sarge?" Corry said from behind.

"Yeah?"

"Ain't you gonna search him?"

A tug on Jeld's collar brought him to a stop.

"Hah! Attaboy! Took ya a block but luckily neither of us got stuck, so worth the lesson. Here, gimme them dogs and get pattin'."

Corry handed off the leashes and stepped in front of Jeld. "Arms up, legs apart, would you?"

Jeld heard a weaselly groan behind him at the last.

"Er, let's go, ah... *boy!*" Corry added.

As the young watchman meticulously patted down his upraised arms, Jeld felt hot, quick breaths against his side. His eyes widened at a sudden, disconcerting realization, and he slowly peered over his shoulder to find Nose's monstrous furry head hovering over his unprotected flank. The hound's mouth hung open, a long, flat tongue lolling from between dagger-like teeth. Jeld clenched his eyes shut as the watchman continued his search.

"If he's a thief he ain't a boot thief," Corry said, coming to his feet. "Ugliest boots I ever saw."

The young watchman started down the street again, Jeld's pack hanging from his shoulders. Longingly eying his pack, Jeld followed to save himself a rap on the back.

"Little crab learns faster than these mutts," the sergeant said from behind.

They continued several blocks through the dark streets before Jeld's stomach sank upon rounding a corner. A cage wagon was parked on the side of the street, a lantern hanging from a tall pole at its front. Three prisoners stared out from within. A chunky watchman sat upon the driver's bench, his head lolled forward.

"Grahh!" the sergeant roared as they neared.

The snoozing watchman cried out and jumped to his feet.

"Blazin' Khapar, Sarge!"

"Watchmen that don't *watch* haven't really done anything to get paid for, have they, Kaddy? And they don't live too long, neither."

"Nearly shat myself, Sarge," Kaddy whined.

"Good. What kinda lesson are you teachin' Corry, a seasoned watchman like yourself?"

Kaddy sat up. "Sorry, Sarge."

"Ay! Up, ya sorry lump! Get this crab in there!"

"Crab?"

"Move!" the sergeant spat, a vein bulging at his temple.

Kaddy walked to the back of the wagon and started trying various keys in the cell lock. Jeld stared past to the prisoners within. Two were ragged, one old and one not, but both looking right at home in a cell. The third was nicely dressed, oddly out of place behind the bars and increasingly familiar.

After several curses and numerous keys, the oafish watchman finally turned the lock.

"Don't anybody try nothin'. Stay put, back of the cell."

Cell...

The word seemed to echo in Jeld's mind. Again his eyes darted about, searching for some means of escape. Before he could piece together anything useful, the sergeant pushed him forward and Kaddy grabbed his arm and swung him into the cell. The door slammed shut behind him as he stumbled to a stop.

"Please!" the familiar prisoner cried. "I didn't do anything! I didn't do anything wrong!"

The man looked to have had a rough night. Fresh dirt covered the front of his otherwise decent clothes, giving him the disheveled look unattainable by the fully wretched. His neatly trimmed beard was caked with filth across one cheek.

Jeld's eyes widened. This was the unconscious man from the alley the night prior—the man he'd tried to rob.

"Uh-huh. Always innocent," Kaddy said, again trying key after key.

The captive's lips seemed to mouth *please* over and over again until they just quivered.

Finally the lock clanged again with a horrible finality. The watchmen climbed up onto the driver's bench, the dogs into their own smaller cage behind them. Corry lowered Jeld's pack out of sight and Jeld's shoulders fell with it.

"Not so bad," a raspy voice said from behind. "I been locked up a time or ten and I'm still alive and good."

Jeld turned to find the older of his filthy cellmates grinning madly at him through a long beard as thin and white as the wispy plume atop his head. One of his wrists ended in a stub, the gruesome sight drawing Jeld's eyes despite his best efforts.

"Oh sure, they put old righty here to the block. Usually though it's just a week in the dark, maybe some lashes at worst, but nothin' that don't grow back."

The man's lips parted in a mostly toothless smile.

"Might not be soo easy gettin' oot thas time, Denin friend," the third of Jeld's cellmates said with the thick brogue of the Isles.

The wagon lurched forward and Jeld had to grab a bar to keep his balance.

"'Ave a seat before yeh 'urt yourself."

Jeld sat beside the islander.

"Noo, Denin, ain't just some drunkard sweep, ain't yeh heard?"

Denin shook his head gravely.

"Good on yeh if yeh have because it just happened the day before. Well, certain yeh know about all the crime been goin' on o'late, what with patrools been rampin' up. Buncha fine shops and homes been hit, rich folk muggins and all that. Well, last night the goovernor's mansion got all busted up. Warst of it though was the pag, it was."

"What?" Denin said.

"Ay?"

"Warst... oaf... pag... *huh?*"

"Oh! The *pag*. Ya, that was the warst yet, it was."

"What? What in the blazes are you sayin'!"

"The pag! *Pag*, I said! Doon't yeh speak a lick of Common?"

"*Ahck!* Idols, you islanders and your gibbertongue, don't—"

"Shut it back there!" the sergeant barked over his shoulder.

"Pag!" Denin scoffed. "Pag, he—"

"Pig," Jeld interrupted before his new cellmates could earn them all a beating. "Worst of it was the pig."

"That's a lad!" the islander said with a slap of his knee. He continued at a whisper, Jeld and Denin leaning in closer to hear. Even the man from the alley stared eagerly.

"Lavonal, by the way. Good meetin' yeh. Anyway, as I said, warst of it was the pag. Whoever it was, they bled that pag out all over the goovernor's garden. And ya know them richies an' their gardens! May as well have pissed on his mother, ain't he have? Rest I'm just guessin', but sure as the Wiseman, the prince called a sweep."

"B-but they can't just go s-snatching up innocent men!" the man from the alley blubbered. "I'm n-not fooling, I've done not a thing. I had a drink or two and next thing I knew..."

"They doon't care none. Crown says sweep and they sweep. Ain't right though, I hear yeh."

"What are they gonna d-do with us?"

"Lock us up for a good while to be sure. A show for all the lordies. Course, they could do worse I suppose...."

Lavonal offered the man a smile, but finding him staring blankly at the ground, he turned back to Jeld and shrugged his eyebrows.

"Soo what's the first order of business to be, then?"

"What do you mean?"

"When you're out. A meal, is it? Or a nap, I'll bet. Muts cut your nap short, am I right?"

"Oh. Yes. They did."

Jeld left it at that. What business of this probable criminal was it when he napped? Lavonal nodded and looked out at the passing city as Jeld found himself nonetheless considering his first order of business.

"I suppose a meal," Jeld said after a while.

"Hard to buy a meal withoot a peb to your name. Weren't plannin' to steal it, were yeh? A *reformed* man such as yourself."

"I've got a coin or two."

"Not in your bag, I hope."

Jeld raised an eyebrow.

"Oh believe yeh me, boy, yeh won't be seein' that bag of yours again."

Jeld's eyes grew distant as he recalled the dark days before his bowl, before his second pair of socks, his coat, his cap, his spare coin. He thought too of the bag itself and the simple luxury of carrying things, but more so the singular connection it seemed to offer to the life behind him... the life beyond the depths.

A loud retching erupted across the cage and Jeld and Lavonal both turned quickly to see their hungover cellmate vomit out onto the street. One hand clenched high up a bar, the man sagged against the cell wall. Jeld felt another stab of remorse over having tried to rob him.

"What about you?" Jeld found himself asking the islander. "Your *first order of business?*"

"Hah, look at us dreamin' like we been locked up for ten years. Well, one meal sounds fine enough, but it's business that'll keep the rest coomin'. I've got to get some goods built back up, seein' as these loovelies saw fit to trash moost my wares and steal the rest."

The concept of thinking beyond one next meal was so out of reach that Jeld couldn't even relate enough to envy, only admire as one might a bird yet make no plans to fly.

"Why did they pick you up?"

"Sold a magic amulet. Noo different than I done a thousand times before."

"We're all wolves," Jeld muttered.

"What's that then?"

"Predators. We're all predators."

"Maybe... maybe. But it seems to me that wolves would sneak up an' tear throoats out, not try'n sell trinkets."

"Maybe we go just far enough, take just enough to not be worth trampling."

"I doon't think the world is so black and white. If I'm a wolf, I think I must be a particularly kind one."

Jeld nodded.

"Aright yeh sheep loover, how're yeh going to get that meal of yours?"

"The hams on the hill don't seem to care enough about their money to keep an eye on it, so I'll probably go west again, at least for the rest of Fallstival."

Lavonal frowned. "Careful there. In case yeh hadn't nooticed they're sweeping up people like us. And watch that word now—*ham*. After that pag, I doon't doubt if they start stringin' us up for sayin' bacon to a butcher."

Jeld fell quiet. West was the only way... Even now, the rising eastern sun pressing against his downcast eyes set his nerves on edge. He wasn't supposed to go east.

"There now, you'll get by just fine. Same as yeh always have for yourself, I'm bettin'. Just doon't go west."

Jeld nodded without looking up. His sullenness seemed to dissuade even the jovial islander, and soon there was only the hollow thud of hooves, the rattle and jingle of the wagon cage, and the hushed murmur of a Tovarian dawn. The cobblestones passed by in a blur behind his rolling prison.

A sudden halt roused Jeld from his fugue. They were stopped before a gate. A small guard shack stood just beyond at the foot of an old tower, not a single window dotting the sheer stone surface as it stretched high into the night sky. Jeld's stomach sank.

"Gally! Got a delivery for ya!" the sergeant called from the front of the wagon.

The door of the guard shack opened and a watchman emerged, his face closely shaven save for a thick mustache.

"Sergeant Alvy. Spending far too much time with you tonight."

"Thinkin' so myself. Got four more to give ya. Three rats and a crab."

"A crab?"

"Found him under the Barking Crab."

Gally pulled the gate open. "Hah! Crab, then."

Jeld looked longingly behind at the still open gate as Gally led their wagon past. Turning to the windowless tower, he shivered. The man from the alley started to sob.

"Thing is, Alvy," Gally began, "we only got room for one. *'Fill up Northwest'*, they said. Well, one of your rats—or *crabs*—will do it. Rest you gotta take to Central."

"Ah!" Lavonal clucked quietly. "Windows there."

"Full?" the watch sergeant said. "It ain't been full since the war."

Gally nodded. "Two-hundred already tonight. Well it's about time we clean things up, if you ask me. Can't keep a city safe by arresting people *after* they do something. It's these street folk that do it all and Prince Dralor knows it, you bet he does."

"That prince's prison opening can't come fast enough, am I right?"

"Tellin' me. Now which one'll it be?"

"Take the old thief. Make for a quieter ride to Central.

"What!" Denin screamed. "I paid my debt! What've these ones paid?"

"Kaddy, get him out."

Kaddy climbed down from the front of the wagon and again began trying keys at the lock.

"No! You can't! It's not fair!" Denin spat.

Lavonal put a hand on Denin's shoulder. "Enough of that, my friend. Just going to get yourself beat doing like that."

"Let off!" Denin growled, swiping Lavonal's hand away with his stumped wrist.

"Come now, yeh weren't soo pissed 'til yeh found out they're not taking the rest of us."

"King's lovelies the lot of you!"

Lavonal winked at Jeld before turning back to Denin.

"Easy now. There it is, there it is. A full prison, they said. What could they do with soo many men anyway but set 'em free after their prince gives his fancy."

Eyeing the cell door, Jeld slid slowly along the bench toward it. Seeming to realize what Jeld was considering, Lavonal discreetly shook his head in warning.

The watchman pulled the cell door open. "Stay on your arses, all of ya. Er, except you there. Out with you."

Denin began to scream and tried pressing himself through the bars. Kaddy sighed and shuffled into the cell as Denin kicked out feebly. He grabbed Denin, stretching him across the cell as the old man clung desperately to a bar with his only hand.

Jeld glanced to the driver's bench. The watchmen all had their backs turned, the hounds caged behind them now slumbering. Again Lavonal shook his head at Jeld, fervently this time, but Jeld only blew out a breath and slipped from the cell behind Kaddy.

Ducking low lest Kaddy spot him through the cell bars, Jeld hurried to the front of the wagon. He peered up at the still turned backs of the two watchmen, rising to peek down into the driver's cab. Jeld spotted his pack, but to his dismay the watch sergeant's foot was planted right inside one of the straps.

He ducked back to the ground and looked about, his gaze passing by one of Nuts's huge paws hanging out from the cage above before snapping back to it as an idea struck him. Jumping up, Jeld punched the dog's paw then rolled beneath the wagon. As he'd hoped, Nuts went wild.

"Ay! Shut it, dog!" came Alvy's bark.

"What's gotten into him?" asked the young watchman.

Nuts only growled and barked more furiously.

Jeld begged himself to reconsider and merely slip away unnoticed, but to no avail. Idols be damned if he was going to let the watch get away with taking his pack after everything else they'd inflicted. Gritting his teeth, he sprung to his feet at the front of the wagon and quickly took in his surroundings. The watchmen atop the wagon were now facing the dog cage. The watch sergeant was no longer standing on his pack. The watchman from the prison was staring right at him.

Jeld's eyes went wide. He snatched his pack and ran, speeding out through the gate. Shouts erupted from behind and he glanced over his shoulder to find the now mad-eyed sergeant already in pursuit a mere three leaps back. His heart racing, Jeld tucked his head nearly to his chest and pressed ahead, but the wiry watchman nearly matched him with unexpected speed.

Jeld turned a corner and looked back again. When the watchman went wide and the gap widened, he knew what he had to do. He zigged and zagged block after block, his lead growing each corner until finally he planted his heel and turned sharply onto the King's Road, racing alongside the storefronts at the edge of the crowd. Not a moment later cries rose up over the hushed morning hum and weaselly shouts shattered any remaining peace.

"Make a... hole!" came the sergeant's breathless bellows. "Step... aside!"

The crowd behind Jeld began to part. His eyes darted about at shops and side streets, the ripple of the parting crowd behind washing ever closer. As he readied to slip into the next alley, something just beyond caught his eye. Two immense doors stood ajar at the front of a towering building of wind-worn stone, intricate etched symbols upon them set aglow by a dim yet warm light radiating from within.

Jeld's gaze lingered upon the doors as he pressed through the crowd. They were familiar somehow, but he couldn't place them. Behind, the last travelers between him and the raving watchman began to part. Jeld looked longingly to the alley and its certain safety even as he darted willfully past, slipping between the massive doors to disappear within.

CHAPTER EIGHT

J eld's eyes traced the ornate carvings upon the ancient-looking doors as he sped between them. Inside, he slowed to a sudden stop. Scattered about a vast room, perhaps three dozen people sat upon long benches of solid stone, their backs turned. Beyond them, a man in a tattered gray robe stood addressing the gathering.

"...would have you believe that our Idols have abandoned us. Given up on us. That *indecency* has pervaded mankind and driven our Idols away. But have you even one neighbor who would not spare you bread should you starve, or water should you thirst?"

Acutely aware of his closing pursuer, Jeld darted inward on silent feet and rolled over the first bench to the floor below, his pack clutched against his chest.

"Evil exists, make no mistake, but know that our Idols have not lost faith in us. They have *not* abandoned us. Trust in the decency of man. Trust in the Idols' eternal love, for such is their faith in us that they have sacrificed everything to bestow upon us the greatest of gifts. It is a gift that began its journey long, long ago when The One first touched dear Idolo..."

As Jeld lay straining to hear any signs of pursuit over the echoing voice and his own heavy breaths, his eyes fell upon a dome high overhead, a soft glow radiating in from countless arched windows around its base.

"On and on this greatest of gifts passed before Lord Reverie dreamt the Halls into being, and on and on did it pass again before the great and wise Tholomas split this singular gift, attuning it to five aspects, that it might bring not one but five to better wield the mantle of the gift. And so did the Halls meld in dreams with the five, sculpting with the Lady her majestic grove, with the Warrior his great hall, the Traveler his tavern, the Craftsman his shop, and the Wiseman his library."

Beneath the dome, a huge eye was etched in shining white tiles high up one of the walls. Jeld craned his neck to the wall opposite and was at once captivated by another symbol. Two flowing lines, like trickling streams or notes of music, faced one another to form the abstract likeness of a lute. It was equally massive and as beautiful as the eye that watched it from across the chamber.

"And when the great enemy *Discord* threatened all, our Idols in their eternal love sacrificed their very bodies to ascend into dreams or beyond, where even now they wage war in our defense. As with their bodies, they could not take the gift into this place, and so like Tholomas before them they split the gift further still, that many the world over might share the Idolic touch, for though some few might wield it unjustly, they trusted in the decency of mankind."

Jeld surveyed the symbols. He fell into the depths of the lute until he was soaring down the open road across a green valley, then above the clouds atop a craggy mountain ridge, then over a great rolling blue sea...

"Remarkable, aren't they?" the disembodied voice continued.

Lost in the majesty of the symbols, a moment passed before a thought struck Jeld and he returned to the present. The voice... had it been different somehow? Softer? Closer? His breathing seeming suddenly louder, Jeld held it and strained to listen, but the place was eerily silent.

"It's alright, nobody followed you," the voice said. "You can breathe."

Jeld sat up slowly until he found the owner of the calm voice sitting upon the stone bench two rows ahead. He had a mop of brown hair atop his head, and the gray robe he wore managed somehow to appear even more ragged than it had from across the chamber. His face showed only the faintest lines, his eyes warm and full of hope. Jeld was at first reminded of the young watchman, Corry, but he quickly realized his mistake. Corry's was a hope untested, naive to the harsh truths of the world, whereas this man had seen much. His was a hope despite. His was faith.

The man smiled to Jeld. Beyond him, the room was vacant save for two young faces staring toward him from the frontmost bench.

"My name is Prishner Walson. I am the attending prishner today—"

The man interrupted himself with a half-hearted laugh.

"Well, I'm the *only* prishner here of late, but regardless, I don't think I've seen you here before, so welcome."

The man extended his hand to Jeld and stared at him with his warm, faithful eyes. Jeld eyed the hand suspiciously.

The prishner let his hand fall. "No matter, son. It's alright. What's your name?"

"Ah, Corr."

"Corr. Can I get you some hot stew? Mostly beans, but the bone broth is quite comforting."

Jeld clenched his jaw closed to stay his famished body's instantaneous affirmation. A man handing out free meals? He glanced behind to the doorway.

"Don't worry, my friend, you're safe here. I know how hard it is out there, believe me. I can't help you there, but I can help you here. This—"

A loud retching sounded from somewhere behind the prishner. He jumped up and turned even as a new voice called out.

"Prishner! He's at fits again!"

It was a girl's voice, urgent and full of concern. It held an accent that, much like its owner's whereabouts, Jeld could not place.

"Turn him on his side!" Prishner Walson called. "Corr, please excuse me, there are others who need tending."

He turned and ran toward the front.

"Fendrith, water and a cloth please! Waller, another cushion please!"

The two boys on the front bench jumped up and darted through doorways to either side.

When the prishner reached the front he crouched, disappearing from view behind the countless rows of benches and leaving Jeld staring past at a sprawling tree etched upon the far wall. He knew it to be the symbol of Syladrya, the Mother, the Lady of the Woods, giver of life, huntress.

"That's better," the prishner's voice echoed softly from ahead. "Should keep him from choking."

Jeld rose to a crouch until he could see Prishner Walson and a girl in boyish street clothes bent over a small, still boy. One of the boys emerged from the doorway on the right carrying a large cushion. He was short and skinny, his plain tunic and trousers badly worn yet enviably clean.

"Tuck it here please, Waller. At the waist. Any higher and it will suffocate him, and any lower and it won't keep him from rolling onto his face."

Waller bent and tucked the cushion into the bend of the sick boy's waist.

"Good. Thank you."

The boy returned to the bench and sat beside a bowl and a hunk of bread. He tore off a piece of bread and began scraping the inside of the bowl with it.

A few moments passed in mouth-watering silence before the other boy emerged from the opposite side holding a large bucket by a cloth-wrapped handle. He was much larger than Jeld, with the bones of a man despite a barely lingering boyishness that put him close still to Jeld's own age. Setting the bucket a few steps from Prishner Walson, he unwrapped the handle and gave the cloth to the prishner.

"Thank you very much, Fendrith," Prishner Walson said.

"You're welcome, Prishner. I should be off. Thank you, Prishner."

"Be safe."

Fendrith hefted a large pack over one of his broad shoulders and started down the aisle toward the door. As he passed, he looked over to where Jeld knelt still upon the floor and nodded.

Jeld flinched away. Footsteps rose and fell and when he looked back, Fendrith was disappearing between the massive doors.

The soothing echo of gently churning water drew Jeld's attention back to the front. The girl beside the prishner wrung the cloth out over the steaming bucket and draped it over the sickly boy's forehead.

"Thank you, my dear lady. You have healing hands," the prishner said. "Would you mind showing our new guest, Corr, about?"

"Of course, Prishner."

She stood and turned to face Jeld. By appearances she seemed perhaps his age. Atop her boyish getup, her dark hair was pulled back into a knot. Her big, ice-blue eyes were fixed onto his.

Realizing he was still kneeling, Jeld came to his feet.

"Corr, is it?" the girl said.

Jeld's eyes flicked back to the doorway.

"My name's Lira. I help here sometimes. Would you like a tour?"

"I, ah..."

Jeld glanced again to the doorway, then to Waller, the bowl of stew, and finally to where the prishner was gently rubbing the boy's forehead.

Prishner Walson cleared his throat. "Waller, help me get Werner to bed, would you please?"

Waller set aside his empty bowl and went to the prishner's aid. Wordlessly, as if both had done it together countless times before, they lifted the sickly boy by the blanket beneath him and shuffled toward a side room.

"It is good to have you here, Corr," the prishner said.

Jeld only stared back as they disappeared through the doorway.

"Come on then," Lira said. "If we liked to eat street boys we certainly wouldn't keep the sick ones."

Jeld met her eyes. *Humor.* He recognized it, but little more. Still, the statement made logical sense. He nodded and walked to her.

"Pleased to meet you, Corr."

"Pleased to meet you," Jeld echoed, his eyes quickly fleeing to the ground.

"How about we start the tour with that meal Prishner Walson promised?"

"That would be... nice. Thank you."

"I'll be right back."

She disappeared through the doorway Fendrith had fetched the water from.

Run! hissed the voice that had kept him alive alone and on the street. *Cult! The stew poisoned the sick boy!*

He glanced yet again toward the exit but the lute etched upon the wall caught his gaze. Certainly the *Traveler* wouldn't flee from innocuous strangers, he reasoned.

The Traveler is dead!

Jeld sat in defiance upon the frontmost bench and surveyed the rest of the room. Upon the wall beside the lute, hidden before from view by the benches he'd lain between, was another symbol. The great sword of the Warrior. Across from it, beside the all-knowing eye, was the open hand of the Craftsman. Jeld turned about the room in full, looking over the eye, the hand, the tree, the sword, and the lute. Again he lost himself in the last.

"Do you whisper to him?" Lira's voice came.

Jeld turned quickly and found her standing in the doorway, a steaming bowl in one hand and a whole loaf of bread in the other.

"Sorry?"

"You were staring at Kelthin's lute. I thought maybe you said your whispers to him. I whisper most often to Vincet. If only I had his wisdom, things would be so much easier. And Tovados sometimes, because, well, for strength. You favor the Traveler, though?"

"Oh. No. I—not really."

She approached, handing over the meal and sitting beside him.

Jeld stared down at the steaming stew with wonder. "Thank you... I—"

"It's nothing. It's what we do. Well, what Prishner Walson does, really."

"What is this place?"

"This is the North Tovarian Temple of One. The prishner does daily tellings here and all that, but these days he spends most of his time helping poor—well, helping kids in need. Nothing much, mind you. A bit of love, a meal now and then. He'd do more if he could, of course, but the temple can hardly afford even that."

"Who *pays* for all this?"

"Hmm? Prishner Walson does. The king pays prishners a modest wage, plus a small upkeep for their temples. Prishner Walson uses all of it to help, even the upkeep money, so he sometimes has to ask his children—the children here—for a helping hand in kind."

Jeld nodded as he ripped a chunk of bread from the loaf, dipped it in the stew, and reveled in its deliciousness. They were silent for a while as he worked at his meal, and Jeld's eyes once again drifted to the symbol of the Traveler.

"Temple of One, you said," Jeld asked. "What does that mean?"

"Oh, yes, confusing isn't it? It was originally built for The One, only later converted to..." She frowned at Jeld's puzzlement. "You know, *The One?*"

Jeld swallowed hard and shook his head.

"Sorry, I thought...."

Looking skyward to gather her thoughts, Lira chuckled and slid down onto the floor. She patted the ground beside her.

"Come down here."

After a moment's hesitation, Jeld slid to the ground beside her, bringing his stew with him.

"You know the Idols, obviously. Like your favorite, the Traveler."

Jeld frowned at her assumption but nodded anyway.

"Well, who made the Idols?" Lira asked.

"They were born normal. So they were just... you know, born."

She laughed. "I mean, who made the Idols *Idols?*"

"The One?" Jeld guessed, remembering the prishner's tale.

Lira nodded. "It was her behind it all, behind The Five and all the others before them. Vincet wrote of it in his histories. Well, he never presumed to know the full of it, but he had his theories."

She tilted her head back and rested it upon the stone bench. Jeld watched her distant, skyward eyes circle as if she could see the stars beyond.

"See?" she said without turning to him.

Jeld followed her gaze to the dome high above. Though undeniably beautiful, he saw nothing of this Idol of Idols. He opened his mouth to feign some affirmation, but then he saw it. A perfect ring of the same pristine white that formed the symbols of the Idols circled the base of the dome. It stretched over the others, greater even than the eye, the tree, the sword, the hand, the lute. It could only be the symbol of The One.

"They say she has been at war with Discord forever," Lira said. "That the Idols leaving was not the beginning, but just another battle in an eternal war."

They were both quiet for a time, eyes fixed upon the circle of The One, the ring of crisp daylight above it and the gray shadows still beyond. Soon though, Jeld found himself staring again past Lira to the symbol of the Traveler.

"He *must* be your favorite," Lira said. "Why does the Traveler fascinate you so? Do you dream of traveling? Or *have* you travelled... you are a traveler, aren't you!"

Travel...

Jeld's focus shifted back to Kelthin's lute behind Lira, and then deeper until the symbol was the faintly discernible currents of a great rolling sea, and then it was in the many-colored leaves of a dark forest, and then the wind-bent grass of a brilliant green hilltop. Then he was sitting atop the hillside. A whisper of familiar laughter sounded beside him. His eyes went wide and he turned toward the sound but the hilltop was gone and he was staring at Lira.

Tears filled her eyes. A single drop had already broken free and was streaming down her face.

She wiped her cheek. "I'm... sorry, I..."

"No, it's nothing."

Jeld forced his attention back to his meal. His impoliteness struck him and he held the bowl and bread out to her.

"Hmm? Oh! No, I couldn't."

"Please."

Lira bit her lip before smiling and tearing a piece from the loaf. Placing her hand upon Jeld's beneath the bowl, she scooped up a pile of stew. When the bite toppled halfway to her mouth, she narrowly caught it and slurped it from her palm before her eyes darted up to find Jeld staring at her. A snort of laughter choked through her nose.

Jeld turned quickly away to save her any embarrassment. It was then that he realized he was smiling. *Smiling*. How warm it felt, and yet how wrong.

The chime of the city bells sounded through the doors behind them. Swallowing the last of her mess, Lira turned to Jeld and sighed.

"Corr, I need to go, I—my shift here is over and I'll be expected back home."

The thought was oddly horrifying to Jeld, a winter sun breaking dawn only to at once descend again beneath the horizon. He searched for words but could think of only one.

"Jeld. It's Jeld, not Corr. I was... being careful."

"Jeld," she tried with a grin. "That fits better."

"Thank you. For the stew, and... talking."

"And thank *you* for sharing a handful of it," Lira said.

A breath of laughter escaped Jeld's lips, Lira responding in kind. They shared a long smile before Lira stood.

"I've really got to go. You should come back—if you need anything, I mean. The prishner can only offer so much, but he will never turn away a visit, or a helping hand."

"Will *you* be okay? Can I see you home?"

She smiled. "No, thank you. I'll be alright. I'm meeting friends nearby."

Jeld nodded wordlessly, his eyes fixed on hers. With a sad smile, Lira turned and started toward the back. She stopped just before the doorway and looked back to him.

"Goodbye, Jeld."

"Goodbye. Lira."

She turned and disappeared between the temple doors. Jeld stared after her for some time before, left alone with his thoughts, the whisperings of his anxiety began anew. He scraped his bowl clean with the remaining bread then shouldered his pack and started for the exit.

Stopping before the massive doors, he looked back at the lute of The Traveler a final time. When his mind began to wander again, though, he forced himself to turn away, an act that felt unnervingly like breaking eye contact. He ran his fingers gently along the strange designs carved into the doors as he slipped between them into the morning light.

The streets were bustling. Jeld turned toward the heart of the city, the North Gate stretching across the road behind him, alien in its immensity. The crowd quickly consumed him, the horrible persuasion of humanity diminished only by its wondrous cloak of anonymity. He turned down a narrow street, the low winter sun pressing reassuringly against the back of his neck. *West.* It had always been the way. Away... but from what, he dared not remember.

Just then the same familiar laughter he'd daydreamed at the temple seemed to whisper from behind. He spun but the sweet sound was gone. Setting his jaw, he started ahead, curiosity, defiance, and an inexplicable sense of purpose driving his steps through the alley and, for the first time in life as he knew it, eastward.

CHAPTER NINE

T he shadows that had followed Jeld eastward now led the way, his meandering course having eaten much of the short winter day. Though a few coins richer since beginning his journey, he was still no closer to finding a decent place to weather the night when the road before him opened into a wide city square.

An imposing stone building not unlike the temple he'd visited that morning towered across the square. *Temple Theater,* he recalled, but eastbound or not he let his rising memories sink again to the place without pain as he took in the sights. A grand staircase spilled from the entry to the feet of a sizable crowd gathered in the street below.

Jeld shivered. Pulling his coat tighter, he pressed into the crowd past men and women in evening finery with swatches of Fallstival colors, and children in full costumes. He settled into a spot with a sliver of a view of the theater doors and cupped his hands before his warm breath.

The huge door of the theater slowly opened with a loud creaking like a wind-blown tree. Hushed cries of excitement washed over the crowd. A young man emerged, stopping just shy of the steps overlooking the crowd. He frowned thoughtfully and peered from person to person.

"Hmm," he said at last. "Not exactly a conventional army by any measure..."

The crowd laughed.

"But... there's a good lot of you, and a fit and hardy folk by the look of it—"

A proud battle cry boomed from somewhere in the crowd.

"Such spirit!" the man continued to more laughter. "Ah, but where are my manners? Good evening, good folk of Corbin!"

The crowd returned his greeting. Just ahead, a little girl tugged at the arm of an old woman.

"Nanna, is the man lost?"

The woman's wrinkled face lit into a bright smile.

"No, my dear, this city was once called Corbin, before there was Tovados to name it after. Long, long ago."

"Even before you, Nanna?"

The old lady chuckled. "Even before me, dear."

"Just last week the myrmidons of mad King Caedis butchered another town," the man atop the steps said. "You people know the dangers and *still* you dare heed my call. Such bravery is precisely why *you-know-who* sent me here. As long as there are people like you, there is hope that—"

Suddenly the clapping of hooves cut through the square.

"Fan out!" a distant voice barked from somewhere behind.

"They've tracked me!" the young performer cried. "Quick, inside the temple! I'll meet you there when it's safe."

He ran along the top of the stairs, stopping just shy of a sizable drop to an adjacent alley and turning back to the crowd.

"Remember, when you're inside, pretend it's just a telling of The One and his *noble* incarnation, King"—he spat—"Caedis. Now go!"

He turned and plunged from sight, Jeld and the rest of the crowd staring after him.

"Come on up, come on up," a voice called from ahead. "Welcome, everyone."

Having taken full advantage of the diversion, a man had positioned himself behind a podium just outside the entry. He was on perhaps the later side of middle age and wore a red suit with gold buttons. Jeld recalled the man's jovial calls, but dared not dwell.

"I'll take your tickets, please. Full show tonight, folks, so we won't be selling any at the door this time."

As Jeld watched the crowd filter past the ticketer, giddy children and adults alike practically dancing into the theater, it occurred to him with a stab of sorrow that nobody else was alone. Again he began to sink away from the pains of past and present, but something gave him pause. The sweet, familiar laughter that had drawn him eastward seemed to echo again through his head, with it a glimpse of rolling green hills and a distant Tovar nestled against the sea.

He looked out again through the crowd, at the people hand in hand, smiling and dressed in their festive getups, and instead of recoiling from the affection he felt drawn toward its warm embrace. Suddenly nothing could be worse than being separated from this, alone and cold and empty on the streets. He had to stay with them. He had to get inside.

"Come on up, folks. Welcome, welcome. We've got drinks for sale inside, snacks for the show. Fallstival toys and more at the shop. No pressure though, just a ticket is all I need from you tonight."

Perhaps he could sneak in, Jeld considered, a coattail shadow amidst a boisterous family. Or maybe just filch a ticket from the festive flock. He surveyed the plentiful array of targets shuffling onward. The same little girl was pleading with her grandmother just ahead.

"Nanna, can I give the man my ticket myself?"

"Yes, my girl, of course you can. Be careful with that. If you lose it we can't see the show."

Jeld's conscience kicked him. He racked his brain for alternatives until a thought struck him. The performer who had jumped into the alley must certainly have gotten back inside somehow. There must be another way in.

Jeld waded through the crowd, spilling from its confines into the empty alley the performer had leapt into. He walked along the side of the theater but passed only solid stone before reaching the alley's end. Emerging onto the next street, his answer loomed ahead— a rear entrance, and not a slight one. The back of the theater opened into a vast warehouse.

For the briefest instant, as if the image were etched upon the backs of his eyelids for but a single blink, it seemed he glimpsed a wagon parked just outside, the backside of a boy with messy hair at its reins. The sight was gone before Jeld could be certain he'd seen it at all, and he found himself staring into the warehouse.

A man was hunched over a desk just inside beneath the farthest of several wide archways. Through rows of shelves Jeld counted four men loading a wagon. Two others conversed in the corner straight back along the wall, one of them the young performer. Jeld retreated into the alley and peered back around the corner.

"... about to start, so keep it down back here ya bunch of monkeys," the performer said playfully and pulled open a door behind him.

"Yeah, yeah. Try not to dance off the stage, ya little priss."

The performer smirked, offered a flamboyant bow, and backed through the doorway, pulling it closed behind him. The other shook his head and set to helping the rest load the wagon.

Jeld's eyes flicked between the workers and the man at the desk. Though the man hadn't once looked up from his ledger, it seemed he would surely glimpse Jeld should he pass. Just then the man frowned and bent behind the desk as if digging through a drawer. All eyes still elsewhere, Jeld bit his lip and darted toward the door. The stone wall to one side and shelves to the other passed by in a blur and he burst through the door, pressing it closed behind him.

His back pressed to the door, Jeld's eyes went wide as he looked out into the room beyond. Dozens of people were buzzing about before the backdrop of a vast crimson curtain. Several were pushing into place the facade of a small earthen hut, it's backside a skeleton of exposed boards. Others dressed in front of mirrors, tugged at ropes and pulleys, or recited lines to nobody in particular.

Jeld looked frantically about as the other voice in his head chastised him. To his left climbed a lengthy staircase, light spilling down from a hallway at its end. Just opposite, another descended just a few steps before twisting into darkness. Even as he considered his next move, a man upon the stage turned his way and he darted down into the unlit stairwell.

Reaching the bottom, he paused in the dim light. Identical narrow hallways opened to either side. Straight ahead the walls fell away, opening into a vast room filled with all manner of oddities—costumes, props, sets, and countless other miscellany. A rough path ran through its center toward a dark doorway set into the far wall.

Footsteps sounded from the stairway behind. Jeld darted into the strange room, cutting sharply off the path after just a few long strides and wading through the clutter. Slipping past a regal throne, his heart skipped a beat as he found himself face to face with a giant black wolf, its teeth bared in a wicked snarl. He hesitantly crouched behind the stuffed beast and peered beneath its belly back toward the entrance.

Jeld watched as a pair of boots stepped into the room and hurried past a tombstone, a portrait of an elderly woman, a rack of dresses, and a small tropical forest before disappearing through the dark doorway at the back of the room. He waited and waited, finally rising before suddenly ducking as the man emerged again. Footsteps passed by, fading in the rhythmic tapping of what Jeld unthinkingly deduced to be carrowood soles upon the stone steps.

Suddenly a rumbling echoed in from the dark doorway, growing from nothing to a thunderous roar like a charging army in but a blink. It broke as suddenly as it had begun, not into silence but rather giving birth to a beautiful melody.

The show.

Jeld crept to the doorway and slipped into the darkness. Countless geometric shapes of light in the ceiling overhead revealed dozens of pillars throughout the shadowy space, like trees amidst a starlit forest. Following the wall to a particularly dark corner, he let out a breath as the shadows embraced him.

The music quieted and a muffled voice began from what seemed to be directly overhead. His gaze following the voice and accompanying footsteps across what he now realized was the underside of the stage, Jeld frowned. He could almost touch the actor and yet it seemed he would not glimpse even a blink of the show.

Just then a faint breeze gently swept a few stray strands of his shaggy hair down over his nose. Jeld looked up at the wall behind him, but having selected his location with the sole criterion of darkness, he saw only that. Blindly feeling along the wall, his fingers bent over a ledge high above. He pulled himself up, his head painfully striking the ceiling, and stared into only more darkness.

Lowering himself back down, he quickly retrieved a lamp from the prop room, pocketing a rusty knife and pair of gloves along the way before returning to the dark corner. He pulled himself up again, careful not to hit his head, and held out the lamp. The lamp revealed a small opening beneath three sloping planks. Beyond it, the planks rose high overhead before leveling off above a narrow passage running into the darkness.

Jeld climbed through the opening. He pressed deeper, the music growing louder until he came to a stop before a nook bubbling out from one wall at perhaps chest height. A sliver of light streamed in from the back of the nook.

He set the lamp and his pack at the mouth of the nook and climbed inward, stopping just before the narrow light and parting a row of short curtains. Beyond, countless faces filled stands to one side, still more upon a balcony above them. On the far wall directly opposite him, a tiny balcony jutted out from the wall, the same thin band of curtain running along its base. To his right, beyond a shallow orchestra pit, a stage was set like a beautiful forest.

A young woman crept through the trees, a fine beam of light from somewhere above encircling her as she stalked ahead. She drew a tall bow and stood completely motionless, eyes focused in an unwavering extension of her arrow. Suddenly a pained, lupine cry cut through the woods and she turned toward it. Her bow still drawn, she emerged into a clearing, where a young wolf lay biting at a snare.

"Oh, poor thing," she said, lowering her bow.

The wolf turned to her and barked.

"I can help you, but you have to promise not to bite me."

The wolf barked again.

"That didn't sound like a promise."

She pulled a limp squirrel from a pouch at her side and eased closer.

"Here," she said, tossing it to the ground at the wolf's side.

The wolf sniffed at it but quickly turned back to her.

"See, I'm not so bad. My name's Syladrya, what's yours?"

The wolf whined.

"How about... *Yip*, then? Now, let me help you, Yip."

She set her bow down and reached to where the snare was fastened to a stake in the ground. The wolf snapped at Syladrya's hand, but she dodged and swatted the side of the beast's head.

"Hey, stupid! I thought we had a deal. Do you want help or not?"

She reached out again and this time the wolf just watched her suspiciously.

"That's better, now let's get you out of that."

She pulled her knife and cut the rope. At once the small wolf pushed itself away only to cry out and limp to a stop.

"You're hurt, Yip. Here, you forgot this."

The girl picked up the discarded squirrel and set it just beyond the wolf's muzzle.

"Now let me see that leg of yours. This might hurt, but remember, I gave you a squirrel. That little fellow cost me a broken arrowhead."

She untied the snare from the wolf's leg and gently palpated it. The wolf cried out.

"It's broken, but everything is still in the right place."

Syladrya began to sing as she worked an ointment into the open wound then set to splinting it with a broken arrow and her belt. Her melody continued unbroken as the scene darkened until the forest was gone and there was only the young girl and the wolf. As the song grew louder and sweeter and more somber, an ethereal door took shape amidst the darkness behind her. It slowly grew clearer, more real, until even the strange symbols etched upon the door could be seen clearly.

Jeld's tear dripping against his hand jarred him from the scene. He began to let himself fall back into the show's spell but something else tugged at his awareness. He let his gaze follow the pull and it fell upon the crowded stands. He looked from person to person, glimmering eye to glimmering eye, surprised to find that where of late he'd glimpsed only emptiness there was again a familiar depth.

When it seemed Syladrya's song could grow no sweeter, and the great door might break free of its ethereal chains and ground itself entirely in reality, a rumble like distant hooves brought her song to a sudden halt and the door disappeared as light returned to the clearing.

"What was that?" she said.

A flickering orange light began to glow in the distance.

"The village! I'm sorry, Yip, I have to go!"

She turned and ran toward the glow of fire. Just as she disappeared into the trees, the young wolf stood and limped after her. The scene went dark, the music stopped, and after a moment's pause, the still wet-faced audience burst into applause.

The show went on to follow the other Idols in their relative youth, the great door appearing before each as they faced trials and tragedy. Jeld's eyes fixed not on the stage but its audience, their every gasp and tear stirring a memory of a time when it was safe to feel, setting images dancing before his eyes and drawing him upward from the depths. He was on the road driving a wagon, then atop cliffs beside the sea, then waking upon a platform in an attic, then stooped over a half-stitched shoe beside—

Cobb...

A choked sob escaped his lips and the epic stole him away again.

Five of the doors lined the stage now all at once, before each standing one of the young Idols. As the Idols reached out, the ethereal doors snapped into reality and the intensity of the audience's emotions climbed to a crescendo that beat like a physical thing against Jeld. Memories flashed before his eyes. He remembered the heat upon his face as he stood in an alleyway watching flames consume the shop. He saw Cobb again, reaching toward the tack hammer, his face contorted with pain. He saw his father, madness in his eyes, blood covering his fists. He saw four boots, their toes skyward within a smuggler's hold. Then he was sitting on a grassy hillside, looking down over Tovar in the distance.

"Do you think we'll stay long this time?" a familiar voice said.

Jeld turned to the voice and there sat Niya. Another sound, wordless and full of anguish, escaped Jeld's lips.

Upon the stage, the hands of the Idols pressed to the five doors and they pushed as one. A single, piercing creak broke the silence and the doors swung open. A flash of light burst from within each and Jeld flinched, his hand shooting up to shield his eyes. Everything went white even through his closed eyes and the awe of hundreds of onlookers crashed against his every sense, then deeper still against senses unnamed. In an instant he burst from the depths into the blinding sun, and as the many painful memories replayed before his eyes, at last he did not look away.

CHAPTER TEN

———◦◦◦———

J eld lowered his hand and opened his tightly clenched eyes to find himself staring into the soft orange glow of an oil lamp. His mind still reeling from the flood of memories and emotions that assailed it, he looked about to gather his bearings.

He was sitting at a table in the common room of an inn. A distant melody and the bustle of countless voices seemed to tease at his ears, though when he tried to focus on the sounds they danced just out of reach. A bar lined with stools ran from one corner of the room, beside it a modest stage raised but a single step, empty despite the music that seemed to hover at the edge of his consciousness. The walls were exposed stone and dingy plaster crossed with dark wooden beams. A staircase at the other end of the bar turned along the wall to climb from sight.

The whole room glowed that perfect hearth light orange that would so entice passersby walking the cold night. So perfect was this place that it seemed it could only be a dream, another repressed memory broken free, but Jeld knew that wasn't so. This place was different. Real. So real that Jeld found himself wondering whether his life before had been the dream, that only now was he truly awake for the first time.

Standing, Jeld's hand brushed something upon the back of his chair and he looked down to find a leather bag hanging by its drawstrings. The bag looked at home there, like its wear and hue matched its surroundings. It was larger than a coin purse, smaller than the sizable pack he only now recalled had been his father's.

He lifted the bag from the chair and thumbed its supple leather before continuing slowly toward the stage. Dozens of instruments—some unrecognizable—decorated the wall beyond it, at the center a beautiful lute which like the bag seemed just to belong. Jeld turned and drifted toward the bar. Feeling quite at ease, he leaned upon it and lost himself in the flickering flame of another lamp.

The easy orange firelight grew to a blinding white and Jeld flinched away. When he opened his eyes, he was looking down over the stage again through the narrow gap in his private curtains. The show continued but Jeld only stared ahead at the memories he had tried so hard to leave behind until, eyes bloodshot and cheeks wet with tears, he blinked and the stage and stands alike were empty.

He made to crawl down from the nook. Only on lowering his hand to the floor did he realize he was holding something. Raising it before the lamp, his mouth fell open as the light fell upon a familiar bag, its leather glowing that perfect orange like the beckoning windows of an inn.

He opened the bag and reached inside. His hand closed on something cold and round and he pulled it out. It was made of metal, its surface inlaid with intricate patterns save for where a deep hole pressed into one side. Noticing the faintest of seams running down the device's center, Jeld dug his nails in and tried to pry it apart. When it didn't give in the least, he wrapped his hands around either side and twisted.

Suddenly the contraption clicked and something hot struck Jeld's palm, the room flashing bright for a fleeting second. Jeld yelped and threw the device down, rubbing his palm before picking it up and gingerly trying again. Again the device clicked as its hemispheres spun, only this time as the room flashed sparks fell from the hole his hand had before covered.

His eyes wide, Jeld loosed another few rounds of sparks before setting the contraption aside and inventorying the rest of the bag's contents. All in all, aside from the device, he produced a set of lockpicks and four badly tarnished silver coins. As he pondered these, he found himself thumbing the supple leather to the rhythm of the melody from his daydream. Again shaking the thought aside, he quickly tucked the strange bag into his pack and set out in search of a safer way out of the theater.

It wasn't long before he hunted not for a way out but rather a way to come and go, realizing that the dark and webby passages could provide a relatively secure bolt-hole. They were dry and warm, free of predators thus far, and there was even live entertainment to be had. The prop room alone was worth a king's ransom, and it was so cluttered Jeld figured he could make off with a full half before anyone would take notice.

Discerning the time was next to impossible within the confines of the theater walls, but he wagered it must have been at least halfway to morning when a faint glow overhead caught his eye. Holding his lamp overhead, the wall lit up in all sorts of colors as it revealed a window of stained glass. At its center, countless pieces of glass formed the likeness of a man in simple brown clothes playing a lute. It seemed at first a tragedy that a treasure so fine might live in such a place, but then he thought it all the more beautiful.

Beneath the window, a board ran along a stone sill. Jeld's heart leapt. He tugged the board and it pulled free, sweet winter air rushing in through the broken panel. Peering out, he found himself looking down into the alley he had traversed in pursuit of the young actor. Though a goodly drop to the ground, it seemed manageable were he to hang from the sill, and the stone wall should offer sufficient holds for an easy return. Jeld closed his eyes, a slow smile spreading across his face and a tear running down one cheek. It was perfect.

After a few silent moments he wiped his cheek and replaced the board then wove his way through the increasingly familiar passages to a small chamber noticeably warmer than the rest. He sat upon a neat pile of blankets he'd borrowed from the prop room and leaned back against the brick wall. Heat radiated from the bricks into his weary bones and he let out a long breath, the immensity of the day at once replaying before his eyes.

Jeld blinked and found his gaze upon his old pack, truly seeing it for the first time since fleeing the shop. Rummaging through it, he set aside his everyday essentials until his eyes widened as he produced a tack hammer. He produced a flint and a buffing brush before his hand closed on a jar of polish. Memories of Cobb flitted through his mind.

He looked down at his boots and groaned at the sight of Cobb's prized boots in such disrepair. He opened the jar of dark brown polish. The surface of the polish was cracked and dry. Letting a drop of spit fall, he worked it in with the worse-off of his five socks until the polish glistened with life.

Jeld spent the rest of the night working that life into Cobb's prized boots until they gleamed like mirrors in the flickering lamplight, then he let his weary eyes fall to rest at last.

***

The streets were quieter and less colorful the next morning, the last of Fallstival now past. Even so, there was a familiar vibrancy to them that Jeld hadn't felt for a long time; a lively thrum like thousands of distant conversations. He tuned out the sensations with only limited success and pressed onward toward the Temple of One.

His travels thus far had proven uneventful thanks no doubt to the clean clothes he had acquired from the bountiful prop room. It had been an altogether pleasant morning save for the agony of having to choose between first bathing or taking a hot meal, but he'd quickly settled the matter by indulging in both at the same time.

Reaching the temple, Jeld passed between its ever-open doors, fingertips brushing the carved runes, and emerged beneath the crisp halo of light inside. Prishner Walson was sitting at a small desk near the front of the temple, bent over a thick book bound in badly worn oak. Over dingy undergarments, he was wrapped in a towel that still managed to appear finer than his usual tattered robes.

"Hello again, Corr."

"Hello, Prishner," Jeld replied, walking down the aisle.

The thicker of the two boys from the night before sat upon the frontmost bench again, a tattered gray robe on his lap and a threaded needle in his teeth. *Fendrith*, Jeld recalled. The large boy looked him up and down, cocking an eyebrow as he passed.

"You seem almost a different person today," the prishner said. "What brings you in?"

"I hoped to speak with Lira. I was nearby. And I brought these for any others."

Jeld pulled three loaves of bread from his pack.

"You're too kind. Let's get those to the kitchen, shall we?"

Jeld followed him into a small kitchen, where the prishner began stowing the loaves in a cupboard.

"She's away, I'm afraid," Prishner Walson said.

"Do you know when she'll be back?"

"It's... hard to say. Lira doesn't come in every day."

Jeld knew at once he was lying, but as Niya had taught him, up to something didn't always mean up to no good.

"I just wanted to thank her. I owe you thanks for the food and shelter, it's just that it turns out what I needed most was to talk."

The prishner closed the cupboard and his shoulders sagged.

"I saw you two. Laughing and talking." He smiled sheepishly. "I couldn't bear to interrupt, so I slipped back in here." Prishner Walson's smile fell away and he began scrubbing a bowl in a wash basin. "But I'm afraid I can't help you. Perhaps you can stop in on occasion and see if she's in. We can always use a helping hand here, as you well know."

Jeld sighed, a trace of the broken boy who last visited the temple creeping back into his face.

"I'm sorry, Corr. I just... well, you're always welcome to check back."

"I'll try. I've got to go. Thank you again, for this place."

"Be safe. You weren't running away from the rain the last time you darted in here. There won't always be a doorway."

Jeld nodded then turned and left the room. He found Fendrith looking his way. In the depths of the large boy's eyes, Jeld beheld a man who had seen too much in his short years. Jeld nodded to him and turned quickly toward the exit.

"Hey, wait a second," came a voice from behind.

Jeld turned to find Fendrith jogging toward him. The large boy slowed to a stop just out of reach and raised an eyebrow.

"You won't need that," Fendrith said.

Realizing his hand was closed around the knife at his belt, Jeld lowered his hand.

"Sorry..."

"It's not such a bad reflex to have." He held out a hand. "I'm Fendrith."

Jeld eyed the hand. He didn't much like the idea of giving his hand over to the much larger fellow, but peering again into those old eyes he saw no malice.

"Corr," he replied and shook Fendrith's hand.

"I've met a lot of people like you. It's another reason I left. No offense, I just didn't want to be like that."

It struck Jeld then just how quickly he'd returned to that darker place. He thought at once of Quintem and shook his head.

"I'm sorry," Jeld said. "I'm not myself. I haven't spoken with many people of late and, well, for the most part that has always been for the best."

Fendrith grinned. "Maybe it's not too late for you after all."

"You've survived worse than the streets, yeah?"

Fendrith frowned.

"You've just got that look," Jeld explained. "Plus, you're too clean—you're making the streets look easy."

"Too clean eh? Look at yourself, little prince."

Jeld found himself smiling.

"I went shopping," he said haughtily.

Fendrith chuckled. "Yeah, I think there's hope for you yet."

"You were a soldier, weren't you?"

"Close, but not quite, little prince. My Da and me were handymen with the armies—tinker and tailor, carpenter and blacksmith all the same. Not soldiers, but we saw plenty of war. A few months back, just before he slept, my Da told me to get away before my eyes went cold, and so I did."

"He sounds like a very wise man."

Fendrith nodded distantly and a heavy silence fell over them.

"It was Thrallsday, if I remember right," Fendrith said after a while. "Two weeks back. And again Thrallsday just yesterday, of course."

"Sorry?"

"When the girl came in. Maybe every other Thrallsday, I'm thinking."

Jeld perked up like a dog catching a lost scent. "Lira?"

"That's her."

"Thrallsdays... thanks, Fendrith."

"Sorry you wasted all that money on a bath just for me."

"It was worth it. I haven't gotten a single dirty look out there since I cleaned myself up and put these clothes on."

"Yeah, I suppose looking clean makes all the difference. Maybe I'll see you some Thrallsday, I've been around a lot helping the prishner with odds and ends. Anyway, I don't think I have to tell you to stay sharp, little prince, but stay sharp. And stay clean, I suppose."

"You too. The blazin' watch is picking up anyone just to fill their prisons. They almost got me."

Fendrith grumbled. "Prince Dralor. War and oppression both—sounds like he is at the root of both our problems."

Jeld feigned raising a mug and started backward toward the doors. "May his pompous head fall off, and the heads of all the pruned-bush Hilltopians alike."

Fendrith returned the gesture. "And may their bushes grow unkempt in their absence."

Jeld drank to their treasonous words, gave another salute, and slipped from the sanctuary into the roaring streets of Tovar.

CHAPTER ELEVEN

J eld glared after a watchman turning from the square and returned his attention to a woman in a long black coat. He swept past her and silently cursed himself as he stuffed her purse into his pocket. *Don't shit where you eat*, his father was keen to say, but the theater crowd was irresistible.

The sky behind the towering theater was only now beginning to darken, the days already growing longer. Despite the steady cadence of performances, Jeld instead marked the passage of time by his Thrallsdays spent at the Temple of One. Two had come and gone already with no sign of Lira.

Slipping into the alley, Jeld glanced behind him before finding his familiar handhold and starting up the side of the theater. Reaching the ledge, he slid aside the board atop it and rolled through the narrow opening beneath the likeness of the Traveler. Dropping to the ground, Jeld let out a breath and filled his lungs with the refreshing dank and dusty air within.

He ducked and weaved his way through the dark and winding passages, stopping only briefly to check a stack of pebs he kept at the most obvious junction to ensure no intruders had paid a visit. Soon the cool air began to warm, an enticing scent of fresh bread and the faint song of a lute growing with each step. Emerging into his bedchamber, he sat upon his ever-thickening pile of blankets and leaned back against the warm brick wall.

A chorus of laughter erupted, bringing a smile to Jeld's face as he set to loosening his boots. Distinct voices soon took shape in the wake of the laughter.

"I didn't *forget* the line, I improvised," came a boy's voice.

"Improvised? You called him the wrong name!" a girl rebutted.

Jeld smiled again. Cass and Hawss. The pair possessed the uncanny ability to communicate exclusively through such bickering. He loosened his other boot and peered through a small hole in the brick wall. In the room beyond, past a table covered in the remnants of a once-mighty meal, the theater crew lounged in an array of mismatched furniture.

Master Edlin sat plucking his lute in the corner, his wrinkled hands tickling the strings with impossible grace. Beside him, a beautiful woman wearing a white apron rose from her chair.

"Sit, sit, Evelyn," Jasselin chided. "Don't you dare touch a dish. Tabe, I do believe it's your turn to tidy up."

The tall, sturdy woman ran everything that happened behind the curtain like a tight ship, menial chores often not excluded.

A young blonde-haired girl wrinkled her nose and trudged toward a wash basin on a counter not far from Jeld's vantage. Though Tabe resembled the Syladrya she'd played on stage, Jeld had learned she possessed none of the Lady's humility.

A grim-faced man drained his tankard and set to clearing the table. *Erol.* It had taken Jeld the better part of a week to realize it was he who played both the serene Wiseman and the jovial ticketer, a testament to the man's acting. Perhaps Erol truthfully only helped clean each night to busy himself after the single tankard *Momma Eve* allowed, but Jeld was quite certain the man was simply more decent than he let on.

"Thank you, darlings," Owan said, daintily sipping a small goblet.

Jeld smiled yet again. Though weeks had passed since the Fallstival show ended, the disparity between the fierce Warrior and the flamboyant actor who played him still tickled Jeld.

In one corner, Alal and Yelana, the Idolic performers who oft plied their trades in the square, lay intertwined on their usual plush chaise. Onders, the quiet but kindly master stagehand who engineered the sets, props, pulleys and whatnot, sat nearby.

Director Sammel came smoothly to his feet. He was an older man, thin but not wispy, just like the short gray hair atop his head.

"I'd best retire. Another fine show, everyone."

"Do stay, sir," Evelyn said.

"Now, you know I'd best see to my scripts."

"Mmhmm. You always manage to make that sound like quite a sacrifice."

Director Sammel smiled. "It's a wonderful thing when one's passions and work are one and the same. Goodnight, everyone."

The crew largely echoed his farewell and the director disappeared down a hallway Jeld knew to be lined on either side with doors to the crew quarters. *Low-enders*, they called those on the far side whose ceilings slanted sharply with the sloping audience stands overhead. Only Director Sammel slept above in a modest room just beside the stage.

Jeld turned from the hole and leaned back against the warm bricks, picturing the familiar faces of the crew as they continued their nightly banter. As the evening pressed on and the voices began to quiet, he hopped up and navigated to the understage, where he crept through the shadows beneath the constellations of trap doors. Coming to a stop under a small ring of light, he climbed to the top of one of the many stone pillars and slid aside a small disk of sky then pulled himself silently through. He emerged onto the stage amidst a cocoon of drawn curtains and leaned back against the frame of the stage.

"What will we do when the men come?" Director Sammel's voice came, only it was higher and soft.

Kalaa, the character was called. It was the director's latest work, a tale of Idolo, the first man touched by The One.

"When the men come, what are we to do?" the same voice came again.

Jeld slowly parted the curtains, peering between the slightest gap. Across the stage and through a cracked doorway, Director Sammel sat at an old desk rubbing his neatly trimmed goatee. He scribbled out a line.

"They *will* come. What then?" the Director tried again, this time nodding and jotting a note.

Jeld smiled and slowly closed the curtains. Leaning back again, he pulled the strange bag from inside his shirt and thumbed its soft leather. He could almost hear the ghostly lute's song from the inn as he listened to the director continue through his script.

So his days went, and then it was another Thrallsday again at last.

***

"Looking good. Should be solid as rock before long," Fendrith said, beginning yet another scrutinizing pass over the temple dome.

Jeld upended his bucket with mutinous arms and scraped the last of the thick mortar onto a final crack.

"Think we're good!" Fendrith called from somewhere beyond the dome.

Smoothing the patch, Jeld pushed himself upright and ran up the dome, careful to dodge the many patches of wet mortar. He spotted Fendrith below on a narrow rim encircling the base of the dome. Jeld looked out beyond him at the thousands of rooftops reaching up from below, and over the low wall that ran as needlessly as venom in a *craaul* bite along the unscalable southern cliffs. Further still, over the great southern sea, a menacing wall of dark clouds stood in stark contrast to the blue sky overhead. Lightning flickered at its center.

"I heard you two were up here," a familiar voice called from somewhere below. Spinning, Jeld spotted Lira's face between the iron bars of a ladder at the roof's edge. "But I didn't really believe you two would be daft enough to play on the rooftop in a storm."

"You've got to come see it from here!" Jeld called, waving.

She lifted both hands and started to wave back but her eyes went wide and she plunged out of sight.

Jeld's heart skipped several beats before Lira's face popped back above the roof's edge with a sheepish smirk.

"*Not* funny," Fendrith said as he walked toward the ladder.

Lira laughed as she climbed onto the roof.

"I'm sor—I'm sorry. I'm horrible!"

Jeld stumbled down the dome clutching his heart.

Lira collapsed against the dome in a fit of laughter, but abruptly cried out and jumped back to her feet. Her side was covered from face to hip in wet, gray mortar.

"What—"

"Bird poop," Jeld interrupted. "They like it up here."

Her lip curled in disgust. "Oh *Mother*..."

Fendrith pulled a trowel from his bucket and set to smoothing the face print from the mortar.

Understanding dawned on Lira's face. "I suppose I deserved that."

Jeld walked past her and sat with his feet dangling over the edge of the temple. Lira followed suit, a chunk of mortar clinging to her hair.

Jeld pointed to the clump. "You've got..."

"Oh." She wiped at it. "Did I get it?"

"It's still..."

Jeld held her hair above the clump so as not to pull it then gently ran his fingers through.

"That was *all* in there?" Lira gasped.

"Eesh, smells like bird poop over here," Fendrith said as he sat beside Lira and kicked his legs over the edge.

"Nonsense!"

"Afraid so."

A low rumble echoed around them. They all looked south over the city and fell into a contented silence, hypnotized by the rolling waves and brooding, flickering storm drawing ever closer.

They sat there in conversation and in silence, legs and concerns alike hanging free in the wind, until the sun neared the horizon and the first drops of rain slapped against the stone.

"We'd best get inside before the lightning cooks us," Fendrith said over a growing chorus of raindrops. "The ladder will get slick too."

"You have way too much good sense, Fen," Lira said, "You'll live to be two hundred years old."

"Not if I keep hanging out with you two. Let's get off this baking pan."

One by one they descended the ladder to a small balcony halfway down the temple wall. Passing through an old door, they descended a narrow, spiraling staircase. They emerged in the kitchen where Prishner Walson was dropping vegetables into a second cauldron that had been added to the fire.

"Oh good," the prishner said. "I couldn't have lived with myself had I sent you slaving to your deaths in return for a bowl of cheap porridge."

"Hungry, Prishner?" Jeld asked with a nod toward the cauldron.

Prishner Walson smiled. "If experience tells, this will be the busiest inn in town shortly."

"It will be rough on the streets tonight," Fendrith said.

"We will be here for them as best we can, as the Mother would have us be."

"How can we help?" Lira asked.

"Would you please serve meals? From the pot on the right, the other won't be ready for a while yet."

Fendrith set to filling bowls. Lira took the first two and Jeld the next before following Lira from the room. Jeld counted sixteen children scattered throughout the temple. Another came in just ahead of a clap of thunder, her clothes drenched and each step leaving a puddle upon the stone floor.

Lira handed off her second bowl of porridge and waved the girl in.

"Roba, it's good to see you. Come to the fire. Let's get you dried off."

She put her arm around the girl and led her into the kitchen.

Jeld looked out over the faces of the others, most eying either him or the porridge he carried. Their gazes carried a healthy suspicion, innocent as scavengers go, but something different tugged at his awareness and he turned to meet a pair of cold eyes in the corner.

Though sitting, the boy looked to be slightly taller than Jeld, his hair a sandy brown and clothing worn. Two larger boys sat with him, and though they too glared, their malice was shallow. Feigned, Jeld somehow knew.

Jeld abruptly handed the bowls to two others and started back toward the kitchen, the glare burning into his back. In the kitchen, Roba was setting a wet sock on the floor beside the fire. She looked up as Jeld approached.

"Hello," she said dreamily.

"Hello, I'm Jeld."

Roba cocked her head and smirked. "Roba."

Fen handed Lira a bowl and turned to Jeld. "Oh sure, tell *her* your real name."

Jeld shrugged sheepishly. "Turns out I'm a nobody by either name, so what's the difference?"

"You should be honored, Roba. I thought we were buds and he still didn't tell me for weeks."

Roba smiled.

"I guess I just like her better," Jeld said. "Where did the prishner go?"

"He went upstairs across the hall to gather some blankets," Fen said. "Said everyone could sleep here beneath the Idols tonight."

"We'd best get the others fed," Lira said.

"Serve those gits in the corner last," Jeld said. "Isn't there some saying about not biting the hand that feeds?"

"I think it might have said *the wise* don't," Roba said.

"Who *are* those scatbags, anyway?"

Lira sighed. "Kaid is the worst of them. The one with the short hair is Depsey, and the big dopey one is... is Vincet."

Roba snickered.

Jeld beamed. "The dumb one's named after the Wiseman?"

"Bet one of his *friends* named him," Roba said.

"I can guess which one."

Lira sighed again. "Alright, this is hardly a place for squabbling, let's just get this over with."

"Alright," Jeld said. "I'll help."

"Very well. Be nice."

"Of course."

Grabbing two more bowls, Jeld turned and led the way back to the corner where Kaid sat.

"Porridge, anyone? A fresh stew is cooking if you prefer to wait."

"Give it here," Kaid demanded.

Jeld took a step backward as Kaid reached out for a bowl.

"Give it here, priss!"

"You think you're *entitled* to this food?"

Kaid only stared back, his eyes revealing a hint of surprise.

"Jeld..." Lira urged.

"This is a *gift!*" Jeld spat through clenched teeth. "The prishner spends his whole life giving, maybe you should show some blazin' appreciation!"

Kaid sneered. "Such an idiot that I don't even have to steal from him, he just gives everything away."

He laughed, his cronies joining in only as he turned to each in turn.

"How *dare* you!" Lira hissed, stepping out from behind Jeld.

"Prishners ain't supposed to take *lovelies,* are they?"

Jeld's blood boiled. A dozen scenes played out all at once in his head—he threw the bowls at Kaid's face, he stomped on his outstretched ankle; he stuck his knife through the monster's boot, then in the gut where he'd die the slowest, then—

"That's enough," Prishner Walson's voice echoed across the temple.

Jeld blinked his fantasies aside and set the bowls on the floor just out of reach then turned away, Lira following suit. Spotting Fen and Roba waving from several rows back, they made their way to them. Fen handed Jeld and Lira each a bowl and they all sat upon the floor facing one another, their backs pressed against the benches to either side.

"You didn't give them spoons," Lira whispered.

"Oops?"

Roba laughed.

"Bastard deserves a lot worse than no spoon," Jeld added. "I'll be right back."

Fendrith and Lira both leveled suspicious looks at him.

"I'm just getting my pack!"

Neither of their stares wavered in the slightest.

"Really? I'll be right back."

Returning to the kitchen, Jeld stopped abruptly just inside as what felt like the heavy weight of a gaze tugged at his senses. He scanned the room, sure that someone was watching, but found it empty. Even so, his eyes lingered on the wall behind which he knew Kaid sat. His pulse quickened as he pictured the three of them sitting there beneath the prishner's roof, eating the prishner's food like parasites.

Taking a deep breath, he grabbed his pack from a cupboard and started back toward his friends. Lightning flashed through the windows lining the dome overhead, a deafening boom of thunder shaking the ground as he walked up the aisle. The hum of the rain rose to a roar through the ever-open doorway.

Sitting upon the bench overlooking his friends, Jeld dug a tunic from his pack and pulled it over his ragged undershirt.

"Why on earth were you up on the roof in your underclothes if you had that in there?" Lira asked.

"I couldn't chance it getting dirty," Jeld answered. "Life is a whole lot easier with clean clothes."

"The watch..."

"They barely see me now that I dress nicer. Before, I was stopped and shaken down, kicked at and chased off too many times to count. And I consider that lucky. You know I almost got thrown into prison? For nothing."

Jeld slid to the floor beside Lira and picked up his bowl.

"I was sleeping under a tavern," he continued. "I bet even the dogs wouldn't have found me if I'd been wearing cleaner clothes. I was probably the foulest smelling thing on the hill."

"That's horrible. I'm so sorry."

"How did you get out?" Roba asked.

"Luck," Jeld said bitterly. "When they were plucking some poor sap from the cell, I was able to escape. They had me, I just got lucky."

"Don't give yourself such a hard time. I'd say everyone in this room is still short their share of luck."

Lira nodded. "I don't think all the luck in the world could have kept me alive in any of your shoes."

"They didn't even care that we hadn't done anything," Jeld said. "Just said some prissy-bushed prince told them the prison better be full by morning."

"I… heard about that. They just don't see it. They think the poor are to blame for all the crime."

"Well, I doubt it's the rich," Fen said. "But yeah, not *all* us rats bite."

"Houses burned, wealthy families harassed on the streets, the pig at the governor's mansion… pardon the metaphor, but *rats* want food, money, clothes. You know what was taken from the houses? From the people? From the mansion? *Nothing.*"

"It isn't *for* the money, it's *about* the money. And the wars, and the fancy balls. People are just mad."

"But they're just making the *Hilltoppers* mad."

"Good," Jeld said. "Not good, but who can blame people. *Nobody* likes Hilltoppers. Of course people are going to do all that."

Lira nodded slowly. "Maybe you're right."

They fell silent, deep in thought then numb from a long day's work, full bellies, and the lullaby of the wind and the rain. The prishner took no such break, however, and guilt soon roused them into service. Over the next two bells Jeld set to repairing mangled shoes and serving meals to the countless newcomers filtering in. Lira gave counsel and helped the prishner with medicines, Fen repairing bed rolls, belts and packs, cutting hair, and sharpening knives, while Roba skillfully mended clothes. The prishner's other children helped as well, all except Kaid, who instead left after managing to score a second meal.

"I must be going," Lira said once the temple was in order and they'd assembled again upon the floor between benches.

"Family again?" Roba asked.

Lira nodded, coming to her feet and flipping on a simple brown cloak.

"My father likes that I help, but he gets worried when I'm away."

"Tell him we're not so bad," Jeld said.

"Oh it's not that at all. It's just, you know, *away.*"

"Some Thrallsday soon?" Roba asked.

Lira hesitated before smiling. "Hopefully so."

"We'll be here," Jeld said, not entirely sure why.

Lira's eyes met Jeld's and her smile turned sad. She cleared her throat.

"Now, do be careful, you three."

"Stay clean," Roba called after her.

A pang of sadness burned in Jeld's chest as Lira turned away, cutting deeper with her every step. When she neared the door, he could bear it no longer and hurried after her.

Lira turned as he approached and beamed a smile that could warm him the next winter through. Jeld opened his mouth to speak but nothing came out.

"I'm going, no need to chase me away," Lira said.

"Will you go to a show with me?" Jeld blurted.

"A show? Oh I... I couldn't."

"Oh..."

"I mean, I *want* to, I just—I'm only supposed to be here. And I couldn't let you spend your money."

"I have seats already."

"My father knows so many people in the city... if they see me, he will find out I wasn't here."

Jeld's hope wilted.

"Although," Lira said, "if I could sneak away somehow..."

"I can get you out!"

A spark emerged amidst her conflicted face.

"I... hope to return in two weeks."

"Two weeks," Jeld echoed.

She smiled again, nodded with finality, and slipped through the doors.

Jeld stood staring after her before breaking free and returning to his friends. He sat with Fen and Roba until the temple fell quiet and his own long blinks threatened to grow much longer.

"I should be going," he said quietly.

"Busy night, eh?" Fen asked.

Jeld eyed the numerous strangers lying about the temple.

"Just... a bit crowded. Are you two okay here?"

"I've slept in worse places. Prishner got me a good spot upstairs anyway, for all the work I've been doing lately."

"I like it here," Roba said.

"You could come visit again sooner. Plenty of work I can pawn off on ya, little prince."

"I hope to," Jeld said. "Stay clean, you two."

"Stay clean," Fen and Roba echoed.

Jeld went to the other corner where Prishner Walson had finally put his work aside and sat sipping hot tea.

"Thank you, Prishner."

"I think you have earned the thanking today, Jeld. You heard it's alright to stay the night this time?"

"Yes, I heard. Thanks, but I'd best be off."

Prishner Walson smiled fleetingly. "I'm afraid caution is a commodity we can't live without, these days. Thank you again for your help today. Take care, Jeld."

"You too, Prishner."

Jeld headed for the door and, with a final wave goodbye to his friends, set out into the storm toward a far more private slumber.

Chapter Twelve

———◆———

J eld sat within his cocoon of curtains, his back pressed against the unseen wall framing the stage. He wore a set of old-fashioned street clothes he'd borrowed from the prop room. Just for the night, he'd told himself. His own clothes, which while also taken from the prop room were admittedly stolen, were drying against the hot bricks of his bedchamber wall.

"The sun must always set, Kalaa. Who am I to stop it?" Director Sammel's voice came.

Mouthing each word in perfect harmony as the director read on, Jeld drew a long breath into lungs stretched and wearied by a hard day's work. The chill that had sunk its teeth into his very bones loosened its grip within the curtain's embrace and a pleasant wave of warmth and contentedness crawled its way through his body.

His eyes grew heavy as he listened to the director's array of voices. So rich with depth were they that Jeld could see the faces of the characters, and soon a scene wove into place around him until there was no director or curtains at all, only Idolo and Kalaa in their small hut.

"I know you, and I know why, but still I ask—why, my I?" Kalaa asked. "Make yourself well, my I! Is it so different than singing a child better, or dancing the rains to our fields?"

She looked down over Idolo with bright blue eyes which, like her bright white mane of curls, stood in striking contrast against her dark, tight skin.

"Ohhh you know," Idolo laughed, his own bright blue eyes shining. "You know!"

He shook his head and the smile fell away. "If *I* stood over *you* though... I know I could not let nature be. I am lucky! Lucky I sleep first."

"Think of the lives you could—"

Idolo's eyes twinkled over a knowing, patient smile.

Kalaa sighed. "I know, my I. I know."

"They say no one but I could understand. I say no, my Kalaa knows. She doesn't like it"—he chuckled—"but she knows."

"Well, now," came another voice.

The sloping walls of the hut rippled like cloth as Jeld's heart jolted him awake. The weight upon his eyelids disappeared and his eyes shot wide open to find Director Sammel standing over him between the curtains.

"An audience already?" the director said. "But the show is still a babe in the womb."

Jeld frantically sat up, pulling his feet back in from where they'd slid beyond the curtains. The part of him that had kept him alive through his worst times re-emerged from the shadows—the thoughtless instinct, the skittish rat. He tensed to roll through the trapdoor.

"What do you think of it?" the director asked.

Jeld froze.

"It's early yet, but a bratty babe oft grows into a brat, I'm afraid, so best fix it young. So, thoughts?"

How strange it felt to be addressed by a man he'd watched for so long now, a man whose work had lifted him from the depths of despair. And yet, he had so many thoughts on the matter...

"Well, the... the second act is brilliant," Jeld said, "but... er, well..."

"Yes? Go on, go on."

"It's just that, well, the villain doesn't show up until the very end of the act and... er, I just thought maybe introducing him earlier might keep the audience more interested. And later, when the soldiers attack the village, Idolo just lets them but... I don't know, he wouldn't do *nothing*, he would talk, plead. If he's brave enough to let himself die at the end, he would have risked his life to stop the soldiers. Also, though Idolo is already perfect... I think it needs another character to relate to, to grow."

Director Sammel cupped his chin in one lean hand and stared silently down at him. Jeld's eyes flicked to the open trapdoor, but a slow smile crept out from beneath the director's hand to stretch across his face.

"Anything else?"

"No, sir. I mean, little things maybe, but I didn't mean to sound—it's very good, I just—"

The director chuckled. "Not another word. If I was going to be offended by feedback I would never have asked for it. What say you we get back to work in my office? You can read the parts of Jakka, Geddana, and Idolo—that'll mostly keep us from talking to ourselves."

"I..."

Jeld's eyes went again to the hole in the stage, but he set his jaw and looked up.

"Alright," he said.

"Excellent!"

The director turned and hurried back toward his office, calling back over his shoulder as if to an old colleague rather than an anonymous trespasser.

"In here. We could just begin where I left off, wouldn't you say?"

Jeld followed him across the stage, standing frozen in the doorway as the director slid a second chair to his desk and sat.

"Just a read through first, then we can circle back and see about your more integral feedback later."

Jeld felt himself start to sweat, certain he'd be cast back to the streets as soon as the director realized he was not only an intruder, but an illiterate one. He forced himself inward and sat.

Director Sammel pointed to a line about halfway down the page.

"Care to start?"

"Ah... please, after you, sir."

"Very well." The director cleared his throat. "I know you, and I know why, but still I ask—why, my I? Make yourself well, my I! Is it so different than singing a child better, or dancing the rains to our fields?"

The director's finger traced the lines as he read until he looked over at Jeld.

Jeld stared at the jumble of symbols. Even were he literate, he doubted he could make sense of it. He'd seen enough writings to know the script was a mess, with entire lines scratched out and rewritten in the margins, sometimes twice again. He let the symbols blur and thought instead of the story he had heard now a hundred times. Letting every aspect of his face and very being fall into Idolo's mold, he laughed the wise old laugh he knew so well.

"Ohhh you know. You know!" Jeld pictured Kalaa's mournful eyes and grew somber. "If *I* stood over *you* though... I know I could not let nature be. I am lucky! Lucky I sleep first."

Eyes fixed on the script, Jeld waited for the director to read his part, but there came only silence. A bead of sweat formed upon his brow. Had he performed miserably? Or worse, did the director know he was faking it? Finally he could bear the silence no longer and he forced a sheepish eye upward.

Beneath raised gray brows, the director's wide, glistening eyes were fixed upon Jeld. Finally he smiled, cleared his throat, and read the next line.

And so they worked, the director scribbling notes atop notes as they went. The final night bell had long since faded into the distance when the director cut Jeld off in the middle of a line.

"Wait wait wait."

"Hmm?" Jeld said, looking up with tired eyes.

"We changed that line on our last pass. It's written above, here."

Jeld looked down at the script. Indeed the line had been crossed out and another squeezed in beside it.

"Ah... right."

"Messy, I know. I think it's about time for a new draft."

Jeld squinted, but he might as well have been staring at tree bark. He silently cursed his ignorance.

"Oh..." Director Sammel gasped. "Mother's touch, you've memorized the whole script."

Jeld's eyes fell to the ground.

"Brilliant!" Director Sammel said with wonder.

Jeld looked up.

"And your *characters!*" the director laughed. "But how? What else have you heard here?"

Jeld managed only a sheepish shrug.

"Do you know who Brandel was?" Director Sammel asked.

"No, sir."

"He was a young gossip peddler in Khapar. Long before it burned, when it was more crowded even than Tovar is today."

Jeld nodded dubiously.

"Very interesting young man, Brandel was. We do a show about him. True story, too. You look a lot like him, though it may just be your clothes..."

He looked to Jeld's shirt.

Jeld's eyes went wide and the director grinned.

"It's quite alright, though I'd appreciate it if you would return the costume before we run that show."

"I mean to, sir. I only borrowed it for the day because the storm soaked my clothes."

"I don't doubt that. You've clearly been a gracious tenant. How long have you been our guest, may I ask?"

Jeld swallowed. It had been a month or more since he'd first taken up residence in the man's walls, watching longingly this diverse band like some pathetic, lonely rat.

"No matter," Director Sammel said. "I only marvel at your dedication. You know, for such a young man, you play a very convincing old man."

Jeld grinned despite himself.

"There's a smile," the director chuckled before yawning. "Well, it's late. Will you return tomorrow? It's nice having a bright brain to bounce ideas off of. You can help out with other things around the theater instead, if you'd prefer. Or you could stay, have a room even. We have an extra. A low-ender, but it's nice. What do you say?"

Even as Jeld looked within for an answer, he felt the director's integrity as plain as a warm campfire. But did the low-ender room lock, he wondered? Did it have another way out, or was it another death trap like beneath the Barking Crab? Could he remain an anonymous shadow in the crowd of deep pockets outside? Still... what must it feel like to sit in the den, on the other side of his bricks sharing stories, laughs, comfortable silences...

"How about you think on it? Come back when you can, if you can. When you want the room, I'll show you there. What's your name, son?"

"It's Jeld." He came to his feet. "Thank you, sir."

"Until next time, my young bard."

Jeld nodded to the director and walked from the office toward the curtains that had once been his cloak of shadows.

"Jeld," Director Sammel called from behind.

Jeld turned to find him standing in the doorway.

"Remember, one who masters shadows is nobody. One who masters *acting* can be anyone at all."

Jeld felt the words sink deep within him. Nodding, he continued across the stage, letting the curtains engulf him and descending through the portal into the comforting concealment of the dark understage.

CHAPTER THIRTEEN

"Well... Brandel you... sh-ould... check your... int-el-lig— intel-lighence?"

Jeld rapped the word with his finger and let his aching neck loll over the back of his chair. The softly glowing stained-glass Traveler stared down at him, a touch of humor in his eyes. A groan escaping Jeld's lips, he bent and traded his script for another upon the floor. He opened it to the back and thumbed through several pages of short lines scribbled in his own hand before his finger came to a stop.

Gen—7, 15, 3.

He flipped to the seventh page and counted down to the fifteenth line, then the third word, finally backing up until he recognized the scene from memory.

"But the *gentry*. Gen-try...." Jeld pulled the other script back into his lap. "In-tel-*lighence*..." He slapped his forehead. "Intelligence."

He sighed. Just as he slid his finger to the next word the midday bell chimed. Jumping to his feet, he set the scripts upon his borrowed chair, tightened his mismatched boot-straps, and climbed beneath the Traveler to the alleyway without.

A crowd in the square ahead awaited the Thrallsday afternoon exhibition. As always it was modest compared to the evening feature crowds Jeld favored, but he hoped to have company later that would preclude his usual pocket shopping. His mind on Lira, he smiled and waded inward toward a well-dressed older man with enough extra girth to mask his handiwork.

Jeld quickly emptied both the man's pockets of their meager coin and looked about for another sheep. As he closed on a strapping young gentleman with a lady on one arm, something gave him pause. It was a familiar feeling, like... like the burn of Kaid's glare at the temple!

He sprung forward through a narrow gap in the crowd even as a firm grip slipped from his shoulder. Behind, a huge man wearing a trim black coat and a stunned expression pulled an empty hand back to his side.

Turning to continue his flight, Jeld slammed into something and suddenly he was lifted off the ground, arms pinned at either side in a vice-like embrace. He sucked in a breath as something sharp poked against his back.

"Yeah, that's a knife," a calm, hard voice said into his ear. "Long one, too, so *behave.*"

Jeld stayed still as the man carried him toward the edge of the crowd. Wresting himself free was out of the question, as the bead of blood running down his back reminded him. Perhaps screaming, then. Surely the man wouldn't stab him in the middle of a crowd, would he? As if sensing his quandary, the knife bit deeper.

"You scream, I stab. You kick, I stab. You talk, I stab. And if you bite me, I'm going to stab *hard.* I *hate* when people bite me. I'll earn some funny looks, but you'll be dead."

As they emerged from the crowd, an approaching woman slowed mid-step and stared. Jeld's captor jostled him playfully and whispered into his ear.

"Smile, puppet."

The knife bit a little deeper. Jeld squirmed playfully and the woman grinned and continued past.

"Nice job, son o' mine. Maybe you can work in the theater someday if I don't stick you."

They entered the familiar alley beside the theater and the huge man Jeld had narrowly evaded fell in step beside them. Halfway down the alley they came to a stop and the larger man set to shaking Jeld down even as he dangled from his captor's arms. Jeld looked longingly up the alley wall at the stained-glass window, the tip of the Traveler's lute barely visible beyond the sill.

Two knives, several purses, and numerous loose coins later, they continued down the alley. Much to Jeld's relief, the coveted bag he'd acquired as if from a dream went unnoticed pressed flat against his chest.

"By the way, real nice grab, Elo," his captor said.

"It was perfect, Ement, just bad luck. He happened to turn."

"Uh huh."

Ement. The name played over and over in Jeld's head until suddenly a memory solidified. It was the man he'd sold his wagons to a lifetime ago. The man working for the mysterious figure at whose mention even Quintem flinched. Jeld's eyes widened as his father's face took shape in his mind.

"Really, the kid just got lucky and turned."

Ement grunted.

Reaching the alley's end, they turned and walked into the warehouse. The man at the desk looked up just long enough to nod before returning his attention to a ledger.

Jeld swallowed hard. Apparently even abducting children didn't warrant a second glance around here. They crossed the warehouse and passed through the back door of the theater. Inside, where Jeld had once turned right and descended to the prop room, his captor instead turned left and started up a staircase.

Jeld eyed the tight walls of the stairwell. A swift kick against the wall was certain to send the lot of them tumbling. Not a bad gamble if certain death lay in wait. Of course, it otherwise might just be a good way to land on a knife already partway into his back. They reached the top before he could decide, continuing down a wood-paneled hallway and through a doorway. A man sat writing behind a polished desk nearly as wide as the room. Windows overlooking the warehouse lined the wall behind him.

Ement dropped Jeld to his feet, clinging to a fistful of his collar. "Found your pest, boss."

The man behind the desk looked up, his grave, dark eyes meeting Jeld's. A close goatee, peppered gray like the hair at his temples, surrounded a slight frown somehow more severe than its meager curvature implied. His clothes were simple in design, yet seemed to be of perfect cut and fine fabrics.

"Well," the man said. "Looks like you were doing alright for yourself, eh?"

"Bread might fill my stomach, but decent clothes are all that keeps the watch off my back," Jeld said.

The man leaned forward in his chair. "How many customers do you think will not return because they were victimized at my theater? How many will never come a first time because they hear of such a thing?"

Jeld searched the man for some chink. Fine but simple clothes—rich but not vain. Piercing eyes, harsh but composed—willing to lash out for need, but not on impulse. Here was a man who respected strength and directness—a man who would not take kindly to being ignored.

"I understand I have done harm to your business. I will stop immediately."

"How many competitors will hear of this and think me weak, that I can't even protect my own place of business?"

Jeld swallowed hard. "I'll make it right. Pay you back, and it'll never happen again."

"A thief promising not to steal. Do you know how to make *certain* a thief never steals again?"

Pay them loads of gold? Jeld knew better than to say it, though. A man like this valued hard and smart work, not witty banter. Or did it just need translating? He thought of Brandel from his script.

"If you won't trust me to stop, you could employ me?" Jeld said. "You'll know I won't steal because I'd earn a wage, and… you'd gain a street source. You'll be the first to hear the talk on the streets. I'll find what your competitors don't want you to know, and leak what you want them to think."

The man only stared back like a cat at a wounded mouse.

"Or I could just be a wagoner," Jeld added, his heart racing. "I was once. I know the trade."

Ement snapped his fingers. "That was it! *Idols* that was buggin' me. You sold me those two wagons. Quintem's boy."

The frown on the man behind the desk deepened.

"I'm *nothing* like him!" Jeld snapped. "All he taught me is what *not* to be."

Still the man said nothing, his eyes flicking to Ement as if to signal the kill.

Jeld took an unconscious step toward the side of the room, out from between the men silently plotting his death. "I'll just disappear forever!" he said, his voice cracking. "You'll never see me again!"

"No," the man behind the desk said, returning his gaze to Jeld. He walked around the desk to stand before Jeld. "What kind of businessman would I be if I simply allowed you to leave?"

Jeld looked behind at the doorway to find Elo filling it. When he looked back, he found the man wearing a slight smile.

"I like you," the man said. "And I like your first proposal much better."

Jeld blinked.

"You're a sharp kid. I'd be a poor investor if I let offers like that pass by, so here's the deal. You stay on top of news. I give you a few jobs to fill your time. Some gossip to spread, people to find, prices to watch. That's it. Each week, one brick. Deal?"

Even as Jeld opened his mouth to accept the offer on account of it not including being murdered, a thought struck him and his brow narrowed. One brick would serve him well enough, but how would a shrewd businessman judge him were he not to negotiate? "How about nothing for the first month, because I owe you, and three bricks per week after that," Jeld countered.

"One and five peb."

"Two and four then?"

"One and nine, and you can walk out of here instead of crawl, thief."

Jeld stared back, his mouth opening and closing before at last he spoke again. "Two and you get another peb's worth of work out of me each week, unless my legs are broken."

The man nodded. "Done. One detail though. I'd like to keep our arrangement... discreet. Just between us here. And Henred—the man at the desk outside. Ement, work with him on how best for us to communicate."

"I can take work at the theater," Jeld said. "Then I can come and go without raising suspicions.

"I might own the theater, but it's not for me to decide who Sammel employs."

"I'll handle that."

Though the man showed no amusement, Jeld somehow felt a hungry delight radiating from him.

"Fair enough. Ement will explain how we can communicate until then as he sees you out."

"Thank you, but no need. I'll be employed at the theater in just two days. Oh, and I need tomorrow off, please. Most Thrallsdays actually, please."

"Very well. Sammel will be informed of your employment here as well. Though he prefers to know little about our goings on, anything less would be... disingenuous."

The man nodded over Jeld's head and Elo stepped aside.

"I'm sorry about the stealing," Jeld said.

"It's done. What's your name?"

"It's Jeld."

Jeld's new employer extended a hand and they shook.

"Krayo Rusrivon. To the beginning of our mutually lucrative partnership, Jeld."

Chapter Fourteen

A couple looked down a side street to Jeld and Lira before passing from view.

"I think they saw! I think they saw me!" Lira hissed.

Jeld laughed. "They saw someone, but they didn't see *you.*"

"They must have!"

"Who are these friends of your father's, magic assassins or something? Your father isn't going to find out. You're just one of the street kids leaving the temple."

She suddenly sprinted ahead, Jeld's heart lurching before he realized she was skipping. He smiled and gave chase.

"What's gotten into you?" Jeld laughed, catching up as she slowed at the next block.

"A wonderful evening on the town, what else! The light is exceptionally lovely this evening, isn't it?"

"*Tovarian dusk.* My favorite time of day. Except maybe for Tovarian dawn, anyway."

"A bit bright yet for dusk, wouldn't you say?"

Jeld raised an eyebrow. "*Tovarian* dusk."

"How do you mean?"

"The sun has fallen below the wall but not the horizon. *Tovarian dusk...* surely you've heard it said?"

"Ah. Of course."

With a quick glance over her shoulder, she pulled her hat off and her hair tumbled down to her shoulders.

"You should take off that old coat too," Jeld said. "Don't want the king's watchmen thinking you're poor."

She frowned. "Can't look like myself or my father will catch me sneaking off. Can't look rich or I'll get mugged. Can't look poor or I'll get jailed."

Jeld steered them onto a busier road to better blend in. Soon after, a distant shouting from somewhere ahead took shape over the evening bustle.

"You! Me! We *all* reap the crop we have sown! Only we can restore the goodness we have extinguished. Only together can we rekindle the beacon that will guide the Idols back to us!"

Jeld and Lira exchanged a look and took the next turn to avoid the Sayer. They continued in silence, Lira looking about the city with wonder, until at last they emerged in Temple Square where a huge crowd was gathered before the theater steps.

"Ever seen a show here?" Jeld asked.

"Actually yes. When I was a little girl, my family came for the Fallstival show. But it's been years. What is the show tonight?"

"*Tale of Tales.* Bunch of folk tales all merged into one story. The White Knight of Havaral, Traveler's Trade, Sisters of Sunndville, Boy in the Stars, Witch of the Mountain. Bunch more."

"I've read them all!"

"You'll love this, then."

"Welcome folks, welcome," called the ticketer as the crowd trickled past. "Come on up, come on up. Let's see those tickets please."

Jeld chuckled despite himself, the sight of grumpy Erol as the jovial ticketer always too much to bear.

"What is it?" Lira asked.

"Nothing really. Come on," Jeld said, leading her through the crowd and into his alley beside the theater.

"Where are you going?"

"To the side entrance!"

Jeld slowed to a stop part way down the block.

"What is it?" Lira asked.

Jeld looked up and she followed his gaze to a window above. Their eyes met and Jeld smiled.

"You don't have tickets..."

"Who needs tickets?"

"You said you had reserved seats!"

"I do! Best in the house."

Jeld waited anxiously for an objection. Instead, Lira started climbing. His smile widening, Jeld climbed up to the other side of the ledge and tugged the board free as Lira came to a stop opposite.

"Like this," Jeld said.

He kicked a leg through and ducked under the window. Turning to check on Lira, he found her already through, her face just a finger from his own.

"And then you just…"

He pulled his other leg through and dropped to the floor. Lira landed beside him and looked up at the window as Jeld replaced the board.

"Your favorite," she whispered.

"Hmm?" Jeld followed her gaze to the Traveler upon the window. "Oh. I guess."

"*Temple* Theater," she mused. "I just never thought about it."

"The other windows have all been bricked in, but I found where each used to be. Wait here a blink?"

He climbed back onto the ledge and retrieved an unlit lamp from atop a beam running overhead then hopped back down. Pulling his sparker from his pocket, he held it over the wick and gave a twist. Sparks flashed in the darkness then the softer glow of firefight stretched across the passage as the lamp caught. Lira's face was alight with wonder.

"How—what is that thing?"

"I don't know. I found it." He turned the sparker over in his hands. "I should show it to Fen, he'd tear it apart until he knew how it worked. Hmm, maybe I shouldn't show it to Fen."

"I've never seen anything like it."

"Me neither." Jeld dropped the sparker into his pocket. "Let's go, I want to show you something before we get to our seats."

Lira smiled.

"What?" Jeld said.

"Nothing. Lead the way."

Jeld held the lamp behind him for Lira and led the way deeper into the theater, raising and lowering it to point out the countless obstacles he navigated from memory alone. He came to a stop where the ceiling sloped sharply down to cut off the corridor.

"Down here," he said, ducking through a small opening and dropping to his feet. "Bit of a—"

Lira landed beside him.

"Drop," he finished. "I want to show you something, but it has to be dark."

Jeld blew the lamp out, leaving them in total darkness.

"What are we looking at?" Lira whispered.

"You'll see. Our eyes just need to adjust."

Gradually, specks and lines of light appeared overhead. A few at first, then dozens. Patterns took shape, circles and squares and triangles.

"It's like the stars," Lira whispered.

"And look." Jeld pointed at the pillars taking shape in the dim light. "I always thought it looked like a forest under the stars."

"It does."

They stood quietly beneath the stars.

"Are we under the stage?" Lira asked after a while.

"Of course not, we're in the woods."

Jeld felt her smile. Music danced toward the opening act.

"A stagehand passes through here soon, we'd best be on our way. Back up through the hole. Watch your head at the top, sharp edge."

She started climbing. "Get you once?"

"Got me good."

Jeld climbed through after Lira and came to his feet. He could just make out her form beside him.

"Let me get this thing lit," Jeld said.

"I bet you do this in the dark."

"It took me a while."

"Let's try."

"Alright, if you say so. This way. There's a beam just ahead."

He felt her probing hand press against his back as he slowed to a stop.

"Here," he said, knocking on a beam. "Find it?"

A moment later Lira's hand fell upon his. He turned his hand over and pressed hers to the beam.

"Just there," he whispered.

He ducked the beam and continued through the passage. Lira's hand clung to the back of his shirt as she followed, but even when it slackened he could sense her there. Just a feeling—exhilaration, or something like it.

"There's a step. Here."

Jeld tapped it with the tip of his boot, careful to use only the sole to avoid a scuff. He stepped up and a moment later the pull on his shirt went slack and her breath tickled his neck. Drawing a breath, he pressed on.

Before long they reached the nook beneath the box seating and Jeld peeled the curtains aside.

Lira gasped. "These *are* the best seats!"

In the dim slice of light passing between the curtains, Jeld saw her glimmering eyes fall upon him.

"How did you find this place?"

"I ran in through the warehouse like an idiot. It connects to the understage. I only found the window afterward."

"It's amazing. This whole place."

"It sure beats the gutters."

The lights dimmed and the music faded until all that remained was the many-voiced song of a single harp. Jeld pulled the curtains slightly wider and turned to Lira to find her staring out at the stage, her mouth hanging open, forgotten in wonder.

Turning to him, she hurriedly closed her mouth then smiled and whispered something Jeld couldn't quite make out. He cocked his ear.

"Thank you," her words came with a warm breath.

Their eyes locked again for a blink that seemed like forever until the show tore her attention away. Jeld watched her for a time as she fell into the story before himself turning to the stage.

So they sat, Lira lost in fantasy and Jeld in her delight, their tearful, shocked, or smiling eyes meeting every so often to share a moment, until at last the curtain fell.

"Amazing," Lira whispered.

Jeld nodded. "And it gets better every night."

"*Every* night?"

"Pretty much. It's not like I have much else to do. Although I might be getting some work soon."

"Oh? You said you were once a wagoner, didn't you?"

"Yeah, but it's something else. Just running errands for the theater."

"That's fantastic!"

"We'll see. I've kinda gotten accustomed to being on my own. But every coin I earn is one less pocket I can get caught in, at least. What about you? What do you do when you're not helping at the temple?"

"Oh, well... plenty? I don't know, I suppose I just play assistant. Or bookkeeper? Bit of a caretaker, honestly. Really I do everything my father doesn't want to do, business or otherwise. Actually, I really should be going."

"Now? Already?"

"I really must, or I could lose my freedom to visit the temple." She crawled out of the nook.

Suddenly angry at her controlling father, Jeld stared after her for a moment before climbing down. He led the way back through the dark passages until soon they were walking beneath the true stars.

As they neared the temple, Lira put the cap Jeld had lent her back on, tucking her hair up beneath it.

"Why should you have to hide?" Jeld blurted. "You help so many people, so what if you treat yourself for a bell or two. Who could have a problem with that?"

"He means well... he really does."

There was something off about her, in her voice or somewhere deeper, perhaps that place beyond the eyes that had of late so availed itself. Jeld again decided it best to drop the subject and they continued in silence.

"Thanks for letting me talk you into this," Jeld said as they turned into an alley.

"Talked me into?" she scoffed. "Don't be silly, you just helped me realize I could get away with it."

Jeld smiled. "It's good to have a talent."

"It was magical. I feel so free—" She froze, her wide eyes staring down the alley.

Jeld followed her gaze to a man charging in from the end of the alley, a heavy club in hand.

"Run!" Jeld yelled.

They spun and fled, but two more men appeared at the other end of the alley.

"Other way!" Jeld said, dashing back toward the lone man.

"Jeld—"

"Stop!" the man with the club called. "Give me—"

Jeld drew his long knife and lashed out toward the man's throat at the last possible moment. The man raised his arms defensively, crying out as the blade scraped along bone. The agonized scream struck Jeld like a physical blow, pervading his senses with a chaotic cloud as if of raw emotion. As Jeld pulled his knife back again, he felt the man's fear, his anger, his anticipation. He felt more than such describable feelings, as if thoughts themselves. Somehow amongst the chaos emerged a discernable pattern— an attack!

He ducked, the club sailing overhead, then darted forward and drove his blade into the man's groin. Without slowing, he pulled his blade free and danced past the man, blood spraying out in his wake as the man loosed another terrible shriek.

The sensation flashed again in Jeld's mind and he spun, but it was too late. The club slammed into his forehead and a flash of light seemed to explode from somewhere behind his eyes. Suddenly he was sitting upon the alley floor, gasping to fill his empty lungs. He strained to bring his eyes into focus on his attacker only to find the man lying upon the ground, Lira standing over him. She pulled a dagger from the man's neck and blood gushed from the wound.

Shouts came from down the alley. He looked to Lira and their wide eyes met through the dark haze. Her mouth moved. *Are you alright?*

"Run!" Jeld tried to shout, tried to scream, but barely a sound escaped his breathless lips.

Lira knelt before him and then she was all he could see in the encroaching darkness. Jeld felt her hand upon his and he clung to it. He managed to pull in a single shallow breath of sweet air.

"Run," he managed to whisper.

But it was too late. Arms reached in and tugged Lira away until there was only her pale hand, bright against the darkness, clinging to his.

"Stop!" Lira's shout came. "No! Let me help him! Wait!"

Suddenly she burst back through the darkness. Her lips pressed to his cheek and Jeld felt something cold against his palm, then the arms stole her away again.

Jeld sucked in a short breath and clawed his way up the wall, but just as he managed to get a single foot flat beneath him, the world spun and he spilled over onto his side.

"Stop! Please!" Lira screamed.

His cheek still warm from her kiss despite the cold cobblestone beneath it, Jeld could just make out three silhouettes and a glare as if from polished armor before there was only darkness.

***

"Ahhhg!" groaned a bloodied man writhing in the dirt road.

"Yeah, shoulda' thought of that before you tried to steal my shit," Quintem said.

Stomping on the bandit's hand, Quintem kicked his sword to Jeld's feet then pulled a knife and walked after another man hobbling toward the tree line.

Jeld picked up the sword and leveled it at the fallen bandit, meeting his pitiful eyes.

"Please, I was just trying to feed my family," the man pleaded.

"Jeld?" Niya said from behind.

"Stay back, Niya," Jeld said.

"What are you going to do?"

Jeld's eyes flicked to the tree line. Quintem grabbed the shoulder of the fleeing bandit and thrust a blade through his back. Pulling the knife free, Quintem booted the man to the ground and turned.

"Jeld!" Niya screamed.

Jeld looked back just as his captive lunged. He thrust his sword but still the man slammed into him, pinning him to the ground. Trying to wrest himself free, Jeld froze as he met his attacker's vacant, unblinking eyes. Pulling his blade free with a sickening wet *squelch*, he rolled the man off him to find Fen staring down, the ring of The One beyond him at the base of the temple dome.

"Lira?" Jeld asked.

"You okay, little prince?"

"Where's Lira?"

Jeld lifted his head from the bench upon which Fen sat, but the room spun and he eased it back down.

"Easy, buddy. I don't know. Lira's not here."

"Is he awake?" Roba's voice came.

Jeld carefully raised his head to find her approaching, Prishner Walson lagging just behind.

Fen nodded. "What happened?"

"They took her!" Jeld shouted. "Someone took her. We have to find her."

"Took Lira?" Roba asked.

She sat cross-legged upon the floor beside the bench as Prishner Walson pressed a hand to Jeld's forehead.

"They attacked us and took her! We need to help her!"

"Mother's touch…" Prishner Walson breathed.

"Who did this?" Roba asked. "Who took her?"

"I... I don't know," Jeld said. "Actually, I'd swear I saw crimson armor beneath their clothes."

"Like... a knight?"

"Why would a knight do this?" Fen asked.

Roba shrugged. "Helping with sweeps?"

"I don't know," Jeld said. "But if we don't go now we'll never find her!"

Reaching back to heft himself onto his feet, Jeld realized one of his hands was clamped shut around something small yet oddly heavy. He held his hand out and opened it.

"Jeld, you've been out for at least a quarter bell, they mu—Mother!"

The object in Jeld's palm caught the light and cast a brilliant golden beam into his eyes. Turning it in his hand until the blinding light moved aside, he found the face of Tovados staring up at him from a golden coin.

"Idols, a gold crown!" Roba hissed. "Where did you get that!"

"I'm... not sure," Jeld said.

A foggy memory of Lira pushing something into his palm flitted through his mind. He clamped his hand around the coin as if clinging still to Lira.

Prishner Walson stood abruptly. "You must be hungry. I'll fetch you some food."

As Jeld watched him go, something tugged at his awareness, a sickening sensation like... arrogance. He turned carefully to find Kaid watching him from several rows back alongside his ever-present familiars Depsey and Vincet.

Kaid took a spoonful of stew and grinned deviously around the heaping bite. Still chewing, he whispered something to his companions and broke into a poorly acted bout of laughter that Depsey and Vincet quickly mimicked even less convincingly. His grin broke abruptly into a glare and Jeld turned to find Roba holding out her pinky with a broad smile on her face.

"Smirk away, ya blazin' pip," Roba muttered.

Kaid wrinkled his nose and turned his back on them.

"Easy," Fen said. "You need rest, Jeld, not a heart attack."

"How can you even think about resting?" Jeld stood, pinching his temples.

"What can we do? I want to help her too, but she was already gone when we found you, and the Watch was already starting to swarm. We barely made it back here."

With a sigh, Jeld lowered himself to the ground, leaning back against the bench. Another flash of pain setting the room spinning, he laid his head upon the bench and closed his eyes.

***

Jeld rolled to his other side, batting down a lump in his mound of borrowed blankets to continue staring into the gold coin in his other hand. Where might she be now, he wondered, a barrage of horrible images assailing him. The scene had been long since cleared by the time he'd returned to the theater late the night prior while Fen and Roba slept, with not a clue to be found. Just an empty alley. Even the hours of sleepless dwelling gleaned nothing more. Emptiness. That's all there was.

The crimson glimmer from beneath the cloak of Lira's abductor seemed to pass again before Jeld's eyes. He scowled. The Watch. The crown. The Mother-bleedin' prince. If they'd taken Lira from him too...

He growled and sat up. Setting the coin down, he had his boot halfway on before abruptly snatching the coin back up. A dusty floor was no place for such a memento. Nor was a clean floor, for that matter. No, he needed someplace secure while he ventured out to get the job with Director Sammel as he'd promised Krayo.

His eyes flitted about for a more worthy hiding spot, looking first toward the purse he kept in his waistband before considering his pack. Or perhaps his sock would have to do again, as it had on his way back to the theater? Jeld frowned. None seemed sufficient to shield the coin that was all he had left of Lira, and was itself worth more than he could hope to steal in years lest he take his craft to the king's palace.

An idea struck him then and he pulled the strange bag from beneath his undershirt. As he looked into the warm, glowing leather his thoughts returned once again to that perfect, warm inn and soon he could almost hear a lute's song. It seemed fitting that one such treasure might contain another.

Brushing off a spot on the ground, he gingerly set the coin down and started feeling his way around a lip of leather that ran around the mouth of the bag. His thumb caught on something and he folded the lip up to find the underside punctuated by tiny buttons. Unfastening one, he peeled up a segment of the liner and crawled his fingers down within. When he turned his hand over and reached for the true bottom, his fingers swiped at empty air.

He frowned and plunged his hand deeper but still his fingers landed upon nothing. Certain that he must have reached through the bottom of the bag, he looked beneath, but the bottom remained intact, his hand nowhere to be seen. His arm now nearly shoulder deep in the bag, he swept it around but again felt nothing.

Jeld jerked his arm back and threw the bag down on the ground. He sat frowning at the audacious curiosity before abruptly grinning and snatching it back up. Removing the tie and letting the bag fall flat open, he unfastened the many buttons and pulled the liner free entirely. Beneath, a circle of perfect black stared up like an empty eye.

Jeld's grin fell away. He held his lamp to the unnerving depths but the fire's light failed to penetrate the void. He cautiously dipped his fingers into it, rubbing them together to be sure they were still intact as they disappeared beneath the surface. Curling his fingers up as if toward the underside of the ice in a winter fishing hole, they fell upon a soft suede. He probed deeper and his fingers slipped off the leather onto what felt like stone.

Pulling his arm free, he stared into the void. He swallowed hard as an unsettling feeling grew in the pit of his stomach, the sinking feeling as when standing atop a cliff, worried not over falling but over one's body betraying him. Soon it seemed he could see Lira standing alone in the darkness, arms emerging from the depths and pulling at her.

Jeld slapped the lining back over the bag. Quickly pulling on his boots, he grabbed up the gold crown and stuffed it into his sock. He reached a copper peb behind the liner of the bag, setting it upon the inexplicable rim of stone within before snatching his hand back and stuffing the bag into his shirt.

His mind raced with questions, but the answers would have to wait. He had a job to start.

What better serves the common good, swords in the hands of the few, or in the hands of the many? Simple logic would seem to suggest both models are equal, that so long as we are more good than not, decency will prevail just the same, in time.

In time... A handy measure to those afforded eternity, but the stricken care not the odds of being struck. What if this sole sword should fall into the hands of a power so absolute, so devastating, that humanity cannot recover? What will time do with naught but ashes?

Clear as the answer may be, I find myself nonetheless unsettled. What if I am mistaken? What if the mighty few are all that hold our world together? Do I risk more in acting, or in not?

—Vincet Ellemere

Chapter Fifteen

J eld dropped to his feet from the theater window and started down the alley. At its end he paused and took a deep breath, his eyes falling closed and failing to reopen. It had been a long and busy night out with Raf, few Upper Hillside walls remaining unmarred by the crude truths they'd slopped on with pig's blood.

Forcing his eyes open, he turned from the alley to the warehouse, his eyes falling immediately upon the man at the desk ever bent over his books. He nodded, and the man nodded back.

Walking through the warehouse, Jeld audited his character the way Director Sammel had the actors do during their rehearsals. Confident but not arrogant, curious but not naive. Youthful but not childish.

One who masters acting can be anyone at all.

In the first bay, two men stood in conversation beside a group of porters loading a wagon. As Jeld neared, one of them turned and he found himself staring into the eyes of Ement Olanson. Jeld raised an eyebrow and continued past toward the backstage door. Out of the corner of his eye he saw Ement turn back to the wagoner.

Jeld felt his nerves ease slightly, having been slightly concerned Krayo would have reconsidered and cut his throat upon arrival. He passed through the door and stepped inside. Familiar faces dotted the stage, not milling about in full-speed rehearsal but reading through parts at the telltale crawl of a new script. *Sir Knight,* Jeld recognized, having recently put the finishing touches on it with Director Sammel. Beyond them, the empty stands towered like an abrupt mountainside.

Spotting the director nodding along as Evelyn performed her lines, Jeld veered toward him. Grumpy old Erol, who would probably seem far less old were he not so grumpy, was the first to see him coming. He frowned at Jeld, or perhaps merely turned an already present frown upon him, but looked away without a word.

"Jeld!" Director Sammel called. "What a pleasant surprise."

The director hurried to Jeld's side and guided him onto the stage with a welcoming hand upon his shoulder.

"Everyone, this is Jeld. He's been helping me with our scripts for quite a while now, so I invited him to help with other odds and ends. Jeld, this isn't quite everyone but let me introduce you to my good friends here?"

"Yes. Please. Thank you."

Director Sammel pointed first to Evelyn. "Here we have the sublime and talented Evelyn."

She smiled warmly and somehow curtsied without seeming to move. "Welcome. Pleased to meet you."

"Pleased to meet you as well," Jeld answered.

The director pointed with a flourish to Hawss, who as usual had the twinkle of an untold joke in his eyes.

"This is Hawss."

"'This is Hawss'?" Hawss said. "'Sublime and talented Evelyn', and just Hawss? Thanks, sir."

"Hawss is a skilled stagehand and actor both."

"That's a stretch," a voice said from behind. "At least he didn't call you sublime."

Jeld turned to find another familiar face. Cass's short hair was as unkempt as usual, her young face stern. She carried a hefty bundle of rope without any apparent effort.

Hawss snorted indignantly then grinned at Jeld. "Welcome aboard, Jelly boy."

The director gestured to Cass. "This is Cass. Cass, in case you didn't hear, this is Jeld. He will be helping out around here."

She crossed the stage to Jeld and an open hand emerged from the bundle of rope she wore.

"Welcome."

Jeld shook her hand. "Hello. Thanks."

Director Sammel turned to Erol. "And this, is the man of a thousand faces. Erol."

"We're still trying to figure out why he picked *that* face," Hawss said.

"Hawss!" Cass scolded.

"What?"

"Nice to meet you," Jeld said.

Erol nodded.

"And this is the amazing Jasselin," the director continued. "Our production manager extraordinaire. She's the real boss of this place."

"Oh nonsense!" she countered, though a proud grin lingered on her face.

The director proceeded to introduce Tabe, Onders, Owan, and even Master Edlin, who apparently joined in memorizing lines to cue his music from.

"That's probably enough new faces and names to set your brain spinning," Director Sammel said. "And that pack of yours probably isn't getting any lighter."

"Cass!" the director called. "Would you mind showing Jeld about, and to his room to get situated?"

"Sure," Cass said.

She cinched a knot around the corner of a hanging curtain then hefted the remaining coil of rope at Hawss's chest. Hawss caught the bulk of it and nearly toppled over, the rest falling in a tangle at his feet.

"Don't work too hard," Cass whispered before turning to face Jeld. "Shall we?"

"Let's," Jeld said, swallowing a grin.

Cass led him backstage and pointed to an open door to one side.

"That's the director's room. And the next door there is the dressing room."

Jeld's gaze lingered on a cocoon of curtains across from the director's room.

"That's the shop across the way. If you think about it, it takes just about every trade in the book to run a show. Carpenter, tailor, painter... you name it." She continued toward the door to the warehouse. "So how did you meet the director?"

"Oh, I shared some ideas once and I guess he liked them because he started sharing his writing with me. Offered me this job and... I really didn't have anything better going for me. What about you?"

"Jasselin is my aunt. She's known the director forever. My mother was an actress here and helped Jasselin get on as a stagehand."

Reaching the door to the warehouse, Cass pointed up the stairwell to her right.

"Don't go upstairs. The man who owns the building works up there. He's a rough fellow."

Cass turned and started down the steps opposite. She paused at the bottom and nodded at the doorway straight ahead.

"That's the prop room. The doorway there at the far side goes under the stage and to the orchestra pit. We can look later, if you want."

To either side of her ran hallways that quickly turned out of sight. She walked down the one to the right.

"These both circle to the den, but your room is on this side."

The narrow hallway turned left and ran for a long while before turning inward again. Doors lined the hallway on either side.

"This is my room," Cass said, brushing her hand along one of the doors before coming to a stop at the next. "And here is yours."

She pushed the door open. A bed stretched from wall to wall across the back of the room beneath a sharply sloping ceiling. A desk with an unlit lamp upon it was pressed against one side of the room, a chest at its side behind the door.

"I know it's not much," Cass said. "Just a low-ender room, but I like mine okay."

"Huh? This is amazing."

"Really?"

Jeld kicked himself for breaking character. Only a transient could be so impressed by the modest quarters.

"I mean, it's very generous to offer a room at all."

"Ah. Yeah, that's always been important to Director Sammel."

She stepped inside and pulled the chest open. "You can put clothes and stuff in here. Try rearranging if you want, but this is the best setup. Trust me, we've tried everything. Oh, and no food in here. We've had a lot of rat problems so best not to feed them. Idols only know what else is living in these old walls."

Jeld swallowed hard. "Right. Got it."

"Well, do you want to get settled and meet me backstage when you're ready for the rest of the tour?"

"I'm ready if you are," he said, setting his pack beside the bed.

"That'll work. Figured you'd want to... you know, unpack and all."

"Oh. Right. Unpack. Well, I wouldn't want to keep you waiting."

Cass shrugged and left the room.

Jeld followed, closing the door behind him and staring at the meager barrier protecting his belongings before finally turning away. They continued into a large room filled with all manner of couches and chairs. Beyond a broad dining table at the back of the room was a brick wall lined with cupboards, a sizable oven at its center. Jeld's eyes locked onto a tiny crack in the mortar beside the oven.

"We call this the den. Everyone shares meals and just hangs out here."

They passed through the den to the hallway opposite and followed it back around into the prop room.

"This is my favorite room," she said, turning off the path into the sea of oddities.

"Did you make any of this stuff?" Jeld asked.

"Oh ya. Loads. How did you know?"

Jeld's heart skipped a beat. Had the director not said as much? Was he not supposed to know that yet?

"I just took you for the builder sort, I guess. Maybe the way you looked at the shop..."

She pointed at a large throne as they passed by. "That was a fun one. And that over there. And that too."

Emerging from between two tropical trees, Jeld found himself face to face with his old friend the massive black wolf.

"How about this thing?"

"Hmm? Oh, her. No, not even Onders made her. They bought her from a taxidermist."

"Wait, you mean it's—*she's* real?"

"To hear Director Sammel tell it."

Jeld followed her through the dark understage to the far wall where she pulled open an unseen door. Passing through it, they emerged at the foot of the stage, the stands towering just opposite.

"This is Master Edlin's orchestra pit," Cass said.

Hearing voices overhead, Jeld backed toward the stands until Erol's head came into view atop the stage opposite. Erol raised an eyebrow at him then turned away. Jeld looked at Cass and they choked back laughter before continuing to the end of the pit and climbing a staircase to the edge of the stage.

Alal and Yelana both turned from rehearsal.

"You must be Jeld." Yelana extended a hand, her lean muscles shifting plainly beneath a thin shirt.

Jeld took her hand, tensing despite himself as if the Idolic's touch might somehow shock him.

"How was the tour?" Alal asked as they too exchanged a handshake. "He didn't see the bodies, did he Cass?"

"Or the... *other*... room?" Hawss added.

Cass shook her head. "Don't mind the children, Jeld. The only room that might have bodies in it is Hawss's, judging by the smell."

Director Sammel cleared his throat. "Why don't we have Onders put you to work for now, Jeld. Then tonight you can just observe how the show runs, and by tomorrow you'll be off and running."

"Whatever you say, sir," Jeld replied.

***

The bar of the door closed with a soft clap. Jeld looked out over the room—*his* room—in silence. It all felt surreal, as if at any minute he might wake up somewhere damp, cold, and dark.

He brushed his backside off and sat gingerly upon the clean bed. Bending over his pack, he unfastened the straps and scattered his belongings over the floor. He sat looking over his many treasures like socks and shoe polish and suspiciously eying the chest before peering beneath the bed. Shaking his head, he sighed and started to stand before his gaze fell upon the wall behind the bed.

Sliding the bed out, he let his fingers trace the top of the lowest board behind it until they slid deeper where the old wood was warped. When a tug proved fruitless, he returned with a pry bar and the board pulled free with only a tired, disapproving groan. Sliding it aside, Jed grinned at the sight of a familiar dusty passageway.

He set to unpacking, stashing the bulk of his belongings in the wall and just enough about the room to avoid arousing suspicion, until upon the floor remained only a handful of items he couldn't bear not to carry.

Jeld looked over the items. There was no way they'd fit on his person, and somehow he didn't figure carrying a pack about the theater would go over well. His eyes fell upon the gold coin and suddenly his eyes went wide. He pulled the mysterious bag from the front of his shirt, removed the lining, and reached slowly down into the void. Creeping his fingers along the stone rim residing somehow within, he pulled out his peb and found it fully intact.

Jeld smiled. There were not many places in the world where even a mere peb could be left unattended for a day without ending up in someone else's pocket. He wrapped Lira's coin in a particularly unattractive sock and dipped it into the void, his hand lingering atop it before managing to leave it upon the rim within.

He looked next to his father's knife and an idea struck him. Moments later he was sewing a ring of button loops onto the inside of his undershirt. A full painstaking bell later, the strange bag was fixed in place against his chest, the liner refastened save for a short gap.

Jeld picked up his father's knife. Of all his possessions it was likely the one he might need with the greatest urgency. He carefully reached it into his collar and beneath the lining of the bag, setting it on the rim where he could most easily draw it. He proceeded to place the remaining items around the rim in positions of varying accessibility, noting each spot with numbers like the hours of a sundial.

When all was settled, Jeld set to practicing his knife draw until a long yawn drained what little energy he had remaining. He pushed the bed back toward the wall, leaving space enough to roll off into the hole should he need to escape in a hurry. Blowing out his lamp, he laid down with his boots hanging off the end of the bed so as to not dirty the bedding. He took a deep breath, nervous at what painful story his eyelids might tell, and closed his eyes.

Lira's terrified scream echoed in his head almost at once, images of arms grabbing at her through the encroaching darkness bombarding his mind. He opened his eyes and they flicked to the door. So thin was the beam securing his room that it barely interrupted the narrow band of light surrounding the door. His heart quickened and he rolled onto his other side.

It was late into the sleepless night when he slid from the bed and squeezed through the hole in the wall. His back pressed into a tight and dusty corner within, he let out a breath and his shoulders sagged, and then dreams took him at last.

Chapter Sixteen

"Prince's Prison opened Ascenday!" Jeld called over the bustle, cutting upstream toward the towering North Gate. "*Sir Knight* running one more week at Temple Theater! Ore supply booms on new quarry!"

Dodging a wagon, he climbed up the back of it and peeked under the canopy.

"Tanner at Riverside Square is hot for hides," Jeld yelled, hopping down and pacing beside the wagon. "They got a big army contract with the crown."

The driver looked down at Jeld and grunted. "What's the rate?"

"Two bricks a side, two pebs per square step."

"Not bad."

"And don't let your wheat go too easy either, it's looking at a quick climb."

The wagoner frowned then flipped a peb down to Jeld. "Thanks."

Jeld tipped his hat and snatched the coin from the air. "Thank you, sir!"

As the wagon pulled away through the crowd, Jeld plucked a scrap of paper from his pocket.

Ore— down

Wheat— up

Final week Sir Knight

Is Semat dealing tar?

Winsted at Tipsy Stool. Fourth bell. Watch, listen.

He nodded along as he read. The ore and wheat bit would keep him busy for a few days, but he'd set plenty in motion already. Half the city ought to have heard his plugs for the show by now, and indeed Semat had been naughty, a second offense that Krayo was certain to make his final. Only the trip to the Tipsy Stool remained, whatever that was about.

Jeld started deeper into the city. At the first vacant alley he reached into his collar and pulled a smith's apron from his seemingly bottomless bag. At the next opportunity he produced a hat, and then a hammer, until he was but a young smith's apprentice walking the busy streets. Splotching black polish onto his face for a finishing touch, he turned a corner to find several armored watchmen herding a line of ragged vagrants from a boarded building into a cage wagon.

"In the wagon! Get! Move it!" a mounted watchman barked as the first of them filed in.

A woman whispered to a shrieking baby. A man with her stared blankly ahead, his shoulders sagging.

Three more watchmen emerged from the doorway, the frontmost pressing his sword to the back of a young boy at the rear of the line.

"Move it!" the watchman yelled and prodded the boy with his sword.

The boy cried out and darted past a woman in front of him.

"Don't you touch him!" the woman spat.

The watchman rapped her across the side with the flat of his sword. She cried out and raised a fist, but a man behind her stayed her wrist.

"Onna, no," the man said.

He gently eased her and the boy into the cage and followed them inside. Through the bars he met Jeld's eyes.

Jeld staggered as the man's shame and sorrow beat against him. He forced himself to look away and soon anger steadied his steps as it did so often now when passing by such tragedies. He walked on, but each time he managed to drag his mind back toward the mission ahead, his eyes flicked up to the prince's new prison tower peeking over the city wall and his pulse would quicken once again.

Turning from the tower, his mind was finally settling on Winsted and the Tipsy Stool when suddenly a piercing scream sounded from just ahead.

"Help! They took... they took my daughter!" the voice wailed.

The memory of Lira's screams seemed to echo in his mind. His eyes widened and he dashed toward the commotion.

Bursting around a corner, Jeld came to a sudden stop. In the middle of the street, a well-dressed man hefted a girthy lady to her feet.

"Did they have armor on?" Jeld shouted. "Under their clothes, even?"

"What's this?" the woman demanded.

"Were they wearing armor!"

"Are you mad? Summon the watch, boy!"

"Which way did they go!"

The man peeked out from behind her and pointed east. "That way! They went that way!"

Jeld was eastbound at full speed without another word. He rapidly scrutinized each person he passed, at first seeing only the clues offered by their clothes, then the subtleties in their eyes, and then deeper still, a distinct sense of each person like a color or taste. Soon it all seemed to flow uninvited, a maelstrom of facts and feelings almost tangible, each lingering upon his mind's eye like a sunburnt retina as he sped past.

Suddenly a terrible horror pierced his open mind. He came to a stop as a girl no older than he spilled from an alley onto the main street. Her eyes were wide with terror and she sobbed with huge sucking breaths as she ran. Jeld's eyes flicked between her and the alley her abductor would be escaping down before biting his lip and darting into the alley.

He emerged from the alley just in time to see two men disappear around another corner. One turned and Jeld looked to the ground, peering up through his scraggly bangs. The man wore his guilt plainly enough for the eye to behold. Jeld fell back and continued his pursuit more discreetly. The pair moved with apparent ease, their clothes clearly not concealing armor. Nearing midtown, they entered a large building of worn, dark stone, closing a soot-stained black door behind them. Sloppy patches of plaster punctuating the walls were all that remained of what must once have been windows, furthering an impression the building had been disfigured by some festering blight.

His lip curling, he pressed an ear to the door and heard the low rumble of voices. Unable to make out the words, he circled the building in search of another vantage. Narrow bands of smoke snaked steadily from any number of unseen vents overhead until he reached the front again having encountered nothing but dying brick and more plastered-over windows.

Suddenly the door burst open. He darted back around the corner and peered out as a woman in tattered black robes emerged. Jeld's eyes widening at the sight of the familiar robes, he slunk after her. After several blocks she came to a stop in the middle of a crowded street.

"Change now or seal our doom!" the robed woman called out. "Serve the light, not your greedy vices! Serve each other and we save ourselves!"

Jeld passed by without another look back, his face a mask of the same annoyance as most others within earshot. Behind the mask, his heart raced. He'd been mostly certain upon first glimpsing the robes, but this confirmed it without question. *Sayers.*

He turned again toward the Tipsy Stool, falling deep into thought as the woman's ranting slowly faded into the distance. What were Sayers doing trying to abduct girls even as they shouted their long-winded preaching of peace? Could they possibly be behind Lira's disappearance? And what of the sheen of armor he'd glimpsed upon Lira's attacker, then? A trick of the light? A concussed imagining? Or a curious alliance?

He sighed. It seemed he'd only gained more questions.

***

Henred nodded at Jeld and set a small stack of coins upon the desk, a tiny scrap of paper tucked discreetly beneath. Smooth as a bard plucking a chord, Jeld snatched up coins and note alike and continued through the warehouse. He greeted Vence and Shane, two porters hard at work with the evening cleaning, and passed through the theater door, nearly colliding with Ement just inside.

"Hey, kid. How was your trip to the Tipsy?"

"Hey Ement. Not much to share. Winsted met some guy named Mendel and they discussed a job moving a good lot of wheat." Jeld lowered his voice. "I saw something else I wanted to tell you."

Ement let the door close and glanced to the busy stage before leading the way upstairs.

"What ya got?" Ement asked, turning into a small office.

"I saw these guys try to kidnap a girl on the street, so I followed them. They went to a sylum."

"Okay."

"A *sylum*. They were Sayers."

"Yeah. So?"

"*Sayers* abducting people?"

"Eh," Ement said. "You offer every poor, worthless crook an ugly robe, food, and a place to sleep in return for spouting off some crazy talk and, well, you end up with a bunch of crooks dressed in robes. Abducting though, you said? Does seem a bit much, even for them..."

"Yeah. Well, trying. She got free."

"Ah. Yeah, see? They probably let her off. Got their coin."

Jeld frowned. "Do you think they would ever do worse? Kidnappings or anything like that? I mean, I just know Krayo doesn't like other organizations causing trouble and all..."

"Right. Hmm. Well, people can ransom or crimp folks for a good haul, but *Sayers?* Naw, they're just bums, drunks, tarheads. I once saw one of those loons so drunk he could barely stand, but still goin' on about *uncleanness* and all that."

Jeld sighed.

"But hey, kid, that don't mean you shouldn't come running the next time you think you see somethin' off. Keep your eyes open."

Ement slapped Jeld on the arm and walked out. Jeld stared after him before sighing and walking back down to the stage. A dozen familiar faces were hard at work, the shining red curtains closed behind them and the murmur of the gathering crowd emanating from beyond.

From the center of the stage, Jasselin pointed a finger at Jeld the moment he emerged then gestured toward a large fake ship. Jeld nodded, and as he came to the ship, Hawss, Onders, and Cass all converged on it. Hawss gave Jeld a whimsical salute and the four of them began pulling it into place.

"Late night with the ladies?" Hawss asked quietly. "Hard to pull away for a show when you've got your own show going on, you know?"

Jeld smiled. "Other job kept me."

"Aren't you out of news to peddle yet? How much money does one kid need, anyway?"

"The idea of two jobs just offends you, doesn't it?" Cass said.

"*Three* with that temple thing!" Hawss said.

"That's not a job. It's a charity."

Hawss stared back in bewilderment.

Easing the ship into position, they started toward two white-capped wave cutouts leaning against the wall.

"And why yes, it does offend me," Hawss said. "Life's too short to always be wanting more. I happen to be perfectly happy as things stand."

When everything was ready, Jasselin signaled to Director Sammel. The director did a cursory inspection then with a broad grin waved the all-ready. Jeld dropped through a trapdoor and ran to the orchestra pit. Behind his lute, Master Edlin gave Jeld a nod and signaled his little ensemble, the music easing seamlessly into the opening theme.

Returning backstage, Jeld darted into a narrow passage beside the curtain and climbed a ramp to a small window. Before the window, a glowing lamp was mounted against a mirrored brass plate, a focused beam of light shining from it onto the floor. Cass's spotlight across the way was already circling through the audience stands below. Jeld turned the plate, walking his beam across to the other spotlight until it jolted aside with a flash. Just as Jeld grinned, Cass's light caught him square in the face and he smiled broader still.

The curtain parted and the show began, and in what seemed both an instant and an eternity the fatigue-giddied crew was melting into the mismatched seating of the den.

"Arrr, he took me cat, too!" Alal shouted in a pirate's brogue, shooting a look to Jeld.

Everyone howled with laughter, except Erol who nonetheless grinned.

Jeld blushed. "The director said improvise!"

"Guess you're all warmed up for improv practice tomorrow," Hawss said.

"Wish I could. Tomorrow's Thrallsday."

"Ahh, right. The temple thing again," Hawss muttered to Master Edlin, who didn't so much as look up from his lute. "I tell ya, no matter how many times I try to tell the kid, he works through the best in life."

Director Sammel appeared in the doorway, the room quieting as he sat in his usual armchair.

"What's got you all so quiet, *cat got yer tongues?*" he said with a thick pirate accent.

The den erupted again with laughter and the banter continued.

***

Jeld growled and rolled onto his back to stare up at the low-ender ceiling sloping just above. What must Lira be enduring while he lay with cheeks aching from smiles and laughter, he wondered. How he yearned for yet another outing with Raf. His thoughts turned once again to the Sayers and the tendrils of smoke seeping from their menacing sylum. Perhaps Ement was right though. Perhaps they were just derelicts at best and thieves at worst. But then, what if Ement was wrong?

Lira's face seemed to take shape in the bumps and lines of the boards above. He cursed and sat up. Even if sleep did come, it was certain to be haunting. Fastening a final bootstrap, he ran a hand through his shaggy hair and walked from his room.

Drifting about the slumbering theater, each shadow was Lira's face alone in the darkness. He heard a faint voice as he roamed the prop room and followed it up the steps to backstage, coming to a stop at the director's open doorway. Inside, Director Sammel sat in a plush chair beside his desk, a steaming mug in one hand, his other turning the page of a book upon the chair's arm.

Jeld knocked gently on the doorframe and Director Sammel looked up with a smile.

"Jeld, my boy. Good show today."

"Thank you, sir. You as well."

"Oh these shows run themselves, more or less. Or rather, you all run them." He gestured to his desk chair. "Have a seat, won't you? How are things?"

"Good," Jeld said quickly and sat.

"Settling in alright?"

"Better than alright. I feel... like I have a home."

Director Sammel beamed. "I'm so glad you feel that way. I feel the same. It's a special bunch."

"I owe you another thanks."

"No, no. Just... give someone else the same chance some day. Besides, you've proven incredibly helpful."

"Your boss would consider it an investment."

"Ahh, Krayo. Perhaps. He would like to think so, anyway. Works very hard to convince himself as much. But don't be surprised if you find one day that Krayo has a good heart."

"I'll keep an eye out for it."

"If anyone can spot it, you can. You're very talented, you know. It's quite uncanny, actually. An attunement with the very heart..."

"Ah... thank you, sir."

The director cleared his throat. "So, anything in particular bring you by today?"

"Actually, I was wondering if there was anything else I might do for you around here."

"I see. Did Krayo's work ease up? Or is it more money that you need?"

"No, nothing like that. I just thought I could... help out more. Learn more."

Director Sammel sat back in his chair and bit his lip thoughtfully.

"You know, Jeld, some people drink away pain. Others *work* it away. I... don't think they end so differently."

Jeld's gaze fell to the floor.

"I want you to be at peace here, but I get the sense you are not at peace with yourself."

"I'm... I'm okay. Really."

"You know you can talk to me, right? About anything that's bothering you. Anything at all. People here, your past—"

"I know!" Jeld snapped, then pinched his eyes closed. "I'm sorry. I know I can talk to you, but I'm okay. I appreciate your concern, really I do."

Director Sammel slowly nodded. "Well, I've got a number of abandoned stories. You know, sometimes the words just stop flowing. Maybe you could make something of them. Share some ideas, or give things a go yourself."

Jeld smiled and nodded.

"Alright then," the director said. "But how about *first* we go through *Times Two* once again? You read Brandon, and I'll read Brandel."

"I've got the spoiled brat again? I do like playing him... but we've been at it for weeks now and haven't made any changes in two reads."

Director Sammel looked down at his desk and Jeld felt a strange melancholy fill the air between them.

"We'll make this the last. What say you?"

Jeld strained to read the director, but all traces of the melancholy had vanished, the veteran actor always proving a difficult study. Raising his chin, Jeld threw his shoulders back, adjusted parts of himself he couldn't begin to name, and spoke in the pretentious Toppertongue of a young noble.

"Well?" Jeld said. "Go on then, street rat. Get on with it."

And so they did.

CHAPTER SEVENTEEN

J eld blinked the script into focus only for a deep yawn to squeeze his eyes closed and leave the words blurry again. The soft sounds of the crew working upon the stage behind him sang like a family's embrace. Just then, a loud crash jolted him awake.

"Sitting on your ass sure does take it out of a guy, doesn't it?" came a voice.

Jeld turned in his chair to see a grinning Hawss standing over a pile of wooden backdrops just outside the shop.

"Intellectual work tires the intellectual, ape work tires the ape," Jeld mused.

Hawss sat on Jeld's desk. "Another long night?"

Jeld's jaw clenched. Despite long hours staking out the Sayers' sylum, all he'd managed so far was to prove Ement right about them.

"Unfortunately."

Hawss shook his head. "I just don't see how that's worth it."

Jeld suppressed a yawn and the effort made his eyes well up.

"And you can't *really* be peddling news all night," Hawss added. "Been hittin' Love Alley I bet ya have? Watch out for them lovelies, they'll tear your—"

Another loud crash sounded from behind. They turned to see Cass already walking away.

Hawss sighed and slid off the desk. "I guess I'd best get back to it. Keep up the good work, my little Vincet."

He started after Cass at a leisurely stroll. "Hey Cass! Cass! Jeld called you an ape! Can you believe it?"

Jeld grinned and turned back to the fuzzy words upon the script, but the smile quickly fell away as his thoughts returned to Lira and his fruitless search.

***

Though the sun had fallen behind the western wall, the clear sky was bright still over Trumbley Market. The shouts of peddlers filled the square. A man in a tattered black robe came to a stop at a fruit stand, and a perfectly ordinary young courier behind him turned to a nearby grain stand.

"One brick per quarter-bushel, one and seven per half!" called a lanky grain peddler.

His eyes fell on Jeld and he smiled.

"Say, kid, any news I can use?"

Jeld tipped his hat to the man. "Not much new. Adolson is doing a quarter bushel for one and five, so you should be fine upping a bit."

Jeld's eyes flicked to the Sayer. It had taken weeks to spot one of the attempted abductors again, and he wasn't about to lose him.

"One and five?" the man said. "I'm already high at one!"

"Bad crop ain't gettin' any better, they're saying."

"No, it ain't. I don't mind selling a bag of wheat for a month's wages, but how long 'til people quit paying and start killing?"

Jeld shrugged. "You know, when I help at the fruit stands I get fruit. When I help at the meat stand I get a chew. The nice thing about a wheat stand is ya got nothing to give but wheat and coin, and you aren't so cruel as to tip a poor gossip some tough seed."

The man pulled a peb from his pocket. "What else have you got?"

Jeld glanced again to the Sayer to find him turning away with an apple in hand. "Gotta be off, actually. Hey, forget the coin and make it double next time I give you something juicy, eh?"

The merchant shrugged and returned a peb to his pocket. "Thanks, kid."

Jeld tipped his hat and hurried after the Sayer.

"Get your wheat! One and four per quarter, two and five per half!" the peddler's pitch called after him.

The sounds of the market faded into the distance as Jeld pursued. After several uneventful blocks, the Sayer made a turn away from the sylum, sending Jeld's heart racing. By the time he turned the corner in pursuit, the man was already passing through the doorway of an establishment. The sign bore the likeness of a knight kneading a pile of what Jeld took to be dough, judging by the wonderful smell of fresh pastries seducing his nose.

He followed him inside and the aroma struck him in full mouth-watering force. A line of patrons snaked through countless packed tables to a counter lined with all sorts of delicacies. Behind the counter, several people in black aprons were pulling fresh treats and bread from a huge oven and exchanging them hand over fist for coins. A jovial man in a white, flour-dusted apron was circulating through the crowded shop exchanging pleasantries and sharing samples from a basket.

Jeld joined the queue, already three people back from the Sayer. The line moved quickly though, and soon he was munching a fresh roll at a table near the Sayer.

He flinched as a hand passed just before him. Looking up, he found the man in the white apron smiling down at him, a square of sweet bread in his outstretched palm. It was an impressive smile, easily reaching his eyes where most salesmen could hardly turn up their lips. Still, it went no further. Suppressing a shiver, Jeld took the sample and nodded his thanks.

The baker reached the Sayer's table and greeted him with the fondness of a regular patron, offering a full three squares of sweet bread. The man spoke but, seeming to make out his words no better than Jeld, the baker knelt and lent him an ear. He stood a short time later, patting the Sayer on his shoulder before turning his smile on an increasingly impatient little girl at the next table.

Jeld's hope dwindled with each innocuous bite as the Sayer finished his pie. He bitterly followed him from the shop all the way back to the sylum without incident, glaring at the festering door as it shut behind another dead end.

***

Jeld looked about the dimly lit understage over the top of a manuscript, his imagination running wild as he blew another breath across his freshly laid ink. Where the prop room served best for inspiring new ideas, and the spotlight walks for writing of ships and tight city streets, the understage remained in general his favorite writing spot. It made a fine forest, dungeon, or even someplace beneath the sea looking up at the world above, and was overall a perfect spot for catching up on the writing he'd let slide far too long in favor of his extracurriculars.

A sudden screech sounded overhead and Jeld's eyes flicked up toward the constellations of trapdoors. He set the script open upon his chair then started toward the stairs. Emerging from the basement, he found Alal sliding some barrel-sized contraption of jumbled wood and steel across the stage, Yelana balanced upon her hands beyond him in some impossibly twisted position.

"What in dreams is that thing?" Jeld called as he approached.

"Oy, Jeld," Alal said, Yelana offering a warm smile from her bizarre pose. "You picked the perfect evening to join us!"

Alal pushed hard on a bar sticking out to one side of the contraption and it locked back with a satisfying metallic click. At the center of the device, Jeld noticed a string pull taut atop what resembled a crossbow.

"If I came sooner I could have advised a few easier methods of suicide, maybe saved you some trouble."

"Oh I'm afraid I'm quite incapable of killing myself. I'm *far* too quick."

Jeld closed his eyes, curled his nose, and in the midst of a monstrous sneeze, lashed out with an open-handed blow toward Alal's gut.

Alal casually slapped the blow aside and laughed. "Wow, that sneeze seemed so real!"

"Apparently acting is no match for—"

Jeld feinted high, then low with a kick, then let his first blow loose.

Alal leaned back just enough for Jeld's slap to fly by and tickle his nose. He laughed again.

"Double feint, neat."

A small hand closed around Alal's throat and his eyes went wide. Yelana stepped out from behind him with a devious smile upon her face.

"Not too quick to die after all," Jeld said and winked at Yelana.

"Rubbish! You two—of *course* I wouldn't bother covering my flank with her there!"

"Aww, only games, my love," Yelana teased.

"That's even worse. If I'm not *really* dead I have to live with my insufficiencies, of which the count now stands at one. Congratulations, I hope you feel good about yourselves."

"Poor baby," Yelana said, gliding back out across the stage.

Alal glared at Jeld.

"At least now you have a reason to use your suicide machine," Jeld said.

Alal laughed. "It's only suicide if *you* try it. Here, let me show you!"

He crouched behind the device, peering through it as he adjusted two knobs. Finally, he produced a crossbow bolt and knocked it against the taut string inside.

"There," Alal said, coming to his feet. "Now, go stand over there."

"There?" Jeld scoffed, following Alal's gesture across the stage. "Across from the sharp thing? I'm afraid you have overestimated my stupidity."

"Only kidding, of course. You're much too not-good. I'll do it." Alal crossed the stage, stopping directly across from the device. "Pull that lever at the bottom, would you?"

"Am I going back to prison?"

"Back?"

Jeld looked over to Yelana, who merely shrugged and turned back to her stretches.

"Ok... I'm pulling it."

Alal gave no acknowledgement, only scratching his ear and looking about the room.

"I'm pulling it, okay?"

"*Idols*, yes, pull it already!"

Jeld looked over at Yelana again, but she seemed unconcerned with her husband's impending death.

"Okay, here goes. Well... bye."

He pulled the lever.

All at once the contraption loosed a sharp click, the string snapped forward with a thrum, and Alal cried out and collapsed to the ground. Jeld's heart leapt in his chest. He snapped to his feet and took a single long stride toward Alal before something brought him to a stop. It was a feeling... familiar but so out of place he almost couldn't place it. *Amusement.*

He returned to the shooting machine and pulled hard on the lever until, with considerable effort, it locked back with another satisfying clink. At the sound, Alal sat upright, the bolt falling from his armpit and clattering to the stage.

"How did you know I wasn't really hurt?"

"You weren't?"

"You're a good lad," Alal said with a smile and crossed the stage. "Remind me of me, just worse."

"Thanks."

Alal patted the top of the contraption. "Pretty good shooter, eh? Onders just finished it today. Works miracles, that man."

"Onders built this?"

"And my last one, too. I think he could have fixed it, but he probably just wanted an excuse to build a new one."

Jeld looked across the stage at the bolt Alal could only have snatched from midair.

"How do you do it? How are you... *Idolic?*"

"How does one guy run faster than the next? I just do it. *Idolic* is just what they call whoever does things the best."

"It's the touch of the Idols," Yelana said, coming to her feet. "I still remember when I felt their touch... I could smell the trees and the flowers of the Lady's grove, and I glimpsed it beneath me."

"Of course you smelled trees, you were in the woods," Alal said. "You think that's how you managed, after all you went through? Naw. I'm fast because I train. You can do what you do because you worked so hard at it."

Yelana sat with her legs dangling over the edge of the stage and smiled out at the stands. "It was like nothing anyone could imagine. More real than real, like I was truly awake for the first time."

Jeld's thoughts turned at once to the warm, perfect inn he'd imagined his first night in the theater. He could still see the scars of a thousand tankards upon the worn table, still feel the warmth of the fire, still hear the lute's melody and the ghostly chorus of voices filling the room.

Jeld cleared his throat and sat beside her. "So, ah... you remember it pretty clearly, then?"

"Clearly as the day it happened. And I *wasn't* in the woods then—not anymore."

Alal shrugged. "Of course you remember it clearly, you were running for your life. Look, I whisper to them too, blazin' shouted when—"

Yelana's eyes went wide then fell to the orchestra pit below. Jeld felt her grief beating against him, nearly drawing tears before he managed to shear his mind from the sensation.

"*Idols*, I'm sorry, my love," Alal said, sitting to her other side.

"That's okay, it's... just something people say these days."

"I should know better."

Yelana turned to Jeld and he realized his eyebrow was raised.

"I'm sorry," Jeld said. "I just don't... maybe I should just—"

"It's nothing really," Yelana said. "Just that phrase. I am from Khapar."

"My love," Alal said. "The boy was asking how we got to be so incredible. Why not tell it in full?"

"I mean, there's not much to tell..."

"If you don't want to talk about it, fine, but if you are going to tell it then tell it right or I'll tell it myself. Do your tale justice."

"Really, I was just—"

"She was only five when—"

Yelana sighed. "Alright, alright. Fine. Well, yes, I was five. There were hundreds of children like me... after the fire. Warm beds, warm meals, warm families one day, then the cold streets with nothing the next. Woefully unprepared, to say the least. Many of us wouldn't have lasted but a week or two had the Citadel not found us.

"Master Sinwo's plan for us was no different than he'd done with others before, really. *Push the limits of humanity*... only, he had an uncommonly ripe selection with us orphans. Young and tempered by tragedy. The perfect crop."

Again her anguish seemed almost to shimmer in the air before her.

"I was in the *sort* for acrobatics, dancing, martial arts, and some shadier skills like most of us got. It was a versatile sort. People paid good money for burglars, performers, and the like. After the rebuild, he made a new program just for the best. *Advanced*, it was called. He handed over the normal programs to other masters and focused all his attention on Advanced. It was all I wanted.

"I was in my final year. My final month, actually. If I didn't improve, I wouldn't make Advanced and I'd be placed. I pushed myself so hard, but... the month passed and I didn't make it. I was to be placed with a patron. A performer for the baron of Gildahen. I don't know what else I expected. It was a fairly typical placement for my sort. A good one, really. But it terrified me. I didn't want to be sent away, to be sold like property. Master Sinwo made other offers, but again I just couldn't. I asked to go unplaced."

Yelana shook her head, Alal placing a hand on her shoulder.

"Master Sinwo accepted, so long as I would pay my debt to the Citadel. I agreed, and left. I was only three days out of the city when my caravan was attacked. They chased me on horseback, so I fled into the boulder fields beneath the Broken Mountain. I knew they were funneling me to the Scar, but I couldn't stop it. By the time I reached the great gorge, I knew what I must do. I didn't stop to think, just leapt. I felt like a soaring bird. The Lady lifted me across that gorge, I know she did. When I landed I just kept running."

Alal wiped a tear from his cheek. "See, that's why she had to tell it. I couldn't do it justice."

Yelana smiled meekly at Jeld. "Sorry for the long-winded version."

"Please, that was beautiful," Jeld said.

"Nothing like fighting for your life to push the limits, eh?" Alal said. "When I was in the tourney—"

Yelana shook her head.

"What?" Alal said. "Okay, fine, not exactly life or death. Anyway, final round of the Avandrian fencing championship. In the great arena of Warrinton, of course. Thousands in the stands holding their breath. It was three points to four, Inado leading. Champion three years running, the bastard was. He lunged. I just remember being so focused, like time itself slowed down..."

He trailed off, eyes distant and proud.

"What happened next?" Jeld asked.

Alal's shoulders slumped. "Er... well, I dodged his lunge quick as a cat, and then three more, like Inado was but a crawling babe. I can only imagine the look on his face, what with the masks and all. And then came the official's call. *'Out!'* Heh, would you believe it, I'd stepped out of the ring. Moment of clarity or no, point and match—*Inado*."

"That's... not a very well-written story."

"Hah! Not exactly the stuff legends are made of, is it?"

"Did you feel it too? The... touch of the Idols? Did you see something?"

"Naw, that's just something people say when they can't explain things," Alal said, his eyes flicking to Yelana.

"You did too, *dear,*" she said.

"A great hall, isn't it?" Jeld blurted. "Tovados's hall. Is that what you saw?"

"I mean, sure maybe I had the Warrior on the mind while I dueled, but what fighter doesn't?"

"You just don't like the idea that you can't take full credit for your own skill," Yelana chided.

"The Lady's grove. Tovados's hall," Jeld began. "Is that how it works? Is that what happens when you... become Idolic? You see the halls?"

Alal shrugged. "Like I said, it's just something people say to try to explain things."

Jeld opened his mind until Alal's uncertainty, his obstinance, his skepticism, his pride, all seemed as if to shine in the air before him. It all made sense now, this... tangible empathy of his, this sense he'd come to trust no less than seeing or smelling or hearing. He thought back through the countless times he'd flexed this unseen muscle, purposefully or not, chasing them back and back until at last he sat again before a burning lamp at the tankard-worn table of what could only be the Traveler's inn.

Jeld's eyes went wide.

"Are you alright?" Yelana asked.

"Oh—ah, fine. Just... remembered I forgot to finish something for Director Sammel. So... you fought again though, right, Alal? Got your championship the next time?"

"I suppose I could have, but the loss put me off the sport. I was never all that into it anyway. Or good at it, for that matter."

Idolic, Jeld marveled, Alal's voice fading into the background. But how? And why him? And what did it mean?

Alal sighed. "Well, there you have it. Now, are you ready to catch an arrow?"

"I don't think that's... quite my specialty."

"You never know 'til you try. Danger makes us stronger, brings out our best. Few arrows and you'll be quick as me. Or dead, I suppose."

"Please, dear," Yelana said. "Jeld's talents lie within head and heart."

She turned to Jeld, her eyes full of wonder. "When I watch you take on a role, I could swear I was looking upon someone else."

"I've... really only done a few small parts."

"I see it even in our exercises and as you work your scripts. Regardless, you don't become a great actor just by being on the stage. It's no different than Alal becoming a great swordsman without being a fighter. I believe we all have a talent—an angle—and if we're lucky, we figure out how to play to it in life. Acting sells it short I think, but lacking better words, I'd say acting is your angle."

An idea hit Jeld quick as a crossbow bolt.

"Forget something else for the director?" Alal asked.

"Hmm? Oh. No, just... you really got me thinking I should try taking my acting to the next level."

"Look what you've done, my love. Now the boy's going to take all of our parts."

Jeld smiled. Alal needn't worry about the competition. There was but one role at which he'd be directing his newfound talents, and that was across town at an old, sickly sylum full of black robes and, with any luck, answers about Lira. It was time to join the Sayers.

Chapter Eighteen

———◦◦———

J eld stared at the blackened doors of the sylum. Too many nights he'd spent watching these foul doors and following their many visitors about the city—all for naught. Even as he grew excited for the answers just beyond, a cold chill ran down his spine and he let his character envelop him until his own self and fears grew distant. Just a cobbler's boy, looking for more in life than soles and stitches.

He silenced his nerves with a deep breath and knocked. A dozen blinks stretched on like an eternity before a man in a tattered black robe appeared in the doorway, barely distinguishable from the darkness behind him. He was clean shaven with warm eyes and seemed of perhaps middle years.

"Hello," the man said. "You needn't knock, you know. The doors do not belong to us any more than do our own bodies. The sylum is open to all."

The Sayer pulled the door wide and stepped aside. Jeld walked into the darkness and the door shut behind him. Countless small glowing braziers were scattered about the chamber within, their faint light hinting at shadowy archways and columns strewn all about. Hushed voices carried throughout the chamber. Jeld could just discern a path running deeper into the shadows.

"Right this way," the man said, walking past him.

Jeld followed him past three robed figures sitting in quiet conversation around a brazier, then past another with a lone woman in plain clothes who looked to be sleeping. Coming to an unoccupied fire, Jeld's guide sat upon the ground beside it.

"What brings you here today?" the man asked, staring down into the fire.

"I... hear your message," Jeld answered, sitting across the fire. "Our bleeding civilization. Our loss of humanity. Our sins that have driven away the Idols. I... want to help."

The man only stared motionless into the flames, his brow furrowed thoughtfully.

"I want to restore the light," Jeld added. "To welcome the Idols back to a world worthy of their presence. There must be an end to this greed and gluttony, sir—"

"Please," the man interrupted. "There are no gentlemen here, just as there are no names. Otherwise, you may call me whatever you wish."

"What would you—how should I...."

"*Adept at the door? One who answered? The man who talks too much?* Whatever you see fit. Most just call me *Adept.* What you call me is for you to decide."

"Why is that so?"

"Names give us pride. Ego. Arrogance. *Identity*. Without names we are equal. Without names we are deeds, and if we are called by our deeds we cannot hide from our sins."

"If we are called by our deeds, could that not invite vanity?"

The adept smiled. "A king might hold his post by winning the hearts of the people or by breaking them. In either case he is a king. What will the people call him, though? The king who bled us? Or the king who bled *for* us? And if a king does great deeds, but for vanity alone, let him be so named."

"That makes sense."

The adept again gave no acknowledgement.

"I... am greedy, Adept. I give nothing back. I want to give. I want to... warm this cold world."

Still the man did not stir.

"How can I help?" Jeld pressed.

"You've already begun. You are wise, *Initiate Who Knocks*. Do as you do. Come as you have. Sit with others, let the light hypnotize your body and set free your mind. Some people you will teach, others will teach you, but from all you will learn. Your deeds today are of the path."

The flames danced their dance.

"I was taken in once by the Temple of One," Jeld said. "Is it similar here?"

"We and they are not so different, and yet... we are *so* different. They believe in The One, whereas we believe in the *many*—that the light binding us all is not some entity, but the very goodness within us. The Idols being missing is, to the Temple, everything. To us it is but a symptom, a manifestation of the problem—sin. Darkness. While we do mean to see them returned, in their return we are not saved *by* them, but have saved ourselves."

"But you both aid the poor?"

"Yes, we have that in common. Should anyone decide to serve humanity, to cast light rather than merely absorb it, we will see them served in kind."

"And if they want only to take?"

"Being poor does not excuse anyone from morality. Just as we do not personify the light within as *The One*, so too do we blame only ourselves for our evils. The Temple's *Discord* does not exist any more than does darkness. There is only light, and light extinguished. But, it has rarely been an issue. The need to serve is in us all. Though none are perfect, those here have much light within." The adept stood. "I trust you'll learn much at other fires. I'll be about should you need anything. You are wise, *Initiate*, I'm pleased you have seen fit to serve."

"Thank you, Adept."

The adept nodded and walked off.

Jeld smiled. Even in the deepest shadows he'd never felt more invisible than he did now, hidden in plain sight behind the mask of his character. Mimicking the adept, he stared into the fire as if entranced. At first it was only an act, but the fire soon set his mind adrift. At least that part of this cult was real, he considered, having in his lifetime lost himself in campfires more days than not. Although, was it really so crazy to rebuke those who foul the city? Those who take and do not give, exploit and do not aid?

He stood and walked slowly about from fire to fire, passing beneath heavy archways and through intimate, shadowy chambers. A robed boy not much younger than Jeld pulled a bed roll from a pack and started laying it out beside an otherwise vacant fire. Two old men sat sharing stories beside another. A pervasive, somber contentedness befitting firelit night wrapped Jeld in its embrace as he wandered on.

Something gave Jeld pause. It was a familiar presence amidst the peaceful chorus. His eyes fixed on a lone hooded figure seated before the fire. He reached out his Idolic sense and sampled the aura, but he couldn't place it. Circling the fire, Jeld found Raf staring gravely into the flames.

Jeld froze. What would his partner in crime be doing in the Sayers were there not something at play here? Yet, what hand could Raf possibly have in any such abductions—and if she was involved, was he complicit?

He shook his head clear. *Lira*. Finding Lira was all that mattered, and at last he felt like he was on the right track.

Jeld sat across from her. "Hello. Spare an initiate some wisdom?"

"Hello, Initi— " Raf looked up from the fire. "Jeld?"

"Surprise."

She looked back to the flames. "What are you doing here? I mean, nice to see you and all, too."

"Maybe I needed a free meal. But why is my vandal friend in the order of righteous nagging?"

Raf laughed nervously. "There's all sorts here."

"I saw two men abduct some girl, and followed them here. They were Sayers, Raf. What's going on?"

Raf lowered her voice. "Jeld, I... I can't—"

"Rekindle the light between us," Jeld mused. "By abducting young girls?"

"No!" Raf hissed. "They let her go, did they not?"

"Let her... I... I suppose so? But why?"

Raf cursed and looked over her shoulder. "Toppers, Jeld. They need to know their evils are not without consequence."

Jeld's mind raced back to the distraught parents of the fleeing girl. They were indeed finely dressed. He thought then of Lira and the ordinary street clothes he'd dressed her in.

"So, they wouldn't just properly take some street girl, then?"

"Idols, no! Jeld, I'm the same person. The same friend. Everything I said about decency, I meant. We're just... not the only ones that feel this way."

Jeld fought back a frown as his only lead for finding Lira went cold.

"But Jeld, you have to promise not to tell a soul, even here. Very few here know what measures we're taking. Most Sayers wouldn't be able to see past the... well, they wouldn't understand. It's necessary."

"The things we did, those were... because of this?"

Raf nodded. "Some were particular missions, like the lord governor's mansion. Others just... well, I suppose when you truly believe in what we're doing, nobody really needs to tell you what to do."

Jeld lost himself in the flames, memories soon dancing within. Hands ripped Lira from his grip, the flash of what could only be a knight's armor catching the light as her attackers fled. Frothing watch-hounds snarled with the flicker of the fire. A tack hammer slipped from Niya's grip as she toppled behind a felled watchman. A cage wagon slammed closed around him.

"How can I join?"

"It's not so simple. The exarch would never let an initiate in. You'd need to learn our ways. To prove yourself."

Jeld frowned. Learning from a band of lunatics was hardly how he cared to spend his time, yet if it came with more opportunities to stick it to the crown, was it such a bad price to pay?

"Alright. Yeah, gotta start somewhere."

"In the meantime, we can keep doing our thing," Raf said. "Off the books still, so to speak. In fact, how's tonight?"

Jeld nodded gravely, his eyes fixed on the dancing flames.

CHAPTER NINETEEN

———◦○◦———

J eld stood just offstage behind a forest backdrop, his tired eyes chasing a spotlight about the stage. Owan walked at the light's center, what little of his armor remained uncovered by mud gleaming brightly. Jeld's eyes lagged further still behind the light. The show grew distant as his mind turned inward to broken glass crashing against the pristine Hilltop cobblestones, then to a haughty cry as a man in evening finery toppled into a puddle.

"Where did I put that blazing map!" Owan shouted in the rich voice of Sir Gilean.

A grin vanished from Jeld's face. The weight of the audience's presence set his pulse thumping in his ear. He took a deep breath and looked over to Director Sammel at the stage wing opposite. Seemingly spotting Jeld's nerves, the director raised his hand and ran it slowly down over his face. *Put your mask on.* Jeld nodded and let out a held breath. *He wasn't going on stage, Squire Percy was.* Percill Carolend. Jeld let the character envelop him and felt his nerves calm.

The floundering, uncertain squire nodded his own altogether different sort of nervous nod to the director, who smiled and tugged his ear. Jeld nodded again and listened for his final cue as the director walked promptly away in a show of confidence that was not lost on Jeld.

"The map, Percy, the *blazing* map!" Sir Gilean shouted.

"Here, sir! Coming, sir!" Jeld called and ran out onto the stage.

Emerging before hundreds of eyes, safely hidden behind the veil of Squire Percy, Jeld started digging through his pockets.

"I swear I've got it right here. Somewhere..."

"No time to waste, Percy, hand it over!" Owan ordered in the prim voice of Sir Gilean.

It wasn't long before there were no masks, no stage, no audience—only Squire Percy and Sir Gilean, and the trees watching over them from either side of the king's road. In the end, Jeld found himself alone upon the stage that was just a stage, before the audience that was just an audience, naked to the world save for the thinnest of veils that he never left home without, and he took a deep bow.

Changing his clothes within his little low-ender room, the boisterous sounds of his friends out in the den soon beckoned him. The euphoria of a show well done melted away as his thoughts turned to the duty note from Krayo within his bag. He sighed. Theater. Sayers. Krayo. His search for Lira had dead-ended at least, but he could hardly take solace in that. He sighed again.

Jeld unfolded the note. It had only one brief line written upon it.

Mendel Emry—see Ement.

***

Jeld's hand closed on a slick rail gleaming in the moonlight and he pulled himself up onto a balcony. Like the others in the area, the house was tall and narrow, had the luxury of alleys to either side separating it from neighbors, and its lower level was not occupied by a business as was the case with many houses down the hill. He produced a long, thin hook from his pocket and fed it between the window panes. It was a perfect fit, having been crafted for this very window earlier that day by a carpenter's apprentice bearing a remarkable resemblance to Jeld.

He silently lifted the latch and pulled the window open on freshly oiled hinges. Slipping inside, he carefully planted the soft soles of his favorite boots upon the floor of Mendel Emry's formal dining room. Pausing there and craning an ear toward the door, Jeld soon heard a snort and what sounded like the purring of some obese cat. He smiled. Snoring, while bane to spouse, was boon to burglar.

Jeld stalked delicately across the room to a staircase. Starting downward, he skipped the third and seventh steps, which the same young carpenter had noted as squealers. He froze as the next loosed an unexpected creak, pausing for yet another comforting snore before leaping to the bottom.

Jeld slid like a shadow down a hallway, paintings to either side lit only in grays by what miniscule Tovarian glow reached from the windows in the sitting room just beyond. His eyes locked onto a doorway at the far side of the next room and a bead of sweat trickled down his forehead.

Suddenly something gave him pause. He listened but heard only the comforting snort and purr of Mendel's snoring, then breathed in deeply but smelled only the stifling, rich incense of cinnamon that pervaded the house alongside just a hint of stale ale. Certain he was missing something, he reached out with his other, nameless sense, and there it was. It flowed like a stream, each ripple a mood, an emotion, a thought. It was concentrated just ahead. Someone in the next room then, but who?

He closed his eyes and the stream came into sharper clarity. There seemed something off about the sensation, a disjointedness discernible only as one might distinguish two languages despite not speaking either. It was as if it were coming from... *two* minds!

Hired swords, Jeld surmised. Why else would two people be staking out the entry in the middle of the night—and *this* night no less, the night Mendel presumed his people would be emptying Krayo's grain stores by cover of darkness. Perhaps Mendel had thrown armed guards into his cocktail of vengeance and ale to further ease himself into dreams.

Sneaking into a side room, Jeld pulled his shirt open at the collar and reached deep inside his bag. His hand closed on a rope at position five and he pulled it bit by bit until a linen sack came free of his shirt. He quickly donned a sharp albeit wrinkled white jacket and gloves from the sack and combed his hair with spit. Idols willing, the darkness would cover the rest for groggy minds.

Jeld snatched up a stocky candle from a small table and wrapped it in the now empty sack. Finally, he lit his lamp with his sparker and started down the hall with the silent yet bold steps of Rinauld Kenswood, apprentice housemaster of Mendel Emry.

His eyes fixed again on the door across the room, Jeld took a deep breath and stepped confidently into the sitting room. Two men looking indeed the part of hired swords sat sleeping upon padded leather chairs. The nearer one, a heavyset bearded man, had rolled onto his side against the pillowy arm of his chair, a sword leaning against a nearby table. Across the room, a rougher-looking fellow remained upright save for his lolled head, and even asleep his hand hovered near the grip of a sword lying across his knees.

Biting his lip, Jeld crept to the closer man, reached slowly back with his makeshift flail, and swung hard. The heavy sellsword spilled onto the floor. The moment his head struck the rug with a heavy thud, the other man's grip closed on his sword and his eyes snapped open.

"Is someone going to get the blazing door?" Jeld said, the bagged candle behind his back.

He looked down as if noticing the splayed man for the first time. "Is this the best help money buys these days? Both of you sleeping is bad enough, but lying on the floor?"

The remaining guard stood, sword in hand. "Who—"

"Shhhh!" Jeld hissed. "Master Mendel hasn't slept this well in days. I dare say neither of us will make a penny or be in his employ long if he is woken. Now, will you get that door or what?"

"I didn't—"

"Of blazing course you didn't hear it, you were sleeping on the job! Woke you right up though, didn't it? Better than your friend at least. Now, get on with it. Probably the happy news our good master is expecting, but I get paid to run the house not get myself mugged, so see to it already."

"Right..." The man walked to the door, cocking an ear for several breaths before turning back to Jeld. "Ain't nobody there. If there was, they—"

A gentle knock came from the door and the sellsword froze.

"Idols, will you get on with it before that racket wakes master Mendel?"

The man walked quickly to his slumbering partner and kicked him in the rear.

"Oy!" he hissed. "Get your arse up!"

The man on the ground groaned but did not stir.

"Lazy bastard!"

He returned to the door and quietly pulled up the two iron bars securing it. Drawing his sword, he cracked the door open and toppled to the ground with a grunt as Jeld's candle-flail struck the side of his head.

By the time the door eased open and Ement peered inside, Jeld had already begun binding the first of the toppled guards with a rope he'd produced from his bag. Ement raised an eyebrow at the scene then stepped casually over the other man. The sizable Elo entered next, then Krayo, frowning at the fallen guards before looking to Jeld.

Jeld shrugged and finished binding and gagging the guards with the help of Ement's practiced hands. After, he led Krayo and company upstairs, the party wordlessly matching Jeld's every move as he again skipped over the more vocal steps. Mendel was still snoring when they reached his door.

Krayo nodded to Ement then led Jeld down the hallway. "Ement can kick things off. I'd prefer Mendel not see your face, anyway."

Ement grinned at Jeld then let the playfulness fall from his face and nodded to Elo, who smashed through the door with a broad shoulder.

Mendel's cry awoke Jeld's conscience. Of course, smashing up Topper shops and pushing Hilltop hams into the mud had exercised his conscience a good bit of late, but Jeld was fairly certain Ement didn't plan to stop at broken windows and mud stains. Jeld had done worse, of course, but it had always been out of necessity. For survival. Whatever this was, though, was more likely to be about padding a purse. His own full purse weighed heavily on him as he stared toward Mendel's door.

"You've done well, Jeld," Krayo said. "With this and more."

"Thanks," Jeld said between Mendel's screams.

"Have you considered what you want next? Your next challenge?"

Jeld forced his eyes from Mendel's doorway. "Ah... no? I suppose not."

"I might have a new opportunity for you soon. In the palace. An informant, of sorts. If you were interested, I mean. Your talents would be quite suited to it."

"Please, please!" came a stammering from Mendel's room.

"The palace," Jeld said. "Wow."

His thoughts turned to his friends at the theater and the temple, to the Sayers, to keeping his head attached.

"I... I don't know," Jeld added. "I've got a lot down here now. A lot going on."

"I understand. Think on it. Let me know if you'd like to discuss it more."

"I appreciate it. I appreciate everything. I hope you don't think—"

Krayo held up a hand. "Say no more. It's no slight. In truth, I feel bad even asking. It's a dangerous job. Now, I'd best not keep Mendel waiting any longer."

Jeld nodded and started back down the stairs to watch over the guards. A door slammed shut behind him. After, there was only silence, leaving him to wonder whether that was for the better or worse of Mendel Emry.

CHAPTER TWENTY

J eld upended a bucket at the base of a sculpted hedge. The foul scent of rancid piss worked its way up his nostrils despite his held breath, and he forced his thoughts to farberries and fresh cream lest he gag again. Despite Director Sammel's best mental exercises, the would-be farberries smelled nonetheless like old piss.

He set the bucket beside half a dozen other empties in the back of a wagon and climbed onto the driver's bench beside Raf. Like Jeld, she was dressed the part of a gardener. They exchanged a grin before Jeld took the reins and they rode off in silence.

As they passed back out through the Hilltop wall, Raf let out a breath then laughed.

"It really worked!"

Jeld smiled. "I told you, people want to believe their eyes. I bet I could walk right into the palace if I just pretended to belong."

"If only I could tell the exarch about you. Think of the jobs we could pull... we could do more than throw rocks, we could really change things!"

"At least I can throw rocks for *you*. And pour piss. Seemed like a good way to do it until I smelled the piss, anyway."

Raf sighed. "How are things progressing with the adept, anyway?"

"Too slowly. Maybe you can just talk to him, hurry things—"

"No, it's the way. You must go through your mentor, the adept. Learn the path. It cannot be helped."

Jeld thought of Krayo's offer. He hesitated before finally speaking.

"Do you suppose if I could... access the palace... would that change the adept's mind?"

Raf blinked. "The palace? I—I suppose it might. But how would you...."

Jeld shook his head. "Just crazy talk. It's nothing. Well, I suppose if ever you tire of my tagalongs, I don't need some secret Sayers sect just to throw rocks at pigs."

"There's that, I suppose."

They rode on to the sylum, where they donned their robes and went their separate ways. Jeld resumed his prescribed rounds, his second stop seeing him across from a newcomer he'd yet to counsel.

"Soon as I broke my foot and couldn't work, it was the gutters for me," the man said through a mouthful of bread. "I guess I was just money to her."

Jeld nodded along. He felt the gaze of the man across the fire, but did not look up from the flames. Such was the way of things at the sylum, and while it had once taken great restraint to stay his gaze, it now came quite naturally.

"It is not of the path to share the bond inauthentically, nor to greed so," Jeld said. "It is good that she left, for it led you here today."

Jeld's words came easily. The cryptic demeanor offered an especially tangible bit of character to latch onto, and while the cultish methods annoyed him, he actually found the teachings mostly agreeable. Of the more eccentric beliefs—that Discord wasn't real, or that the Idols would return—he couldn't well say, but fighting greed and gluttony was an easy enough sell.

The man nodded and bit off another chunk of bread. "I'm feelin' a... a *purpose* for the first time in my life. I weren't meant for workin' in that life-suckin' mine forever, ya know?"

"There is no greater purpose than to spread—"

Jeld turned toward the sound of footfalls to find the adept who'd first welcomed him approaching.

"Join me when you have a moment?" the adept whispered into his ear, a gentle hand patting one shoulder.

Jeld turned back to the man across the fire. "Than to... ah... no greater purpose than to help see the world on a path to being healed. Will you excuse me, please?"

"Course, course. Good chattin'."

"You as well. Stay the path. Those on the path are always welcome here."

Jeld stood and followed the adept across the sylum and down a dark stairwell. He had yet to explore the lower level, which as best he could tell was reserved for those at least called *neophytes*, though the ways of the sylum were far too vague to directly say as much. Below, countless pillars fought back a heavy stone ceiling just out of reach, the glow of firelight flickering down a dozen narrow passages.

He followed the adept down one of the passages, making several turns before emerging into a small chamber. The embers of a dying fire glowed atop a brazier at the center of the room. They sat and the adept began stirring the meager fire to life.

"How may I serve, Adept?" Jeld said quietly.

"You've done well on short order."

"Thank you, Adept."

"You've sat with many, learned from the most lost of souls and wisest of adepts alike. I've watched you turn many to the path, even in your short months here. You are wise beyond your years."

"I'm... pleased to serve the light between us, Adept.

"I think it's time you were the light's *voice*, Neophyte."

"Thank you, Adept. However I may best serve."

"You spread the message well. You have a way with words, I think. It will serve you well sharing our ways out on the streets."

"The words come easy when you believe," Jeld said.

His excitement melted away as he spoke the words. For how long must he spew cultish dogma before he could properly join the sect punishing the rich hams, instead of just tagging along with Raf as an outsider? There had to be a way to speed things along...

Jeld let his gaze fall to the ground.

"This displeases you somehow?" the adept asked.

"Hmm? Oh. No, I just—well, sometimes it just seems we talk, but the ones we mean to change are the ones who don't listen. And honestly they're not the worst offenders. It's the rich that sin the most, is it not?"

"Ah. I... see. Perhaps so, but we must be patient. We must all do our little parts. One little spark of light at a time."

"Yes, I know. I know, but doesn't it seem like we could be more... aggressive in our methods?"

Jeld felt the adept's eyes diverge from the fire to land upon him, a deep conflict seeming to do battle behind his gaze.

"I don't think so," the adept said firmly. "Know that what you do matters. We all do our part, Neophyte."

"Of—of course. Thank you for entrusting this part to me. I'm honored to serve."

"Good. You will find in sharing our path to redemption that you learn as much as you teach."

"When do I begin?"

"It is never too soon to do the light's work."

***

Light streamed in through the many windows lining the dome beyond the white circle of The One, casting a bright ring onto the stone benches below. As was typical of warmer, drier days, the temple was mostly empty. Two old women sat quietly talking midway up the chamber. The only other soft voices in the Temple of One were those of two young men and a young woman sitting side by side near the back.

"How's your mum?" Fendrith asked Roba.

"Today? Fine. She's doing stitchwork for the tailor again. She's best when she's sewing. Was pretty bad a couple weeks back, though. I had to take my sister again for a bit."

"Damn..."

"Oh it's fine. It's great, now. This is the best she's been in a long time. What's new with you?"

"Not much. Finished up most of the work around here. A few odd jobs for the city through the guild calls. Mostly, I've been at the new prison helping with just about everything."

"What!" Jeld blurted before lowering his voice. "You're helping build Prince's Prison? How could you help that bastard lock up half the city?"

"Yeah, yeah. What, you gonna throw rocks at me too? That place was going to get built whether I helped or not. I might as well get a coin or two out of it."

"How can you say that? How many people have to die before a coin or two isn't enough!"

"Woh, Jeld. I get it. It's not as if I like helping the guy, but I do like not starving."

Shouts of the City Watch filled Jeld's mind. The cold touch of Niya's nose seemed to chill his cheek and he rubbed it unconsciously.

Jeld shook his head. "Sorry. It's my... nothing. I thought the prison was done, anyway?"

"It's open, but there's plenty left to do."

"What's it like?" Roba asked.

"Well, you've seen the tower," Fen said. "Most of the cells are done, but I got to go to the top last week to work on a lookout deck. You wouldn't believe the view. Apparently

Prince Dralor figured if he was going to build a menacing prison tower it might as well provide a military advantage too. Smart bastard."

"Why not build it *in* the city if he wants everyone to see it?" Jeld asked.

"Space. It's not just a tower, there are to be dozens of outbuildings too. And it'll have its own little wall."

"All for more prisoners... blazin' bastard."

They fell quiet and Jeld loosed a big yawn, his eyes squeezing shut and failing to reopen.

"You look terrible," Roba said.

Jeld forced his eyes open. "Gee, thanks."

"She's right," Fen said. "You need a break, man. The theater, your... sketchy thing, your *other* sketchy thing. Something's gotta give."

"It's fine. Really, I'm fine."

"I think you need a break, buddy. You've been through... a lot. Have you even taken a moment to breathe since... since any of it? Taken time to deal with all that?"

"I'm fine!" Jeld snapped. "You sound *just* like Director Sammel. I'm not in denial! My sister is *dead*, my father is *dead*, my... Cobb is *dead*, and Lira is probably dead too. I know they are gone, I get it!"

"Jeld... there's a difference between not denying something, and actually... coming to terms with it."

"I'm okay. Really. Thank you, but I'm okay."

Fen glared at Jeld and gave him a shove. "Take. Some. Time."

"Alright, alright."

"So, you and your Sayer friend are still stickin' it to the Toppers good?" Roba asked, earning her own glare from Fen.

Footsteps sounded behind them and all three spun to see Kaid enter the temple, both his cronies in tow. On noticing Jeld and his companions, Kaid quickly looked away and walked past.

"Traveler's crack, I hate that pip," Roba murmured.

"I almost feel slighted, where's my glare?" Fen said.

"Anyway. Sayers, Jeld. Sayers."

"Nothing new," Jeld said. "I'll get in with this *exarch* fella before long, I think. Start to finally do some good, maybe. Until then, keep doing my thing."

Fen shook his head. "Something's not right about it."

"Oh sure, defend them. Already building their prisons, might as well."

"I like it," Roba said, earning another irritated look from Fen.

"It's not just what you're doing, but who you're doing it with," Fen said.

"You know I could care less about them," Jeld answered. "Hey you know what else? These Sayer robes are better than being invisible. I can go anywhere. Really handy for staking places out for Krayo."

"You're going to get yourself killed," Fen said.

"If they murder me, consider it proof that abduction isn't beyond them."

Prishner Walson emerged from a side room with a broom and set to sweeping.

Jeld frowned. "Guess we'd best lend a hand."

They spent the next three bells cleaning and otherwise helping out in their own unique ways. There was much still to do when Jeld gave a mended pair of shoes a final inspection then crossed the room to where Fen and Roba sat sewing beside a bench.

"I'd best be off," Jeld said, nonetheless sitting on the floor beside them and stretching out his legs.

"You look pretty content to stay," Fen said.

"Are you going to the sylum?" Roba whispered.

"Naw, not today," Jeld said. "I'm... supposed to drop off a payment in some guy's house."

"That's not strange at all," Fen mumbled.

"It's not like I'm killing the guy. I'm *paying* him."

"Delivery right to his nightstand, what service," Roba said distantly, holding up a pair of trousers and inspecting her progress.

Jeld forced himself to his feet. "Alright. Until next time. Stay clean."

"You too!"

"Stay clean, little prince," Fen said.

Jeld left and made his way west toward the dwelling of the magistrate's assistant to whom Krayo owed his ominous payment. Not far from his destination, he came to a quiet and winding road. The falling sun pierced occasionally between the silhouettes of shops lining the street, leaving the otherwise shadowy block feeling even darker.

Rounding a curve, Jeld's unnamed sense screamed out in alarm. His groggy mind came alive at once and he spun, but it was too late. A dark blur of motion filled his vision and something slammed against his chest. Hurtling backward, he glimpsed a figure in dark clothing before tucking his chin down to stave off another concussion as the stone wall behind drew invariably closer.

A Sayer, Jeld thought in the instant he waited for impact, but contact never came. Instead, something grabbed him from behind and jerked him violently backward faster still. Alley walls raced by to either side and suddenly he was facing the narrow band of sky above. His back struck the hard alley floor, a grunt escaping his lips.

Men to either side pinned his arms painfully to the ground. Jeld kicked out but they pinned his legs beneath their own. He bucked and struggled every which way to break free, but to no avail. A face appeared above him then, its nose wrinkled in disgust, mouth a bitter frown. It was no Sayer, but Kaid. At that, Jeld recognized the forms of Vincet and Depsey atop him.

"Help!" Jeld screamed as Kaid knelt before him. "Somebody hel—"

Kaid's fist slammed into his cheek.

"Scream again and you're dead, rat!" Kaid spat and swung again.

Pain exploded in Jeld's gut and his breath escaped in a wheezing grunt.

Kaid began rifling through Jeld's pockets. "Where's the crown?"

"Your Mu—" Jeld managed to say before falling into a coughing fit.

"What?" Kaid demanded eagerly. "My what!"

"The Watch," Jeld choked out, thankful his cough had interrupted him. "The Watch took it!"

A fist came down across his jaw, spinning his chin into the cobblestones and setting off a flash of light behind his eyes.

"Lie all you want," Kaid said breathlessly. "I'm walking away with either a gold crown in my pocket or a heap of guts behind me."

Jeld grunted as a fist struck his temple. "Okay, okay! It's in a bank. There's a bank behind Temple Theater. Take me there and it's yours."

Kaid shook his head. "You know, you cost me a lot of money ruining my deal with the slavers. They were going to pay well for your wretched girlfriend!"

Jeld barely flinched as another blow struck his side, only staring up at Kaid with wide eyes.

"But that coin of yours should more than make up for it," Kaid continued, searching the tops of Jeld's boots. "Where is it!"

Jeld gritted his teeth. A low growl escaped his lips, then a roar as he fought with a newfound strength. His arms came slowly upward, lifting Depsey and Vincet, but the two thugs shifted their weight and slammed his arms back to the ground.

"Last chance, rat, or we're tearing you apart piece by piece!"

Kaid reached way back and swung a fist down at Jeld's chest, but the impact never came. Instead, Kaid spilled over onto Jeld before scrambling off to stare in horror at a gaping black hole in Jeld's chest.

The pressure eased up on Jeld's limbs as Depsey and Vincet too gawked, and Jeld seized the moment. Kicking up with both feet, he was rewarded with two breathy grunts as his ankles struck home between their legs. As they both toppled onto their sides, Jeld rolled onto his feet and charged after Kaid, who had already found his footing and was fleeing down the street.

Kaid took a sudden turn into an alley but it only narrowed the gap as Jeld took the corner even more sharply. Just a leap ahead now, Kaid glanced over his shoulder and his eyes widened. He leaned frantically into flight and the gap began slowly to widen, but Jeld roared again and put on an extra burst of speed.

Suddenly the gap was gone and Jeld lunged forward, grabbing Kaid around the waist. Kaid took the brunt of the fall, spilling forward and grinding to a halt along the rough cobblestones. Jeld climbed atop him and only as he wound up a blow did he realize he was holding his father's long knife.

"Stop! No, wait!" Kaid shrieked and held up his hands.

Jeld plunged the knife down, turning it at the last moment and slamming his fist into Kaid's nose.

"What slavers? Who were they!" Jeld demanded.

"I don't know! My guy—I told him about a pretty rich girl, and... and he set up a deal. I don't know anything else!"

Jeld pressed his blade to Kaid's neck.

"I don't know anything! I-I heard him mention some knight. A-a knight in need—that's all I know!"

The glimmer of armor Jeld had glimpsed upon Lira's attackers flashed in his mind, and with it a spark of hope.

"A knight?"

"I—that's all I heard. Please!"

Jeld pressed the knife deeper until a bead of blood seeped from Kaid's neck.

"Name! Your guy, what's his name!"

"He's dead!" Kaid screamed, his voice cracking. "You killed him!"

Jeld's hope melted away.

"Look, it's done," Kaid groveled. "It won't happen again, so what's it matter? I'll get you money! I'll disappear!"

"What's it matter? What does *selling Lira to slavers* matter?"

Suddenly Kaid was not just Kaid but rather everything that had ever pained Jeld, everyone that had taken from him. Voices from the past whispered then spoke then shouted into his ear.

Treacherous bitch, you ruined me! Slavers. Ten blinks until I let Nose and Nuts at ya! Slavers. No! Let me help him! Slavers. Slavers. Slavers.

Kaid's eyes went wide as madness stretched across Jeld's face.

"Wait! She—"

Jeld raised his knife and plunged it into Kaid's chest.

Kaid loosed a terrible cry and his eyes fell to the knife protruding from his chest.

"No," Kaid managed. "No, no."

Jeld's eyes welled with tears as Kaid's horror and hopelessness consumed him, but he tapped his anger and it all fell away beneath the flames. He twisted the blade. Kaid groaned and his head fell back to stare at the sky above, his mouth opening and closing wordlessly like a caught fish. Jeld heard his own primal scream as if from afar and he drove the blade deeper and deeper.

"Stop, City Watch!" a voice called, but Jeld heeded it not.

Footsteps and the jingle of chainmail neared. A boot slammed against Jeld's shoulder, sending him toppling onto his back. He let the knife fall from his grip, screamed up at the sky, and began to sob.

Chapter Twenty-One

J eld shivered in a corner of his cell. The meager glow from a small barred window high up one wall narrowly staved off total darkness. That he could no longer smell the once incapacitating stench of urine and excrement was somehow worse, knowing the filth entered his lungs unnoticed with each breath.

A long moan echoed into the cell and his eyes flicked to a writhing form in the shadowy cell across the hall. This neighbor had proven well cast for the dismal setting, having performed dreadful convulsive fits throughout the evening and into the night. Jeld had often encountered his sort out on the streets—tar junkies who failed to steal enough to get their next fix.

"I'm hungry, Muma," came the now familiar voice of a little girl from down the hall.

"I know, sweet girl, I know," a woman said, a gut-wrenching despair beneath her gentle voice. "Muma's hungry too. Everything's going to be okay."

Jeld's gaze fell into the shadows. Though the darkness did little to mend his broken spirits, it befit both mind and setting.

He sat awake the night through, his back pressed to the cold stone wall despite the bitter chill. Time passed slowly, with little to occupy his raw mind but the past he had before been so careful to avoid.

It seemed the night would never end when at last dawn's light pierced Jeld's captivity and kindled a slumbering hope to live another day. He had two lockpicks in his cell's lock when the sound of footsteps and jingling armor echoed down the hall.

Jeld quickly stuffed the picks back into the bottomless bag pressed still to his chest and slid to the ground against the wall of the cell. The sound grew louder and louder until a watchman, fatter and paler than most, stopped outside the cell with an ominous set of iron manacles in hand. The watchman stared appraisingly at Jeld before exchanging the manacles for a keyring at his belt and pulling the door open with a shriek. He waved Jeld forward with a single fat finger.

Jeld approached cautiously, coming to a stop just outside the cell before a surprisingly gentle prod started him down the hall. He followed the dark passageway, pausing at every turn until another poke turned him left or right, up or down. *Down, down, down,* he would silently wish at each stairwell, remembering only climbing on his albeit fuzzy journey inward, and every time the fat finger obliged.

Finally they came to a stop before a gate. Across the room beyond, light streamed seductively through a wooden door.

"Here," said the watchman from behind.

Beyond the gate, another watchman peered around the corner.

"No manacles," the smaller watchman said bluntly.

"Afraid of the boy?"

The other watchmen scowled back then unlocked the gate and turned from sight. A hand reached over Jeld's head and pushed the gate open before prodding him onward. Jeld crossed the room, optimistically veering toward the door and the light beyond. The watchman did not intervene, even pushing it open as they approached.

Jeld recoiled from the light as it rushed in and blinded him in bittersweet welcome. Another prod and Jeld staggered out the door, a hand over his eyes. He walked on in what he hoped was a generally straight path. Peering past his hand, shapes emerged amidst the blinding light. There was a gate, and another large shape beyond—a wagon. His meager hope sunk. It could only be another rolling cage, no doubt destined for the Prince's Prison.

A hand at the back of his collar hoisted him up and into the carriage until a bench against the backs of his legs bid him sit. The door slammed closed, the wagon lurched forward, and Jeld looked up to find himself staring across the carriage into the grave eyes of Krayo.

"Jeld," Krayo said, his eyes flicking down to Jeld's chest.

Blinking away surprise, Jeld followed Krayo's gaze and found his shirt covered in dark red stains.

"Krayo..."

"You had us worried."

"I'm okay. I got... there were these... they took Li—"

Jeld stopped short, his chin quivering. For Krayo to be here now could only mean he already knew. He knew how it went down—how they'd found him screaming, sobbing. Jeld's chin quivered again and he clenched his jaw to still it.

"Okay. It's okay. Who did you... who did this?"

"This guy from... this miserable guy and his thugs. They took... my friend has been missing, and I found out he... he sold her. He sold her to slavers."

"I'm... so sorry. A terrible trade. I have always intended to see it ended here." Krayo pursed his lips. "It... sounds like you made certain he will never do that to anyone again. You should be proud of that."

"It's not that. I'm not upset I killed him. I'm *glad* he's dead."

"Oh... I see."

"It's... I *lost* it. I... I just lost my mind!"

Jeld's voice cracked as he looked down at his blood-soaked shirt, at the total collapse of his judgment, his logic, his will.

"It's... it will be okay. These are exciting times. We've got much to—" Krayo sighed and shook his head. "I'm sorry. I'm terrible at... these things. Mostly."

Krayo produced a clean shirt from a burlap sack at his feet. Jeld managed a smile and changed into the new shirt.

"You know," Krayo said, "Sammel has been worried about you. Perhaps you should talk to him. Ease your concerns. He's good at that."

Jeld turned away to hide his tears and stared out a small window. Of all people, Krayo was the last he wished to see him like this.

"Is there anything I can do to help?" Krayo offered, the kindness somehow only weakening Jeld's resolve.

"I'm alright. Don't worry, I'm solid. Sure, I'll talk to—" A familiar intersection caught Jeld's eye. "Actually... would you mind if I got out here? I have friends nearby. I think I'd do well to talk to them."

Krayo stared back before knocking on the wall behind him. The carriage came to a stop.

"Are you sure?" he asked.

"Afraid I'll kill someone else?"

"No, afraid you'll get *caught* killing someone. Again, mind you."

Jeld smiled despite himself. "Really. I'm going to be okay. I hope you don't think me—"

"Not another word. These really are important times, and I need you well for them. I'll tell Sammel you'll be back at the theater tonight, then?"

The carriage door came open.

"I'll be there," Jeld said.

"Excellent."

Jeld's eyes flicked briefly to the door. "I'm... sorry. It won't happen again,"

"The only person you owe an apology is yourself."

"How about *thank you*. I do owe you that."

"You are most welcome. Well, go on."

Jeld ducked through the doorway, nodding to Elo outside.

"Jeld," Krayo called.

Jeld turned as Krayo unwrapped his father's knife from a white cloth and reached it out to him. The blade was covered still in dark, dried blood.

"Don't forget this," Krayo said.

The depth of Krayo's words not lost on him, Jeld took his knife.

"See you soon," Krayo said. "Elo."

Elo closed the door, nodded to Jeld, and drove the wagon onward. Jeld stared after it for a while before making his way down toward the Temple of One.

Arriving at the temple, he paused outside its parted doors, took a deep breath, and stepped inside. It was bright inside. Looking about, he found only unfamiliar faces sitting upon the benches. His pulse quickened, his eyes searching the same faces and empty benches again and again.

"Why hello again, Jeld," Prishner Walson's voice came.

Emerging from a side room, the prishner started toward Jeld before coming to a sudden stop. His usual smile fell away as he stared into Jeld's eyes.

"They are just inside, Jeld," the prishner said, stepping aside.

Jeld nodded, took another deep breath, and walked into the side room. Fen and Roba were standing by the fire, filling bowls from a cauldron. Roba turned with a steaming bowl.

"Jeld! Hey—" She froze. "Jeld, what is it?"

Fen turned and only stared back.

Roba set down the bowl then hurried across the room and wrapped Jeld in a tight hug. Again the kindness seemed only to bring him closer to tears, but it was a good pain.

"Come on," she said and hurried to the stairwell at the far side of the room.

Jeld and Fen followed her up to an intimate circular landing.

"What happened?" Fen asked as they all sat.

"You were right," Jeld said. "Something's wrong with me."

"What do you mean?"

"It was all so—it all just hit me. I lost it. I totally lost it!"

"Jeld," Roba said. "What happened?"

"Kaid's dead. He and his goons attacked me. He wanted Lira's coin, and he said it was slavers who took her. And *he* put them up to it!"

"Kaid... sold Lira to slavers?" Fen said with horror.

"He's dead?" Roba asked. "You killed Kaid?"

Jeld stilled his jaw with a hand. "I lost it. Everything just... *everything*. You were right."

Fen nodded and Roba put a hand on Jeld's shoulder. They sat in silence.

"It was just the three of us," Jeld began at last. "Four, in the winters. Me, my father, Cobb, and my sister—Niya. It was always just us."

Jeld wiped his tears and continued his story for the first time, his friends at his side.

CHAPTER TWENTY-TWO

"You'd best turn that hand toward something green before you reach for anything else, young man," Evelyn chided, inarguable as the tides as she turned from the oven bearing fresh bread.

Jeld let his hand pass over a platter of sweet rolls and grabbed a spoonful of steamed beans from the bowl beyond.

"Mmhmm. You might fool an audience but I'm not impressed."

"You might just be able to save the boy from whatever malnourishment befell *that* one," Jasselin said, stabbing a fork across the table toward Hawss.

Beside Jeld, Hawss's mouth fell open. Cass snickered to Jeld's other side.

"Now Jasselin, we'll have none of that at the dinner table," Evelyn said.

Jeld grinned and took another bite. His eyes wandered over the lively faces of friends, all framed in the explosion of red, white, green, black, and brown decorations filling the den. It was hard to believe Fallsday had come again, and even more surreal that he was spending it amidst family.

Owan's theatrical voice caught Jeld's ear from the far end of the table.

"So the sergeant grabbed the halberd and spat, 'Like this ya blazin' spud sprout!' And he rapped the other private across the head."

Beside Owan, Erol grunted a laugh. "Bless a good sarge."

And so the meal went, as they always had, with many sharp instruments gesturing in Hawss's direction, many tales, and many laughs. When finally the forks surrendered to the endless hordes of delicious food and the conversation slowed as heavy stomachs turned to heavy eyelids, still they sat there in the den late into the night, together.

***

"Come in."

Jeld opened the door to find Krayo behind his desk. "Good evening, sir"

"Come in. Sit. What brings you by today?"

Jeld sat in a fine yet practical leather chair across from Krayo.

"It's something you said. An opportunity in the palace. Is that still on the table?"

"Ah. I see. Change of heart?"

"Maybe," Jeld said. "I was hoping you could tell me a bit more."

"Of course. But before we get into that, there's something I want to share."

Jeld swallowed. "Alright."

"I'm doubling your wage."

"You're—uh... thank you."

"Thank *you*. Not me. You earned it, I just want to keep you."

"Well... thank you for the opportunity."

Krayo nodded and leaned back in his chair. "Now, this new opportunity. It goes without saying that if I tell you more, it stays between us, yeah?"

"Of course."

Krayo nodded again and pursed his lips before speaking. "There is a lot going on right now. This rash of crime, Prince Dralor and his city sweeping, the tension with the Isles flaring up again... the list goes on. With all this, there is growing attention on the king's coffers, which means attention on import taxes.

"Now, some people say stability— normalcy—is the best for business. Bah! No, they are the best for bad businessmen. *Change, disruption* though... that's where the real opportunities lie. But there is one key to coming out ahead in such an arena."

Krayo raised his eyebrows at Jeld.

"Information?" Jeld guessed.

"Precisely! To see the opportunity, and be the first to act on it."

Krayo leaned forward in his chair and his voice fell to a whisper. "All that's happening in the city... there is a common hub where every bit of chaos converges."

Jeld's heart leapt. "Prince Dralor!"

Krayo blinked. "Why do you say that?"

"I just... guessed. Go on."

"Well, you're not wrong. But more broadly, the *crown*. It all meets at the crown."

"Right. Of course."

"I need to be the first to act," Krayo continued. "I need to know what to act *on*. I need to know the crown. I need you to be my eyes and ears. I need you in the palace."

The palace. Sure, that was the plan, but never before did it seem so very real, nor the blade of the king's headsman so sharp. Jeld managed only barely to keep from making unintelligible noises.

"I know, it's a big job," Krayo said. "But it's worth a lot to me—and to you. What's your take now with the raise, four bricks a week? You do this and I'll make it seven."

Jeld reeled at the sum. Though he wanted for little beyond his warm bed and regular meals, he could hear the coins clanking against his old wooden bowl.

"It's risky," Krayo said. "A lesser offer wouldn't cover it."

How foolish it seemed to uproot himself from the stable new life he had at last achieved, yet chaos called to him like an old friend. More than anything, how else could he prove his worth to the elusive Sayer exarch and begin to truly bring the fight to the crown, not just pour rancid piss on their gardens?

"I understand if you'd prefer to remain in your current position," Krayo said. "The doubled wage stands even so. It's yours."

Jeld pursed his lips. "How would I... even begin?"

Krayo smiled. "Suppose a respected member of the king's council has a... *nephew* that needs some time in court to introduce him to the noble ways. Say, Sir Olind Emry?"

"Emry? As in *Mendel* Emry?"

"A cousin. Olind couldn't have cared less, but a mutual aunt quite close to him somehow caught wind of Mendel's woes and saw fit to lobby for his aid."

"Somehow. What luck."

"What luck indeed."

"Why not just have Olind be your eyes and ears himself?"

"Why indeed? I do, and he does... but I don't trust him to be entirely forthcoming. At the end of the day, he's still something of a competitor. Plus, he isn't so much... *willing* to help as he is *obligated*, and when you force someone's hand, they don't always provide the best service. Plus, while he is a fair businessman, he isn't you."

"What... ah, exactly are you looking for from me?"

"Nothing in particular. There won't be regular reporting, or any instructions really. You just live. Build relationships, build trust. I know you'll sniff out valuable tidbits; you can't help yourself."

"When would I start?"

"The sooner the better. I just need a few days' notice to get you prepped and set your insertion in motion."

Jeld shook his head. It was risky, far too much so even for such a sum, but already the clanking of coins had faded behind as Jeld's thoughts soared to the spires of the royal palace.

"Eight bricks," Jeld said, his distant eyes jumping up to meet Krayo's.

Krayo grinned. "A small price to pay for such a job, and such a skillset. Fair enough."

"So, what now?"

"I start the ball rolling, and you get with Ement tomorrow first thing."

Jeld nodded, his eyes already distant again. He took a deep breath and stood.

"Don't worry, we'll get you ready."

Jeld didn't doubt that, however what disturbed him was not worry over what lay ahead, but mourning for his life behind. Still, he offered a polite smile.

"Suppose I'd best go see to some things, then."

"Thank you for your help, Jeld. I'll be seeing you."

"Thanks, boss."

Jeld left the room. He made his way downstairs and looked out at the empty stage. His eyes fell upon Director Sammel's door and a sudden thought drew him to it.

"Ah, Jeld!" Director Sammel said from behind an upheld book. "Come in, my boy. Pretty smooth show, eh?"

He slid Jeld's usual chair across from his own.

Jeld sat. "It was. And I never grow tired of watching Alal and Yelana spar."

"Like currents in the sea."

Jeld pursed his lips. "Tell me again why you always wanted me to read the part of Brandon instead of Brandel?"

The director blinked. Frowning, Jeld took in every detail of Director Sammel's face and his very aura, turning it over in his mind like a familiar spice across the palate. The taste of guilt was unmistakable.

"Krayo told you, then," Jeld said.

The director's eyes fell closed. "I knew he offered you an assignment, but... you took it, didn't you?"

"You knew about this all along. You used a part to train me."

Director Sammel sighed. "I didn't want you to go, but what right do I have to dictate your life? I only gave you the training—the opportunity—so you could choose your own path."

Jeld's eyes fell shut at the director's confession, but the sting of betrayal diminished as the director's words sunk in. He looked up into the director's glistening eyes and nodded.

"Thank you, sir."

Director Sammel let out a breath. "You have no idea how much that means to me."

"Well, it meant a lot when you took me in instead of squashing me like the rat I was."

"I don't know exactly where you'll be going, truly. I could guess but even that I'd rather not. It's always been best that I know as little about Krayo's business as possible. When will you leave us?"

"A few days, I think. I'm not sure when I'll be back."

Director Sammel nodded and came to his feet with a groan. "Well, I suppose that means you should go enjoy this evening as much as possible."

Jeld followed the director to the door, pursing his lips when he could think of nothing more to say.

"Jeld, it's been a pleasure. You are talented beyond measure. More than an actor, you... transform. Thanks for all your help, and for your friendship."

Jeld felt his eyes well up. "You too, sir. Thank you. For everything."

"Be careful."

Jeld gave his mentor a final nod and walked out. He came to a stop just before the door to the warehouse as Director Sammel's voice called after him.

"You remember what I said that first night?"

Jeld turned. "'One who masters shadows is nobody. One who masters *acting* can be anyone at all.'"

The old director smiled. "Well, remember too... *anyone* can die, but *nobody* lives forever."

***

At the snowy edge of the River Kline, the worn stones beneath the shallows turned to bricks and swept aside a narrow branch from the river. Upward the channel seemed to rise as the hillside itself fell away, until it flowed upon a great viaduct bounding across the valley to the royal palace of Tovar, where it filled the royal stores and flushed the royal latrines. Beneath the cobbled streets of Tovar and its many public privies, the now filthy torrent ran on before reemerging above ground to sweep out the gutters of Riverside, bringing with it the stink of the entire city above.

"Idols, how do these people stand it?" Jeld said, stepping over a missing cobblestone onto a merely cracked one.

"You know it stops under Midtown until the tide is going out?" Fen marveled. "To make sure it all gets sucked out to sea."

"Midtown? Bet the Riversiders love the pileup."

"Does it all automatically too, you know," Fen said. "Can you even imagine building that..."

"I bet they like it, actually. So what if their gutters stack up, at least it means they only have to smell their *own* shit for a while."

"I think this is the place."

Jeld followed Fen's gaze just ahead to a slouching shop with a battered sign bearing a needle and a swirl of thread. Across the street, two old men sat in equally decrepit chairs smoking through still more neglected teeth. One with a long white necklace stared at Jeld and Fen as they approached the shop.

Jeld climbed the single step to the door, his foot sinking as the wood bowed under his weight.

"Careful, Fen. Rotten step. If it bent under me, you will probably fall through it."

"Big words, little man."

Jeld pushed the door open and peered inside. Several tables were covered in tools, scraps of fabric, and half-stitched garments. Nobody in sight, he knocked on the door frame and slipped inside.

"Anyone in here?" Fen called over Jeld's head.

Jeld slowed beside one of the tables, an old leather punch catching his eye. Cobb had one so similar it could have shared the same maker. Jeld rested his hand upon it.

"Can I help ya?" a voice that was not Fen's called from behind.

Jeld jerked his hand back and spun. One of the old men from across the street stood in the doorway, only now Jeld could see the long white necklace was in actuality a measuring tape the same yellow as the man's teeth.

"We're looking for a friend," Fen said. "She lives here, I think. Roba?"

"Ah-ha. Upstairs. There." He pointed to a narrow gap in the shelving along the wall. "Second door on the left."

"Right. Thanks."

"Mmhmm," the tailor hummed, walking back outside.

Jeld and Fen exchanged a shrug and walked to the passage, starting up a stairway just beyond. At the top they emerged into a dark, musty hallway lined with doors on either side. With each step down the hall the wood creaked but, much to Jeld's relief, sagged only slightly. They came to a stop before the second door on the left.

"Roba?" Fen called through the door.

A baby cried within for a long stretch before the door was pulled open and Roba popped her head out.

"Jeld? Fen? What are you guys doing here?"

"What a strange coincidence, we were just out for a stroll," Jeld replied, going to her.

"Do you always call my name when you go for strolls?"

"You are always top of mind."

"Want to go out?" Fen asked. "On the city, I mean."

"I...." Her eyes flicked back toward her apartment.

"Roba?" a woman's voice called softly from within. "Roba, who is that?"

"I can't. I've got to go. Sorry!" Roba retreated inside and shut the door.

"Roba, wait!" Jeld called. "I'm leaving town. For a while."

There was a long silence.

"I'll meet you downstairs," came Roba's voice at last. "It's nobody, Mum! Just finish your leggings."

"But they called your name. Who is that?" the other voice said, growing closer.

"Some people I know. I told them to go away."

"Friends? What do they want?"

"Nothing, Mum!"

The door creaked open and a woman appeared in the doorway. Thin and pale with hair much the same, she looked at Jeld and Fen each in turn with wild, suspicious eyes.

"What do you want?" she said.

"We just wanted Roba to join us for a walk..." Fen answered.

"Why?"

"Because she is our friend."

"Please, Mum, just let them go!" Roba's voice pleaded from within.

The woman stared silently at them for a moment before her brow fell. "Don't come back."

The door slammed shut.

Jeld exchanged a bewildered look with Fen before brushing past him and rapping on the door.

"Miss! Miss! It's about the Prince's Prison! I just want to make sure Roba knows what *they* are planning."

A long silence ensued before Roba's mother pulled the door open, her suspicious stare giving way to a desperate need.

"What is it? What do you know?"

Jeld let his eyes flick to either side. "Best not talk here. And I'll only speak to Roba."

The woman frowned before nodding.

"Roba, go with these boys. They know things about the others." She disappeared inside without another word.

Roba appeared in the doorway and looked at Jeld as if she'd never truly seen him before.

"I'll get my things," she said and closed the door.

Jeld turned to Fen, looking quite impressed with himself, but when his friend only raised an eyebrow, he shrugged and started down the hall. He stopped partway down the steps and sat.

"Poor Roba," Fen said as he sat beside Jeld.

"Hopefully that's the extent of it. There are worse things than paranoia, especially these days."

"Sure, well, not everyone has as low a standard as you."

"Sorry, I just mean... she's tough enough. Somehow she still finds the funny in things."

A creaking came from behind and they both turned. Roba closed the door behind her and leaned back against it, her eyes falling closed. After a moment, she sucked in a deep breath and started toward the stairs. Jeld and Fen turned quickly away.

"Sorry about all that," Roba said as the stairs groaned.

"Hey, don't be," Jeld said, starting down the stairs.

"Hey Roba," Fen greeted.

"What's all this about?" Roba asked. "What do you mean you're leaving? And that *Prince's Prison* business you fed my mother? You are a mysterious person."

Roba stepped over the rotten doorstep and waved to the old tailor across the street.

"You mean a *pain in the arse* person," Fen said.

Jeld sighed. "I hope it's no trouble. I just thought she seemed a bit... off, and figured she'd only let you out if she knew we were on her side."

"Ok, not a pain in the arse. You're *evil*. An evil little man."

"Well, you were right about her," Roba said. "Sad thing is, she's not entirely wrong. Crown really is out to get us, ya know?"

"Exactly," Jeld said. "See, Fen? No lies."

Beneath the afternoon sun, the party wandered south and west. They walked until only a short stone wall and a lengthy fall stood between them and the sea, and upon this wall they sat, watching the waves break against the rocks below. Behind them, a park stood like an oasis in the city, with old trees reaching their arms out over the green grass.

"And you said *yes?*" Fen said, throwing another stone up into the sky.

They all watched as the rock fell toward the rolling sea below.

"Why not?" Jeld asked. "Krayo needs it, and... well, it'll come with a hefty purse."

"Oh I don't know, because you'll lose your head when you get caught?"

"*If* he gets caught," Roba corrected.

"What! Are you condoning this?"

"No... no way, it's just that if he doesn't listen to us, I don't want him to get caught just because we said he would."

"Look, guys," Jeld said. "I appreciate it, but what else would I do? The same thing I've been doing, every day, *forever?* Honestly, it just sounds... interesting. "

"I've heard that logic before," Fen grumbled. "That's what young guys all say right before leaving their perfectly safe, perfectly ordinary lives to join an army and die for a lord that doesn't even know their name. What's in it for you, anyway?"

Fen threw a rock straight down toward the water. "Jeld, there isn't anything else, you know. Life is just living. Best we can do is make it to our next meal and hopefully have a little fun before the one after. Whatever you're looking for, it isn't there. You've got it good here!"

"I know, I... I know, but...." Jeld sighed. "It's stupid. I get it, but what if this new thing *is* my fun?"

"Nothing quite like getting your head chopped off to brighten the day," Roba said.

Jeld frowned. "I shouldn't have said anything."

"Of course you should have. How else would we get to talk you out of it?"

Jeld sighed again.

"We're just messing with you, Jelly," Roba said. "I mean, you *are* being an idiot, but we just care about you. What about your thing at the theater? You've got a great thing going there."

"It'll have to wait. They'll take me back later. You know, they could use some help around there. You are quick with a needle, and Fen—handy guy like you—Onders could put you to good use on the sets."

Fen frowned. "Might check it out, thanks. So, when do you go?"

"A few days, I think."

"Few days! And you just found out? What, are you just going to walk in and say you're the lord of Riverside?"

"'*The lord of Riverside*'," Roba mused. "I like the sound of that. Sounds like a story."

"My next performance," Jeld said with a grin. "Krayo has a plan. I'll be some noble's nephew."

"Idols, man! This is serious stuff," Fen said, then squeezed Jeld's shoulder. "You need to be careful. Never let your guard down."

"You know me. I won't."

Suddenly Jeld's eyes widened and he tried to roll his shoulder from Fen's grasp, but it was too late. Fen's hand clamped down and tugged him into a headlock. Jeld pulled his legs up beneath him until his heels rested atop the wall then pushed off, sending the both of them toppling backwards. Fen grunted as he landed on his back with a hollow thud, then again as Jeld landed upon his chest.

Jeld loosed but a single laugh before suddenly finding himself slammed to the ground beside his friend. Laying side by side in the grass, they wheezed in breathless laughter. On the wall above, a broad grin stretched across Roba's face.

When Jeld's lungs were restored at least mostly to working order, he rolled to his feet and turned sharply away from his friends. Reaching into his collar, he turned back after but a blink with a head-sized leather ball in hand.

"How'd you do that!" Roba demanded.

"Sleight of hand!"

Jeld kicked the ball toward a huge tree deeper in the park then raised an eyebrow at Roba and raced after it. Roba slid off the wall and gave chase. Fen came slowly to his feet, sighed, then chuckled to himself and ran after them.

They played into the evening beneath the sprawling tree before climbing it to watch the sun fall. Jeld grew quiet as the sun set on safe slumbers, on the easy breaths of days spent working the streets, and on laughter and warm silences shared with good friends.

In these final days, I find myself pondering the meaning of it all. I can conclude only that our purpose is our pleasure. That ultimately, we will never make a single selfless decision. Why do we give? Why do we take? Pleasure, and pleasure only.

The spider preys. The thief steals. But I fear we cannot fault spider nor thief, only stomp and stone them in kind for impeding our own pleasures. This thought leaves me feeling filthy as I make my final arrangements. I acknowledge it must only be for my own pleasure that I aim to serve the greater good, but if I must spin a web to do so, am I not a spider?

—Vincet Ellemere

CHAPTER TWENTY-THREE

J eld sat upon a beautiful yet rigid couch of jet-black wood and gleaming leather the deep crimson of only the rarest, most pristine strawberry. It was an odd thing to be in someone's home and yet still feel so distant from them. As best he could tell, the room in which he waited served no purpose save to do exactly that—to wait. It was offensive on multiple levels, but to the credit of his would-be uncle, it was a most interesting room in which to wait.

He tore his gaze from a single picturesque strawberry atop a nearby arrangement of delicacies and looked about the room. It was perhaps five times the size of Director Sammel's office, with towering ceilings giving it the appearance of being far larger still. The walls were dotted with paintings large and small, the floor cluttered with furniture as if empty space implied an inability to afford filling it. A small bookshelf near the center of the room caught his eye in that, while fine, it was not excessive like everything else. He went to it and scanned the books. *Rise and Fall of the Mad King by Avela Farol, Economicon Volume One by Sir Radrid Gavins. Economicon Volume Two by Sir Radrid Gavins. Economics of Post-Idols Avandria by Sir Olind Emry.*

The name of Jeld's soon-to-be uncle gave him pause. He pulled the volume out and flipped it open, certain any man who stocks his waiting room with his own books could be easily flattered with a reference or eight. It opened to a map covered in symbols of crops, livestock, and goods of all sorts. While an impressive collection of information, the clutter reminded Jeld of the very room in which he sat.

He flipped to another page, this one blanketed entirely in text, and began to read.

While the principles of supply and demand carry forth from trade into the realm of mercantile, they are not the cornerstone of the art. Of the cornerstones of the merchant is first and foremost location. And of course this is so, as what could be more important to a business than an ample flow of customers, but be cautioned that population and customers are not one and the same. The next—

The sound of footsteps approaching tore Jeld's attention from the book. It was a slow, hoof-like clap of fine wooden soles, easily distinguishable from the prompt, subdued taps of the leather soles worn by the pleasant old chamberlain who had seen him in. Jeld found himself growing angrier with each step, certain it must be by design that a Hilltopper's shoes should clap arrogantly while his servant's fall quietly.

"Arvin," came a soft and painfully proper voice.

Jeld looked up from the book in feigned surprise. A man not far beyond middle years stood just inside the doorway. The top of his head was bald, the sides brown and bushy. He wore a flowing red tunic with cape-like sleeves and gold embroidery, tight black leggings, and pointy black shoes.

"Uncle!" Jeld said, coming to his feet. "I'm sorry, I was lost in this book. It's fascinating."

Olind's smile stretched to his eyes and beyond. "I should hope so, there is a lifetime of wisdom in those pages. I'm sure I only hurt myself giving such a weapon to competitors the world over, but, for the good of the kingd—"

Olind's eyes widened as if he realized he was speaking to a snake.

Jeld pretended not to notice. "Thank you so much for welcoming me here."

Motionless, Olind stared back before at last sucking in a breath and managing a smile.

"Of course, of course. Well, sorry to have kept you cooped up in here. How about a tour while Hamry readies us a meal?"

Jeld glanced at the mountain of delectables already laid out.

"That sounds splendid."

"Right this way, then."

Jeld followed Olind into the next room, though it was more comparable in size to a public square. The furniture, refreshingly sparse compared to the cluttered waiting room, was well organized to break the vastness of the place into several distinct spaces. Pale sandstone walls glowed bright with the light of several large chandeliers and a huge fireplace hosting a sizable forest fire. A grand staircase spiraled along the bend of another wall. The far wall was almost entirely made up of broad wooden panels.

"It opens to the gardens," Olind said. "We'll open it on warmer days. The view of the palace over the gardens is beautiful, and the outside air is always refreshing. Come, then."

As Olind led the way across the room, he pointed to a marble-topped standing desk before a narrow doorway.

"Should you ever need anything, Hamry or one of his staff can usually be found there."

"Very good," Jeld said rigidly, resisting the urge to slap himself.

They passed through a broad archway, huge open doors framing it like spread wings to either side. Inside, a massive table filled much of another room.

"The dining room, of course. Oh, that reminds me. We'll have company tonight. I thought it proper to host a dinner to welcome you to court. I doubt we'll get the best of them for such an occasion, but we'll draw our share."

"A welcome dinner? That's very kind."

"It's expected. Plus, it will be a good start for your... politicking." Olind paled and grew distant before abruptly turning.

"Hamry, we'll do the gardens!" he called as he marched from the room and toward a door beside the paneled wall.

In but a blink Hamry sped past, pulling open a wardrobe and wrapping Olind in a rich green coat. He whisked a heavy red coat from the wardrobe next and Jeld squirmed awkwardly into it. By the time Jeld looked up, the old chamberlain was already standing beside an open doorway, his head bowed slightly and eyes to the ground.

Jeld followed Olind through, nearly making it past Hamry before caving to decency and nodding his thanks. Hamry's eyes flicked up to Jeld and, after a moment's hesitation, he seemed to return the faintest suggestion of a nod.

Grinning, Jeld stepped out into the crisp, cool air onto a vast patio amidst beautiful gardens. Beyond a perimeter of sculpted hedges other mansions could be seen climbing still higher up the hill. In the distance, a dozen spires stretched into the sky.

Leading the way toward a bench at the patio's edge, Olind let out a breath as the door clicked closed behind them.

"This is madness!" Olind blurted.

"What—"

"Madness!"

Olind stopped before the bench and stared out toward the spires. Eventually his shoulders sagged and he slumped onto the bench.

"So how does one's... *career* lead to such a task as this?" Olind whined.

Jeld raised an eyebrow and sat beside him.

"Oh, *Idols*! Come now, let's not fool ourselves any more than we must."

"If you insist. Well, just... training. Observing people. Listening. Learning to... blend in."

"You're one of his actors, aren't you?"

"Well, not by trade, but—"

"Hah!" Olind whimpered. "An *amateur* actor, no less."

"It's only part of the gig. Among... *other* things I do for Krayo."

Olind tensed.

"So you two go way back?" Jeld asked.

"Yes. Fair bit of history."

"Business, then?"

"Mutually beneficial," Olind said defensively. "Though in this affair I dare say I'm getting the better of our friend. I'm foolish to accept, given the obvious risks, but from a purely financial perspective, it's a meager cost for the favorable terms I negotiated to save my foolish cousin's livelihood. Or life, for that matter."

"*Negotiation*. Is that one of your cornerstones?"

Olind nodded distantly. "Tell me, what does Krayo want of you? Not *exactly*, of course, but if I knew where you needed to get, or who you wanted to get close to, we could both be through with this madness sooner."

Jeld paused to consider the question. Krayo sought information, but from where? And from whom? And about what? *The crown*, he had said. Not much to go on, but as the good director often said—*in the absence of direction, improvise.*

"He wasn't precisely clear, but I think perhaps the prince?" Jeld lied.

"The prince!" Olind yipped. "Just the toughest man in the damned kingdom."

"Only guessing. And we wouldn't need to rush anything, but perhaps that gives you an idea where to start."

"Well, I suppose that changes little to nothing, really. Gaining favor with the prince is already the reason anyone does anything. We'll just have to work up to it. Perhaps in time I can request that you be allowed to accompany me to the council."

Jeld's eyes traced a winding topiary nearby. "That sounds like a fine start. So, what else do I... do? I mean, Arvin. Or anyone my age, really."

"Well, if we do start council that will be at least one day a week. We'll have balls about every month, the first being next Thrallsday, and this one is at the palace, no less. There's the occasional ceremony or games, sporting, studies, dinners. We'll host occasionally for one reason or another—"

"Studies, you said?"

"Yes, of course. *Idols*, you do know how to read, don't you?"

Jeld's jaw clenched before he managed to force out a haughty laugh. "How are studies conducted hereabout?"

"There's a schoolhouse you'll attend five days a week. You will cover all manner of topics."

"I see. Alright, and what else will I be doing?"

"What *else?* That's nearly something each day, often more!"

"Ah, yes, of course," Jeld said. "Quite busy. So, who will be attending the dinner tonight?"

"It should be a fair group. Lady Edenwood will be in attendance. Old money, and Edenwood itself is of course still prosperous. Wonderful lady, a true businesswoman. Lord Carsidge as well, more old money. Truth be told they're almost all old money. Anyway, Carsidge might be your best in. He was a knight in his day so he's warm with Prince Dralor. Sir Hepsbry and his devils, wife and children all. Nice fellow, but painful to watch the poor sap let his wretched flock peck him to bits. Renae Warrin, sent to court by his father to strengthen ties. Roughly your age. High station but not too connected here at court. Some of my business partners should be joining us as well.

"Anyway. Among others," he added, coming to his feet. "Much more to discuss, but we'd best see to your clothing for this evening."

Jeld stood and followed Olind back inside. Hamry stripped off their coats smooth as a pickpocket as they crossed to the grand staircase.

"We'll see to Arvin's clothing now," Olind stated as if to the mansion itself.

"Right away, sir," Hamry answered.

At the top of the stairs, Jeld followed Olind down a wide hallway with bright red carpet and walls punctuated by regal portraits that, to Jeld's relief, did not depict Olind. Stopping outside the first door, Olind waved Jeld past.

"Your room," Olind said. "I hope you'll find it to your liking."

Jeld paused just inside and looked about. A four-post bed with wispy drapes towered at the room's center, piles of crisply-folded clothes covering the mattress. Also in the room, trying futilely to fill the vast space, were a beautiful writing desk, a bookshelf that Jeld couldn't help but scan for additional copies of Olind's works, a leather sofa, and a broad wardrobe.

"It's incredible," Jeld said, holding his hands out to a crackling fireplace as he passed.

"The tailor will be up shortly to fit your clothing and see that you have something suitable for tonight. Your belongings are in the wardrobe. When you're finished with the fittings, make yourself at home. You can usually find me in my study at the end of the hall if you need anything, and you know where to find Hamry."

"Thank you so much, Uncle. For everything."

Olind grimaced slightly before returning an unconvincing smile and leaving the room, closing the door behind him.

Jeld made his way to the back of the room and peered through a doorway into the room beyond. A bath seemingly shaped from a single piece of polished stone stood at the room's center. Light streamed in from an open window beyond, beneath it a beautifully carved wooden throne padded with fine leather cushions.

Crossing to the window to orient himself, Jeld spotted a polished ring of marble upon the seat of the throne and realized he was looking not at any throne but rather a kingly toilet. He clenched his now aching jaw and looked out the window.

The excessiveness of the looming palace spires proved a poor diversion from his anger, but as he relieved himself into the fancy toilet whilst staring out at the king's palace, he found himself grinning.

***

A woman's fingers danced along the strings of her lute, a flute grieving along and a harp whispering of better days behind her song. Her eyes came open, the flames of the fireplace beyond flickering amidst her tears, and she sang.

We danced, we sang, traveled the land
Oh her smile, those eyes, toes upon the white sands
Our love young forever, two hearts afire
Afire in Khapar

Jeld sat amidst a spattering of Hilltoppers upon one of a dozen or more couches Hamry's staff had arranged around the great room fireplace. He wore black leggings and tall boots to match, with a rich blue doublet shying just short of aesthetic perfection thanks to the extra chest space he'd negotiated for easier access to his bag.

My lord's forgiveness I have I pray
For from my post I fled that day
High in the sky, black smoke afar
The fires of Khapar

"In the end he opted to wed Poleni Barettol," Mabel Hepsbry chided over the music, her shrill voice shattering the pristine melancholy. Her light blonde hair was done up in a bejeweled nest.

"Thin as a sickly child, that one, but a seductress next to Miura. Dull as a log, too. It'd be like rumping a starved simpleton!"

The others had all quieted their voices since *"Fires of Khapar"* had begun, or at least limited their conversing to between the verses, but not Mabel Hepsbry. Sir Del Hepsbry sat next to her, a diminutive fellow with a ring of dark hair surrounding his bald head. Beside him sat their four boys and a lone girl, each topped with their mother's light blonde hair as if their father's blood were as docile as he. Devin Hepsbry, the smallest of the Hepsbry horde, sunk lower into his chair as his mother droned on.

So I came before the shattered gate
Despite my haste I feared too late
The thought aside I ran inside
Into the fires of Khapar

"Just arrived, haven't you?" Lord Carsidge whispered to Jeld from the seat beside him. He was an imposing man with a thick black goatee.

"Yes, my lord," Jeld said, carefully tailoring his accent.

"How are you settling in?"

"Quite well, honestly. All things considered, of course."

"Of course. I'm quite sorry for your loss."

"Thank you. It's done, anyway. I'm... just grateful for my uncle. In the end, I can't think of a place with more opportunity to grow."

Lord Carsidge smiled. "You're strong. And right, somewhat. Opportunity, yes, but too much of it makes one grow only at the waist. And opportunity must be seized, not... *bathed in,* as many here often do. You will seize it, though. I think you will."

"Thank you, my lord," Jeld said, the man's words refreshingly grounded.

At last I came to the home we'd raised
Alas the flames I would have braved
If more than rubble had remained
Beneath the fires of Khapar

"Quite a change, it must be," Lord Carsidge said.

"As different as night and day, if I'm honest. It's a simpler life down there. Tough, but simpler, I imagine."

"You're in a different world, that's for sure. Honest work you did there before. That's what makes a man."

"I hear you were a knight. I'm sure nothing better makes a man."

Lord Carsidge nodded. "War makes a man like nothing else. Or perhaps it just leaves only the men standing... but I think the former."

Snowflakes dance amidst ash each swing
And as I dig I hear her sing
In the dust, a ring, a ring
The fires of Khapar

"Oh!" Del Hepsbry sighed from the chair beside his wife. "That song always does me in."

"Oh don't be such a whibzy," Lady Hepsbry chided as a servant chased after her goblet with a full decanter. "It's nothing to celebrate, anyway. Soldiers abandoning their posts when they are needed most? What message does that send our soldiers? Whoever he was, he should be jailed for desertion, not... not be gallivanting about bragging of it!"

"Yes yes, of course dear, of course," Del Hepsbry muttered distantly.

The servant deftly cut off his pour as the lady lifted her goblet to her lips as if it had never been empty. The musicians began a peppier tune, the whole room seeming to brighten with it.

"What say you all we make our way to the dining room?" Olind said, rising from his seat beside Lady Edenwood.

Olind offered his hand to the older lady, who took it with a polite smile before coming quickly to her feet. They walked hand in arm toward the dining hall on slow, patient steps.

"Excuse me, won't you," Lord Carsidge stated and stepped off toward the privy.

"I'm famished. Yourself?" Renae Warrin said, falling into step beside Jeld as he followed the crowd toward the dining hall.

"I as well, somehow," Jeld said. "Between you and me, I don't know how you all aren't fat around here."

Renae laughed. "I do think you'll find it rather top-heavy hereabouts. Don't let the extra layers fool you though. Many have shed blood, in the Vanishing Wars or otherwise. Too proud to wipe their own arses, but many can ride and swing a sword."

"What about you? Do you wipe your own arse?"

"Why bother? It'll only be fouled again."

"And swordplay?"

"*Play?* Does a true swordsman play?"

"Shall we find a true swordsman to consult?"

Renae grinned. "Alas, I merely dabble. I'm told I do quite well, but I've not cut my teeth in battle, only little skirmishes back home."

"Skirmishes?"

"On the frontier. The north has a dozen cities protecting it, but the east has only Warrinton. My father keeps me from the worst of it, but I suppose the small chance of my being killed is worth mitigating the high chance of my otherwise becoming"—he leaned in and whispered—"a *whibzy.*"

Jeld laughed.

"What of you?" Renae asked.

"Arse or sword?"

Renae frowned in contemplation. "Sword."

"Ah. Well... none, really."

"None? Never battled? Trained?"

Jeld's mind conjured a memory of a writhing bandit beyond his upraised sword. "Never anything. Nothing. Maybe picked one up once."

"What!"

"I've always been too busy with business."

"I must say, I'm disappointed. I thought being a... *er*, from the country, that perhaps you'd give me a good run."

"Country... yes, us country folk just shovel shit and sword fight all day. And fight with our shit shovels, while we're at it."

Renae grinned as they entered the dining room.

"Arvin!" Olind called from the head of the table as he made a show of helping Lady Edenwood into her chair. "What's my dear guest of honor doing back there? Please, join me."

Perhaps the wine was easing Olind's nerves, Jeld considered, but it seemed his dear uncle was better at this than he'd thought. Jeld stared deeper into him, first at his faint sheen of sweat, then at a smile that found his eyes but did not quite convince them, then deeper still to a thing no eyes could behold. It was faint, and more a feeling or a color than a word—the color of bitterness.

"Most of the guys do fencing every other day," Renae said as Jeld began to turn away. "Tomorrow, third bell. The sporting hall at the royal armory. I'll show you the ropes."

"Right, ah... right. Thanks, Renae," Jeld said with a heavy swallow. "Best be off."

Returning a nod as Renae took his seat, Jeld turned and went to Olind's side at the head of the table. Looking out over the room, he found everyone seated, silent, and staring singularly at him.

"Thank you, my friends," Olind began. "My lords. My ladies. Thank you for sharing your company with me this evening. Let me interrupt for only a moment, please, to welcome a new young gentleman to the table. I am pleased to introduce my dear nephew, Arvin Emry. Nephew, have you a word to share?"

"Thank you, Uncle. Yes, I have."

Jeld's pulse began to drum in his ears as he looked out at so many powerful men and women.

Arvin, he reminded himself. They looked not upon him, but upon Arvin. He wrapped himself even tighter in the warm cloak of anonymity that was his character and considered the scene from Arvin's perspective. The panic of a spy beneath a magnifying lens quickly became merely the nerves of a young man addressing for the first time a distinguished group of elites.

"Right. Ah, thank you all for the most gracious welcome. I am fortunate to have such wonderful people to count among friends. And to my dear uncle, thank you most of all for inviting me to Tovar when... well, thank you for everything, Uncle."

Olind raised a goblet, the others all following suit. "To my nephew, Arvin Emry. Welcome to the great city of Tovar."

"To Arvin," everyone echoed back.

Olind drank and again the others followed his lead.

"Now. Please, friends, let us bother you no longer. Enjoy."

The room broke into boisterous chatter at once. Olind nodded to Jeld then sat and resumed his conversation with Lady Edenwood.

The evening went on, food the likes of which Jeld had never before tasted coming in wave after wave. After dinner the gathering returned to the great room and mingled as the musicians graced the hall with song that both filled the silences and complemented the conversation. Servants delivered sweets and kept goblets topped off, and while Jeld ate more than his share, he was careful to nurse his drink slowly for fear his acting, or merely morning, might otherwise suffer. Despite Lady Hepsbry's nose turning further upward in his presence, Jeld found himself actually enjoying the superfluous affair and its company, particularly the young Renae Warrin.

Pleasant as he'd found the gathering, Jeld's shoulders and heart alike sagged with fatigue when finally the last of the guests had departed and his bedroom door closed behind him. He quickly heeded the beckoning of his heavenly new bed, his mind racing behind closed eyes through the fresh memories of his wild day before turning to times ahead. He thought of his first day of lessons tomorrow, and the definite trouncing he would receive in fencing, which he'd already decided on attending. Also occupying no small part of his mind was the inescapable fact that he was now a spy in the court of the most powerful people in the kingdom. Even so, his concerns were soon but dreams.

CHAPTER TWENTY-FOUR

Jeld woke the next morning to the sound of someone struggling with the door.

"Master Arvin?" Hamry's voice came amidst a knocking.

Jeld jumped out of bed. "Yes, one moment please!"

He scrambled to untie a rope binding the door handles together. Loosing a final knot, he threw the rope across the room and swung the doors open even as the rope slapped against the wall and slid out of sight behind his dresser. Turning, he found Hamry standing in the doorway with a tray bearing a glass of juice and a steaming washcloth.

"Good morning, Master Arvin."

"Good morning, Hamry. Ah... sorry about that."

"Sorry? Whatever for?" Hamry asked, the slightest twinkle in his eyes. "May I, sir?"

Jeld stepped aside and Hamry marched promptly past, setting the tray upon his desk.

"Will you be joining Master Olind for breakfast after you are dressed?"

"Is that his wish?"

Hamry frowned. "I can only assume, Master Arvin. In any case, he will be dining shortly."

"Very good. I'll be down soon."

"Very good, sir."

Hamry offered a nod and left the room without another word, pulling the doors closed behind him.

Jeld made good use of the warm cloth to clean himself up, enjoyed the sweet juice while he dressed, and made his way downstairs. When he arrived in the dining hall, Olind was already stooped over a stack of letters beside a tray of half-eaten food.

"Good morning, Uncle."

"Good morning," Olind replied without looking up.

Jeld sat across from Olind before an untouched tray of food.

"I... slept very well. The rooms you've afforded me are most comfortable."

"Mm. Good. Good."

Olind dipped a quill and began penning a letter.

"Lessons today," Jeld said, smearing jam over a roll. "Should be most interesting."

Olind's pen twitched ever so slightly. "Yes. Yes, most interesting."

Jeld continued his breakfast in silence.

***

"Questions on that?" Tutor Reiman asked, pausing his pacing to look out over the class.

The old tutor's pale skin and white beard seemed almost aglow against the black wall of solid slate at the front of the classroom. The stone wall, so broad it seemed the schoolhouse could only be pressed against the side of a mountain, was covered in strange symbols scribbled almost illegibly over earlier lessons the tutor had not bothered to erase. Even a large map from Geographies hours before was still visible far beneath.

Algebra, Tutor Reiman had called this latest bit, and while Jeld found the topic somewhat intriguing, he hoped the excuse of being new would last a good while.

"No questions?" Tutor Reiman asked. "Very well, let's move on. The next topic is a very important one."

He picked up a handful of dirt from atop a large table at the front of the room and let it run slowly from his fist.

"Agriculture. Farming practices."

A snicker from behind Jeld broke the silence.

"Funny, is it, Calane?"

"Why are you teaching us a peasant trade?" came a voice from behind.

Jeld felt more than heard a collective groan fill the room with the exception of a giggle from Jodith Hepsbry across the aisle. Turning, Jeld found a boy staring smugly down at him. He was tall with black hair and a strikingly handsome face if not for the arrogance in his eyes.

"Mm. Peasant trade. I see, I see," Tutor Reiman said.

He wiped his hands clean, crossed them behind his back, and resumed his invariable pacing. Even as Jeld marveled at the consistency of his route, Tutor Reiman abruptly stopped before a shelf along the far side of the room and pulled out a book. He thumbed through it as he returned to the front then began to read, tracing along it with a wiry finger.

"'Most notable of the agrarian houses of the era was that of Demerious, which the great Tennefor Demerious grew from but a single infertile plot, eventually usurping his lord and further...'"

He slid his finger down the page. "Ahh, perhaps we should read about House Pendrian too?"

A red-haired girl across the aisle sunk lower in her chair.

"Warrin, perhaps?" he added with a nod to Renae beside Jeld.

The old tutor pressed the book closed and brushed some dirt from its cover.

"Land is the source of wealth for nearly every noble house. But dirt itself is hardly valuable, so you see it was your ancestors' ability to *cultivate* which has enabled you all to sit now atop the kingdom knowing not even what a shovel looks like."

He lifted a handful of wheat grains from the front table. "Crop rotation. Irrigation. And do you think wheat was always so big? *Selective breeding.* Lord Camish Havaral, that one. Innovations aside, many of you will one day be responsible for land, and if you pay attention, we may yet keep this civilization alive another generation."

"Maybe Emry can just show us how to shovel cow shit," Calane said, Jodith Hepsbry snickering once again.

"Enough!" Tutor Reiman scolded. "Another disruption from you, Calane, and I'll see that you cross wits with your father. Understood?"

"Of course, Tutor. My apologies."

Tutor Reiman stared coolly at Calane before nodding and continuing his lesson.

Jeld's blood boiled. Petty children wanting for naught, their minds forced instead to find conflict in frivolities. *Ignore it,* he told himself. *You need favor, not enemies.*

Enemies... Perhaps that was his path to favor. Perhaps this audience needed a hero.

He turned to Calane and whispered, "Perhaps you're a better fit for a demonstration on cow shit, having taken such good care of your mother all these years."

"How *dare* you, you filthy peasant—"

"Calane!" Tutor Reiman roared. "I'll be having words with your father! Shall I plan to explain why you were *expelled*, or will that be all from you today?"

Seething, Calane shook his head.

The tutor straightened his robe and took a breath. "Now. Who can tell me about crop rotations?"

Calane stayed silent for the remainder of the lessons, though his scowl burned loudly against the back of Jeld's neck. When finally Tutor Reiman dismissed the class, Renae led Jeld out of the hall and down the street in the opposite direction Calane stormed.

"Well now, you certainly made a wonderful impression on your first day," Renae said as they walked.

"I'm not the one who called someone a *filthy peasant.*"

"No, you only called the wife of one of the most powerful lords in Avandria a cow."

"After he called *me* a filthy peasant."

Renae led Jeld into an establishment with a steaming bowl etched into its sign.

"Technically it was after he *implied* you were a filthy peasant, but before he actually called you one." Renae shook his head and sighed. "Why do I get the feeling I'm going to regret associating with you?"

Jeld sat across from Renae at a corner table and looked about the establishment. It had a refreshing grittiness that Jeld hadn't encountered since ascending to Hilltop. He let out a breath and leaned back in his chair, but something gave him pause. The chair hadn't loosed even a whisper of a creak. Wiping a single finger across the yellowed wall beside him, Jeld turned it around and showed Renae a perfectly clean finger.

"Fake dinge. Nice. So let me get this straight... you picked a spot with scratched tables to try to make me feel at home? What's the name of this place anyway, *The Filthy Peasant?*"

Renae laughed. "It's called Sigmoore's Soups & Spirits. That mustache behind the bar there is Sigmoore. And despite what you might think about people up here on the hill, they love a little grit. Most of them, anyway."

"Yeah, long as they can't taste it, smell it, or get it on their clothes."

A group Jeld recognized from lessons entered and sat around a distant table.

"Guess you're right," Jeld said. "So what does everyone do after lessons, just... eat soup?"

"There's that. Some return to their families. Others have tutors for music, language, dancing. Most of the boys just kill time until fencing. Some of the girls, too. Just *stunning* in their shapeless fencing suits."

"Ahh, right. Fencing. I'd almost managed to forget."

"I was thinking we could even go early so I can show you a thing or two before everyone else arrives to embarrass you."

"That's very kind," Jeld said.

***

Tiled white fighting rings covered the stone floor of the vast sporting hall. One wall was made up entirely of sloping audience stands, a more intimate balcony protruding from the top. At the center of the hall, a single ring was raised a step above the rest.

"Got all that?" Renae asked from across the raised ring.

He pressed closed a little door in the front of his mask. The rest of his upper body was protected in heavy leathers, thick padded undergarments showing through at the joints.

Jeld slashed his sword about. It bowed ponderously, hissing as it cut through the air despite bearing no edge and being capped at the end.

"I think so. No touching, stay in the circle, stabbing only, first stab wins."

Renae frowned. "Actually, that sums it up. Alright, go to your line and stand like this. And close your mask."

Jeld matched Renae's stance, stepping one foot out before the other and raising his sword. He snapped his mask shut with a grimace, the cursed thing feeling every bit the face cage it resembled.

"Good. Now, salute." Renae raised the pommel of his foil to his chin.

Jeld saluted back. "What now, Sir Renae?"

"Now, you stab me."

"At long last."

Jeld prodded a haphazard blow at his friend's chest and Renae slapped it aside with his blade.

"That's called a parry. Deflecting an attack with your sword. Come at me again, and *please*, don't hold back this time."

Jeld thrust again, and even as his sword was slapped aside, Renae's bowed against his chest.

"That, was a parry and riposte. Deflect and counterattack."

They went on to cover the basics before others began to arrive. Hopping down from the ring, Jeld and Renae sat atop a large storage chest and discussed the sport as the room filled with more people. Among the last to enter was Calane.

"Wonderful," Jeld groaned as the others all suited up.

"Best ignore him," Renae said before pointing to a pair of girls practicing in a nearby ring. "See that lunge? Snappy, like a striking snake."

As Renae went on pointing out various maneuvers, it became painfully clear to Jeld that every single person in the room had been at this a very long time. Before long, a man dressed already in fencing getup stormed into the room. His suit was trim and clean, and he looked somehow more at home in it than did a pig in mud. He had long dark hair and a strong jaw covered in a week's worth of whiskers.

"That's our instructor," Renae said. "Master Inado Allsglade."

The name set Jeld's brain churning as Renae went on until at last he placed it. This was the man from Alal's story, the fencer who had defeated him in the championship.

"Four-time champion of the King's Games," Renae continued. "After his second win, he was given title and invited to instruct here in Tovar."

Master Inado drew his sword as he jumped gracefully onto the platform, sword at the ready before he landed.

"Viktor, show me what you have learned," he commanded.

A wave of relief washed over the hall as jeers and cheers erupted from a group of nearby pupils. A tall blond boy worked his way to the front and stepped onto the platform.

Jeld leaned over to Renae. "Is this how it always goes?"

"Often. Keeps people on their toes, and it does provide good instruction. After he is done with Viktor he will probably have us do practice bouts amongst ourselves, then usually a few duels up there."

Jeld swallowed audibly.

"Remember," Master Inado began, "speed, finesse, initiative, misdirection, anticipation."

He closed his mask, stepped to his line, and exchanged a salute with Viktor.

"Now, parry drills!"

The instructor lunged forward at once, his sword bowing against Viktor's abdomen in the blink of an eye.

"Your opponent will never wait until you are prepared. Again. Ready yourself."

Inado lashed out again and this time Viktor swept the blow aside.

"Good. Again."

Viktor caught the next attack with the tip of his sword, but Inado flicked it aside and struck Viktor's side.

"Parrying with the tip has its place, but it affords no control. Again."

He lunged, crossing the ring in one long step, but Viktor swatted the attack aside lower on his sword.

"Good. Low on the sword for control."

Master Inado began a slow, rhythmic series of attacks. Viktor parried attack after attack as Inado continued his lecture.

"What we cannot forget is that a parry is worthless if it doesn't put us in a position to riposte or disengage to attack again. Otherwise, a parry merely delays the inevitable. Now, a bout."

He returned to the line and they exchanged a salute.

"Arms!"

Viktor attacked immediately. Master Inado caught the blow low on his sword and pushed it aside, turning his sword inward and striking Viktor's shoulder not a blink before Viktor's bent against his own.

"A parry without control is worthless," Inado said as he reset. "Again!"

They did several more bouts, Master Inado issuing some lesson after each. Most ended with both striking a blow, though Viktor's always lagged just slightly.

"This guy is awful!" Jeld whisperer to Renae. "Four-time champion? He's died a dozen times!"

Renae laughed, Jeld only staring back. "Oh. You're serious. Sorry. Maybe I didn't mention it before, but it's just the first strike that counts."

"But... how can you win if you're dead?"

Renae shrugged. "They've got to draw the line somewhere, unless they want people fighting to the death."

Jeld watched the last few bouts, shaking his head each time Master Inado got stuck until finally the instructor flipped his mask open and returned his sword to a loop at his waist.

"Well done, Mister Colligaugh. To rings, everyone! Remember what you've learned, or you'll only reinforce poor form."

Renae hurried Jeld to an unclaimed circle in a corner of the room as everyone dispersed.

"We'll just go at half speed to get the feel of things," Renae said, closing his mask and saluting.

Returning the gesture, Jeld stood at the ready, his heart racing. Renae lunged. Jeld knocked aside the slow attack and countered, but Renae easily swept it aside and riposted. As Jeld caught the blow, Renae pivoted, pressing his attack toward Jeld's shoulder. Jeld tried to twist away but the blow came too fast, bowing mostly painlessly against his shoulder. Despite the loss, Jeld grinned like a child at play and they started again.

"Not bad, Arvin," Renae said breathlessly after several rounds, pulling his mask open and taking a big swig from his waterskin before tossing it to Jeld.

Jeld nodded his thanks and started chugging. Between the exercise, the thrill, and the thick armor, he'd sweated more than he could ever recall.

"Not bad at all," came a voice from behind.

Jeld turned to find Master Inado standing outside the ring.

"You've got speed, focus. You're a mover. Anyone's strikes would be clumsy so early, but I think you'll always be more mover than striker. Don't let me label you, though. Fight and learn your way. Blossom beneath the rain of combat." He smiled and gave a slight bow. "Welcome, Mister Emry."

"Thank you, Master," Jeld replied, returning the bow.

"Mister Warrin, thank you for taking our newest pupil under your wing. He's lucky to have you."

Master Inado returned to the platform and the clatter of swords soon fell silent.

"Are there any challenges?" Inado bellowed, stalking around the edge of the ring.

"Emry," a cringeworthy voice answered.

Jeld's pulse pounded in his neck as Calane Demerious stepped up into the ring.

"Nonsense," Master Inado said without so much as looking at Calane. "Anyone?"

Jeld clenched his mouth shut, Renae's cautionary words echoing through his mind.

"Master Inado," Jeld blurted despite himself.

Renae threw his hands up and began rubbing his temple.

"I don't mind," Jeld said. "I imagine fighting is the best way to learn."

Master Inado stared back.

"I... suppose I wouldn't be the swordsman I am today without the trial by fire of two older brothers. Very well. As you wish."

Stepping up onto the platform, Jeld looked back and offered Renae an innocent shrug as his friend tried to bury a grin. Movement beyond Renae caught Jeld's attention and he looked up to find perhaps a dozen people occupying the balcony atop the stands. Though they looked mostly to be conversing, all eyes were fixed on the ring.

He swallowed hard. The curtain was drawn, as it were, and he didn't know his lines. His eyes flicking to Calane's sneering face, Jeld sucked in a deep breath, closed his mask, and stepped up to the ready line.

He waited for a salute, but when Calane didn't budge— no doubt thinking himself too important to salute a *lowly peasant*— Jeld started to salute but jerked his sword back as Calane returned it in full.

"Too kind," Jeld said, returning the salute.

"You—"

"Arms!" called Master Inado.

Jeld lunged, crossing half the ring before the echo of Inado's call was finished, and struck Calane's chest.

"Strike!" Master Inado shouted.

Calane swatted Jeld's sword aside. "Of course you'd fight like a rat!"

"And of course *you* would fight like a *cow*," Jeld countered. "Considering... you know, the mother thing."

Laughter erupted all around as Jeld reset to the ready and offered a salute.

"Arms!"

Jeld faked the same attack. When Calane tried to parry, Jeld turned his attack toward an exposed flank, but still Calane swept his sword aside and lashed out. Rolling his shoulder beneath the blow, Jeld saw an opening and countered, his sword bending against Calane's thigh.

Grinning beneath his mask, Jeld turned back to the ready line, taking only a single step before suddenly a sword bit painfully into his lightly armored back.

"Strike!" Master Inado called.

Stumbling to a stop, Jeld turned a puzzled look upon Master Inado.

"You were off target. Torso, Mister Emry."

Jeld found himself speechless. It seemed there were no bounds to the length at which the sport went to crown the dead.

"To the ready!"

Jeld and Calane exchanged another salute.

"Arms!"

Calane lunged, passing Jeld's guard in a flash. Too close to parry, Jeld raised his sword along his torso and spun. His blade turned the blow aside with a sharp *clink* and he charged past Calane. They both spun to face one another, swords held out at the ready.

They circled like prowling cats, the room falling completely silent. Suddenly Calane charged forward and lashed out high. Jeld narrowly slapped the attack aside and struck out toward an exposed side, but Calane's sword turned suddenly down at him. He jumped backward but he was too slow, Calane's sword bowing against his shoulder.

"Strike! Emry, don't disengage to defend yourself if you can strike first. You could have had the point."

Of course, I should have just let myself get stabbed second!

Calane took the next two points, easily parrying Jeld's clumsy strikes. Resetting to the ready line, Jeld closed his eyes and took in a deep breath. His pounding heartbeat slowing, he felt Calane's prideful yet anxious presence like a shining light through his eyelids. Suddenly he felt pity for Calane as deep insecurities began to unfurl. How starved he was for love and affection. How desperately he craved validation. How miserably he loathed Jeld for standing in his way.

A sudden current of frustration pulsed amidst Calane's aura and Jeld blinked open his eyes to find Calane rendering a salute.

"Sorry," Jeld said and quickly saluted back.

"Arms!" Master Inado called.

Jeld stared into Calane as they circled the ring, watching for the twitch of a muscle or the slightest chink in Calane's defenses, then deeper again into the raw feelings beyond. Patterns emerged within the chaotic torrent undulating before his opponent, like a shadow leading his every next move. Soon Jeld found himself reacting to each shift, adjusting the angle of his sword, the bend in his knees, the plane of his body, the weight in his every step.

Calane lunged, but Jeld saw it coming and easily parried. He attacked again, but already Jeld had pivoted and the blow stabbed at the air beside him. Jeld dodged another, parried a fourth, and as another closed on him he fought the instinct to disengage and instead lashed out toward Calane's exposed abdomen, landing the blow just before Calane struck his shoulder.

"Strike!" Master Inado called and raised an arm toward Calane.

"I struck first!" Jeld said, flipping open his mask. "His torso, even."

"Right-of-way, young Arvin. His attack, his point. Even if you land first. You must riposte or disengage to reset the initiative."

Jeld fought to keep his jaw from dropping.

"And, match—Calane. Well fought." The master turned to Jeld. "Well fought indeed."

Jeld started back across the platform toward Renae. Beyond his friend, a striking man in the balcony stood promptly and marched down the stands toward the exit.

"Who's that?" Jeld said, hopping down beside Renae.

Though the man's hair had given much ground to age in both color and quantity, he glided smooth as a skilled swimmer through water, each effortless stride carrying him farther than it seemed it should.

"Ah. That's General Tovaine."

"Who's next?" Master Inado called behind them, several swords rising into the air.

"Handan Tovaine?" Jeld hissed.

"Someone you've actually heard of? I'm shocked."

"Of course I've heard of him!" Jeld groaned.

"What's the problem?"

"I'm so bad the blazin' leader of the kingdom's armies couldn't bear to watch me!"

"Idols, are you still playing at that?"

"At what?"

Renae shook his head and turned to the next duel.

"At what!" Jeld pressed.

"You could have let me in on it, that's all."

"What the blazes are you going on about?"

"This ploy of yours. Pretending not to know how to fence to lure Calane into a fight. I'm just saying, you didn't have to deceive me too. I would have gone along if you'd just told me you were having a go."

"Renae," Jeld said sternly. "No tricks. I've never fenced before. In case you didn't notice, I lost."

Renae stared back skeptically before frowning. "Well, if you're being honest, you might have found your calling."

"Strike!" Master Inado called.

Chapter Twenty-Five

———◆◇◆———

J eld could just make out the shapes of the spires through the moonlit mists above. Far
beneath them, a clean line of torches lit a long rampart crossing over the road ahead.
Iron lamp posts lined the road, casting perfectly spaced circles of light all the way down
the slope and setting aglow the breath of the team pulling just ahead.

"Close that, would you?" Olind said. "It's terribly cold out there."

Jeld looked one last time through the carriage window to the shadowy silhouette of
the spires then pulled his head back inside and closed the shutters. He stared at the vel-
vet-padded wall, his mind on the palace ahead as the carriage creaked, hoofbeats clapped,
and the wheels rumbled and clunked their quick cobblestone rhythm.

"How old is the palace?" Jeld asked after a while.

"The bones... three centuries or so. Much is newer, added after the Idols claimed the
city as their capital. Tovados didn't want a new keep any more than he wanted a new name
for the city, to hear it told, but they say Vincet set him straight. Nice as the Demerious
keep was, Vincet knew a kingdom needed a kingly estate."

"Did you know him? Tovados, I mean."

"Know Tovados? Oh no. I was just a lowly merchant's son until well after he had gone,
though our operations *had* taken a turn for the better by then. My father met the Traveler
though, would you believe. He stopped by the shop and bought quite a haul—stuffed his
pockets with enough food to feed a horse. Or so my father told it, anyway, and he told it
plenty."

Jeld's eyes flicked down to his bottomless bag just as the carriage came to a stop. He
made to rise but Olind shook his head.

"This is just the outer gate. Hamry will deliver us to the great hall."

Jeld looked over to the shuttered window as the carriage lurched into motion once
more.

"Oh go on," Olind said. "We're nearly there anyway."

Jeld pushed the shutters open and poked his head through the window. The carriage pulled away from the gate and his pulse quickened as the castle wall seemed to wrap around behind him. Ahead, the keep loomed like a mountain, so massive it seemed to grow no larger even as they continued toward it through manicured lawns.

The carriage veered toward a lower section of the keep that stretched out from the rest. Brightly lit arched windows punctuated the entirety of the expanse. A carriage in front of them passed between two massive pillars and stopped beneath an overhang large enough to cover a riding arena.

Jeld pulled his head back inside and straightened his jacket. A few moments later, the carriage came to a stop.

"*Now* we've arrived," Olind said.

The carriage door opened soon after and finally Olind stepped out, Jeld following after. Atop a rise of steps that spilled out like ripples of water, a pair of knights in glimmering armor flanked two giant doors. Muffled music from beyond whispered out into the night.

With a nod over his shoulder to Hamry, Jeld started up the steps after Olind.

"It sounds as though we've managed to be nobly on time," Olind said.

"I rather thought it sounded as if we were late."

Olind laughed.

"What is it?" Jeld asked.

"It's an expression. *Nobly on time.* It means... to arrive fashionably, and as is appropriate to one's station. One must avoid being too early, as if desperate for favor or unbusied by important affairs, but one must also take care to arrive no later than those of higher station."

"I see."

Jeld's nerves brought a sudden sweat to his forehead. Did the intricacies of this vain ham dance know no bounds? Could any such slight breach of obscure protocol expose him to the lions whose den he now entered? He took a deep breath and let Arvin envelope him like a veil, his nerves easing as he looked out through his character's eyes at the doors ahead.

The knights faced inward with a snap of their heels and pulled the doors open.

Jeld squinted as brilliant light, music, and warm air crashed out into the night from the confines of the great hall. The first thing he saw was the color gold. *Gold* sewn into clothes and decorating fingers and wrists and necklaces of the dozens of nobles milling and dancing about. *Gold* intricately etched into pillars and the very walls. More than anything it was the radiant golden light spilling from the hall, as if the king waged war against the very night.

Jeld followed Olind inside. Servants stripped their coats and disappeared like muggers into the golden woodwork. As his would-be uncle surveyed the political battlefield, Jeld marveled at the royal ballroom. Laughter and whispers and the clinking of glasses played behind the song of a small band across the way. The tall arched windows that from outside had offered glimpses of the glowing decadence within now punctuated the gilded walls with jet black reminders of the dangers beyond the king's embrace. Beside each such window rose a spiraling staircase from the shining marble floor to a balcony circling the hall above.

"Aha," Olind said, continuing inward.

Jeld followed him toward a more intimate space beneath the balcony where several people were seated around a low table. As they neared, Jeld recognized Lady Edenwood among them.

"My," Lady Edenwood gasped. "Two Emry men so dressed is a right unfair employ, is it not?"

Olind smiled and kissed her hand. "My lady. You flatter us, such words from a lady of your beauty."

"Bah! I've seen prunes less wrinkled than this old face."

"Are you enjoying the festivities, my lady?"

Lady Edenwood turned an impressed frown to Jeld. "Masterfully avoided, was it not?"

"I'm sure I don't know what you mean, my lady," Jeld said.

"Rather look daft than call an old lady for what she is? Safe, anyway."

"It *is* only my first ball. Perhaps with time I shall become as bold as you, my lady."

She stared back gravely. Jeld felt Olind flush with embarrassment and outrage. The others in their gathering went still. Then suddenly Lady Edenwood cackled. "Marvelous! Oh marvelous! Olind, you've brought us a treasure."

"Ah, of course," Olind choked. "Thank you, my lady. A splendid lad indeed."

The man in the chair beside Lady Edenwood stood, drink in hand. He was cleanly shaven and fit, his hair receding in the fashionable manner that began with the sides rather than the more unfortunate wispy crown that afflicted Olind.

"Allow me to introduce my nephew," Lady Edenwood began. "Lasken Edenwood, commander of the City Watch."

Jeld swallowed hard. "Pleased to meet you, sir."

"And you. Any man that can make my aunt laugh so is a friend of mine. She's quite the judge of character, you know."

"Thank you, sir. I'm sure the feat pales in comparison to the difficulty of running the Watch."

The bliss of drink and music fell from the man's face.

"An understatement of late, I'm afraid."

"I'm quite new to Tovar, but I've heard there has been much unrest of late. Muggings in the streets, mobs, and the like?"

Sir Lasken sighed. "Quite right, quite right. And bolder every day. Well, nothing bolder than the... *pig incident* outside Lord Governor Demerious's place, but working their way up to its like again, I've no doubt."

"I heard someone at lessons tell the tale! I didn't believe it."

"Oh it's true. Believe me, it's true. Blazing bastards, the lot of them. Not doing themselves much good in all this anyway, are they?"

Jeld recalled the despairing faces of ragged men, women, and children filing out of a dilapidated building before a squad of watchmen and fought back a flash of anger.

"Indeed, sir. I can't see as all this will work out well for them."

"A wretched lot. They want to take our wealth, even as they squander theirs on whores, tankards, and tar."

Jeld grunted in agreement. "Did I hear right that a new prison was raised?"

"True again. Prince Dralor saw to that. Can't expect things to change if we just keep turning people loose before the booze even wears off. We've got to make a lesson of it, not to mention keeping them off the streets longer."

"Prince Dralor sounds like a sensible man."

"He is. And a hard man. Gives the watch what we need, but... well, he has high expectations." He drained his goblet and looked down into it. "Interesting times indeed. If you'll excuse me, young friend, I seem to have run dry."

"Wonderful to meet you, sir."

"And you."

Lasken turned and started across the hall toward a bar barely visible through the crowd. Behind the bar a tower of meandering iron poles reached skyward before fanning out in the likeness of a sprawling tree, its branches winding around the upper balcony to form another bar for the level above.

"Did you call Sir Lasken *ancient* as well?" Olind whispered.

"No, I—" Jeld looked over to find a rare smirk upon Olind's face. "It would seem that talking about his post requires a goodly flow of drink."

Olind nodded before something seemed to catch his eye. "Interesting. He doesn't often show up. Brother must have talked him into it."

"Who?"

"Prince Dralor. In the gathering just there. And Queen Darene. The king himself is likely buried in there. Not one for fanfare, King Loris. Just slips in like the rest of us. Come, I'd best introduce you."

Olind turned to Lady Edenwood. "If you'll excuse us, dear lady?"

She nodded. "Gentlemen."

Jeld followed Olind into the crowd. His steps suddenly felt clumsy. Or did they merely seem so because he was thinking about them? He swallowed hard, an increasingly familiar sensation, and pulled tighter his albeit similarly nervous cloak of Arvin.

Olind exchanged smiles, nods, and greetings while they slowly meandered across the great hall as if purposelessly adrift. As Olind reached out to pluck the last goblet from a passing servant's tray, a woman turned and frowned. She was slightly taller than Jeld, with dark hair and a light complexion not unlike most of the gentry.

"Ah, Your Grace!" Olind said. "Please, after you. It seems we share a vice, Your Grace."

The woman smiled deviously at Olind and took the goblet then turned to Jeld.

"It's not so bad as vices go, is it, young sir?"

"Well, it's basically just fruit juice, is it not, Your Grace?" Jeld said and raised a toast.

"Hmm, yes. Not so bad at all then."

She smiled her devious smile then clinked her goblet against his and took a sip. Lowering her drink, her eyes fell closed and she seemed to breathe in the life of the ball.

"Your Grace," Olind began, "allow me to present my nephew, Arvin Emry. He only just joined me here in Tovar a few weeks past. Arvin, I have the honor of presenting Her Grace, Queen Darene."

"I'm honored to be among your company, Your Grace," Jeld said.

"And I yours," she said to no one in particular before turning back to Olind. "Oh Olind, you simply must come share a dance with me later."

"Of course, Your Grace. It would be my honor."

The queen gave no sign of noticing Olind's response, her eyes already wandering about the ballroom.

"Ah, Your Grace, I don't suppose you would introduce my nephew to your noteworthy party there?"

Smiling distantly, Queen Darene reached behind her and tugged on the back of a tall man's doublet.

"Dral, dear," she said over her shoulder when the man seemed not to notice.

The man turned, a look of annoyance upon his face. He wore a black doublet reminiscent of a military coat, a silver pin of the sword of Tovados glistening upon one shoulder. Like his neatly trimmed goatee, the otherwise black hair at his temple was dusted with gray. His eyes flicked to Olind, then to Jeld.

"Pardon the interruption, my dear prince," Queen Darene said before leaning closer to whisper in his ear. "Though you seemed *dreadfully* bored. May I introduce Arvin Emry, nephew of our very own master of commerce."

"Arvin Emry," the prince tried, his voice deep and gaze heavy. "I heard hardship brought you here. I hope you'll find Tovar a suitable place to nurse your wounds and cast new roots. You are welcome here."

"Thank you, Your Grace," Jeld said. "You are most kind. I'll have no trouble being at ease here. You've crafted a magnificent city, Your Grace."

A weight fell over Prince Dralor and his eyes grew even more troubled. He quickly set his jaw and nodded.

"My brother has done a fine job indeed," another man said, stepping out from behind the prince.

The man bore an unmistakable resemblance to Prince Dralor, though his black hair was notably thicker and his eyes, while similar at their surface, were kindly where the prince's were grave. He wore all white save for a decorative crimson cape over one shoulder. The sword of his house was embroidered in a discreet silver over the full of his chest.

"And I'm sorry to have bored my brother so, my dear," the man said, raising an eyebrow to Queen Darene.

The queen smiled and put her arm around the newcomer's waist. "You heard me introduce our new guest then, I trust?"

"Indeed I did. I echo my brother's eloquent sentiments, young sir. Pleased to meet you, and welcome to Tovar."

Jeld could feel Olind's nerves rising as the man spoke, as if Jeld might fail to realize who he stood before.

"The pleasure is mine, Your Highness. Your family and court have been gracious beyond words, Your Highness."

"Your Highness!" a thick bearded man called out, barging between Jeld and the king.

"Ralegus!" King Loris greeted. "I trust you've tried the ham hock? Best pigs to ever grace this table."

"Aye and aye, my friend. Now I know why our Tovados truly planted his throne here. The hogs about Odsgaard just taste like tusks and hair and mean."

The king stepped back around his large friend. "My apologies, my dear Emrys. If you'll excuse me? Olind, find me later to discuss this influx of eastern ore, won't you?"

"Of course, Your Highness!"

Suddenly aglow, Olind nodded to the others despite their having already entangled themselves in new conversations, then nudged Jeld toward the bar.

Jeld loosed a breath as he followed Olind from his unlikely encounter with a prince, queen, and king alike. Weaving through the crowd, he issued smiles and nods with every important click of his heels upon the marble floor.

"It seems you are highly respected in court, Uncle."

"I've helped Tovar thrive in trying times."

"And you've no small talent in court politicking."

"I spent my early years in trade. In sales, you must convince people to give you money. In politicking, all you must extract is a worthless smile."

A servant behind the bar greeted them and Olind placed a lengthy order of seemingly nonsensical words interspersed with the occasional herb.

"Olind, good evening," came a voice from just down the bar.

The owner of the voice was dressed in a fine but simple green doublet, a white tree pin at one epaulet, and another of a sword upon his other. He had short gray hair, a neat beard, and warm green eyes.

"Sir Benam! Good evening. I didn't recognize you so close to the bar."

The man chuckled. "If these magicians can craft so tasty a spirit, imagine how delicious are their more innocuous conjurings?"

"None can argue with logic sound as that. Forgive me, this is my nephew, Arvin. Arvin, I present Sir Benam—friend, advisor, and chief healer to the king. A knight, scholar, and tutor to the princess herself."

"Former knight," Sir Benam corrected. "Pleased to meet you, Arvin."

"You've earned many names, Sir Knight," Jeld said. "You must do much for the king and his lands."

"There are many who if bestowed a name for each skill they possessed or deed they've done would have far more than I, young sir. But I thank you all the same for your compliments."

The bartender sprinkled bright blue crystals atop two goblets of pulpy pink juice and placed them on the bar before Sir Benam, who nodded his thanks. A small hand plucked one from the bar and whisked it away behind Sir Benam.

"Ah, I must beg forgiveness as well," Sir Benam said, grabbing his drink and taking a step back from the bar.

Jeld's breath caught as he beheld an impossibly familiar pair of bright blue eyes shining over the top of the pink goblet. It was unmistakably Lira.

"Sir Arvin," Benam continued, "I present Her Grace Princess Liraelle, daughter of His Royal Highness King Loris."

Jeld stood frozen. He wanted so badly to run to her embrace, and yet also to flee before a mere look could see him hanged. Her eyes seemed to widen for but a fleeting moment before a blink washed away the trace of surprise. It was a masterful subterfuge, an indifference that might even have offended Jeld were a less disguised wonder not pouring from deeper within her.

Lira lowered her drink and cleared her throat. "Arvin Emry, is it? Most pleased to meet you."

Jeld tried to speak but no sound escaped his mouth. He mentally slapped himself and tried again.

"The pleasure is mine, Your Grace. Thank you for welcoming me into your home."

Lira smiled. "I'm *certain* you'd welcome me into yours just as graciously. This is your first ball, I believe?"

"It is, Your Grace."

"They certainly leave little to be desired. I imagine, though, this must be somewhat overwhelming for you, and it's become quite too warm for my taste. Would you care to join me in the gardens?"

"Ah... of course, Your Grace."

"Wonderful. Gentlemen, if you'll excuse us?"

"Of course, Princess," Sir Benam said.

Olind swallowed audibly before offering Lira a smile and a bow.

"Shall we, then?" Lira said, turning away without another word.

Jeld nodded to Olind and Sir Benam and hurried through the crowd after Lira. Each obsequious smile to Lira turned to an appraising frown on falling upon Jeld, until at last they reached a door at the foot of one of the arched windows. Jeld slipped out into the night and continued after Lira along a cobbled walk.

Perhaps a dozen steps along, Lira let out a breath.

"What the blazes are you doing here, Jeld!"

Jeld fell in step beside Lira as she quickly swatted a tear from her cheek. Longing to embrace her, his eyes flicked back to the ballroom windows.

"How did—*Idols*, I thought you were..." Jeld shook his head. "How did you escape? What did they—are you alright?"

"Escape? Jeld, what are you talking about?"

"The men in the alley. The slavers, they took you!"

"Jeld, we stopped him. My—oh no. Jeld, the other two were Sir Krisharc and Sir Aarend—my knights. They dragged me back to the keep. I tried to stop them so I could help you. I tried so hard, I was so worried about you, I—"

"Knights..."

"They always shadowed me when I left the hill. Jeld, I... did you say *slavers?*"

Jeld shook his head in disbelief, his mouth opening and closing wordlessly as he stared at the passing cobblestones underfoot.

"Jeld?"

"Knights? Then you were never..." Jeld loosed a breathy laugh. "And you're a *princess?*"

Lira looked down sheepishly.

"I suppose that makes sense of things, really," Jeld said.

"But why are you... how did you...?"

"How did poor, dirty Jeld become a courtly noble's nephew?"

"I mean, not like that, but... yes, how?"

"I... I don't know if you'd—I mean, you're a..."

"A princess? Okay, you're dirty and poor, and I'm a snobby princess. Now that that's done, *how?*"

Jeld looked down at the walk again and more stones passed in silence. Of course she wouldn't mean him harm, but how could someone in her station even begin to understand his purpose? Certainly not his personal motive, but even Krayo's?

He followed Lira across an expanse of manicured grass to a small stone gazebo and sat beside her upon a bench within.

"Lira, if you tell anyone... anyone at all, I'm dead. You understand that, right?"

"Are you doing something bad?"

"Bad? No—well, that depends who you ask, but—"

"I'm asking *you.*"

"Then... no. I'm... working for a man who wants to know what madness the crown is bringing about. For business reasons, mind you, but I like to think I can do more good with it." He continued as Lira only returned a puzzled look. "War, trade, the watch... it's all just conversations over tea here. But down the hill, it's life or death."

"I see," Lira said.

"You know from helping at the temple. You know all the shit that flows down the hill. *That's* why I'm here—to see what the next wave of shit is. Well, I think so, anyway."

"You *think* so?"

"Well, I don't actually have any real... directions. Just... watch and listen."

"I see. So, you're... a spy."

"What? No. Well... no, a spy is a snoop for an enemy. I'm just listening, but not for the enemy."

Lira laughed suddenly then shivered and wrapped one of the many layers of her skirts over her arms.

"So you're a *noble* spy."

"Spy is such a *sinister* word. I like to think of myself as a... hero of the people."

"You know, my uncle is quite afraid *the people* really are rising up. If he knew..."

"He'd waste no time in seeing my head removed. I know. And I'm *not* part of anything like that. I can't say as I'd fully blame the people for not liking Hilltoppers all that much, though."

"Nor can I," she said somberly.

"So... you won't have me executed for treason?"

"You said *slavers* before. That man who attacked us was a slaver?"

Jeld nodded. "Kaid told me. Turns out our good friend tried to sell you to slavers."

"He *what!*"

"He said they might be working for some knight, that they mentioned a... *knight in need*, or something like that."

"Why would a knight need to abduct me?"

Jeld shook his head. "You wouldn't believe the things I did to try to find you, but nothing went anywhere. Do you think one of your knights could... you know, be in on it?"

"And then rescue me from their own plot?"

"Well, maybe a different—"

"Absolutely not. No, not a chance."

Jeld sighed. "I really did try. So hard."

"I can't believe this whole time you thought I was in some slave pit or... worse. I had my own fears for you, you know. When my knights dragged me away and you were just lying there in the alley..." She looked Jeld in the eye, setting her jaw to still a trembling lip before continuing. "I never forgave them. Or myself. How could they whisk me away to safety while you lie there dying for all we knew? As if my life were more important than yours!"

"You didn't have a choice. And neither did your knights. Of course they chose the princess over some street kid. I'm sure they were just trying to protect the kingdom."

"It's not right. It shouldn't matter who my father is. And it's not just that my life was given higher value, it's that yours was given *none*. They could have seen you to a healer, or even just a room, but they just left you there!"

"Station shouldn't matter, but it does. Of course it does."

They fell quiet. Jeld looked about the elaborate gardens then behind him where, through the many windows of the great hall, the golden light of the ball shined as if from a different world.

He shook his head in disbelief. "Here I am sitting with Princess Lira-*elle* outside the royal ballroom."

Lira smiled and came to her feet. "Walk with me more?"

Jeld followed her back to the path.

"You must be disgusted," Lira said, her eyes on the spires above. "Here it is, your taxes spent on castles, expensive wines, exotic foods..."

"Just one king, at least. Never excess, here on the hill. Now, could we go back to the *not executing me* question?"

Lira grinned. "I promise we won't eat you, at least. You're much too filthy."

Jeld laughed.

"So Olind... is a spy?" Lira asked.

"Hah! Olind? No, Olind is just Olind. He was put up to this. It's just me."

The muffled music grew suddenly louder behind them and Jeld turned to find General Handan Tovaine emerging from a doorway. Jeld's thoughts returned at once to the celebrated general marching from the stands after his embarrassing defeat at fencing.

Legends had the man seven feet tall with shoulders nearly as wide, wrestling dragons and lifting ships. Maybe such deeds were true, but while tall and broad to be sure, his proportions were in fact more modest. He wore a military coat not unlike the prince's, only crimson in color and simpler in design.

"The best company can always be found *outside* a party," General Handan called as he neared.

"So say those of us outside parties," Lira answered.

"Hmm. Yes, wise as always, Your Grace. Still, I think we have the right of it." He turned to Jeld. "Arvin, isn't it?"

"Yes, sir," Jeld said.

"You two have met then?" Lira asked.

"Not exactly, Your Grace. The good general watched my first fencing duel. Somehow he lasted to the end of my feeble display before fleeing to witness no more."

The general's brow furrowed. "Ahh. You misunderstand. It wasn't your skills that turned me away, it's that awful sport. In a real fight that boy would have been two legs and a head shorter before getting a blow in."

Jeld swelled with pride.

"No man would expose his gut to a blow just to strike first," General Handan continued. "And don't get me started with those flimsy twigs they call swords!"

"Pardon me, sir, but watching bouts seems a strange pastime if you dislike the sport so."

"You hate the sport and you were the one fighting, am I right?"

Jeld smiled. "I despise it. So many rules. What business do rules have in a fight?"

"Indeed. So you're a fighter, are you?"

"Not really, no. Honestly I don't think I've swung a real sword but once or twice."

When the general said nothing, Jeld realized he and Lira were locked in some kind of silent negotiation. Lira raised her brow again and again, Handan countering each time with a shake of his head until at last the general's shoulders sagged and he nodded.

Lira smiled and turned back to Jeld. "General Handan has been kind enough to start teaching me swordplay. *Real* swordplay, not fencing. You could join us."

"I—yes. Of course. I'd be honored."

Jeld and Lira exchanged miserably suppressed smiles.

The music from within the great hall cut suddenly to silence.

"Come," Lira said. "Let's hear what's to be said."

She led the way back inside, warm air and hushed voices washing over them as they slipped through the door. Everyone within had their backs turned and was looking up at the balcony.

"We lost General Handan," Jeld said as he followed Lira up a spiral staircase.

Lira turned and grinned down at the general, who stood against the rear wall.

"He hates politics. Rather fight a war than attend a ball, I'm quite sure."

Reaching the top, Jeld followed Lira to a vacant spot at the railing and quickly spotted King Loris, Queen Darene, and Prince Dralor across the way. In front of all three, at the center of the rail before the mass of attendees below, stood an older man Jeld did not recognize. His short hair was wispy and white, and he wore an intricate white robe.

"Who is that?" Jeld whispered.

"High Priest Naelis."

Jeld had heard of the priest, of course. Once the foremost disciple of Vincet himself, he had been the voice of the Idols ever since the Vanishing.

"Ladies and gentlemen of the court," High Priest Naelis began, his voice soft yet filling the hall. "By the Idols' good graces, today we gather here once again as the shepherds of the kingdom. May your night be magical and leave you feeling nigh as full as the Mother's touch.

"Remember, though. Remember why we gather. Why we bond. Why we build our kinship tonight through shared bread and drink. Our Idols ascended long ago to quell dark forces that threatened to turn we mere men against one another, and they fight that enemy still.

"Discord acts even now on Tovar. But where with devious whispers he moves wicked men like pawns against peace, *we* must be the Idols' arms. We share their burden. Our hands are their weapons, our unity their message of peace. Our king, their lieutenant on this battlefield of Avandria.

"Tonight we owe thanks to the king for his resolve in preserving the safety and sanctity of the kingdom in the name of his forefather and the other Idols. May they watch over you now, and in dreams."

"In dreams," everyone echoed back as one, including Lira.

King Loris took the priest's place at the center of the balcony.

"Thank you, High Priest, for your beautiful words. Welcome, everyone. And a special welcome to those who traveled to join us here today. I thank you for all you do for your lands and for the kingdom."

He raised a goblet. "To Avandria."

"To Avandria!" everyone echoed back.

"Make yourselves at home. Enjoy the festivities."

The music resumed almost at once as the king turned away, and soon the thrum of activity surpassed even its prior heights.

"You get all that?" Lira asked. "We're all saving the kingdom, one ball at a time."

CHAPTER TWENTY-SIX

T he night's first stars in the dark blue sky silhouetted the spires towering above. Jeld's mount huffed impatiently beneath him and he tore his gaze from the royal keep. He gave her a gentle tap with his heel and she resumed her rhythmic walk.

His nerves began to rattle as he neared the gate, his visit for the ball just a few days prior offering little to prepare him for riding alone up to the royal keep—and to meet the king's daughter, no less. Two armored guards stood before the gate, two others bearing torches atop the wall above. Jeld straightened his posture and pressed ahead.

"Sir, your business this evening?" asked one beside the gate.

He was young and fit in contrast to his older, somewhat thicker partner who nonetheless looked perfectly able to remove Jeld's head with ease.

"Good evening, gentlemen. My name is Arvin Emry. General Handan is expecting me tonight, and each Moonsday, Thrallsday, and Citizensday after."

"Aye, sir, we were so informed." The guard looked up over his shoulder. "Passage!"

A moment later a heavy clank rang out and the young guard pulled open an iron door set within the larger gate. He stepped aside and snapped to attention.

"Gentlemen," Jeld said, kicking his horse ahead.

"Good night to you, Sir Arvin."

Jeld rode past without a word before suddenly reining in his mount. Perhaps a show of respect was out of character, but if Olind's accounts on supply and demand held true... that only made it all the more valuable hereabouts.

He turned his horse. "Your name, guardsman?"

The younger guard stood speechless until his colleague nudged him.

"Lucas, sir."

"Good night to you as well, Lucas."

Jeld turned his horse and started down the road, staying straight toward the keep itself where before his carriage had veered right toward the great hall. As he drew closer the spires seemed to stretch higher, the massive keep blotting out more and more of the stars until he found himself contemplating why he felt more a pawn at the king's very doorstep than striding alongside His Royal Highness's shit at the gutters of Riverside.

Two more guards in shining armor snapped to attention as Jeld approached the doors of the keep. He repeated his prior exchange, handed his horse over to his new acquaintance—a gruff former spearman named Andren—and soon found himself standing alone within the king's palace.

At once he dubbed his whereabouts *The Great Hallway*. With high ceilings and a seemingly endless stretch of broad archways piercing deep inside, it didn't itself seem to serve any purpose beyond accessing whatever rooms lay beyond. Jeld found himself wondering why the walls of the keep couldn't simply have been built further back.

"Good evening, sir."

Jeld spun. A man stood before a narrow passageway set inconspicuously into the wall beside the entrance. He was dressed in white servant's garb of the typical fashion save for a handful of discreet embellishments.

"Sir Arvin, is it not, sir?"

"Yes. And you are?"

"I am *at your service*, sir," he said with a bow.

"I see. Pleased to meet you. I've an appointment with General Handan."

"Moonsdays, Thrallsdays, and Citizensdays. Yes, sir. Right this way, sir."

The servant led him inward. With each turn deeper into the keep the air grew colder, the halls darker, and the walls somehow more raw, like they were boring into the very heart of a mountain. Step by step it became more apparent to Jeld that he walked the halls of a fortress, built with a purpose far different than the lavish mansions just outside the castle walls.

They climbed a spiraling staircase until the servant stopped and pointed down a short hallway with a single door at its end.

"General Handan's apartments, sir."

"Thank you, *at your service*."

The servant grinned despite himself. "As you wish, sir. It's Master Servant Darrelin. Will there be anything else, sir?"

"No, thank you, Master Servant Darrelin."

Darrelin bowed and disappeared back down the stairwell.

Jeld walked down the hall to the door, straightened his posture, and knocked. A few short breaths later, General Handan pulled the door open. He wore simple linen clothes of an off-white resembling dry grass. Loose as they were, the curves of his muscles were plain to see.

"Arvin. I'm pleased you made it. Come in."

"I wouldn't miss it."

Jeld entered. The room was modest, with stone walls and thick wooden beams running across the ceiling. A door flanked by shuttered windows stood at the center of the far wall. Another wall was covered in maps, a table before it bearing the remnants of a meal and a spattering of more maps.

"This way," General Handan said.

Jeld followed him through an arched doorway into a broad, circular room. Firelight from two braziers flickered over countless weapons of varying obscurity mounted upon the single curved wall. Like the first room, one expanse was lined with shuttered windows surrounding a sturdy door. At the center of the room, Lira sat stretching, dressed like the general in simple light linens.

She smiled. "Hello, Arvin. Guards give you any trouble?"

"Not at all. They were very helpful. General, your apartment is beautiful. Are we in one of the towers?"

"The southeastern tower." He effortlessly hefted a huge sword with a gleaming double-edged blade from the wall. "Teach him, Liraelle? I'll return. There are clothes for you in my changing room, Arvin."

He turned and left the room.

Lira rocked onto her feet and lit the room with a smile.

"It's so strange seeing you here," she said. "Like you're from a different life, or a story I read."

"I hope I don't seem so out of place to everyone else."

"It's not that. I just... those trips down into the city were the only times I've ever felt... *free*. And it's been so long since."

She walked to one of the windows and pushed it open, a deep rumbling rushing in at once.

Jeld joined her at the window. Beyond a modest balcony, the rolling sea churned far below, stretching uninterrupted to the horizon. The rhythmic crashing beat like the heart of the sea as the waves broke against the very rocks upon which the keep was built.

"In summer we train on the balcony there," Lira said.

"Amazing. So, you are to be my master-at-arms?"

"Only for the basics. I'm sure he just figures it'll be good for me to teach it. You'd best get changed."

Jeld nodded and left the chamber. When he returned wearing his new attire, Lira was still at the window.

"Perfect fit," Jeld said. "How did he manage that?"

"The servants have a tight network. I'm sure Sir Olind's chamberlain provided your measurements."

She crossed the room and pulled two matching wooden swords from the wall, tossing one to Jeld. He caught it and tried a swing, finding it far heavier than the flimsy swords they used in fencing.

"Sit. Stretches first, then bantae." She sat and bent forward over her legs.

"What's bantae?"

"It's an Eastern warrior practice. Bantae is... like fencing drills, but by yourself."

Jeld set his sword down and matched her pose.

"Don't set a sword on the blade like that, you'll dull it."

Jeld looked up at her.

"I know, I know," she said. "Wood, right? Well, try telling Handan that. And always keep it close, too. Try like I have it."

Jeld picked up his training sword and leaned forward again, this time resting its end upon his other outstretched arm.

"Perfect," she said. "It makes sense at least, right?"

She folded her legs in, set her sword on her lap, and arched her back until she was looking up at the ceiling. Jeld followed her lead, his chest and neck burning wondrously. The sea sang its lullaby. His breath slowed and his eyes fell shut.

"People don't ever just take a moment to themselves anymore," Lira said.

Jeld matched her next pose. "It's a nice luxury."

"Luxury? A moment? A deep breath? It is a precious thing that costs nothing."

"Maybe it just doesn't have the same effect when your *deep breath* reeks of sewage, and closing your eyes can mean a beating from a watchman or worse. Sorry, I—"

"No. You're right."

She came to her feet after several more stretches. The sword looked at home in her hands.

"Now, bantae. Imagine an opponent. Feel the weight of their sword upon yours."

She held her sword out in front of her and began to slowly move both sword and body fluidly through all manner of steps and swings and parries.

Reminded of the improvisational drills at the theater, Jeld raised his own sword as if to ward off some unseen blow. Feeling his enemy's sword against his, he let its weight slide to his hand guard then ducked beneath it and struck a blow to his opponent's shoulder.

Lowering his sword, he stole a look at Lira. She seemed to dance around a foe, darting in for quick thrusts before bouncing nimbly out with swift parries. Jeld smiled and raised his sword, his imagination at once running wild again. He fought foe after foe, each one fighting a little bit differently. He learned the balance of his sword wherever his opponent might strike it. He learned when to dodge and when to block, when to slash and when to thrust, when to press forward and when to fall back.

Suddenly he sensed another attack from behind. Spinning, he raised his sword and another slapped against it. His other senses caught up and he found General Handan standing over him with a training sword.

"Very good," General Handan said, his breath short and forehead glistening with sweat. "I could see your opponent clear as I see you, and still you didn't let your fight blind you to the battle."

"It's surprisingly natural."

"Not for most. People think imaginations are just for artists and daydreamers, but it's not so."

Suddenly Jeld's sword tore free of his grip and flew across the room, General Handan's blade seeming only barely to twitch before leveling at Jeld's face.

"Now, who wants to fight?"

***

Gritting his teeth, Jeld willed his aching fingers to close as they worked the last tie atop his collar, but they only shook harder and dropped the ties.

"Not bad," Lira said, taking up the strings and nimbly tying a bow. "I could hardly walk for three days after my first day with Handan. Ready?"

Jeld nodded and pulled General Handan's door open with a groan. He followed Lira from the quarters, trailing a step behind the princess per protocol. Perhaps halfway back through the keep she turned down an unfamiliar hallway.

"Decided to take me to the dungeon after all?"

"Oh yes. No sense resisting, now. Just make this easy on yourself."

After a few more twists and turns they passed through a door. Shelves packed with books filled the room as far as could be seen in the meager light of two lamps flickering upon a nearby table. An empty track running along the top of the outer shelves hinted at a ladder left deeper within at the end of some knowledge-seeker's journey.

"You showed me your favorite place," Lira said. "This is mine."

Marveling at the collection, Jeld followed Lira as she grabbed one of the lamps and started down an aisle. They wound deeper and deeper before emerging into a small space with a little desk to one side and a pile of velvety cushions at the other.

Lira sat upon the cushions. "It's like pushing aside a branch in the woods and finding a grassy clearing, I've always thought. Or what I imagine that to be like, anyway."

Certain it wouldn't do either of them any good to be caught sharing a cushion, Jeld slid one across from her and sat, his aching legs giving out just halfway down.

"I've seen many clearings like that. We would often sleep in them on clear nights so we could look up at the stars. I always wondered what caused them. Why did the trees grow everywhere but that one spot?"

Lira sighed. "I envy you."

"Envy *me?* You're mad..."

"You've seen so many places, though! You've *lived*. I've just..." She gestured about the room.

"You've dined with lords, been tutored by knights. You've... you live in a castle! You're a blazin' princess!"

She laughed. "It's no hardship, of course, I just... oh I must sound awful. Born to a king and I'm complaining."

"No, it's okay. I understand. To be honest, I don't know how people can stand it up here. All the vanity, the ceremony, the manners!"

Lira lit up a little, as if she'd ever longed for even the slightest pity.

"You know I've never slept outside?"

"Never?"

"Pathetic, isn't it? For a while, before that night those men attacked us, I could at least get out on the town and be normal."

"I'm sure I can sneak you out some time."

"You know, you really make me question the security of the keep."

"Isn't *security* the reason you're saying you haven't lived?"

"Now you're making me question my sanity."

The sound of a creaking hinge came suddenly from what Jeld believed to be the direction of the entry. Lira blew out the lamp at once, tugging Jeld to his feet and steering him into an even darker aisle. Soon there came the quiet murmuring of two voices. They grew louder until distinct words began to emerge, the first voice at once recognizable as Prince Dralor.

"I don't need you to give me the Idols' approval, I need you to calm the *blazing* people."

"It's difficult to lead the unwilling to the Mother's light," High Priest Naelis's voice answered. "You are a just leader, Prince. The mantle of the Idols weighs heavily, but your will is strong."

Prince Dralor grunted dismissively. "What is it you wished to show me?"

High Priest Naelis chuckled. "Patience. Yes, it is a difficult opponent we face. Discontent cannot be seen nor killed, it just *is*. But we must forgive those who seek forgiveness, welcome them with open arms."

"Thieves, vandals, arsonists, traitors," Prince Dralor spat. "My arms will not open to them."

"That is not unjust. While still they do harm to others, you do the kingdom a great favor in seeing them stopped. It is no different in war, you well know. One must not accept surrender while still his enemy holds a weapon. You can forgive only those who change their ways."

The prince said nothing. The once still light of the remaining lamp shifted and started deeper into the library, the occasional beam managing to pierce through to Jeld's hiding place as the voices and footsteps grew ever louder.

High Priest Naelis continued. "Vincet told me long ago, near the end, that defeating the mad king was easier than defeating discontent in all the years after. That at times, methods not unlike those of the mad king were discussed."

"What I'm doing and *the mad king* do not belong in the same discussion. This is justice, not madness."

"I mean only to say that your grandfather and his brethren were aware of that distinction as well in defining their methods. Too lax and the unchecked deeds of the wicked might as well be a docile leader's own doing. Too harsh and a leader is himself wicked. You and the king must find this balance."

Much to Jeld's relief, the light stayed a safe distance, the voices beginning to grow quieter as it passed by. Jeld nudged Lira toward the diminishing voices. She resisted at first before relenting with a sigh, grabbing Jeld's hand and pulling him deeper into the library in pursuit.

"My brother doesn't make this easy," the prince said. "He's weak."

"The king is... gentle. A good trait in a king, so long as he has strong counsel. A perfect pair, you two make.

"Here," Naelis added. *"Of Rule.* I think you'll find it offers many applicable insights."

"This says—my grandfather wrote this? Why have I not seen it?"

The light started back toward the entrance.

"The Idols wrote many things. And... well, while their later troubles were no secret, few would benefit from seeing how early they wrestled with such things. Anyway, quite relevant. Hard times and hard choices."

The voices faded, the door creaked, and the library fell silent.

"Fool!" Lira said. "Doesn't he get that imprisoning the city is just making the people even angrier?"

She sighed and led the way back to their clearing. "None of this makes sense anyway. How do they not see it?"

"See what?" Jeld said, pulling his sparker from his shirt and relighting the lamp.

"Nothing, just—well, Benam says it's nothing, or that there's nothing we can do about it anyway, but, it's just a theory—"

"Lira..."

"Sorry," she said, sitting at the desk. "There's just something off about all this. The poor don't mug rich people and leave their purses behind. The hungry don't leave fat pigs on the governor's doorstep. But it's more than that—why is this happening all at once? In *Of Kingdoms,* Avela Farol wrote that there's always a catalyst for this sort of thing. A thousand years, a hundred civilizations rising and falling, and there's always been a catalyst. Taxes, laws, wars... *something.*"

Jeld sat upon a cushion. "What if the people started it?"

"What? Of everyone I know, how could you blame the people?"

"No, I mean... a while back, I saw these people attack some Hilltoppers. I followed them because... well, I thought maybe it would lead back to you somehow. It turns out they were Sayers, and they've got this... *sect* trying to punish the nobility. What if the people are just getting blamed for it all?"

"The Sayers? Why would they do that?"

"Actually it perfectly fits everything they preach. Greed and gluttony and all that—begging your pardon. The Sayers usually focus on commoners, but it's worse at the top, you know?"

"The Sayers..." Lira mused.

"It's probably nothing, it—"

"Jeld, what if they're the catalyst? What if this whole time Dral has been pushing back, he's been pushing back on the wrong people? We've got to figure out what's going on."

"Can you talk to someone? The ki—your father?"

"I could, but how sure are you about this?"

"I'm sure, I..."

"Jeld?"

"It's got to be true, but, it's just that... well, I suppose I've actually only heard about it from one person. But—"

"Jeld, if I tell my father, he'll tell Dral. Dral would... No, we can't risk being wrong." She stood and started pacing. "We need to be certain so we don't get innocent people killed. So we have enough to act on... enough to convince my father—"

She spun to face Jeld. "We need to infiltrate the Sayers."

Jeld laughed.

"What?" Lira asked.

"I already did that. That's how I know about this."

"Oh. Well, we need to infiltrate them *more*. We need to be certain."

Jeld nodded. "I think it's time to dust off the old robe."

CHAPTER TWENTY-SEVEN

"**M**usta been a blazin' hundred of them greedy, lazy, whiney animals!" Sergeant Alvy shouted over his tankard.

He took a big swig and slammed the tankard down, a grizzled watchman across the table effortlessly dodging an ensuing splash.

"Gettin' bolder and bolder, they are!" the sergeant continued. "Well this street ain't your bed, and that food ain't free! And that shithole you broke into ain't your house, even if you look right at home in a shithole!"

His three companions barked out in laughter. All were dressed in the Watch uniform of dark leather and mail beneath a red tabard.

"It's like digging a hole in the sand," said a large watchman softly from beside Sergeant Alvy. "Spend all day cleaning them out, and the city just fills in with them again."

The table fell silent.

Sergeant Alvy loosed a weaselly laugh and smacked the big watchman on his shoulder. "Thank you, Corporal *Vincet!* Can always count on our watch philosopher!"

The watchmen again filled the room with laughter, the pub falling quiet in its wake.

Another voice carried in from somewhere outside. "—drink to fill a void, but only the light can fill—"

"Idols!" The ale-dodger interrupted. "I can't take it anymore, I'm going to go kill that rober bastard."

"—is no future but darkness should we stay our course of greed and gluttony and wickedness! Only we can restore decency. Only we can win back the Idols and fill with warm light the empty void within us all!"

"Yup, killing him!" the watchman added and came uneasily to his feet.

"Sit down, Donny," Sergeant Alvy said, tugging the man back into his chair. "You know we can't touch them maniacs."

"Bullshit! They're worse than a whole pub of drunks!"

"I know, I know. But we don't get paid to *like*, we get paid to *do*."

"It's to keep the peace," the large corporal said. "They are priests, Sayers or not, and if we go locking them up, the whole city will be up in arms."

"Bah!" Donny barked into his tankard. "The city is *already* up in arms. And I never met nobody that didn't hate them creepy robers. I bet if we started cleanin' them up we'd have the people kissin' our feet!"

"Alright, Donny, I'll pass your feedback to the king next time we do tea," Sergeant Alvy said, draining his tankard and coming to his feet. "I'm off. I can ignore the damn Sayer but I can't ignore your bitchin'. You boys wrap up soon."

"G'night, Sarge," Donny grumbled, the others raising their tankards in salute.

The sergeant threw a few coins on the table and started off with a smile. *Good lads*, he considered as he made his way to the door. *Even Donny.*

Emerging from the Tipsy Stool, he started toward his modest apartment. He was halfway down the block when a shout startled him. Turning, he found a young Sayer, little more than a boy, preaching to a stumbling passerby.

"Even as Tholomas cast the light upon our Five, he knew we would one day drive them away with our foulness. He knew that we would murder the Mother herself. For he knew it all to be necessary for the final peace."

Breaking off his dramatic pursuit of the drunk, the Sayer spun, his accusatory finger locking onto Sergeant Alvy.

"And now—" The boy froze as his gaze fell upon the sergeant.

The veteran watchman's eyes narrowed.

"Now... we face the darkness within!" the Sayer continued, cowering as if before some unseen enemy. "But alas! Alas we must steel our will! Face our fears! Make ready to face our final test!"

Alvy shook his head, his suspicion falling away. The kid best work on his acting if he wanted to make a career in brainwashing. Of course, he was at least smart enough to milk the robers for easy food and a dry spot, never mind a blazin' free pass to disturb the peace! Not bad for just standing around yelling.

He shook his head and continued on toward home, where he could strip off his cursed uniform and collapse upon the fine bed he'd bought with his very first sergeant's pay way back when. His thoughts were already there as he continued along the quiet streets.

***

Jeld sat before an open fire in the maze-like lower level of the sylum, unable to see the flames as anything but sword fighters dancing smoothly at bantae.

"Jeld?" Raf said.

"Hm? Oh, sorry."

"Don't be. It is only when we are not lost in flames that we are truly lost."

Just then his mentor emerged from the shadows. Raf stood, exchanging a nod with the adept and placing a hand on Jeld's shoulder.

"Really good to see you again," Raf said to Jeld, then walked off.

The adept sat across the fire.

"Good evening, Neophyte. What do you know?"

"I know that there is goodness in even the most wretched, and wickedness in even the most polished."

"That is true. What else do you know?"

"That I will never know the full truth of things."

"Wise. Do you know why the Wiseman wore black, Neophyte?"

"No, why?"

"For that very reason. Black is emptiness. Vincet wore it to show that even *he* knew nothing, not but a speck of all there is to know."

Jeld nodded into the fire.

"What you have learned may be the wisest thing there is to know. It comes as well with humility, which of course is of the path."

Jeld nodded again. *Nodding... always nodding.* How much longer could he sit and stroke the egos of old, eerie men with riddled answers and fireside nods? His mind returned to his and Lira's theory, then to boarded up shops, the Prince's Prison looming ever above, the wretched poor shuffling before the watch's sword.

"See, Neophyte? The path reveals itself to you most when *you* reveal *it* to the world. I've watched you, listened to your words. The light burns bright within you, I think."

Jeld suppressed the instinct to offer thanks. One cannot possess a compliment, just as one cannot possess a name. Or some rubbish like that.

"I am pleased to serve the light well. Still... I know I should not want for more, but I can't help but wonder if there is more I can do to serve."

"Ah. Yes... I believe you have mentioned that before."

"It's just—the crown has grown so cruel... it just seems we would do the people—the light—a disservice to ignore such cruelty and preach instead to the common drunk."

The adept frowned. "You are right, of course. Any wealth at all is a peb not given, and the crown has many. Pebs or not, they might be the most wicked of them all. But... I'm afraid our words resonate the loudest in the hearts of the... more grounded."

"Yes, I'm sure you're right."

Jeld feigned a sigh, his heart pounding as he readied his next words. Whether to prevent oppression by shutting down this secret sect, or punish oppression by joining it, it all rode on this risky next move.

"It's just... so difficult to walk among them in the palace and not pass judgment."

The adept shifted. "The palace, you say?"

"My work has brought me there oft of late."

"I see..."

"Have I upset you, Adept? I only thought my mentor should know I want to do all I can to serve the cause."

The adept said nothing, just staring gravely into the fire, concern dancing before him as plainly as the flickering flames.

Jeld opened his mouth to speak but thought better of it. *Patience*, the adept often told him. Patience.

Finally, the adept sighed. "Return in three days. Ascenday. Seventh bell. Above. I will meet you in the exarch's chamber."

***

Jeld winced as Renae's sword bit into his shoulder.

"That move of yours would have been impressive," Renae said, flipping open his mask. "Had it worked, I mean."

Jeld slapped open his own mask. "These damn bendy swords!"

"Master thy weapon at hand, mate. Where did you learn that little move anyway?"

"Saw someone do it in a fight once."

"Ahh. Poor sap."

"Well he's not dead! They weren't using flimsy swords, so it worked just fine."

"Ahh. Poor *other* sap, then. If only he'd been using a bendy sword."

Renae shook his head mournfully and had his mask halfway closed when there came a pained yelp. A small boy spilled from the next ring, crashing onto his back. The boy's opponent was quick to pursue, kicking away a fallen sword and pulling his mask off to reveal the sneering face of Calane Demerious.

Calane laughed haughtily. "You're lucky this isn't a duel or you'd be bleeding out, Hepsbry!"

He raised his sword and swung again toward the boy's ankles.

Jeld sprang forward and swung his sword down hard against Calane's hand. Calane cried out, his sword clattering to the ground. Before Calane could turn, Jeld slapped him across the back of the head, spinning his mask around. Calane struggled futilely to right his mask before ripping it off. His eyes narrowed in a venomous glare as they fell upon Jeld.

"Filthy rat! I'll have your head for this!"

"Come take it, *Cowlane.*"

Calane bent to pick up his sword, but the fallen boy grabbed it and lashed out. The blade crashed suddenly to a stop just a finger from Calane's face, another sword crossed before it.

"That'll do," Renae said, lowering his sword.

Calane snarled and threw his mask violently across the room, sending a number of people ducking and dodging out of its path before it was snatched from the air by Master Inado.

"What's going on over here!" the swordmaster snapped.

"This rat broke my hand!" Calane spat.

"You must learn to protect your hands while dueling, young sir."

"We weren't dueling, he just came over here and attacked me!"

"Is this true? Sportsmanship is of utmost—"

"Master," Jeld interrupted, "you might ask Calane if it is sportsmanlike to throw a boy to the ground and rap him across the back."

"Outrageous!" Calane snapped.

"It's true!" a small but seething voice said.

Jeld turned as the fallen boy stood and pulled off his mask. Devin Hepsbry, youngest of the Hepsbry horde, looked to Jeld and nodded.

"If this is true, your father would be most disappointed, Calane!" Master Inado said. "He was quite the fencer, you know."

Calane scowled at Devin, then at the swordmaster. "Yes, yes. I've *heard* about my father!"

"It's fine, Master. We'll just go cool down," Renae said, wrapping an arm around Devin. He flashed a dirty look at Jeld and started toward the door.

Eyeing Calane's injured hand, Jeld extended his own. "No hard feelings."

Calane scowled back before storming off.

Jeld shook his head. "I'm sorry for the trouble, Master. I only meant to help Devin."

"Most noble, young sir. You are not the one who owes an apology."

"Thank you, Master." Jeld glanced toward Renae.

"Yes, yes," the swordmaster said. "Off you go, then."

Jeld smiled and jogged after Renae and Devin.

"What in dreams were you thinking?" Renae said as the door swung closed behind them.

"You're going to scold me for protecting Devin while he's right next to you?"

"Has it ever occurred to you that there are worse things than being bullied?"

"I think what you did is great," Devin said. "Calane deserved it. Maybe now he will think twice before picking on somebody."

"So you're *both* fools!" Renae snapped. "Don't you get it? Calane might stop trying to hit you with a blunt sword, but he's just going to find something sharper!"

"Renae," Jeld said, "I think you're overestimating our dumb friend."

"Idols, how are you two still alive? This isn't about Calane, it's about House Demerious."

"What's to worry about?"

"You don't understand, relationships here can mean war or peace for entire *regions*. Lord Governor Tydel has done far worse than ruin some merchant and his nephew."

Jeld sighed. "I'm usually careful. Calane just brings out the worst in me."

"And you, Devin—you've been here plenty long enough to know better. What if I hadn't stopped you? What if Lord Tydel decided to stop doing business with your father because you slashed Calane across the face?"

Devin hung his head.

They came naturally to Sigmoore's without any need for discussion. Jeld had come to quite like the place and its fake grit. Fake grit, Jeld had decided, was better than no grit. Plus, he found food itself was far better without any grit at all. They sat at their favorite corner table, not considering it was only set for two until Devin pulled up another chair.

"I hate to be the mother, guys, but you just can't play with fire like that," Renae said.

Devin sighed. "You're right, of course. Thank you for stopping me. That would have been... bad. *Really* bad."

"You all talk about Lord Tydel like he's as bad as Calane," Jeld said.

"Oh he is. Worse. I think he's *still* bitter the Idols took his family's city. Well maybe they wouldn't have if his grandfather didn't fight for the mad blazin' king! See, it's that whole blazin' family. Runs in the blood. He's lucky the Idols let them keep their title at all."

"It was no luck," Renae said. "The Demerious army would have fallen to the Idols eventually, but not before it took many more lives. Demerious knew it, and his price for turning on the mad king was title and pardon."

"Yeah, I know," Devin said. "Doesn't mean I wouldn't have lobbed his head off if it was me. Then Calane would be better than dead."

As soon as he said it, Devin looked nervously over his shoulder. When he turned back, his nose was wrinkled in disgust.

"*Idols,* this place is foul."

"Have you *ever* been off the hill?" Jeld asked.

"More than once, I'll have you know."

"Twice, then?"

"This place is filthier than the street," Devin said, ignoring the question.

Jeld couldn't help but see a glimpse of Devin's awful mother in him. "It's not filthy, it's just dark and not made of gold. A little grit makes for better conversation."

"My father would rather I stab Calane in the eye forty times than be seen in such a place."

Jeld smiled. At least the Topper boy shared his affinity for stabbing Calane in the eye.

"Have a third today, do ya?" Sigmoore called from behind the bar, clapping a third tankard onto the counter.

"Make it a fine brew," Devin said without turning. "I owe my friends a drink."

CHAPTER TWENTY-EIGHT

J eld stared across the dining room table to Olind, managing a smile to Hamry as the old chamberlain set a tray upon the table and slipped from the room. There was something more today beyond Olind's usual coldness chilling the room, and it took no extraordinary empathy to perceive, nor even eyes. His would-be uncle's breath blew and sucked loudly through his flaring nostrils, his pen scratching fast and furiously upon a letter.

Shaking his head, Jeld snatched a steaming roll from the tray and slathered it with butter and jam. He was especially hungry this morning, having endured half the night awake in anticipation of his meeting with the exarch later. Lira had been giddy at the news. Only Olind's demeanor that morning hampered Jeld's enthusiasm.

"Something is bothering you. What is it?"

Olind offered an annoyed glance before looking back down into another letter.

"It's me, isn't it?" Jeld pressed. "I've offended you somehow. Uncle, what is it that I've done wrong?"

Olind shrunk as he did whenever Jeld called him *Uncle*, then balled his fist and snatched up another letter from the table.

"This! You. Your... *antics!*"

He shook the letter violently then threw it. When it landed atop the tray, he swatted it aside and began nervously picking at one of the rolls.

Jeld grabbed the letter and unfolded it. In a tall, flowing script somehow reminiscent of a light-footed dancer, it read:

To Sir Olind Emry,

Due to ungentlemanly conduct within the sporting ring, I regret to inform you that your nephew, Sir Arvin Emry, has been expelled from further training. Reentrance may be requested in one year's time.

Well regards,

Master Inado Allsglade

Below the swordmaster's signature was another, more lavish one that took Jeld a few tries to decipher. *Lord Tydel Demerious*, it read. At the very bottom, two final words were hastily scribbled in the prior script.

I'm sorry.

"That rotten hammy bastard," Jeld said.

He shook his head and loosed a breath of laughter. What a strange world, that his obscure, windy path might see him expelled from fencing by the lord governor of Tovar. And that said lord could actually be as petty as rumor told, no less.

Olind huffed. "I fail to see the humor in this."

"Calane did this, the blazin' bastard."

"I'm certain he did, and *you* let him! Snapping at every problem like some wild dog! You and your games. Your *ego!*"

"Uncle, he was tormenting Devin Hepsbry. I couldn't just do nothing."

"That's right, *you* couldn't! That's your problem, you don't know how to mind your own business!"

"I'm sorry. But—I think it will turn out for the best. Nobody likes the Demeriouses, but the Hepsbrys are one of the richest families in the city, and I helped one."

"Money and power are not one and the same!" Olind sighed before continuing. "You just don't understand. You'll ruin me. And—" He glanced over his shoulder. "And Krayo's absurd plan, too. You're playing with fire. Calculated, patient, vindictive, *Demerious* fire."

"I'm sorry, Olind. You're right, of course. I've been foolish."

"Yes, you have been."

"I'll not do it again, I promise."

"No, you won't. And you'll be doubly respectful in council tomorrow."

"In council? I thought you were still awaiting the king's invitation?"

"I lied. The king offered weeks ago, you've just been so reckless I've made every excuse not to bring you. But if I arrive without you now, everyone will think me weak for hiding you from Tydel. Now you *must* come, Idols help me."

***

Spotting a familiar tack shop called the Bridle and Bit through the cracked carriage shutters, Jeld's pulse quickened. He closed his eyes and took a deep breath, opening his mind to the world around. The steady clap of hooves beat with the rocking carriage, and the wheels of the wagon ground against stone and axle. Something else whispered at his awareness and he pushed out his senses, but it was as futile as flexing one's eyes to see in the dark. With another deep breath, he reached not outward but rather welcomed the sensation inward, sampling it as if upon his palette until his awareness spanned like a map about him and he recognized amidst it the familiar presence of Hamry at the reins.

Putting little trust in the practice, he waited for the carriage to near the next alley before hopping out onto the street as if merely rounding a corner. Slipping away from the wagon without so much as a nod to Hamry, he felt his usual pang of guilt. Of course, it was all part of the arrangement—discretion for a side of Olind's business best kept quiet.

His precautions felt more unnecessary with each trip down to the sylum, the streets growing ever quieter. What few people he encountered passed by with downcast gazes. He could scarcely recall the sight of children playing in the streets.

Jeld turned into an alley and pulled a black robe from his collar. His heart quickened anew as he donned the robe before venturing the remaining few blocks to the sylum. He made his way inside and to the shadowy central walk, the dim glow of countless little fires bleeding through the many archways that defined its shape. Deeper still, the archways became walls and the light faded quickly to darkness.

In the distance, a faint glow stood alone in the thick shadows like a single star in the night sky. The suggestion of a staircase began to take shape in the distant light as he pressed on. When at last he reached it, he paused in the firelight flickering down from above and listened. Faint, unintelligible voices echoed down the steps.

With a deep breath he started up the stairs, his very footfalls shifting further into character with each step. Halfway up, the sound of footsteps from above brought him to a sudden stop. They grew louder until a Sayer came into view from above, face a mask of pure shadow beneath a hood. Jeld pressed his back to the wall and the figure slunk past, the void of a face like a single hungry eye turning after him with each step before at last disappearing around the bend.

Jeld shook away an uneasy feeling and continued climbing until, over the remaining steps, he saw the staircase open into a circular chamber. Bookshelves lined most of the walls, interrupted only by several narrow doors and a desk. Jeld was surprised to see sunlight streaming in from a ring of windows above.

At the center of the room, Jeld's adept sat across the fire from another Sayer, their words just unintelligible whispers from his vantage. Jeld was surprised again to find the second man familiar somehow, though he couldn't quite place him. He let the man's face churn through his memory.

The man smiled into the fire as he mouthed more inaudible words, sending Jeld's mind darting back toward a feeling, then to a face. It was not the smile itself that was unmistakable, but the way it so starkly contrasted the emotion behind it. Even the black robes, where before the man had been neatly dressed with a white apron, did little to disguise it. This was unmistakably the proprietor of the bakery he'd once followed Raf to—one of the many cold trail ends from his sleepless nights searching for Lira.

The man turned as if noticing Jeld's alarm and their eyes met over the top of the steps. He smiled and Jeld fought back a shudder.

"Join me at the fire, won't you?" the exarch beckoned then turned back to the adept. "Thank you, Adept. You do the Idols a great favor."

"Thank you, Exarch, that is all I can hope to do."

Jeld walked inward as the adept started toward the door. When their paths crossed, the adept stopped and put a hand on Jeld's shoulder, meeting his eyes with a conflicted gaze before nodding resolutely and walking past.

"Please," the exarch said as Jeld approached. "Let us get to know one another."

The adept's footsteps echoing up the stairwell behind him, Jeld returned the exarch's smile and sat in his mentor's place.

"So, you are the young man my adept tells me so much about."

Jeld looked down into the fire. "I am but the Idols' servant."

"Yes, yes. That's what we say, isn't it?" He chuckled. "'The evils of individuality...'" Jeld blinked.

"Black and white works well for most of our colleagues. Keeps their little minds on the path, right? But I think you and I both know it isn't so simple."

Jeld forced his eyes from the fire to find the exarch staring at him.

"Yes, exactly like that," the exarch said. "Individuality is real, never mind what we often say here. Otherwise everyone would be around my fire, instead of just you."

"And everyone would have such quarters, instead of just you."

The exarch smiled. "We each have our own talents and experiences. You, for example. Quite the package, I'm told. Already teaching the path better than our eldest? Remarkable."

"It's nothing, Exarch. Theatrics."

"What are theatrics but seeing into a heart and showing it what it most needs? But... no amount of staring into fires or yelling on the streets will fix all the world's hearts, no matter how talented. We face an enemy that starts at the top, where our voices cannot reach."

"I told the adept as much—that the crown and nobility are the worst of them. Sending men warring over flags, sitting in golden castles while the people they tax haven't a peb for bread, filling gardens with fruitless shrubs while we labor to grow a meal between the king's cobblestones..."

Somewhere in the midst of his rant, Jeld had stopped acting.

"You know them for their true selves, then," the exarch said.

"I see too much of them. But I thought, maybe, I could turn that into a good thing."

"The adept told me. He was wise to. He knows you and I have this perspective in common."

"Isn't there some way we can right things?"

The exarch stared back silently, his usually conflicting demeanor aligning in a singularly hungry gaze.

"I think there may be something. But... there are others involved I must protect, so I can't too carelessly go letting people into our small circle. With you, if I'm honest, it's more a formality, but you'll humor me with a... test of loyalty, won't you?"

"It's good to know those under your wing are well protected."

The exarch smiled. "Hmm. Protocol should call for evidence that you have access to the palace, and that you can be trusted. Hmm... gold? No, if you were the king's man that would prove a simple matter. Perhaps a mission, then. Something only a genuine Sayer would carry out..."

A heavy silence lingered between them.

"Do you have others in the palace?" Jeld blurted.

The exarch stared appraisingly back before speaking. "Yes."

"Then you'll know I'm your man when you hear reports of Lord Tydel's new black eye."

The exarch returned a grave stare. Time seemed to drag on under his scrutiny until suddenly he laughed uproariously.

"*My!* Bold, but should you fail I'm afraid you'd be in no condition to try again. We'd lose this rare opportunity."

"If I fail, perhaps it was not meant to be."

"Or perhaps Demerious cuts your fingers off until you tell him about me."

"I like my fingers. I'll keep them."

The exarch let out a breath of laughter and looked down into the fire. After a few long breaths, he began to nod.

"Yes, I think you will."

━━━◆━━━

Chapter Twenty-Nine

J eld found himself staring across the massive round council table to Lord Tydel Demerious, weighing a hundred different methods for giving the man a black eye.

"They reject the crown," General Handan said firmly. "We've managed to take every other island around Caerghallad at one point or another, but when we leave they send our magistrate away, give our flag to a mother for a swaddle cloth, and go about their business."

"It would give us a place to stage a fleet in the west," Prince Dralor said.

"Unless you care to wipe every island clean and siege Caerghallad by sea, you're wasting your time."

"Perhaps that's precisely what we should do. It's unheard of to allow such a parasite to linger on a great kingdom's back. We stand to raise significant taxes, and they will benefit from our protection. All of Avandria will benefit from the stability and security such a territory would afford."

"Perhaps..." King Loris mused.

Rubbing his beard, the king tapped at the table distantly. The matching throne beside him was vacant. The air in the chamber seemed to grow thick with tension before at last the king spoke again.

"But whatever taxes we'd gain would just be spent waging a war. Anyway, I won't have us invading the Isles when we can hardly keep the lands we have under control."

Prince Dralor set his jaw. Jeld stole a glance at Lira, finding her unphased by the exchange.

"Nonetheless," King Loris added, "we should always be prepared. General, would you see that occupation plans are updated, as well as our defensive scenarios pertaining to the Isles?"

"Yes, Your Highness."

The plump little Chancellor Cerus cleared his throat after a conclusive silence. "The... next order of business then, Your Highness. Sir Lasken on the state of the... unrest."

King Loris nodded.

"Your Highness," Lasken said. "We have fully deployed all of our bolstered ranks. We've concentrated our efforts on public gathering places—the markets, main avenues, ports. The gates, of course. I'm pleased to report that the observation deck at the new prison is complete, however the cells are... ah, full, Your Highness. We've been quite thorough with our sweeps."

Jeld's cheek twitched as he fought to hold a scowl at bay.

"Full?" King Loris asked. "Already?"

"Most efficient, Commander," Prince Dralor said. "Empty space would just mean it took longer to find the people who should occupy it. So long as there is crime, it's *empty* cells we should be worried about."

The king stared gravely down at the table. "And what shall we do with any new prisoners?"

Sir Lasken looked over to Prince Dralor, who offered a short nod.

"A prison camp," Lasken said. "It will surround the new tower. Much cheaper to construct. Easier to scale. And it will have industry. The city will have a free labor source for cutting bricks from the quarry rock, processing fish, or whatever the case. I mean to say, it could offset its own cost."

"Your Highness, if I may?" Sir Benam asked, continuing nonetheless. "The prisons are not full of murderers and rapists, but of beggars and street dwellers. You are hesitant to abandon this barbarous approach so far along, I think, but far along is never a good reason to continue a faulty pursuit. And *industry?* Such a practice has another name—*slavery*. Mercy, Your Highness. Be a king of the people again."

"Your words are always most moving," Prince Dralor said, "but the king *remains* a king of the people, just as he was when first the commoners turned unruly—*before* we employed any of the methods you like to blame, you'd do well to remember."

"Your Highness, you—"

"There are *serpents* among us. There are serpents, and they harm Tovar's people, and our order. This is not some child's tale in which love might stay their strikes!" The prince took a breath and shook his head. "I commend your compassion, but naivety—righteous as it may sound—will not restore order. We need to lock this city down, deploy our army, restore order before it's too late. Finish this and turn our attention back to the whole of Avandria."

"Compassion motivates us both, Your Grace," Sir Benam said, even his legendary patience showing wear. "It is *methods* upon which we disagree. A city is not a battlefield, won by might. A city is a beating heart, won like a friend or a lover."

"Perhaps flowers and poetry, then?" Prince Dralor shouted.

"Come now, my friends," High Priest Naelis said. "Indeed the city is like a loved one, for nothing wounds us like rejection... *twists* our emotions every which way. But let us not forget that we fight a war greater than ourselves. Individually our lives are too small for the eyes of this war's titans to even behold, but together as a kingdom we have a place on the battlefield beside the Idols. If we let the city fall to those whose minds have been corrupted, we lose ground to Discord. We must love, but in loving we must protect."

King Loris's eyes darted back and forth across the surface of the table before at last looking up to Sir Lasken.

"Keep me apprised, Commander."

Sir Benam's eyes fell closed, the weight of his sorrow nearly drawing tears to Jeld's eyes.

"Of course, Your Highness," Lasken said with a bow.

Chancellor Cerus cleared his throat and looked around the table. "Onward, then. Sir Brayold with the counts."

A portly man with a ring of disorderly gray hair shuffled several documents, his pointed beard twitching as he pursed his lips before at last speaking.

"Your Highness. Tax counts are indeed in, and we're nearing our final tallies. We... ah, even if we consider outstanding numbers, it seems unlikely we will come within even, perhaps... fifty percent of last year's total."

Olind gasped.

"Fifty percent?" King Loris said. "Sir Olind, didn't you say prices were generally up?"

"Yes, Your Highness," Olind said. "Prices on commodities are up a bit, but little else is even changing hands. That is to say, people are not buying anything but the bare essentials. Also, in times of depression, people have historically taken less kindly to taxation and thus evaded, or merely begun doing so out of desperation. And as buying is down, so too is importing, which—"

"This system is rubbish," Lord Tydel snapped. "For years, through good and bad, the kingdom taxed landowners alone, not traders at the gates. Tax milk at the cow, not by chasing every blazing bladder of it across the kingdom. The current economic state was irrelevant. If milk was being made in Avandria, or steel or lumber or wheat, the crown collected its dues."

Several new black eye ideas were running through Jeld's imagination by the time the rant concluded and Olind cleared his throat.

"Go on, Olind," the king said.

"My Lord Tydel is wise to suggest changes to simplify and guarantee collection at a time such as this. However, I must caution the council that even today's abysmal count is far higher than any in the life of that system. Perhaps we should... draw inspiration from Lord Tydel's wisdom, to craft a solution more appropriate to our current troubles."

The king nodded. "We need a solution. A growing kingdom cannot afford a shrinking purse."

Sir Brayold held up two documents. "Your Highness, I have calculated two courses of action. Our largest sources are still reporting, so increasing our rate on them by a mere ten percent will almost cover our other losses. Our other option is to improve our auditing and go after those with illegitimate revenue drop-offs from last year."

"Try the latter. If we raise taxes any more, the people will tax our heads. Plus, the law abiding should not suffer for the crimes of the evaders."

"Very good, Your Highness."

Chancellor Cerus cleared his throat. And so the council went, for nearly four bells.

***

Jeld ducked Lira's blade, eyes tracking it as it passed just inches overhead before turning toward the back of his neck. He spun and the blow crashed at once against his sword. Now inside her guard, he charged inward, turning the edge of his blade out toward her throat as it slid free.

Lira jumped aside, spinning her sword overhead then down at Jeld's back as he passed. Jeld spun with a counter and their swords locked between them. Circling, they stared past crossed swords into each other's eyes. Sweat poured down Jeld's forehead as he considered his next move. After nearly two full circles, he let his sword begin to give under the weight of Lira's attack and slid his hand down the back of his sword as if to support it. When his charade brought his hand near the tip of her sword, he grabbed it then pulled his sword free and struck her chest.

"Good," General Handan said. "Very good exchange. You are both watching now instead of hoping."

Lira tugged her sword free and swatted Jeld's hand aside. "That would *never* work with a real sword!"

Jeld shrugged. "You're dangerous, sacrificing a finger might be worth it."

"It happens," the general agreed. "You can't fight by rules. Desperate people do desperate things. I've seen better ideas fail and worse ideas succeed."

General Handan picked up a practice sword from the rack and swept it defensively before him.

"Remember that moving your sword around your body is slow. And moving your body around your sword is even slower. Do *both*."

The general swept his upraised sword one way and shuffled the other, placing himself behind his weapon almost at once.

A knocking came from outside the dueling chamber.

"Take a break," Handan said and jogged from the room. "What news?" his voice came before the door creaked closed behind it.

Jeld turned to Lira. "I had a nice little chat with the exarch."

"What did you—tell me more!"

"It's all true. It's them."

Lira's eyes went wide. "For sure? You heard it from him?"

"Well, I don't know *exactly* what they're doing, but the exarch is definitely operating against the crown. Or against Hilltoppers, anyway."

"That's... a good step."

"It's solid! He's behind the crime wave. Basically said as much himself." Jeld shook his head. "I was so close before. I once followed a Sayer I'd caught mugging Hilltoppers to a meeting with the exarch, only at the time I'd thought he was just some baker."

"A baker?"

"They met in some bakery. He owned it, I think. Nice place, line almost out the door."

Jeld pictured the sign hanging outside the bakery, upon it the likeness of an armored man working a pile of dough.

"The Kneading Knight," he realized with a chuckle. "It was just so loud inside I couldn't—"

"J—Arvin!" Lira gasped.

"What?"

"The *knight in need!* That's what Kaid said, right? About the slavers?"

"The wha—"

Jeld's words halted. Of course the Sayers sect meant to do the crown harm, but somehow this was different. It was they who'd attacked Lira and seen her dragged from his life.

"The Sayers tried to abduct me..." Lira mused.

Jeld's mouth opened and closed wordlessly. Finally, he set his jaw and spoke.

"You need to tell someone."

It would ruin everything, of course, but sparing the people the crown's wrath would do them far better than whatever else he could hope to accomplish here, black eyes or otherwise.

"I... want to, but we can't," Lira said.

"What? But this is your catalyst! This is tearing up the city! Tell your uncle. He might be half of the problem, but he's also the only one who can fix it. There's no way he wouldn't act on this."

"Oh he would act. Well, if he believed us, but yes he would act. He'd tear the man's head right off."

"I could be proof. Tell him you enlisted my help—*Arvin's* help—to investigate."

"You're missing the point. We can't tell him precisely *because* he'll act. The Sayers may have started it, but thanks to Dral the people really *are* rising up. Imagine what they would do if he rode down the hill and massacred a bunch of priests!"

Jeld prodded the ground with his sword. "Well we have to do something."

"We could tell Benam. Not to convince my father, just for guidance. I told him my theory, you know, and this will prove it!"

"As in your father's best friend? As in, *can't-tell-a-lie* Sir Benam?"

"He doesn't have to lie, he just has to keep a secret. Besides, I'll make him promise not to tell, and he won't break a promise."

Jeld stared skeptically back.

"He's the wisest man I know," Lira added. "He'll know how to deal with Dral, how to deal with the Sayers... how to restore order. He'll know what to do."

"Oh fine. Tell him if you must, but leave me out of it. And Arvin too."

"See, now we'll have an ally! But you have to keep digging. Keep building trust. We need to know more. We need to see how wide this web stretches if we're to stop it."

"In the works," Jeld said with a grin. "I told the exarch I work in the palace."

Lira gasped.

"Don't worry, he just thinks I'm a servant. Anyway, he gave me a little task to prove he can trust me. I'm to give Lord Tydel a black eye."

Lira's eyes narrowed. "He gave you this task, did he?"

"Well, he approved it, anyway "

A creak came from the next room and a moment later General Handan entered the chamber, a vexed look upon his face. He took a deep breath and spun his training sword to the ready, a calm washing clear his troubles as he looked down the back of his blade.

"Alright," the general said. "Let's see how you two fare today."

Chapter Thirty

Jeld let his eyes trace an ornate carving around the perimeter of the wood-paneled ceiling. Where Olind's sitting room was crammed with luxuries, the sitting room of Lord Tydel Demerious was *itself* luxurious. The very walls and windows, marble floors and carved ceiling, all of intricate craftsmanship. He turned his attention to a tall window, in particular the latch mechanism he'd face should he need to make an unannounced visit. Bad as it seemed, he had yet to formulate any better idea than burglary for delivering the black eye Tydel had long been begging for.

The door behind him swung open and the old but prim-postured chamberlain who had seen Jeld in appeared in the doorway.

"Sir Arvin, Lord Tydel will see you now, if you please."

"Excellent, thank you."

Jeld followed the chamberlain out and across a luxurious great room to a door flanked on either side by imposing, life-like suits of armor. Each held at its waist a sword that rose to pass before the vacant eye of a helm topping it. The plinth upon which one sat had a smashed corner, a matching dent in the door where the two might meet.

A shout echoed down the polished floors of a nearby hallway and Jeld gritted his teeth as the familiar voice brought to mind the face of Calane Demerious. The laughter of another boy followed after it.

The chamberlain knocked on the door.

"Enter," came Lord Tydel's voice, sounding even more annoyed than usual.

Jeld swallowed hard as the chamberlain pulled the door open. Behind a broad desk of polished wood, a window framed in bookshelves provided a view of the gardens to all but the very man seated before it. Lord Tydel didn't look up as Jeld entered.

Jeld was only a few steps in when he heard the door close behind him, his host seeming still not to have noticed. He continued inward and stopped in front of a vacant chair centered before the desk. His nerves gave way to anger as he stood ignored until, able to bear it no longer, he sucked in a breath to speak.

"You wished to discuss something?" Lord Tydel said, looking up at last.

"Not discuss, my lord. I—"

Calane's muffled shout came again, barely audible through the closed door. Lord Tydel flinched, his jaw clenching until the voice subsided.

"I... only want to apologize," Jeld continued. "I was wrong to fight Calane. He may have deserved it, but it's not my place to disrespect you and your noble house by doing what I did."

"No. It most certainly is not your place."

"Not that you need my approval by any means, but I think your reaction is just. A bold statement that you and your affairs are not to be trifled with."

Lord Tydel just stared back coolly. Another muffled shout broke the silence and he gritted his teeth.

"It seems you have the gist of it," Tyden said with a short nod. "It's good to see that your generation has at least one person with a mostly developed brain. Very well, I'll pen a note to Inado to have you reinstated in four weeks."

Lord Tydel slid a fresh parchment onto the desk and dipped his quill.

"You are very kind, my lord, but I only meant to pay my respect. Your punishment is fair and deserved."

"Ah. I see. Why go back when you've got Handan teaching you proper swordplay."

Jeld hid his surprise. "I like the practicality of the sword. Fencing teaches the fundamentals nicely, though. My limited time with Master Inado helped me no small amount. I'm told you were quite an exceptional fencer?"

"It is a good sport. My instructor said I could have made something of it, but my father did not care for sport and busied me instead with house matters."

"I assume those skills better befit your station."

"Yes, for the most part. Until we lords find ourselves in front armies. Then, the fencing seems quite practical."

"Of course. Well, I don't mean to dismiss myself, but I know you are a busy man."

"Very well. Take your leave."

"Thank you for seeing me, my lord."

"Good day," Lord Tydel said without pretense and turned back to his work.

"Good day, my lord."

Jeld hurried from the room, closing the door behind him. Another of Calane's shouts echoed down the hall and Jeld pictured Lord Tydel gritting his teeth. His eyes fought their way to one of the armored statues as he tried and failed to shake a miserable idea from his mind. With a quick glance about the room, he sighed, pressed his back to the plinth of one of the statues, and let a character play out in his head until soon he was enveloped in a perfect veil of petulant jackassery.

***

Not so bad for a lowborn boy, Tydel Demerious mused as he peeked from a blank parchment to the closing door. A bit too confident, perhaps, but that would do the boy well in later years if he survived long enough.

"Hey, rat!" Calane's voice called from the next room.

Feeling his pulse throb in his neck, Tydel closed his eyes and took a deep breath. *Idols, let the Emry boy break Calane's other hand.*

"Ow—hey!" came the Emry boy's voice. "Calane, stop, I—"

A deafening crash erupted outside and Tydel snapped to his feet, his nostrils flaring. Crossing the room in an instant, he threw his weight against the door and shouted.

"Cala—!"

Pain exploded at the base of his nose and he staggered backward as the door slammed back into him. Doubled over, Tydel stared through ringing silence in the cacophony's wake to the blurry and spinning marble floor. Blood slapped against the surface, and a more frantic slap of footsteps faded into the distance.

Tydel righted his posture, set his jaw, and pressed his shoulder to the door. With great resistance and a terrible screeching, it gave way. Peering through the gap, his jaw clenched harder still at the sight of one of his great grandfather's knights lying scattered across the floor. He stepped over it and looked up to find Calane staring dumbly back. Tydel's already swelling face twisted painfully into a venomous scowl.

CHAPTER THIRTY-ONE

A heavy boot splashed into the mud beside a large sunken hoof. Water streamed down from a dark cloak into countless black pools filling the ravaged ground, setting dancing the many reflections of a lantern dangling at the figure's side. Though scant light pierced the thick shadows beneath the traveler's hood, two green eyes shined bright and warm against the cold night.

Before the figure stood a broad gate of thick iron, a wall thrice his height running into the night to either side. The traveler stared through the gate into the darkness beyond. Light from torches mounted high up the walls within pierced just enough to catch the edges of countless barracks running in a perfect grid as far as he could see.

A heavy weight, felt more than seen, pressed down from above. To the eye it was a void of perfect darkness high above where instead there should be the brighter black of night clouds. To the heart, it was hopelessness. The traveler remained there before the wall, beneath the rains and the oppressive shadow pressing down against his spirit like some great encumbering burden. Beside him, Myr whinnied uneasily.

The lantern lit the man's breaths as his shoulders rose and fell in a solemn cadence, until finally, in a billow of hot breath, his shoulders stayed tall and his heel sucked free of the mud. He turned from the gate and started toward a single door set into the wall beside it. Myr followed closely behind even before her guide rope was taut, mud splashing up with each step to cover what few white spots of hair the rain had managed to uncover.

He tied his mount off beside the door then raised a balled fist to knock before setting his jaw and barging in instead. Across the small room within, a wiry watchman behind a barred window looked up from a steaming cup. The traveler lowered his hood. Short locks of gray hair snaked down his wet forehead. His green eyes, though warm, were tired.

A smug grin as if of some untold joke bent up toward the corners of the watchman's droopy eyes.

"Good evening again, Sir Benam," the watchman said.

"Good evening. Kindly see me in, please."

"Can't help ya this time, sir. Nobody's to enter. Or leave, of course. Heh. New orders from the prince."

Benam stared back coolly.

"Of course, there may be other ways in...."

"Oh? How do you mean?"

The watchman only blinked then fought back a grin.

"Watchman, I asked you a question."

"Never mind, sir."

"You want a bribe! That's what you mean, isn't it?"

"Of course not! Just... trying to think of ways to help you out, sir."

"We have no place for corruption in our city, watchman. I should have you stripped of rank for this."

The watchman's smirk vanished and he jumped to his feet. "Sir, I didn't mean that at all! Actually... you know what, I think we both know the prince must not have intended for his new rule to keep *you* out, of all people!"

He hurried from view then reappeared behind a barred door with a keyring in hand. Turning the lock over, he swung the door open and waved Benam past.

"Come along, sir. Come by any time and I'll let ya right in. Except Ascendays, as I'm not in. Of course, I'll come in if ya like..."

Benam glared at the watchman. As if soliciting a bribe were not bad enough, now this wretched watchman had the audacity to disregard a direct order from the prince by letting him through! With a sigh, he shook his mind from its moral grappling and walked through the door. Lives were at stake. Nothing else mattered.

The door crashed closed behind him, sending a cold shiver running down his spine as he continued down the narrow corridor toward a wooden door. He pulled it open and the night rushed in through another barred door just beyond.

"Clear south door!" the watchman called from just behind him.

"South door clear!" a voice answered a moment later.

Brushing past, the watchman peered out then unlocked the door and swung it open.

"Come on, sir. These dogs aren't keen to stay in their kennel."

Benam stopped within the open doorway and turned an icy stare upon the man.

The watchman's eyes flicked nervously out into the darkness. "Sir, we really—"

"We are *all* in cages, watchman. You too are a dog to those outside it."

Benam turned and walked out into the night, the gate closing behind him at once. Rain beat upon his forehead and he made to raise his hood before letting his hands fall and continuing uncovered toward a row of barracks. He came to a stop at the mouth of a central walk, barracks lining either side as it ran into the night. The dark weight loomed still in the sky above.

He started down the walk. Steam seeped between the boards of the crudely constructed barracks walls. A hushed murmur of breath filled what small silences punctuated the rain and wind. As he passed by each row of buildings, another appeared in the distance. By the tenth row, the weight above had grown heavier and the shadow wider. After the twentieth the sky was completely dominated by it. Beyond the thirtieth, Benam came to the base of a massive tower, the grid of barracks continuing in every direction around it.

He began to circle the tower toward the northeast quadrant. Despite his numerous visits he had not yet reached the sector, having always found too many in need along the way. When the dark, wet stone of the tower was within reach, he let his fingertips brush the bricks as he walked. Something gave him pause and he turned to face the tower, pressing his hand solidly against the wet stone. His eyes grew distant until a shiver ran down his spine and he jerked his hand back.

Pulling his cloak tighter, he turned away and took a single step before sucking in a breath, his hand reaching for a hilt that hadn't been there in many years. A figure in a long white cloak stood just before him, head cocked to the side with only a vacant frown visible beneath his hood.

"Knight," the man said coolly.

Benam glared back. "Inquisitor."

"You waste your time," the man said, his words thick with an Eastern accent.

"My time is not my own."

"Your dedication shines brightly, but your charity is misplaced. The Mother has greater needs for your service."

"You presume to know the Mother's will? You who keeps men and women and children locked away in filth and bondage?"

"Justice done upon the wicked is as love upon the pure."

"I sense but few wicked here."

Benam started past but a hand shot out from beneath the man's cloak with unnatural speed to hover like a claw over his chest.

"You have no business here, knight."

Benam fought to keep from looking down at the claw that seemed to grip his pounding heart. When his eyes fell upon the endless rows of barracks, his brow narrowed sharply.

"Step. Aside!" Benam shouted through clenched teeth.

Beneath the raised hood, the edges of the inquisitor's mouth seemed to turn downward.

Benam felt the inquisitor's fingertips press lightly against his chest and sweat beaded on his already-wet forehead. Even so, as he stared the man down his fear and anger both gave way to pity. How misguided. How misled these shadows of men that haunted the prison. What must have befallen them to empty them so, he wondered.

The inquisitor recoiled. He met Benam's glistening eyes once more before turning quickly away and stalking off into the night.

Benam sucked in a quavering breath as he stared after the man. Shaking his head, he gave the tower a last lingering pat before continuing toward a wider road that marked at last the border of the northeast quadrant. Just steps down the road, a distant shout from behind broke through the night and brought him to a stop. Looking mournfully into the northeast quadrant, Benam sighed and slipped between a row of barracks back to the south.

The sound soon came again—not a shout, but a cough—and he quickened his pace. Then again, just ahead. He went toward it and held his ear before the loosely fixed boards of a barracks. After several blinks there came a terrible raspy cough from just inside.

He circled the building to a door that was little more than a few of the same misshapen boards hanging crookedly by worn leather straps. Gently pulling the door open, he stepped inside. A chorus of slow, dry breaths greeted him through the darkness. The air was thick with the putrid scent of life at its most reduced. It was both sickly and familiar, a smell he'd once made every effort to escape.

Benam blinked away memories of grisly battlefields and pulled off his cloak. Catching himself looking about for a clean place to hang his cloak, he pointedly let it fall to the muddy floor. He made a fruitless effort to scrape his boots off and followed another cough down a narrow aisle, bunks three high passing by to either side.

A raspy breath brought him to a stop. Setting his lantern on the ground, he squeezed into a miniscule space between two bunks and looked about the six slumbering men packing it. On the lowest bunk lay a man curled in a ball beneath a ragged blanket, his closed eyes fluttering restlessly with his erratic breath. His skin was darkened by sun but not yet leathered, and like so many others in the prison his beard was just long enough to safely trim with sharp rocks.

Benam carefully sat upon the bedside and put the back of his hand to the man's forehead. He closed his eyes and let the man's ailments speak to him. Heat and a sticky sweat pressed against his hand. A noxious odor stowed away in the man's breath. Then came the cough again, wet at the top but dry and wheezing at the bottom. With a silent whisper to the Mother that his own strength be given the poor man, Benam began to hum a low tune as he took in the man's pains.

Continuing his song, he pulled a small wooden box out of a bag slung at his side and plucked from it a small vial of greenish-brown flakes. Closing his box, he froze save for his unbroken song, the room having gone otherwise silent. Turning slowly over his shoulder, he found a dozen faces staring out at him from bunks high and low, the aisle packed with still more men. Young and old, tired and ragged, each stared in wonder.

Benam nodded to the onlookers and turned back to his patient to find the man's eyes upon him.

"Hello, friend," Benam whispered, but the man only stared back.

"It's alright, friend. I've some things to get you right."

Benam unstoppered his waterskin and held it out to the man.

"Fresh water?"

The man's eyes flicked between Benam's and the waterskin several times before he struggled upright with a pained groan and took it. He cautiously raised it to his chapped lips and drank, slowly at first, then voraciously.

"Easy there. Easy. Forgive me, I beg you, but there are so many thirsty here."

The man's grip loosened.

"What's your name, sir?" Benam asked.

The man's eyes fell away and seemed to wander.

"Yence," he said at last, almost a question.

"Mine is Benam. Good to know you, Yence."

The man looked up at him again. The fear had disappeared from his eyes and a different man stared back—a man named Yence. Yence nodded.

Benam produced a chunk of bread from his bag, splashed it with water, and dropped a pinch of green flakes from the vial onto it.

"I think you can beat this, friend Yence, but you need the help of medicine. One pinch, twice each day. With food, if you can. If not, just drop it on your tongue and swallow. Understand?"

Yence nodded.

"Good, my friend. Here, eat this."

"Thank you. Thank you, sir."

Taking the bread, Yence devoured several bites before freezing and looking about at the many watching faces.

"Give it to another," he said through a mouth full of bread.

"Most noble, sir, but you must eat it."

"Please."

"Andlock will help you, but it will only harm them. I'm sorry, but you must."

With another look about the room, Yence nodded and took another bite.

Benam smiled. "Rest easy knowing that at life's hardest it still pained you more to take than to give."

He took Yence's hand and pressed the vial into it.

"Take care, good Yence. Survive and share your strength and kindness with the world around you."

Tears welled up in Yence's eyes. "Thank you."

Benam fought back the urge to protest. What thanks had he earned? Despite having the king's ear, what had he managed? To comfort a handful of the dying? To tend some few stricken ill? But out of how many? How had he failed so to convince Loris?

He smiled warmly to Yence despite his woes. What else could he do? With Andlock already working its mischievous way through the man's veins, all he had left to offer was hope. If a kindly smile offered a sliver of hope, then by the Idols he could spare a thousand more. Standing, he turned to face the others.

"Hello, friends."

A bald, stern-faced man pushed his way to the front of the gathering. "Who are you? What are you doing here?"

"Save your fight, friend," Benam said. "You'll need it, but not for me. Tell me, friend, who are the sickest among you? Who can I help the most?"

"The women," another man said quickly. "They're in Third, I think."

Benam nodded. "They are, yes, and I will. But who *here* is in need?"

"Who are you, I said!" demanded the bald man.

"He's the one they all speak of, Arnelt!" called a young man barely more than a boy. "The one Hamar told of. The healer who comes out of the night."

"Oh no, son. Nothing so spectacular as that," Benam said. "I am only a healer with sway enough to enter, if just barely." He turned to the bald man. "If you think I do the bidding of this place, you need only open your eyes and look upon me again."

Arnelt opened his mouth but only closed it again.

"Tomisch needs you," the young one said. "His cut. It was only a small wound from the brickyard, but it's all festered now. You can help him, can't you? You're the healer Hamar spoke of, right?"

Benam nearly began to protest before stopping himself short. *Hope.*

"Yes, young sir. I can help."

Long do I dream now. Even in wakefulness my mind is in the Halls, some foreign shell of me left walking Avandria. I dread this wonderous place, where once I was whole. Every quiet corner and warm hearth is a reminder of dear lost Syladrya and our treasured talks. My other beloved brethren remain, yet I must distance myself, lest I be unable to do what must be done next.

—Vincet Ellemere

CHAPTER THIRTY-TWO

S moke rose from the fire before Jeld to crawl along the ceiling of the exarch's chamber and cascade from the high windows like some black waterfall.

"They are monstrous, be it in oblivion, apathy, or intent," the exarch said from across the fire.

Jeld nodded. "I wish I could give them *all* black eyes."

The exarch raised an eyebrow. "Broken noses, you mean?"

"Close enough. The bruising *did* nearly reach his eye. I wonder... when they waged war to defend the values of the Idols, was it a lie then? Or have they just changed?"

"What does your heart tell you?"

Jeld looked for answers in the fire dancing between them at the center of the exarch's chamber. "I think they lost their way. It's easy for the warm and full-bellied to forget."

"I think you are wise. Yes, it's in our nature to fight for more, but it takes an extraordinary person to fight for less."

"It's true," Jeld said. "Already I sometimes find myself growing too comfortable, taking things for granted."

"Already?"

Jeld silently cursed himself for forgetting his role. "At so young an age, I mean. Hilltop masks problems of survival and freedom with struggles of wardrobe and palate. I promise, I will not let myself be spoiled so."

The exarch smiled hungrily. "I have no doubt you'll do great with—"

An agonized scream echoed up the stairwell into the chamber. The crashing and shouting of men at arms erupted in its wake.

Jeld jumped to his feet. "We've got to get you out of here!"

The exarch stood and pulled a dagger from his robe. "I think not. There's no way out."

Jeld turned as another terrible cry echoed up the stairs. His other sense reeled beneath an onslaught of horror pouring from those below, but there was something else amidst the sensation... a sinister chill, only it seemed to come from—

He spun as a glimmer of steel flashed toward him. Jeld jumped back but it was too late. He cried out as the exarch's dagger bit into his side. The dagger came away glistening red as his own momentum pulled him free of it. Staggering back, Jeld scrambled aside to put the fire between him and the exarch.

"I'm sorry, but they can't know we have infiltrated the palace," the exarch said, stalking around the fire. "It puts the others at risk. We must give our lives to the light, else the crown force the truth from us."

Jeld reached his hand into his robe on his injured side, wincing in pain and staggering aside. Seizing the moment, the exarch dashed around the fire and lashed out with his dagger. Catching the exarch's wrist, Jeld darted inside his guard and slammed into him.

The exarch sucked in a sharp breath, his dagger tumbling to the ground with a clatter barely heard over the melee below. Falling to his knees, his eyes landed on a bloody blade protruding from Jeld's robe and he collapsed to the ground, motionless.

Not sparing the exarch another glance, Jeld pulled his robe off and sawed a strip from it, hastily tying a bandage atop his blood-soaked tunic. He groaned as he cinched the knot, the room spinning and seeming to fall into the distance. Terrible screams, still louder than before, set the maniacal scene with such perfection that it could only be a nightmare.

Anchoring his gaze upon a flickering torch to steady the spinning pandemonium, an idea struck Jeld. He threw what remained of his robe into the fire and traded his still-wet blade for a length of rope from his bottomless bag. Jeld ripped the flattened bag free, drew it back into some semblance of a bag, and stuffed it into his pants lest it be looted. Staggering, he started toward the torch with the rope in hand.

Not halfway across the room Jeld's knees buckled and he spilled onto the cold stone floor. He dragged himself across the floor and clawed his way up the wall, throwing the torch aside and threading his rope through its ring. The clink of armored footsteps sounded from the stairs as he set desperately to binding his hands overhead. The steps grew louder. He cinched a final knot with the last of his strength and went limp just as knights armored in the king's colors spilled into the room. Somewhere in Jeld's lingering consciousness he audited his character. *Prisoner. Defeated. Injured. Bleeding. Slipping away. Slipping away. Slipping away.* A humorless laugh escaped his lips. His final role, a dead man pretending to die.

"Another rober here!" one of the knights yelled. "He's... dead."

"Dagger right in his blazin' heart," another said.

The shadows deepened and Jeld's eyes fell shut, his body sagging further along the wall.

"Killed himself?"

"Blazin' fanatics."

"Another here!"

"A prisoner? He alive?"

"Breathing. Barely. He's bleeding bad."

"Don't just stand there. See to his wounds and get him outside! He may know something."

Jeld felt strong hands upon him, a sense of floating, and then nothing.

CHAPTER THIRTY-THREE

L ira stood beside the bar in the radiant royal ballroom. She turned and her eyes met Jeld's. Her whole face smiled and she reached out her hand to him...

Jeld took her warm hand and led her through the darkness of the understage. A hushed song hummed through the walls from the orchestra pit, a lone familiar voice among it singing a low, warming tune. They watched from the nook beneath the box seats as a huge door opened upon the stage and light spilled from within...

The faces of Jeld's friends were alight with the perfect, warm glow of the pub. A smaller, peppier jig played from nowhere in particular, the same familiar voice continuing harmoniously behind it. Lira and Fen wore big smiles as Roba told an animated story...

A hand gripped Jeld's shoulder and he turned to find Krayo holding a long knife out to him by its tip. A coin purse sat on the table between them. Jeld took both and peered down into the purse, falling into the cold, empty void within...

Darkness only, and silence save for the same distant song. A metallic plink broke the relative silence and a gold coin gleamed brightly against the darkness. He looked up from his bowl to a young girl with warm, curious eyes. Her father whisked her away and all warmth left with her. Jeld shivered where he lay atop the cold ground and watched the boots of a thousand travelers pass by around him. One stopped just before him and in its sheen he saw Quintem's face staring back...

A buffer brush flew by and kissed the side of the boot. Old Cobb dipped the brush and held it out before Niya and Jeld. Niya stared intently at Cobb as his mouth moved ever in lessons. She looked to Jeld and her eyes went wide as the reflection of a bandit appeared suddenly within them. Jeld spun and lashed out with his sword. Quintem collapsed lifelessly atop him, throwing him to the ground and enveloping him in darkness...

The comforting presence of his wagon overhead seemed to press down on him in a warm embrace. Rolling onto his side, he looked out at the thin strip of stars pressed between the darkness of the horizon below and underside of his wagon above. The stars grew brighter and brighter until they cut the darkness in a solid band of white light. The strip of light widened, pushing the darkness away. In the light something began to take shape.

The distant song stopped and another sound came. A man's voice, clear enough but somehow indiscernible. The sounds of the voice did not change, but rather began somehow to make sense, to resemble words.

"Arvin? Arvin?"

Colors and lines converged into focus until suddenly Jeld recognized the face of Sir Benam.

"Welcome back, Arvin."

Hamry's face came into view behind him.

"Fine to see you, young sir," Hamry said. "I'll go inform your uncle."

Watching Hamry go, Jeld took in his surroundings. The bed was thick with fine dressings, the walls hung with tapestries. An open window framed a square of perfect blue sky. His sluggish mind raced to place his whereabouts. Not only that, but how had he come to be here? Why couldn't he remember? Panic rose up within him. He tried to push himself upright but pain exploded from his side and a memory flashed in his mind—the exarch lashed out, a dagger biting into his side. Jeld slumped back into the bed as a flood of memories bombarded him.

"Easy there," Sir Benam said. "You'll pull out your sutures."

"The Sayers..."

Jeld shivered and put a hand to his side, finding it thickly bandaged.

"You're safe now," Sir Benam said.

"How did you all find me?"

Benam's eyes fell. "The Sayers were... found to be organizing crimes against the people and the crown. The prince ordered a raid."

"The exarch spoke openly about such plots. I... don't think he ever intended that I leave."

Benam sighed. "At least some good came out of this atrocity, then. Quite a scar you'll have, mind you. Had us quite worried for a while there. Liraelle was... well, that girl cares quite a lot, I'll say."

"Atrocity, you said?"

"Well they certainly weren't *all* culpable. A small few, maybe, but even they deserved better."

"He killed them all..." Jeld breathed. He thought of Raf.

Sir Benam nodded, his gaze dropping to the floor.

"I didn't think I would make it," Jeld said. "I don't know how you saved me."

Sir Benam patted Jeld on the shoulder. "You'll be just fine. If you're careful to take good care of that wound, mind you. I gave instructions to your man. Hamry, wasn't it?"

The door swung open and Renae entered, a grin stretching across his face.

Sir Benam gave Jeld another pat and stood. "I'll leave you two. Do as Hamry will tell you. Remember, add *more* bandages, don't rip off the old ones yet. I don't care if it gets so thick you can't even fit your shirt. Rest up, Arvin."

Suddenly Jeld sucked in a breath, bringing a flash of pain to his side.

"What is it, son? Are you alright?"

"Er, yes. Fine. Sorry. It's... my things. Do you know where my things are?"

"Ah. There was nothing, I'm afraid. I assume the Sayers took anything of worth."

Jeld's guts wrenched. "My... my bag, sir?"

Benam shook his head. "Empty, I'm afraid."

"Empty!" Jeld laughed. "Is—it wasn't thrown out, was it?"

"Ah, no... it was given with your clothes to Hamry."

Jeld let out a breath. "Ahh. Excellent. Thank you. Sentimental, is all."

"I can appreciate a man who values a purse more than its contents." With a warm smile, he turned and started away.

Renae nodded to Benam as he passed by, then began shaking his head and started toward the bed.

"You ever start to wonder if, just maybe, the reason you attract trouble is because you invite it?"

Jeld grinned. "How was I to know that the Sayers were covertly engaged in a war against the privileged and would abduct and nearly murder me for my vast exploits against the common folk?"

Renae snickered and sat at Jeld's side. "You are so very oppressive. And influential. You have pretty much single-handedly waged the war of classes."

Jeld feigned polishing a ring upon his bandages.

"How are you doing, Arvin? Stabbed through and through, I heard."

"Through and through? Well, you heard more than I, it seems."

Renae shook his head. "*Idols*, what were the odds?"

"Have to ask Benam, he did the stitching."

"Not those odds. Being taken by the Sayers, I mean."

"Ah. Yeah. Some luck, eh?"

"Think you'll be able to make it tomorrow?"

"Make what?"

"Council. Didn't Benam tell you? The prince wants you to share your story with the council."

Jeld groaned.

"Benam probably didn't tell you so you'd stay in bed and heal up. Guess I'm a bad friend."

"Naw. Probably good to get out of this bed. Idols, what day is it, anyway?"

"Onesday. You've been here two nights."

"Onesday! Yeah, I'm going. Say, where am I anyway?"

"Fourth floor, east wing."

"Okay, yeah I can crawl my way to council from here."

Renae smiled, but it seemed somehow forced.

Jeld cursed his perception. "Out with it, man. Say what you'll say."

Renae sighed. "Guess I'm as bad as Benam. Didn't want to worry you, but... the city's a mess. Apparently massacring dozens of people, even Sayers, isn't such a good idea in times like these."

"Dralor," Jeld cursed. "Blazin' fool. What did he expect?"

"People are up in arms. Two watchmen were beaten to death by a mob. The prince is in true form. I expect if you don't come to council you may get a personal visit."

Jeld's thoughts drifted back to the many decent Sayers he'd sat across a fire from. He fought to keep a growing rage from showing upon his face until there came another knock at the door and Lira hurried in.

Renae stood. "Your Grace."

"Hello Renae," she answered, her eyes never leaving Jeld.

"I'd... best be off. Some affairs to attend to. See you soon, Arvin. Your Grace."

"Thanks, Renae," Jeld said.

Renae bowed to Lira and left the room, closing the door behind him.

"Thank the Mother!" Lira said, taking Jeld's hand. "I was so worried when I heard there were to be raids. I knew you would be there, but I didn't know what to do. I felt so helpless but... you're alright, right?"

Jeld chuckled then winced. "I'm alright, thanks to Benam."

"He's been at your side since your wagon got halfway up the hill, you know. Benam has a big heart."

"He must think his favorite student would be troubled by my untimely demise."

"He came running before knowing who you were, actually."

"Saved my butt, that's for sure."

Lira closed her eyes and sighed. "Well he also nearly got you killed. He let slip our little secret, and Dral found out."

"What! How could he not see what Dralor would do?"

"He didn't tell him. Or my father, even. He confessed it to High Priest Naelis, and Naelis felt obligated to tell the council."

"I knew something was off with Benam. He seemed... guilty."

Lira squeezed his hand.

"What do we do now?" Jeld asked. "We proved it was the Sayers' fooling about that started this mess, and now they're dead. Lot of good that did."

"I'll talk to my father, but... I don't know. I think we just forget what *started* the fire and try to put it out. We'll just... help out where we can?" She sighed. "At least you have one less identity to keep straight."

Jeld's eyes grew distant. The Sayers' sect was gone. Just Krayo's spy now. Just Arvin. It certainly simplified matters with Lira at least, seeing as this seemed a definitive end to actively conspiring against her family, but for what reason was he here at all then? What did that leave of himself?"

Jeld forced a smile. "I'll have to pick up a new part."

"I've got an idea." Lira leaned down and whispered into his ear. "Just try to get healthy." She picked up a book from the bedside table. "You can read this while you recover. It's brilliant."

"*Governance and Sovereignty?* Why do you want to hurt me so?"

"Your body needs to rest, but your *mind* doesn't."

"It's perfect," Jeld said. A smile pinched his eyes closed and he fought them back open.

"Maybe your mind could do with some rest too, actually. Perhaps you will adventure yet in dreams."

Jeld smiled again, and this time his eyes did not reopen. He remembered little beyond that, only that he still held Lira's hand.

***

"You heard them say things, did you? Speak against the crown?" Sir Lasken asked.

The council chamber was unusually quiet, and Jeld felt the council's scrutiny as clearly as he saw their eyes upon him.

"Yes. Well, there were those who attacked me, but technically I only heard the exarch speak against the crown. It seemed like a secret even there, as if most were not supposed to know."

Sir Benam huffed.

"The exarch said the crown—" Jeld looked to the king. "You'll forgive me won't you, Your Highness? These words are not my own."

King Loris nodded. "Of course."

"He said the crown had... 'filled the seats of the Idols with thieves'. And something about... 'building their palaces upon the bodies of common men.' And—"

"Go on, son."

Jeld sighed. "Something like 'fattening their guts and coffers with their takings'... and, ah... 'befouling the names of the Idols.' And, well, he just went on like that, Your Highness."

"Terrible," High Priest Naelis muttered.

"What else?" the king prompted.

"He... said they had bled a pig at the lord governor's door. And that they had punished the crown by attacking the wealthy, and—"

"And now they're dead and we have new problems to turn our attention to," Prince Dralor snapped.

Sir Benam drew a sharp breath. "You have *massacred* dozens of innocent people to kill a handful of the guilty!"

Jeld's eyes fell to the ground.

"It's a cult!" Dralor shouted. "They're all brainwashed. All part of the problem! Now, shall we turn our attention to restoring order to the city, or must we spend more time bickering over the fate of a coven of criminals?"

"They are no more guilty as a collective than the city is for the crimes of its few. But then, you've already been punishing Tovar just the same, haven't you? Locking everyone up in your heinous *work camp*. Don't you see where it's gotten us? *You* have created *that!*" Benam stabbed a finger out toward the riotous city.

"And *you* would let them raze our city!"

"Enough!" another voice bellowed.

They all turned to find King Loris standing, fists pressed against the table and his throne-like chair toppled behind. Two servants were the first to unfreeze, an older man and the young red-haired servant girl of the high priest both hurrying to right the fallen chair. The king slowly sat back down.

"Fighting fire with fire leaves only ashes," King Loris said. "Many kings have made that mistake. My own grandfather, Tovados, razed Khapar. The mad king before him brought the whole of the kingdom to its knees. I will not allow our misguided fear and vengeance to see this city ruined nor tormented. This is *our* doing, and we will set things right."

"What would you propose, Your Highness?" Lord Tydel said after a silence, his voice nasally through a still-swollen nose.

Jeld suppressed a smile.

"Gather the people in two days," the king said. "Citizensday. Seventh bell, in the palace gardens."

"Inside the wall?" Prince Dralor scoffed. "Are you *mad?*"

"I can hardly address the people as equals from atop a golden tower, now can I? How well will an apology be received from a man who will not walk amongst his people?"

"Apology? You would apologize to looters and beggars? To those who would take up arms against us?"

"I would apologize to those I have wronged!"

Prince Dralor only glared back.

Chancellor Cerus cleared his throat. "If the matter is settled then, we'll move on to the next topic?"

King Loris nodded.

"Very good. The next matter for your attention is regarding tax revenue and, in particular, an external proposal to help reverse the dwindling returns."

Jeld's heart slowed as the spotlight pivoted from him, and soon the chancellor's voice melted into the background. His eyes grew heavier and his breaths deepened until suddenly a distant name jolted him back into focus.

"Krayo Rusrivon?" Sir Brayold scoffed. "The smuggler strong-armer? You can't be serious."

"His Royal Highness has seen fit to hear him speak," Cerus said. "Sir Olind has vouched for the man's qualifications."

Olind nodded. "He is among the city's most accomplished businessmen. Trade, portering, and all manner of local establishments alike."

"See him in," the king said.

A servant exited through a small passage in the corner of the room. A few moments later the more substantial doors pulled open and there stood Krayo Rusrivon. He followed the servant to a vacant seat directly across from the king, stopping behind it and offering a deep and graceful bow.

"Your Highness."

"Welcome, Mister Rusrivon," King Loris said. "Please, sit."

Krayo sat. "Thank you, Your Highness. I'm honored to be invited to your company, and the company of your great council."

"You may address the council," Chancellor Cerus said.

"I will jump right into business. Tax revenues are falling, as you know. I wager you have a plan to fix it. Audits, probably, but that will hardly cover it, and most people will just make excuses anyway. Inevitably, you'll increase tax rates. On imports first, I'd wager? Some new sweeps, perhaps?"

Sir Brayold's mouth came open and Krayo promptly continued. "Pardon my saying so but you've got a mess down there. Do you really want to tell them you're raising the rates? Or adding new sweeps? I don't advise it. In fact, if you raise rates any more, in addition to pissing off the citizenry, I can guarantee you will make *less* money. Do you know why?"

Jeld opened his mouth and shut it.

Krayo looked about the room. "Nobody?"

"Because if you raise taxes, people will just smuggle more," Jeld said finally. "Or they'll tear down the city. Both not good."

Krayo smiled and looked to Olind. "Your nephew, isn't he, Sir Olind? You've done well with him. Yes, precisely. Which is exactly why I propose we *lower* taxes."

Sir Brayold scoffed. "Of course he wants to lower taxes, he's a trader! Must we endure this pitch any longer?"

Krayo leaned forward in his chair and continued at a whisper. "The tax rate is fifteen percent. Nearly half of imports are smuggled. Yes, *half*. Some traders bypass the magistrates entirely, others only partially. Next, about sixty percent of commerce is big operations.

"The idea is simple, really. You lower taxes to ten percent for smaller operations, twelve for the large. This way it's definitely not worth the risk to smuggle, and you get your cut. Today, you're getting fifteen percent on half of everything coming through that gate.

That's seven and a half. With my proposal, you'll make twelve percent on sixty and ten percent on forty. That's up nearly fifty percent."

Krayo held up a finger as if to reserve his place before continuing again.

"Now, that's just with the current valuation process. I also happen to know that goods are being undervalued during tax assessments. Goods targeting Hillside and beyond sell for higher than goods targeting Riverside. The catch? Most are the same goods! Did you know the smart traders polish their apples *after* they are in the city, so they are taxed as a poor crop? Clothing and materials too are made to look shabby so as to be assessed at a low price. Just improving our valuation processes has the potential to see returns of *thirty percent!*"

He plucked a goblet from the table.

"Now, all this is great on the coffers, but you know the real treat? It's *fair* to the people. Our city—*your* city—is up in arms. The mobs are growing. The stones they bear are turning to swords and torches. With this plan, you can demonstrate to the people that you are unquestionably on their side, *and* make more money doing it." Krayo spread his arms. "I apologize, I can be quite long-winded on the matter. But, I'm done." He took a sip.

"What has the council to say on the matter?" Chancellor Cerus said after a while.

Sir Brayold shifted in his chair.

Finally, Tutor Reiman spoke in his deep singsong voice as he frowned down at nothing in particular. "Economics are beyond the complexities of even the sciences. The variables are too great to count, like predicting the ripples of an ocean. Worse, the problem is not just physical, but psychological. Still... that isn't to say we cannot make educated decisions to model these tides. It would seem counter to common sense that lowering the tax rates should net more income, yet, the model *is* quite logical. Tax reduction, a graduated rate, closing valuation loopholes... mmm, mhmm..."

Nodding approvingly down at the table, the old tutor trailed off.

Lord Tydel Demerious sat forward in his chair. "What *exactly* brings you to this council today, Mister Rusrivon."

Krayo nodded. "My proposal is good, but we both have a problem. I cannot implement this in my current station, and *you* cannot implement it without me. You see, lowering the tax rate will only loosen so many purse strings. The others will require an extra little push—a push that, after a lifetime fighting the likes of these smugglers, I am uniquely equipped to issue.

"So the question is not what I want, but how can we together get what *you* want. I propose you order the establishment of a new guild. The Trade Guild. Appoint me leader of the guild, and allocate one percent of trade tax proceeds to the guild. In return I will fill your coffers, and the people will love you for it."

The council went quiet. All watched the king, his eyes brimming with interest.

Chapter Thirty-Four

I t was a bell-less hour of a cool and foggy Thrallsday night. *Thrallsday*. The symbolism was not lost on the mobs filling the streets and packing the public squares, for it was the day so named after the long years the people were but slaves under a mad king's rule.

To those watching nervously from their Hilltop mansions or the towers of the keep itself, the mobs were a glow of torches snaking through the city, an ominous roar filling the gaps between the crash of waves precluding any escape. Were the torches coming closer, they wondered as their untouched tea grew cold? Was the roar growing louder?

The masses of humanity marched through the city like the annual Fallsday parade, only with neither color nor joy. They hurled curses and rocks at anything remotely symbolic of the crown, marching and shouting with such energy as the old, tired, broken, and disheartened had not felt for years. Their zeal rose and rose and it seemed the energy might carry the mobs to the doorstep of the king himself when suddenly there came a message spreading through the city like a great wave over wildfire.

The king will speak in two days.

The fervor and froth melted away. Torches fell and the crowds dispersed as the people of Tovar, numb from their rage, shuffled back to beds and pubs. Fireside thoughts churned back over foreign memories of chants and shouts and waving torches as people recalled through their own eyes the deeds their rage had driven.

They sleeplessly wondered at the king's speech. Let it bring change, they whispered, that they might never again need give their bodies over to the fury. But then, let it change nothing. Let no crown placate them with its lies and send them scurrying back down the hill to live docile amongst the rats. Soon enough. Soon enough. The king would speak on Citizensday.

***

The keep was running wild, the household staff literally so and the gentry running merely their mouths in a nervous spat of barked orders. In the gardens before the palace, tables had been erected and were piled with mountains of cheese and bread. Knights and watch captains surrounded another table covered in maps. Before it all stood a new platform raised for the king's speech, far shorter than it had been just bells before when Sir Benam had ordered it lowered to a less ostentatious height.

Jeld had done very little that day, perhaps less even than the plumpest of lords, if it could be believed. A tending by Benam, a few rounds about the keep to befriend no few servants, and a chance encounter with Krayo, who Jeld learned had spent the better part of the morning assisting the king with his speech. His only other stop had been at General Handan's quarters after realizing he was suddenly the only man on Hilltop without a sword at his waist.

It was midday when Jeld made his way back through the buzzing keep to the quarters lent him for his recovery, a sword upon his belt and no shortage of bread and cheese tucked onto his bottomless bag. It was then, as he set out his lunch upon the bedside table, that he saw a note lying upon his pillow.

Scanning the room, he picked up the note, broke an unsigned seal of red wax, and unfolded it.

Burn the palace gardener's shop to the ground at sixth bell.

It could only be from the Sayers, but how could they have endured after the prince's massacre? And—his eyes widened—*they knew who he was*. How much did they know, though? Just of Arvin, or of he himself? And how?

Jeld sped toward the door to go find Lira only to stop halfway across the room, his eyes growing distant. His mind drifted over the mobs packing the streets just short days before, then to a watchman kicking him into the gutters, dogs snapping at his heels, a looming black tower stretching into the sky. An arson was sure to spoil the king's offering and throw the city into disarray, but was that such a bad thing? Should not the people be spared the crown's hollow apologies? Was this not the moment he'd been waiting for? The very reason he'd accepted this insane job from Krayo to begin with?

His thoughts returning to Lira, Jeld hurried from the room. He made straight away for the servant's station, where Darrelin kindly agreed to deliver a note summoning Lira, then promptly ventured to the library.

Mind racing as he impatiently paced Lira's little clearing, he took a deep breath and forced his thoughts into focus upon the passing titles. A book with a particularly cracked spine caught his attention. He flipped it open.

... if only the cowardly beasts of the plains might turn their unified strength upon the lion. It is just so with the common man. It is not in the nature of the docile masses to rise against their keepers, but make no mistake, when he is cornered his teeth might bare. It is vital as such that the masses must at all costs never realize the strength of their numbers, else...

Jeld's nostrils flared. *Cattle.* That's all the commoners were to the crown. A resource to be kept just well enough fed to produce their milk, to build their castles, to fight their wars.

A creak issued from the direction of the entrance. Closing his eyes, Jeld tracked Lira's familiar presence until at last she emerged wearing a bright green dress with a long golden necklace.

"I got your message," she said. "What is it? Is something wrong?"

Jeld thumbed the note within his pocket.

"Is that Nadir's *Civilizations?*" Lira asked.

"Hmm?"

"Your book there."

"Oh. *This* piece of trash."

"*Trash?* You must be joking."

Jeld let the note fall deeper into his pocket. "Who is this Nadir guy? You'd think he was raising pigs for slaughter rather than real people."

"*She* is only the most renowned advisor of Tovados's rule. We could learn a thing or two from her to put down this revolt."

"A revolt against men shitting on them from ivory towers! Maybe a kingdom without a crown wouldn't be so bad."

"And everyone will live in harmony as equals forever after?"

"Well, no, but—"

"Kingdoms don't work like fishing villages. People vie for resources. For land. For power. Without order it's a bloodbath."

"*With* order it's a bloodbath, but only the king wins."

"More people have died trying to *become* kings than in service to them!"

Jeld sighed and collapsed against a pile of cushions, wincing in pain.

"It's not as if I have a better idea," he said. "I just... well, I don't blame people for rising up."

"But they are rising up against a false enemy, remember? Everything was fine before the Sayers started to turn us all against one another."

"*Finer*. Yeah. Maybe so."

Lira sat upon the cushions where Jeld lay. "Did you summon me here just to debate philosophy from old books?"

"Do you really think we've seen the last of them? Of the Sayers? Dralor only wiped out one sylum, and certainly there were people absent even there."

"Does it matter? The damage is done."

Jeld's eyes flicked down toward the note in his pocket.

"Maybe. But any plans they had for me, they'll just assign to someone else now. Don't you wonder what they have planned?"

"I suppose so. Yes. Honestly, it's probably for the best that you are out, though."

"You... think so?"

"As soon as they asked for something really bad, you would have had to disobey them. After your last encounter with their little cult, I don't figure they leave loose ends alive for too long. At least now they think you're dead, so they don't have to kill you. Again."

"Yeah... yeah, that's true."

Jeld fell silent, his mind on the Sayers, the city watch, the black prison tower, the prince, the note. The note.

"Do you think there will always be classes?" Jeld asked. "Rich and poor? Master and servant? Lord and soldier?"

Lira laughed. "You really did just want to talk philosophy?"

Jeld forced a smile. "Sounds like I've got your number, eh?"

Lira laid down beside him, the back of her hand against his. "It *is* pretty well my favorite thing to do. Classes... I hope not. But I don't see how."

"It's not right."

"No, it's not."

"Do you think we can change things? Improve them, even just a little?"

"Yes. I do."

Jeld met her bright blue eyes. He opened his hand and the backs of their fingertips intertwined.

Lira returned his gaze. "I have something you should probably know."

"Oh?"

"There is this commoner boy I rather like. He showed me how to live. We had a wonderful night out to a play once, and he even saved my life that night."

"Ah. Well, I suppose it's for the best, because there is this commoner girl…. She saved my life one day long ago at the Temple of One. Gave me life where food and water could not."

Lira smiled. "It's hard to believe we're here now together. Or that that time was even real."

"I'm glad you decided not to turn me in. It'd be a long slog up the hill only to be beheaded on arrival."

Lira leaned forward until her forehead was pressed against his.

"Try not to get yourself killed," she whispered, her breath warm.

"I should like to keep my head *precisely* where it is."

He kissed her, managing even to forget about the note within his pocket if but for a moment.

***

Jeld walked down a corridor toward the royal ballroom. Like much of the keep it felt as military as it did opulent, its cold stone walls punctuated at precise intervals with alcoves hosting beautiful works of art. As he neared the corridor's end, voices echoed from somewhere ahead and he froze. His heart racing, he audited his character, wrapping it around himself like a cloak. He pulled a sweet roll from his pocket and resumed walking. A trip to the kitchens was a perfectly viable cover, he had to remind himself as the voices neared. The hall behind him led indeed to the kitchens and any number of other places, yet all he could think about was the winding route to the little gardeners shop that even now would be filling with flames.

Glancing down to his sweet roll, Jeld's eyes widened at the sight of soot staining the side of his hand. He shot a look down the hallway. The shadows of whoever was approaching showed upon the floor at the corner now. In an instant, Jeld darted into one of the alcoves and hid behind a large statue. He began hastily scrubbing the soot away with the cloth that had wrapped the roll.

"For what it's worth, I still think it's a terrible idea, Lor," Prince Dralor's voice came from afar.

King Loris laughed. "Of course you do, Brother. You think everything is a bad idea."

Prince Dralor chuckled, a sound Jeld had not before heard from the man. The voices grew clearer, the click of heels louder with each step.

"I trust you've been up all night crafting your words?" the prince asked.

"Indeed. I thought it would come together more quickly, seeing as the words are truly from my heart, but in fact that made things all the more difficult."

The king's words burst into clarity beyond the alcove before beginning to fade.

"I wouldn't expect it to be easy," the prince said. "It'll take nothing short of magic to do any good."

"It turned out well enough, I think. Magic though? I'm afraid I..."

Their voices faded until all that remained was an unintelligible echo bouncing down the corridor. Jeld inspected his hands again then continued down a tangle of corridors and emerged into the royal ballroom.

The vast room was dim, lit only by the evening light silhouetting the many nobles staring sullenly through the windows to the gathered crowds. Lira, Benam, and Queen Darene stood before a window overlooking the king's modest dais. In the center of the room, several platoons of the royal army stood in formation, a smartly dressed officer at the front of each. No less than two dozen armored knights lounged in a corner, their individuality somehow more fearsome than the soldiers' rigid uniformity. At the back of the ballroom, a single mass of watchmen stood in a rough formation.

Jeld made his way quietly inward, coming to a stop within earshot of Lira and company. He and Lira exchanged a nod.

"Just dreadful," Queen Darene cursed. "I don't see the harm in a little more light."

"Apologies, Your Grace," Sir Benam said. "King Loris wished to—"

"Yes yes, I know what he said. Well if you ask me, we should be making it *more* clear just who holds the power here, not acting as if we're some... poor friend of theirs."

Lira's ensuing groan was cut short by heavy footfalls from the corridor to the keep. Prince Dralor emerged, stopping just inside and indiscriminately scrutinizing the crowd before crossing to where General Handan, Sir Lasken, Lord Tydel, and High Priest Naelis stood not far from Jeld.

"Is everything in order?" the prince asked.

General Handan nodded. "Yes, Your Grace."

"The cavalry is staged?"

"It is. And all is peaceful."

The prince nodded, perhaps a hint of disappointment upon his face. As if to appease him, a single cry issued from the crowd, then a thousand more. People pointed and hollered, their many voices seeming to converge on a single word.

"What's that?" High Priest Naelis asked. "What are they saying?"

"Fire," Prince Dralor said distantly.

Hushed murmuring filled the ballroom but the stirring nobles did little more than look at one another.

"Lasken," Prince Dralor said. "Get men over there to find the fire. Have some troughs and buckets loaded onto wagons in preparation. Report back here with a location. Understood?"

"Yes, Your Grace!" Lasken said and ran toward his men at the back of the ballroom.

The prince shook his head. "Absurd. Invite a stray dog into our home and we are surprised to be bitten. I should like to bring the cavalry around."

"Patience, Prince," High Priest Naelis said softly. "Patience. Some fires go out easier than others. Let us not start one to put out another."

Prince Dralor said nothing further. Lasken led a file of watchmen outside at a jog, leaving the ballroom silent in their wake. The seventh bell chimed as all remaining stood quietly awaiting news of the fire.

Finally, the sound of rapid footsteps rose from the corridor and all turned in anticipation of Lasken's news, but it was Master Servant Darrelin who burst into the room. He was pale and panting. His mouth opened and closed several times before sound finally escaped his lips.

"The k—"

Darrelin's wide eyes flicked to Lira. He sucked in a short breath.

"The king is... dead."

Jeld's world seemed to tunnel inward. His eyes shot over to Lira. She stood frozen and expressionless, but her horror beat against him and nearly buckled his knees.

"How?" Prince Dralor breathed.

"It seems he was... stabbed, Your Grace. In—in the back, Your Grace."

"Clear them out," the prince said quietly then turned to General Handan. "Clear them out now, General."

"You can't!" Sir Benam said. "They didn't do this. *They* are not your assassin! The people came to hear us. We must speak."

Prince Dralor grabbed Sir Benam's collar. "Enough! Your weakness already killed my brother, you naive fool!"

The prince shoved Benam, sending him staggering backward.

Regaining his footing, Benam straightened his posture. "You don't even know who to be angry at. You just bark at whatever is in front of you, clean yourself of blame by casting it upon everyone else."

Dralor's hand wrenched the hilt of his sword and he stepped toward Benam, but High Priest Naelis put a hand upon his arm.

The prince turned his glare upon the high priest, who shook his head disapprovingly. His nostrils flaring, Prince Dralor looked back to Sir Benam and spoke through clenched teeth.

"Out. Do not show your face here again or I'll see your treacherous head removed. Out!"

Sir Benam looked aside and Jeld followed his gaze to Lira's tear-filled eyes. Benam gave her a nod then shook his head at Prince Dralor and walked from the ballroom.

Dralor stared after him, his eyes falling sullenly to the ground once Benam had gone.

"He's right," Lira said with a shaky breath. "You can't—"

"Bring the cavalry around," the prince interrupted, turning back to General Handan. "Clear them out, General."

The prince marched off toward the corridor Darrelin had emerged from.

"Show me to my brother," he commanded without looking back.

Darrelin looked again to Lira then ran after him.

CHAPTER THIRTY-FIVE

A grizzled army commander passed by a pale watch captain being consoled by High Priest Naelis. He exchanged a smirk with a knight sharpening his blade nearby and continued past to the center of Lord Tydel Demerious's great room, where General Handan and Sir Lasken stood over a map. Offering a brief report, he joined his colleagues around a fireplace.

General Handan moved three blue stones from the base of Hillside up to the lower wall.

"But... we'd be giving back so much ground," Lasken said. "We only just cleared the hill a few bells ago."

"Yes," General Handan said distantly as he studied the map. "Better to give what we cannot defend than to retreat bloodied from it. We'd never recover from a defeat out there. We tighten our line and hold."

"I... I see. Perhaps we should distribute our reserves across the line, then?"

General Handan shook his head as he rearranged another stone. "We don't need a slightly thicker line everywhere, we need a sizable force wherever we are engaged. The reserves stay in reserve."

Lasken fidgeted. "Might we also consider, ah... an advance? A show of force could turn the odds, could it not?"

Handan exchanged words with another passing commander before turning to Lasken. "We hold."

"I see. It's just that, according to your own accounts, against superior numbers a forcible advance can demoralize the enemy and—"

The general leveled an icy glare on Lasken, who swallowed audibly.

"Ah—of course, General."

A commotion swept over the room and General Handan turned as a pair of servants heaved open the massive double doors of the entry. In the doorway, Prince Dralor sat atop a black horse barely visible against the night sky, his armor dark red like old blood. As the prince dismounted and stormed inward, two men in white silken clothes emerged from the night behind him and scanned the room with cold eyes.

"Handan!" Prince Dralor snapped. "Why are your men not moving? Was I not clear?"

"I'm holding the city," General Handan said shortly.

"Ridiculous! It was your gentleness clearing the keep earlier that emboldened them so. Handan—clean up your mess!"

The two men in white fell in behind the prince.

"It would be a massacre. An *unwarranted* massacre," General Handan said.

"Unwarranted? They killed Loris! They are sacking the city! They are coming here, *to kill us!*"

"I've bled for them my whole life. We both have."

"Yes, earned a place in their hearts, haven't we? What's wrong with you? Has Benam filled your head with this foolishness?"

"Two good hearts can disagree, my young friends," High Priest Naelis said, joining them. "That is why you two have done so well together over the years, is it not? Two tacticians are hardly better than one if they think alike.

"However," the high priest continued, "while I often find myself dissuading the prince from his... more *firm* methods, I must agree that we cannot allow this wickedness any more than we should allow thieves to go unpunished. We owe it to the many decent bystanders of the realm to apply justice and maintain order, lest Discord spread her chaos like a disease."

General Handan looked back to Prince Dralor and found him staring appraisingly back.

Shaking his head, the prince turned to Sir Lasken. "Lasken, you have command. Ready the men for an assault."

"Ah... y-yes, Your Grace," Lasken said and turned from the table. "You all heard the prince! Prepare the cavalry, all the watch teams, and the infantry for advance." Lasken's eyes flicked to General Handan. "But keep the reserves on standby."

The watch captains moved at once, but the room quickly fell still and silent. Lasken looked about to find several army commanders and knights had discreetly positioned themselves between the watchmen and the exit. Some stilled their mark with a firm hand upon the shoulder, but most with only a look, an eye fixed all the while upon their general.

"That's enough, Dral," General Handan said. "We've done plenty of war, you and me. But I'd sooner lay down my sword than wage war on our own people."

"How *dare* you!" Prince Dralor spat. "You would commit treason to hand the city over to a mob of beggars? Even our priest has more courage than you!"

"Please, gentlemen," the high priest began. "We are better than—"

"Beggars?" Handan said. "They ask only for words, and you'd rather give them death! Call this off. I won't ask again."

"Enough!" Dralor shouted. "Do not forget your place, soldier!"

Handan's eyes narrowed. "*My place.* When your grandfather gave me his name, he charged me with being a protector of this kingdom. I *know* my place."

He drew his sword in a slow movement of incomprehensible strength, like a glacier carving out the mountains.

Prince Dralor took a step backwards. The high priest and the two men in white melted aside at once. Two watch captains drew swords and ran to stand before the prince, who made no attempt to draw his own.

The general began a slow advance, not cautious but impending. There was a blur of motion and the general's blade came down on the hilt of one of the watchman's swords, sending it speeding toward the ground. Another blur—the flat of Handan's sword slammed down against the tip of the other watchman's sword. The watchman grunted and fell backward as his own hilt bit into his lightly armored gut. The general continued his advance uninterrupted as the first watchman's sword clattered at last to the ground.

Handan's breath caught and he spun with his sword held high just as something crashed against it. Beyond a wooden bo pressing against his blade, one of the men in white glared back. A momentary flicker of confusion passed over Handan before his eyes widened. He flicked his sword in a nearly unmoving pulse of force that sent his attacker stumbling backward then spun, but he was too late.

Pain exploded at the side of his head and a bright light flashed behind his eyes. A short iron rod clattered to the ground at his feet. In the distance, barely visible in the blur of blinding light, the other man in white drew another iron rod from his shirt.

Handan staggered to a knee. The flash faded, and faded, and faded, until instead the darkness grew. Another explosion of pain erupted in the back of his head and he spilled over, catching himself with one hand and pushing away the ground that pulled at him. He lashed out blindly in a broad sweep of his sword, but the force of it spun him off balance and he landed on his back. He could just make out two white shapes standing in the darkness above him. He roared and lifted his sword, but there was another flash of pain, and then nothing.

***

"Will our taxes craft our chains!" a single voice called out over the masses gathered in Temple Square.

"No! Resist! Resist! Resist!" thousands roared back as one.

Beneath the faint glow of dawn, a lone man paced back and forth atop the stairs of Temple Theater. He stopped abruptly and turned again to the crowd.

"Will chains silence our voices!"

"No! Resist! Resist! Resist!" the people bellowed, their torches stabbing at the sky.

"You can't tax our hope!"

"Can't tax our hope!"

"You can't chain our voices!"

"Can't chain our voices!"

"The Black Prince killed our king, but can he silence us?"

"No! Resist! Resist! Resist!" the people roared back.

Even over the commotion, another chant began to echo into the square as if from the city itself.

"Which way!"

"Up!"

"Which way!"

"Up!"

"Which way!"

"Up!"

The man on the steps pointed toward Hilltop and bellowed over the crowd. "Which way!"

"Up!" the mob shouted, their voices joining the rest.

The crowd twisted and churned like converging sea currents until it began steadily to flow west from the square. Still, the crowd did not thin. Person after person poured in from every eastern street and alley as all of Tovar swept west and south.

"Which way!"

"Up!"

Louder and louder the crowds grew as they surged along the avenues and trickled down the alleys like rivers and streams, only upward. Ever upward.

"Which way!"

"Up!

Tax offices, watch stations, and mansions burned behind them as the people climbed Hillside. Chants quieted as people neared the lower wall, anger and hope tempering to a cool resolve. Men and women, porters and merchants, bakers, sailors, and fishermen alike all pressed on side by side. Few eyes did not glisten as the people spilled through and over the lower Hilltop wall and marched across manicured gardens toward the towering mansions built upon their backs for too many years past. Toward the keep of the Black Prince who would enslave them.

Suddenly a stir passed through the crowds like the flutter of a dreaming eye and they slowed to a stop in the gardens and back on Hillside where still their tail followed. A sound. A rumble...

Cries of alarm rose up over the crowd as the rumble broke into the distinctive beat of hooves, and then the prince's army was upon them, crashing through bodies and hope alike, the world reduced to the terrible faces of screaming warhorses, the flash of steel raining from above, and the smell of blood.

***

Gil polished the bar top in slow, smooth circles with one hand as his other held a tankard beneath a tap. One of the regular lovelies sat at a small table with his only other customer. Her show was off—her game, her luster, her slither—but the man with her had no interest in that anyway. They just sat quietly beside one another, each with a nearly empty drink in hand.

An empty pub was an ominous thing. In good times and bad there was always life at the pub, but not anymore. The streets too were quiet now. People looked down as they walked, if they must travel at all. Down, away from the eyes of the watchmen and the soldiers that had joined their ranks. Down at the still bloodstained streets, a reminder of the price of hope.

The barkeep flinched as ale spilled over his hand. He quietly cursed his wandering mind and swapped out the overflowing tankard. With a great effort he focused on the task at hand and stoppered the tap as the ale foamed into a perfect dome just beyond the top of the next tankard. Nodding at his handiwork, he toweled off the first tankard and delivered both to his sole customers. He returned to the bar with the empties, gave them a dunk in his wash bin, and set to polishing them clean. Again his mind wandered.

The city still stood, he reassured himself. He still had his pub. Still polished his counter. In some ways, for those fortunate enough to have survived the quelling and maintained some semblance of their livelihoods, perhaps little had changed. And yet, so much had changed. It was the difference between a room locked from within and a room locked from without. Tovar was still Tovar, but it had betrayed them—it had locked the door, and for that, everything was changed.

CHAPTER THIRTY-SIX

J eld blocked and dodged attack after attack, the crack of wooden swords echoing off the walls of General Handan's training room. Though he glimpsed himself in Lira's enraged eyes, Jeld knew she saw not him but her father's assassin, the crown's oppression, Dralor and his reckless massacre—every pain she couldn't kill, couldn't mend, couldn't solve. How terrible the thought that her hatred should certainly be his were she to discover he'd as good as put the knife in her father with his gardener's shop fire.

"Well don't just stand there!" Lira said.

Still Jeld only fell back beneath her onslaught. He couldn't bring himself to strike her, which was convenient because each opening closed as fast as it appeared, her very recklessness patching its every flaw with yet another ferocious attack. His heel struck the wall behind him and General Handan's distant voice seemed to scold him even as the point of Lira's sword came to a stop just before his neck.

Lira wiped her sweaty brow. "Handan would have let you hear about that one."

"Oh he did," Jeld said, pointing at his head.

It seemed she might smile, but she grew distant as her eyes fell upon a vacant spot on the wall where the general's blade once hung.

"Don't worry," Jeld said. "Even Thennaly Island can't hold General Handan Tovaine."

"If he's there at all. He's certainly dead, and this whole exile story is just to keep his loyal men at bay."

"You don't really think he would let those priests get the best of him, do you?"

Lira smiled ever so slightly, but it faded like the sun behind clouds. She hung her sword upon the wall.

"I need to be going," she said. "I'm to help my mother host a dinner this evening after council, and she'll no doubt need me to oversee preparations."

"Isn't that what servants are for?"

"Oh I'm sure we won't do any *real* work ourselves."

Jeld shook his head. "Fancy dinners. Sounds horrible. Or a nice distraction, maybe?"

"I don't want a distraction. I don't want everyone pretending nothing happened. *Khapar*, we don't even *know* what happened!"

Jeld just nodded. There were no words. He took her hand and squeezed it, the best answer he could think of.

"The people all think Dral killed my father," Lira said. "But it had to be the Sayers, right?"

A wave crashed against the cliffsides somewhere outside as guilt stabbed at Jeld's heart.

"It... was the Sayers," Jeld said at last.

"It had to be. It certainly wasn't Dral, that's for sure." Lira wiped away tears. "I really must be off."

"But, I mean—"

"I'll be late. My mother will no doubt chastise me for not properly fussing over who sits where, and what color napkins to tell the servants to use."

Jeld sighed. "I'll walk with you. It's not safe in the palace until we find out who ki— er, find out what happened."

"And who is going to escort *you* after that?"

"Escort *me?* Your Grace, I am not important enough to be at risk. Nobody cares about Arvin Emry."

"Maybe they should. Maybe they should care a lot about both of us."

Jeld walked with her, parting only once they had neared the royal dining room. With lessons cancelled, swordplay abbreviated, fencing off-limits, and little else to occupy his time, he returned to Olind's mansion.

"Welcome, Master Arvin," Hamry greeted just inside.

"Thank you kindly, Master Hamry."

Hamry squirmed slightly at the honorific as usual.

"How might I serve you, sir?"

"Would you please have a bath drawn? I don't want to offend the council this evening. They've enough to worry about of late."

"Of course, sir."

A young servant was off before Hamry could manage to issue her a nod.

"Ah, I nearly forgot!" Hamry said, pulling open a drawer in his tall desk.

He produced a letter sealed in unsigned red wax and held it out to Jeld.

"This came for you perhaps a quarter bell ago."

Jeld's pulse quickened. He took the letter far less fervently than he was inclined and nodded.

"Who, may I ask, sent it?"

"It arrived by the royal courier. They didn't know with whom it originated, I'm afraid."

"I see. All the same. Thank you Hamry."

"It is my distinct pleasure, Master Arvin."

Jeld managed a smile and, again with much restraint, walked to his room. Once inside, he ripped the letter open.

Meet at fourth bell. Northwest spire. Central observation deck.

Jeld's mind spun. A meeting at last? But for what purpose? Another mission? Or could it be a trap to clean up loose ends? Perhaps he'd be wise to just disappear, but what mysteries would then remain uncovered? What would Krayo think of him? And Lira? Would he see her still? Would she be safe?

Fourth bell...

He dressed rapidly, combed his hair, dabbed clean his sweaty forehead, and burst out of his room. On the stairs, two confounded servants bearing trays of hot stones scurried aside as he charged downward three steps at a time.

"I'm so sorry!" Jeld called. "I must attend to an urgent matter at the palace!"

Seeing Jeld's haste, Hamry pulled the door open and Jeld sailed past, calling out his thanks behind him. Outside, he made for the stables and had the carriage moving on short order.

He arrived at the palace just after third bell and continued on foot at a less suspicious pace toward the northwest spire. Jeld climbed the narrow, spiraling stairs to the central observation deck where broad windows offered breathtaking views in every direction. The sea glimmered in the western sun. So far below were the white capped waves stretching across the sea that they seemed not even to move. The palace sprawled below, the other spires piercing high into the deep blue sky above. If this was to be an ambush, it was at least a good place to die.

But he didn't intend to die today. He pulled his longest rope from his bag then leaned out a window and looped it back around into the next. Tying a snug knot, then another, he let the rope fall to the gardens below. Finally, he dug out a jar of shoe polish he kept around for makeup, fuel, and sometimes even polishing shoes, and gave the rope a stony gray complexion.

An escape in place, he went back into the stairwell and climbed until he came to a small landing beside a slit window, little more than a nook for a plump noble to catch his breath. There, with mathematics notes upon his lap for a cover story, he closed his eyes, took a deep breath, and expanded his awareness. And then he waited.

It was shortly after the chimes of the fourth bell rang through the narrow window that something tugged at Jeld's sense. It was a calm presence, collected and unusually complex. Jeld could appreciate yet not understand it, like fine penmanship of an unknown language. When finally it seemed the presence was growing no nearer, he counted out a dozen more breaths and descended the steps.

Peering into the observation deck, Jeld found a man in a white robe gazing out the windows at the far side of the room. Fighting back his nerves, Jeld crept to the center of the room and let his final step slap against the stone floor.

High Priest Naelis turned from the window and smiled.

"It's a pleasure to finally meet you," Naelis said. "In this capacity, that is."

"And you as well... High Priest."

"You don't seem surprised. Tell me, did I betray myself somehow?"

"Oh, no. It's just that I've had to teach myself to... hide my feelings in order to survive here amongst these people."

The high priest approached and put a hand upon Jeld's shoulder. "And because of your talents you've done so much more than survive, haven't you?"

Jeld felt a chill and turned as another man in a white robe appeared in the doorway. The man had the dark skin of an Easterner, and his cold gaze sent a chill down Jeld's spine. He crossed his arms beneath his robe and turned his back.

"My inquisitors," the high priest said. "Priests. The world will have much need of them soon."

Jeld turned back to the high priest. "They dispatched General Handan."

"Yes. You know, I was quite worried when I thought you'd been caught in the temple raid. Then I heard you'd not been captured, but rather *rescued*. Just brilliant!"

"I was rather proud of that one. Thought I was done for, for a moment there. Even before the exarch tried to kill me."

Naelis frowned. "The standing orders have always been to protect our secrets at all cost. I'm afraid the late exarch was not as creative in his methods as you."

"I admire his dedication, anyway."

"Poor Davend. He and I shared a bond that bridged even the great divide between the Sayers and the followers of The One. I think you'll find in time the Sayers were more right about many things."

Naelis gave Jeld's shoulder a pat then went to a window overlooking the city.

"Join me, won't you?"

Jeld followed Naelis to the window, making sure to choose the side closest to his escape rope just in case.

"So much wickedness out there still after all these years, even in our own capital," High Priest Naelis said. "The Sayers have done their part, and our order as well. We've spread the light. Served justice. But... so little ground has been gained." The high priest sighed. "I have a confession to make, Arvin. It weighs... so heavily upon me. Haunts my dreams. But it has been... necessary."

"Doing the right thing is rarely easy."

"Oh how very true. How terribly, painfully true." He sighed again. "You know well our aims to grow the light, but I've not been entirely truthful in our... *methods* to do so. We are so insignificant, you see, so vastly outnumbered both on Hilltop and below that it was the only way. We could never win the war ourselves, but where allies run thin we must turn to other enemies."

"I... don't understand."

"Davend's Sayers weren't punishing the crown, they were provoking it. It was always best Davend not be aware of that distinction, but it is true all the same. I had to start a war between our enemies, a war we could never fight on our own. Do you understand?"

"But... what light can come of such destruction?"

"Oh it's not destruction we seek. There... will be costs, yes. The greatest forests are sown with fire from time to time... but believe me, if I could fell even one less tree to save the masses I would. There is only one way to ensure the kingdom lives as Vincet—as the Idols—would have us live. We must again crown the Idols as our kings, Arvin, and in their absence only *we* can rule in their name. The war is not to punish, but to embrace. Only then can Avandria heal."

Jeld looked out over Tovar and nodded slowly. "No war, no matter how righteous, is without loss. What must we do next?"

"You... would forgive me then?"

"Forgive you? The kingdom is in your debt."

The high priest's eyes fell closed, sending a tear rolling down his cheek. "Your kindness heals my wounds. And your courage sustains me."

"How might I serve?"

"For now you need only stand ready to be called upon. Very soon there will be much to do for our cause. Tonight at council, the one man who stands in our way will be dealt with. Dralor has proven himself a most valuable tinder, but he is blind to the sins of the powerful."

Jeld fought to keep his eyes from widening. All he had to do was nothing, and the prince would be dead at last. The prince who had built and filled his death camps and his dreaded prison tower. The prince who had set his terrible watchmen loose on the city, watchmen who had tried to wrest Cobb's shop from Jeld and forced sweet Niya to fight when she'd had nothing left to give but her life itself. At last he could do more than throw rocks with Raf, more than bleeding pigs in the lord governor's gardens.

Jeld's breath caught at this last thought. It had been these very antics by Raf, the Sayers, and even he himself that had so provoked the prince to begin with, then. Naelis had said as much. *Naelis.* Naelis was behind it all.

"You've crafted this most masterfully, High Priest," Jeld said.

"Vincet lights my path, I need only follow it. It has always been so, when I walked beside him and even now in dreams and whispers."

"Well, you serve him well. You need only guide my path as he guides yours, and we'll see the kingdom back to the light."

The high priest smiled and patted him on the shoulder again. "Thank you again. For all you've done, not least of all for forgiving my deeds to get us this far."

Jeld returned the smile.

"Now," the priest said, "I must see to things before our eventful evening. If things go poorly, I know I have another capable and loyal servant of the Idols to come to my aid or take up my burden. I will see you soon, my young friend."

"I will be there, High Priest."

Naelis gave him a lingering, appraising look before issuing a final smile and starting toward the stairs. The man in the doorway turned a cold, expressionless gaze upon Jeld then followed the high priest down the steps.

Jeld waited until the sound of their steps faded then pulled a notebook, quill, and ink from his bag and frantically penned a note.

Naelis is leader of Sayers. Wants throne. Killed your father. Going to kill Dralor at council tonight. You must warn him!

Staring down at the note, Jeld folded it and unfolded it before finally sighing and pressing it closed. He hurried across the keep and found Master Servant Darrelin standing sharply outside of the servant's office.

"Darrelin. Would you please see that Princess Liraelle gets this at once?"

Jeld held out the note, a silver royal atop it in place of a seal.

"Of... course, Sir Arvin," Darrelin replied.

"It is of utmost importance. Please, do not let any nonsense stand in your way. And please see it directly into the princess's hands, would you? Personally."

"Of course, sir. I shall see to it this instant."

"Thank you, my friend."

Darrelin took the note with a bow and hurried off.

Jeld's mind raced, but with the unfortunate luxury of more time to worry than preparations to make, he made for the library and paced the aisles impatiently. After the better part of a bell, he straightened his sword belt and started toward the council chamber and the certain bloodletting ahead.

Chapter Thirty-Seven

J eld dabbed a nervous sweat from his forehead and turned the final corner toward the council chamber. Approaching the chamber door from the opposite direction, Olind frowned at him before managing a half smile.

"Hello, Uncle. Ready for another evening of managing the kingdom?"

Olind waved Jeld ahead through the door. "I hope you are learning a great deal. Very few have an opportunity such as this."

"That is not lost on me, Uncle. I am—"

Jeld's words cut short as he stepped into the room. Across the table already sat High Priest Naelis, two of his unnerving inquisitors standing just behind in their white robes. They all looked at Jeld as he entered, the two inquisitors with their cold eyes and Naelis with his usual tranquil smile. Behind Naelis's smile though, Jeld could feel a thick tension like a snake ready to strike... a knowing arrogance, a devious treachery.

Jeld suppressed the urge to grin. It was going to feel good to see that smugness beaten out of Naelis when Lira and the prince arrived with men. He offered the slightest of nods. Krayo, now a fixture at council after having been granted his request, gave Jeld a curious look.

"I am very grateful and learning more and more each day," Jeld continued as they took their seats.

"Very good," Olind said, trying so hard not to look at Krayo that he might as well have been staring at him.

"Anything new with the business? Still managing to work around all... all this?"

Olind perked up at the mention of business. "Dreadful! I saw all this coming of course and divested myself of my luxury dealings, but even commodity storefronts suffer in depressions. Luckily I don't hold onto a great deal of inventory, so it's not as if I am losing money so much as not making as much."

The council chamber filled as Olind continued to speak of his woes and purport-edly brilliant countermeasures. Soon only two notable attendees were missing—Prince Dralor, and Lira.

Jeld looked over to High Priest Naelis. Still behind that priestly peacefulness lurked an irksome smugness. Jeld turned to Olind and nodded along, only vaguely aware that his dear uncle was still talking. Soon even Olind quieted as the council's chatter turned from business to gossip over the missing pair, then gossip to uncomfortable silence as the absence weighed on.

High Priest Naelis cleared his throat. "My lords. Already we face trying times, I know, but I'm afraid I have most... *distressing* news."

A murmur of alarm passed through the chamber.

"It's about our prince. He—" Naelis took a deep breath. "I'm sorry, it pains me to say, but I've come to learn that it was he who... who murdered our dear King Loris."

The chamber erupted with gasps, curses, and cries. A few seats away, Renae looked over at Jeld to share a moment of shock, which Jeld obliged.

"I know. I know. This is most disturbing. Violence, power, oppression... all enticing aspects of Discord. It was the great will in Dralor's heart to protect our kingdom that, in the end, proved his greatest vulnerability to Discord's seduction. I fear the last of the prince we all knew died with the very blow that struck down his brother."

As chaos broke out amongst the council, Jeld's eyes flicked to Naelis to find him staring back. Their eyes met and the terrible arrogance, the serpentine readiness, the devious treachery, all washed over Jeld. It wasn't directed at the council, he realized with a start. It wasn't for the prince. It was aimed at *him*.

Before Jeld could suppress his alarm, the high priest's eyes narrowed in a menacing glare. Jeld stood and the inquisitors tensed, but the high priest shook his head ever so slightly and the pair seemed to stand down. He glanced to Renae, then to Krayo, finding the latter staring gravely back. Without a word, Jeld mouthed his pardon then walked quickly from the room as Olind looked on in dismay.

Clear of the room, Jeld ran toward the main entrance. Turning a corner, he narrowly dodged around a veritable wall of gold and red, spinning to find a burly knight closing his fist around the hilt of a sizable sword. Behind the knight's other outstretched arm stood Lira.

"Lira! Did you warn the prince?" Jeld asked rapidly.

"What's this?" the knight said.

"It's okay, Krisharc, he's a friend," Lira said, ducking past the knight. "Yes, Dral's on his way with men."

"Where is he? It's a trap, we have to warn him!"

"Ah... Arvin, I did. I warned him."

"No, Naelis *wanted* us to warn Dralor. *That's* the trap!"

"What? How? How would he know?"

"No idea, but we need to warn your uncle, now!"

"Why would he want us to warn Dralor? He's bringing men to—"

"It's what Naelis wants. If he wants it, we don't! That's all there is to it. And if those priests can stop Handan...."

Lira stared gravely back before turning to Sir Krisharc. "Let's go."

The knight took the lead as they ran toward the entrance, servants and soldiers melting from their path. As they neared a young servant girl, something screamed out in Jeld's mind and he froze.

"Watch out!" Jeld shouted.

The servant jumped out at the knight with unnatural speed. There was a gleam of steel, a flash of bright red blood, then a gruesome gurgle as Krisharc fell to his knees.

"Run!" Jeld yelled, tugging Lira into flight.

He stole a glance over his shoulder as the servant pulled a knife from the toppling knight and looked up to meet his eyes. Her hair red and complexion freckled, Jeld recognized her then as the high priest's servant. She frowned venomously and sped in pursuit, two daggers flashing as she pumped her arms in a mechanical sprint.

Jeld led Lira around a corner and flew down the next corridor. He took two more turns before looking back again, his eyes widening at the sight of his pursuer just a few leaps behind.

"Hide in there!" he yelled, pointing at a doorway ahead.

When Lira looked at him incredulously, Jeld winked and drew his sword. With a nod, she darted ahead into the next room as Jeld came to a stop, turning with his sword at the ready.

The servant slowed from her sprint and stalked toward him, a dagger gleaming red in each hand. Jeld could almost hear General Handan's voice in his head—*keep a dual wielder on the defensive*. He lunged forward.

The would-be servant caught the blow on one dagger and attacked with the other. Jeld darted backward and her dagger snapped to a stop just shy of his neck. She jabbed several times in a flurry of blows, each one driving Jeld back a step as he dodged or slapped them aside with a flick of his sword.

Jeld swept a blow across her midsection, but she caught it upon crossed daggers then pulled one away and lashed out toward his thigh. He jumped backward and swung to cut off her pursuit, but she sidestepped and darted forward. When Jeld desperately swung again, she caught it on her rear blade and stabbed at his chest. He leapt back again, narrowly evading and surrendering another few steps.

Sweat poured down Jeld's forehead. She was too fast, every attack in her intricate dance improving her position... if not for but one fatal flaw. Jeld backpedaled another step.

She charged forward and lashed out in a blur of speed. Jeld slashed aside a high attack, then a low one, loosing another defensive sweep. Again she crossed her daggers and caught his sword, only this time she held onto it and charged inside his guard. His sword held at bay, Jeld could only look on in terror as she pulled a dagger free and plunged it toward his neck.

Suddenly she sucked in a short breath and her eyes went wide. She spun with a dagger but there came a crash of steel and she fell to her knees. Lira stood behind her, a bloody knife in her hand.

Jeld brought his sword down hard. It bit deep into the servant's neck and she folded lifelessly to the ground. He let out a quavering breath and looked to Lira with wild eyes.

"Come on!" Lira yelled. "Dralor must be nearly to council!"

The sure sounds of battle echoed down the hall as they neared the council chamber. Turning the last corner, they came to a sudden stop. A dozen watchmen spilled from the chamber with swords in hand. At their center, two men carried a bloodied Prince Dralor. Behind them all was one of Naelis's priests, a long wooden bo held out before him.

"Back!" Jeld hissed.

Before they made it back around the corner, the priest's eyes snapped onto Jeld.

"Run!" Jeld called, but this time it was Lira who dragged him into flight.

Portraits of kings and nobles of old flew by on either side. Jeld glanced over his shoulder. The priest was charging after them in the same mechanical sprint as the servant girl, his expression cold, inevitable.

"This way!" Jeld said between breaths and took a turn.

He pulled a pair of leather gloves from his collar and passed them to Lira.

"Put these on!"

"What?" Lira said even as she pulled them on.

Jeld took another turn. "Ever climbed a rope?"

"Rope? No!"

"Loose hands, tight feet," Jeld panted. "Not too fast or it burns. Not too slow or we die. Most important—don't let go!"

He glanced over his shoulder. A maelstrom of white robes stormed in pursuit, those cold eyes at its center.

Jeld lurched ahead faster still, Lira keeping pace without prompting.

"Left!" he yelled.

They flew up spiraling steps two and three at a time. Jeld reached again into his collar and produced his sparker.

"Next door. When I say jump, just jump!"

He pulled his belt off as rapid footfalls echoed up after them.

"In here!"

Jeld turned into the observation deck, slamming to a stop against the wall beside one of the windows and thrusting his escape rope into Lira's hand.

"Jump!" Jeld yelled.

Staring beyond the rope to the sprawling city far below, Lira's eyes widened even as her fist tightened and she leapt out the window, plunging from sight.

Jeld looped his belt around the rope then rolled over the sill and clamped his heels to the rope. Cursing himself for having but two hands as the priest spilled into the room, Jeld fumbled to twist the top of his sparker with what few fingers he could spare. It slipped from his grip just as the top twisted and threw out a spark. Meeting the priest's eyes as a flame raced across the rope, Jeld eased his grip and plunged downward.

He landed hard on his feet in the neat green grass of the inner gardens and looked around in a panic before spotting Lira perhaps a dozen leaps away. The smoldering rope tumbled down beside him and he looked up the tower, but there was no sign of Naelis's man.

"Come on!" Lira shouted.

Jeld scanned the grass for his sparker.

"Jeld!"

With a final glance through the grass, he ran to her and together they sped toward the gate.

"Open the gate!" Lira called ahead as they ran.

In the distance, the gate guard appeared to turn toward them but said nothing.

"Open the gate!" Jeld bellowed.

"Arvin?" one of them called.

Lira shot Jeld an irritated look and he shrugged innocently as they charged ahead.

"Lucas! Open the gate please! Quickly please!"

"Okay!" The young guardsman looked up to his counterpart atop the wall. "You heard him!"

There was a heavy metallic clank and Lucas pulled open the iron door set into the gate. As Jeld and Lira neared, Lucas frowned at Lira.

"Princess Liraelle?"

"Good day."

"Princess is in a spot of trouble," Jeld said, flipping a coin at Lucas. "Don't dare put up a fight for the next guy, but maybe your hearing isn't so good when they need that door unlocked?"

"Wha—ah, sure thing, Arvin."

"Thank ya!"

They sped through the gate, the crash of the door and Lucas's call to lock it echoing in their wake. Their legs burning and lungs aching, they charged onward.

"What now!" Lira huffed.

"There," Jeld said, pointing to Lord Demerious's mansion just ahead. "We need horses."

"Why would Tydel give us horses?"

Jeld raised an eyebrow.

"Oh," she said. "Right."

Circling the mansion, Jeld led Lira charging into the stables past a wide-eyed stableman. He had a horse free of its stall before the stableman appeared in the doorway.

"Come on then!" Jeld shouted. "Let's have another. A good one, too. Don't give me rubbish."

The stableman took a few steps toward the stalls then turned back to Jeld and Lira.

"Sir—ma'am, ah...who—"

"I think you mean 'Your Grace', "Lira snapped. "And I'm certain you haven't another blink to spare!"

The young stableman swallowed audibly then jumped into action. Leading his horse outside, Jeld frowned at Lira and she shrugged innocently. Grinning, Jeld handed her the reins with a bow. The stableman followed closely behind and not two breaths later, Jeld and Lira each sat atop one of Lord Tydel Demerious's finest horses. They were off at a gallop as the still stunned stableman caught a silver brick from the air.

With the help of another confounded guard, they were soon through the lower Hilltop wall and galloping down the streets of Upper Hillside. Spilling out into a wide intersection, they nearly collided with a squad of mounted watchmen.

"What's all this?" shouted a burly sergeant as he reined in his mount.

"Form a blockade!" Jeld ordered with a glance over his shoulder. "Stop the white-robed men, and the mutinous soldiers riding with them! Defend your princess!"

As the watchman turned a dumb look upon Lira, Jeld kicked his mount into motion and rode through their ranks. When he looked back, the watchmen had drawn their swords and were forming a line across the street.

Near the base of the hill, Jeld led Lira into a side street and slowed to a stop before a pair of thick men with tanned skin and sun-dried hair.

"Gents. I've got a silver royal for you to share if you'll lend me a hand?"

The two looked at one another then back up to Jeld.

"Yeah?" one of them said.

"These horses need to go all the way to the river. Don't care where. Sell 'em to a trader down there if you want another good bit of coin. Best you disappear soon after."

They exchanged another look before the same man spoke again. "One royal *each* and you got a deal."

Jeld pulled a small purse out of his collar and dumped two silver royals into his palm. He flipped a coin to each and dismounted, Lira following suit.

"Your lucky day, gents, had two in there today. Alright then. You'd best be on your way, and I must recommend haste."

The pair exchanged a final look then mounted Lord Demerious's best steeds and sped away.

Jeld reached deep into his collar and fished out a sack fashioned from a tapestry and piece of rope. He threw it to Lira.

"Change of clothes. Hurry."

"Don't I know this pattern?"

Jeld pulled out another. "Would you believe they were just going to toss them out over a few wine spots?"

"And how did you do that? Gloves, these sacks, that little—oh, that reminds me."

She tossed Jeld's sparker to him.

"You found it!" Jeld said, stuffing it into his collar. "We need to get changed. I'll explain later."

She blinked at him, shrugged, and stepped into a doorway to change.

Soon they were walking openly down the street in simple attire, Lira with a headscarf covering her too-clean hair and each bearing a heavy bag of jingling metal upon one shoulder.

"I can't believe you stole all this," Lira said as they walked south.

"I didn't *steal* anything. They were throwing most of it out, and this cutlery was just wasting away in some dusty chest anyway. I don't think anyone would have noticed if I'd stolen the whole blazin' room."

They fell silent as they walked, a now familiar somberness pressing against Jeld. Beside him, Lira's distant stare dragged along the ground. Once more Jeld could find no words, and though it seemed as futile as reaching to touch a rainbow, he imagined his own presence embracing the weight of her sorrow.

When finally they had passed through Midtown and Jeld was soon to turn north again, a bell rang frantic and without measure. Soon a hundred more across the city echoed its discordant call. Jeld had heard its like each night since the king's death, but he'd been above it then. It felt so different beneath its heavy assault, subject to it. It was the curfew bell, only it was earlier than usual.

"Naelis is closing us in..." Lira said.

Jeld nodded. "Our only edge has been being ahead of the news. That's over. We need to stop for the day. It won't do us well to be the only ones walking the streets."

He led the way twisting and turning through the city streets as others scurried for shelter.

"Where will we find a room?" Lira asked.

"We shouldn't. If they go offering a life's wages to turn us in, people will be lining up to hand over their own children."

He turned down a nondescript alleyway toward the steady clink of a hammer.

"Where will we go then?" Lira asked.

Jeld came to a stop halfway down the alley, crammed their bags of cutlery back into his collar as Lira stared quizzically, and patted high up the wall.

"After you. Be careful."

Jeld followed her up, the position of every next hold coming back to him as he climbed. When he reached the top, Lira was sitting on a small overturned crate. Beyond her was a broad brick chimney, a narrow overhang running across it to form a small nook beneath. A familiar hammering echoed up the chimney. He sat beside Lira atop the crate.

"You lived here..." she whispered.

"Yeah. Survived, anyway. Ate when I could. Drank when I could. Slept when—" He chuckled. "Actually I slept quite a lot."

A pillow beneath the overhang had at some point been made into a bird's nest. What appeared to have once been a blanket was plastered with mud into one corner, a filthy ceramic bowl beside it. Remembering fondly the many uses of his own bowl, Jeld wondered what must have befallen this one's owner for such a prize to be left behind.

The hammering stopped, jarring Jeld from his daydreams.

"This place isn't quite as nice as I remember."

"Hilltop life certainly couldn't have made it feel any fancier."

"Well, at least I've got good company this time. That might have been the worst part about all that anyway. Poor and frozen and starving, sure, but utterly alone...."

Her eyes glistening, Lira fell quiet for a time before speaking.

"You know what my mother said when I told her I had to warn Dral? 'Oh sweetie, don't fret over silly politics. Just stand tall and put on a strong face.'" She laughed humorlessly then sniffled. "Do you think she'll be alright?"

Jeld took her hand. "I think so. She's not in the succession, so she isn't a threat. And wasn't it an alliance with Havaral that drove your father and her to be bound to begin with? She's still a Cross, and Naelis needs Havaral now more than ever."

"She'll be no better than a prisoner. Although I'm not sure she'd mind so long as she gets her servants and balls."

"We'll figure something out."

"I'm really never going back. I'll never see the library again. Or spar with Handan. Or study with Benam—" She shook her head. "What does it matter, they're both gone anyway. Just like father."

"Of course it matters, it's your home. I don't know, I figure... somehow we're going to have to see that Naelis pays for all this, and then maybe you can go back. For now, I think we're just lucky to be alive after everything today."

When Lira only nodded, Jeld pulled two tightly packed bedrolls from his bag and set to arranging them beneath the overhang. Lira silently joined him in setting up camp, and soon they sat upon their bedrolls leaning back against the chimney.

"It's warm," Lira said with surprise.

"One of the best spots in town."

Jeld bundled up the ropes that had held the bedrolls together and stuffed them back into his collar.

"How do you do that?"

"I... don't really know. It's this bag. Here."

Jeld unbuttoned the flattened circle of leather from the inside of his shirt and bunched it back up into some semblance of a bag.

"See, it's a bag, but reach in here."

Jeld pulled away part of the liner and Lira reached inside. When her elbow passed through the top of the bag, her eyes went wide and she pulled her arm free.

"How..."

"I don't know. It's just... bottomless. Well, sort of. You remember when I showed you beneath the stage at the theater, with all the trapdoors overhead? It's like reaching up through one of those. I can set things around the rim. So it's actually more... *topless*."

Jeld removed the liner and laid the bag open. They sat staring into the void before Lira gingerly dipped her hand inside.

"How—where did you get this?"

"It's... well, I was watching the Fallsday show at the theater and...."

"And?"

Jeld shook his head. "Sorry. You know when you think something really happened, but then you realize it was a dream?"

Lira nodded.

"Sometimes it seems like that's bound to happen... only I haven't realized it's a dream yet." Jeld shook his head again. "It *must* have been a dream. I must have just happened upon the bag. It was dark after all, and—"

"Jeld, what happened?"

Jeld bit his lip then sighed. "I was at the show. I was... in a really dark place then. Vacant, I guess. I hadn't really felt anything for so long, but the audience... there was so much awe and sorrow and excitement pouring off them that I could actually feel it. The show, the people... it just hit me. There was a flash and..."

Jeld closed his eyes. "I was in a tavern. It was perfect. Warm. There was this soft music. And the place had this wonderful glow. Orange, like firelight. Like... the Traveler's tavern."

Lira shook her head. "Kelthin's Tavern was in the show, right? It was probably just on the stage and set your imagination—"

"No, it was just the doors to the Halls. You know, the part where all the young Idols walk through them for the first time."

"But it may have reminded you of the other part and, you know, set your imagination—"

Jeld nodded down to the bag and Lira frowned.

"There's something else," he added. "I meant to tell you before, but I guess it never seemed like the right time."

"What is it?"

"Ever since that same day, I've been able to... I don't know, feel people? Really *feel*, like—" Jeld reached out and ran his fingers through the air between them. "Like it's all right here. I can feel what people feel. What they think even, sort of."

"Handan once said that in a battle during the Vanishing Wars, he glimpsed the Warrior's great hall. He said it's often like that with..."

"Idolics," Jeld supplied.

"That's how you fight so well," Lira breathed.

"And how I knew Naelis was setting up your uncle." He closed his hand loosely as if letting sand trickle through it.

"What do you see?"

Tears welled up in Jeld's eyes as he studied her deep sorrow.

"You."

A tear ran down Lira's cheek.

"You know," Jeld whispered, "that day it happened was the same day I first met you. I don't think I would have even watched the show otherwise, never mind felt anything from it. It's like you opened me back up."

Lira smiled. "The stories say the Traveler could pull anything from his cloak. Maybe it's like that. Maybe he had this bag?"

"So I stole the Traveler's bag? No wonder I have nightmares."

"Well, I don't think the Idols are going to be needing it."

They both fell somber at that.

"We should probably get some sleep," Lira said after a while.

She laid down and pulled her blankets up around her. Jeld laid beside her and they both stared up at the early stars.

"We're going to your theater, aren't we?" Lira whispered.

"We can be safe there."

"Just... in the walls?"

"I was still thinking that through. I'm sure Director Sammel would put us right to work, but a boy and a pretty Hilltopper girl showing up the day after the princess and her friend go missing? It'd stand out."

"You really think so?"

"Yeah, it's risky."

"Not that. The other thing. About a pretty girl going missing."

Jeld blushed. "Oh."

Lira smirked. "So, you don't think we could just disguise me? Blend in?"

"Probably. Maybe. Change your hair, lose the Toppertongue, make up a good story. Sure, it might work... but I think we should just disappear for at least a little while first."

"Yes. Yes, of course."

"Oh!" Jeld said after a silence.

"What is it?"

"You're outside. You once said you've never slept outside."

"Ohh."

Lira gazed out at the first stars, but soon her distant eyes seemed to look still beyond as the sky grew darker. Despite their worries, exhaustion brought sleep quickly, though it was a fitful sleep full of unkind dreams for both. Their hands found one another late into the night, and while their dreams did not turn kinder, they faced their demons alone no longer.

***

The next morning Jeld and Lira made their way to the theater. When they reached what had once been Jeld's bedroom within the old walls, he found it almost unrecognizable. It was clean—pristinely so. No scraps of wood, no carpet of dust nor valances of spiderweb. Where his filthy makeshift bed once lay beside the warm bricks behind Evelyn's oven, a plush feather mattress now gleamed a perfect white. Plump pillows floated upon it beside a basket of exotic fruits. Atop the pillow was a note. They read it together beside a flickering candle.

Welcome, Her Grace Princess Liraelle Tovados and Sir Arvin. Won't you join me for breakfast in my office come morning?

-KR

CHAPTER THIRTY-EIGHT

J eld savored a deep breath of fresh air. It seemed a month must have passed within the confines of the dusty theater walls, but in fact he'd lasted only two days before venturing out to survey the state of the city and its pursuit of Princess Liraelle. Krayo had of course offered to keep him apprised, but seeing as Krayo's top sneak was confined to quarters, it seemed a look for himself couldn't hurt.

He shrugged a courier sack higher onto his shoulder and turned out onto the main road. The lively buzz of the city was gone, the lingering travelers skittish and suspicious. The buildings themselves were at first glance much as Jeld remembered. Only on closer examination did the signs of vacancy and hardship reveal themselves—a smokeless chimney, an empty table, eyes peering longingly through the shutters of a dark but free captivity. Just as he of soiled clothes, it seemed the people had learned that to let a shop fall into disrepair was to invite trouble with the watch.

Presently, a squad of watchmen was stopped beside a large group of soldiers, their sergeants in a heated conversation just across the street. Both groups were armed and armored for war. Jeld pulled a letter from his sack and pretended to scrutinize it as he passed by the patrols. Just a few blocks ahead, the familiar sight of The North Tovarian Temple of One brought an irresistible grin to his lips.

He wanted so badly to go inside and see Prishner Walson, to fill the dear man's kitchen for the many children he looked after. Had their numbers swelled in these hard times? Or were they all wasting away now in the Prince's Prison? Jeld sighed and walked past the temple. It was certain to be the one place Naelis would think to look for Lira, which was precisely why it was just the place to investigate the state of the pursuit.

Scanning the crowds, Jeld took a deep breath and opened his other sense to the world around him. The city's collective despair pressed against him. He flexed his will and from the chaos emerged individual stories. From the stone walls of the temple itself seemed to emanate a comforting warmth. At its front, the etchings upon the temple doors seemed almost to glow. He turned and scanned the storefronts across the street, a likely vantage for anyone staking the place out. A woman wrapped in a thick blanket was sewing winter caps outside a tailor's shop. Through the window of the next shop, a barber woman was trimming a man's beard. In another, a man sat by himself behind a tankard.

Jeld blinked at the man. He drifted closer, peering discreetly past another letter into the tavern window. The man's tankard was full, it's handle opposite him as if untouched since the barkeep had placed it. His green eyes flicked over the top of the tankard toward the temple. Though unshaven and plainly dressed, there was no mistaking Sir Benam.

Shaking his head with a grin, Jeld turned into the tavern, got a drink from the bar, and slapped his tankard onto the man's table.

"Mind if I join yeh?"

"Please," Sir Benam said, his eyes fixed upon the temple.

Jeld summoned up Arvin's voice. "Too kind. Looking for something? Someone?"

"Never mind, frien—"

Benam looked over at Jeld, who raised a finger to his lips.

"Arvin!" Benam whispered. He loosed a breath of laughter. "You're—where's the princess? Is she alright?"

Jeld smiled back and nodded. "She's safe. Hurting, understandably, but well enough."

A great weight fell away from Benam.

"You knew she would come back here, then?" Jeld asked. "Have you seen others? Anyone looking for her?"

"Plenty of patrols. Who can say? Arvin, what happened? What's this nonsense about Dralor murdering Loris? And Naelis naming himself king?"

"You're right that Prince Dralor didn't murder the king. Naelis did. It was him behind the Sayers all along, too. Behind *everything*."

"The high priest... dear Mother."

"Yeah. But naming himself king... that one I hadn't yet heard. Can't say I'm surprised."

Shaking his head, Benam reached for his tankard but let his hand fall and only tapped at the handle. "How did you escape?"

"Narrowly. Naelis brought in these... guards. Eerie fellas, and faster than they have a right to be. Idolics for sure. Even stopped Handan. They almost had us."

"White robes?"

Jeld nodded.

Benam frowned. "Inquisitors."

"Who are they?"

Benam's eyes grew distant. "I don't know much. They serve in the prison camps, and that's what they call them there. *Inquisitors*. Easterners, most of them. There's something altogether... *wrong* about them. Evil, I dare say. That's all I know. Arvin, where is Lira? I need to see her."

Jeld took a slow sip as he considered his answer. He had fresh scars from Benam's last round of good intentions, and Krayo wasn't likely to appreciate such an exposure. Still, what would he tell Lira should he turn Benam away?

"We're hiding out in Temple Theater. Krayo is helping to keep the princess safe."

"Krayo Rusrivon? He's risking a lot helping Liraelle, after everything he went through for his position."

"Maybe he just expects that helping the royal family will come back around one day. Or maybe he's just, you know, doing the right thing."

"Yes, probably expects Lira will pay him back somehow," Benam said. "Dear Idols, I can't believe I found her. Let's be off."

He started to rise.

"Woh there!" Jeld hissed. "We don't know who might be watching. I'll leave first. Give me... say, until that guy there finishes his drink, then go to the warehouse behind the theater. Cut through some crowds on your way. Empty alleys are a great way to see if you're being followed. At the warehouse, tell them you have an appointment with Ement. Got it?"

Benam settled in his chair and nodded.

Jeld stood. "I'm glad to see you well."

"You also, Arvin. And thank you. For saving Liraelle."

Jeld gave Benam a nod. "Thanks for saving *me.*"

He slapped a coin on the table beside the two full tankards and set off in a winding path toward the theater.

At the theater, he gathered Lira, Ement, and Krayo in an austere dining room beside Krayo's office. A sharply dressed servant from Krayo's newly opened Red Curtain Eatery across the square set a final covered platter upon the table and slipped from the room. Nearly colliding with the servant, Henred appeared in the doorway and waved Benam into the room.

"Benam!" Lira cried, jumping up and running into his arms.

"Oh, my girl!"

Henred nodded to Krayo and stepped out of the room, pulling the door closed behind him.

"Sir Benam," Krayo greeted. "Fine to see you again."

Benam's green eyes flicked back to Lira before he grasped Krayo's hand.

"You as well."

"Won't you dine with us? Please, have a seat."

Ement set to uncovering the many silver platters as Sir Benam took his seat.

"Enjoy, everyone. Eat, we have much to discuss."

"You're doing well enough?" Lira asked Sir Benam.

"Well enough, yes," Benam said. "That is all I could ever ask. It's not for myself that I grieve, my princess, but for our kingdom. For your father. Even for your uncle. He doesn't deserve to be executed."

Lira gasped.

"Ah... executed?" Jeld said. "I thought he was—er, dead?"

Ement shook his head and spoke around a mouthful of food. "What're you, living under a theater? Two more days. Can't come fast enough, if you ask me. Beggin' your pardon, Princess."

"Come now," Benam pleaded. "Let us not speak ill. Believe me, I know Dralor is a harsh man, but if High Priest Naelis truly is behind all this then Dralor is more a victim than anyone."

"I hear you've spent some time at *Prince's* Prison, sir. That prince sure runs a nice clean camp, eh?"

Benam shifted in his chair but said nothing.

"Sir Benam is right," Lira said. "Dral has been a monster, but I don't think he wanted any of this. It's Naelis playing to his weaknesses, turning all his passion into hatred. Naelis ruined him, and now he's going to finish the job."

"Yes, exactly," Benam agreed. "Ever have I disagreed with the prince's methods, but I don't believe I can let this happen. I can't allow Naelis this last victory over Dralor. Over the crown."

"My friends," Krayo said. "Let us not dwell on the inevitable. Now, we've got the matter of the princess's safety to discuss."

Benam shook his head. "We can't let this happen."

"What could we do? And to what end, anyway? Where could he go? You think Prince Dralor would hide in the walls?"

"I don't intend we hide," Benam said, turning to Lira. "We must go to Delvarad. My father will not stand for this usurpation. We'll be safe there, and find a way to set things right."

Krayo frowned. "I don't presume to know your father, but I don't see Lord Relthid as particularly... *sensitive* to the crown's hardships."

"I thought much the same for many years. Only recently have I begun to understand him. He never hated the Idols or Loris's father when he stood against them. What he hated was loyalty for sake of loyalty. Faith for the sake of faith. He only opposed failure, and the Idols were admittedly... failing. Even before Khapar, they spent far more time in dreams than awake."

Krayo nodded. "Well, if the princess will be safe there then perhaps you should consider making the journey. We can help you get outside the walls and past the checkpoints. We can make arrangements immediately."

"The prince as well," Benam said firmly. "We can't let him die. *Maybe* a citizen deserves to take Dral's life, but Naelis cannot have him."

Krayo closed his eyes and rubbed his temples. "It's risky enough helping the princess, let alone having you here. Look, we have a chance to protect the princess if we don't do anything stupid. I'm sorry, but saving Dralor is stupid. And there's nothing we can do, anyway. He's in the keep jails. It can't be helped."

Krayo set to his food again, the others all picking at theirs in silence.

"Huhm," Jeld said after a while, his eyes distant. "There might be a way..."

CHAPTER THIRTY-NINE

E verything lurched suddenly downward in the darkness and Jeld's forehead slapped against a board above. The toe of Alal's shoe rapped his ear. Jeld whispered a curse and his hot, dusty breath bounced back against him. He sighed. Another dusty hole.

In time the darkness drew his thoughts again from the constriction and abuse. Arvin Emry's stint was up, the Sayers had stabbed and now chased off their once promising young initiate, and if somehow he survived the night, all hope of returning to his simple existence at the theater was lost. Once again life was but ashes behind him.

There came another bump and while he managed to avoid hitting his forehead, Alal's shoe once again hit him in the ear. Jeld cut Alal's snickering short with a kick of his own.

"Ouch!" Alal cried. "*Khap—*"

"Shut it!" Erol's muffled voice came from above.

Jeld managed a smile and they drove onward in silence until more voices outside shared a brief exchange. There came the unmistakable ratcheting of a gate opening, then its closing faded behind them.

Not soon enough, the carriage came to a stop. It rocked as the floorboards above creaked. The wall just beyond the top of Jeld's head fell away and crisp night air rushed in. Jeld craned his neck around to find a figure standing over him, silhouetted against the starry sky. The figure glanced behind and the starlight traced the profile of Krayo.

Jeld took Krayo's hand and pulled free of the smuggler's hold. His hair was dyed a light blond, his meager lines deepened with the magic touch of Evelyn's makeup brush. Patting off his white clothes and straightening his high servant's shoulder cord, his pulse eased as his feet hit the open road. Overhead, a tree's canopy concealed them from whatever patrols might be walking the keep walls above. Krayo was dressed in ballroom finery that only just managed to convey his usual practicalities. Beside him, dressed the part of a chauffeur, Erol pulled Alal from the hold.

Alal shivered. "Well that was unpleasant. Not Onders' finest work."

He dusted off his white inquisitor's robe and pulled up the hood.

"Tough to be fast in a smuggler's hold, eh?" Erol said.

"Quite unsettling. And quite boring. At least Jeld lent me his ear."

Krayo met Jeld's eyes before issuing a curt nod.

"Good luck," he said, climbing back into the carriage.

Alal cleared his throat. "Best hurry back."

Erol grunted, climbing atop the carriage and pulling away.

"Right," Alal said. "We'll just be here, standing in the king's garden. No hurry."

Jeld led Alal off the road and into the trees.

"Perfect," Alal said, eyes darting about. "What could go wrong?"

"Nobody will see us here. If they do, just act like you are supposed to be here. It works every time."

"Ah. I'm *supposed* to be lurking in the king's trees. Yes, that ought to work."

Jeld smiled, his own nerves easing with it. He tried to nudge Alal but his friend casually dodged.

"Just give them your best inquisitor dead-eyes," Jeld said. "Nobody will say a word."

Alal smirked and nudged Jeld.

They fell silent as hoofbeats drew near. Jeld's pulse beat faster and faster until the sound began to fade into the distance. The faint sound of music emerged amidst the silence.

Jeld blew out a breath. "I definitely liked it better when my character got to *attend* balls instead of just stalking around outside them."

"Prefer eating the king's pork over trying not to get beheaded? Yes, I imagine so."

Another carriage went by, Jeld and Alal remaining silent this time even after it passed. They said not another word as dozens more rattled by, the breaths dragging on painfully slow. Eighth bell chimed in the distance.

Alal bit his lip. "He should be back by—"

Hoofbeats approached once again, only this time they seemed to slow nearby. The rattle of the carriage seemed more metallic, a steely jingle. A memory of a cage wagon flashed in Jeld's mind and he caught Alal's shoulder as his friend made to peer around the tree.

"Wait," Jeld hissed.

Alal froze and they could only wait as the sound drew nearer. Jeld clenched his sheathed knife, Alal slowly drawing a short, skinny sword from his robe.

"Jeld? Alal?" Erol's voice came at last.

Jeld let out his breath and stepped into the open to find Erol atop a cage wagon, dressed the part of a watch sergeant.

"What are you—"

"Yeah I know," Erol grunted. "Drop Krayo off, get the cage together. Well, there it was with nobody watching, so?"

"I don't suppose you've got the prince back there already, too?" Alal asked.

"Nice job," Jeld said.

He hurried up onto the bench beside Erol, Alal following closely behind. Erol rapped the reins, and not a moment later other hoofbeats approached.

"Characters," Erol said, his posture slackening.

Jeld brought to mind an officious servant he'd once encountered and let it envelop him until all that remained of himself was a distant whisper to steer this other man occupying his body. His posture shifted, his face twisted, and as he approached the stables he was Farence Chornsby, former aid of house affairs to the royal family and now high servant generalist to the high priest.

Glancing aside to Alal, Jeld found his friend cold-eyed and sneering beneath his white hood. With a shiver, Jeld turned back to the road. A carriage approached, its driver taking one look at Alal before averting eye contact and passing them by.

Jeld pointed at a turn. "There."

Erol turned and they followed a smaller road toward the eastern wall. Soon Jeld could see the faint shapes of two guards flanking an unlit archway.

"I could just kill them," Alal whispered.

Ignoring his friend, Jeld gave his character a final audit before they came to a stop in front of the guards.

"Guardsmen," Jeld greeted.

He climbed down and handed a note to a grizzled old corporal.

"Orders from the high priest," Jeld said. "We're to deliver the prince tonight to a watch detachment in Lormster Square for execution tomorrow."

The corporal took the note. Atop it gleamed a freshly pressed seal of white wax bearing the symbols of the Idols, compliments of Fen's handiwork.

"I thought we were moving him tomorrow?" the younger guardsman asked.

"Something about a threat to the planned route tomorrow," Jeld said. "Came in no more than a bell ago from one of the—well, from him."

Jeld pointed to Alal, but the guards were already staring at him.

The younger guard glanced to his partner, who shifted uneasily.

"Go on, tell him, Bren" the corporal said.

"Right. We... don't have the key."

Jeld swallowed. "Isn't it... fairly typical of jail guards to have keys?"

"Prince Dralor had a lot of friends," the corporal said. "Or allies, anyway. Don't think Lasken is quite sure who can be trusted to keep a key to his cell."

"I see. So... only Sir Lasken knows?"

"More than knows, he's got it."

"I see. Well, that won't be a problem. I'll return shortly with the key. Thank you, guardsmen."

Jeld turned to Alal. "Perhaps you'd best wait here. Much as I trust the good guardsmen, if whoever leaked the execution route finds out about our plan, they'll come for Dralor."

Bren looked nervously to his corporal as Alal climbed down.

"Very good," the corporal said, then patted his partner on the arm. "I'm going with them."

"But—" Bren and Jeld said at the same time.

"No, no. I insist," the corporal interrupted, eyes darting from Alal. "Happy to... help."

Following the guardsman onto the wagon, Jeld shrugged at Erol, who grunted then turned the wagon toward the distant music of the ball.

"Back right quick, Bren," the corporal said. "You two have fun."

"Hah!" Erol said when they were out of earshot. "Can't say I blame ya. Shared a bench with that fella longer than I like, myself."

The corporal bit his lip and looked over at Jeld.

"Oh have your fun," Jeld said as the wagon clapped along. "I serve High Priest Naelis, not those... *those*. Truth be told, I'm not sure how fond of them the high priest is. Finds their skills quite handy though, to be sure."

The corporal shrugged. "Well, you said it."

When Erol and Jeld said nothing further, the corporal filled the silence.

"So where do you usually serve, Sergeant?"

"Ah... sorry," Erol said. "With the leak of the route, I'd best not give any hints where we might take him."

"Ah. Right, right."

They rounded a curve and the music grew louder as they found themselves approaching the ballroom, its tall arched windows setting the gardens alight.

"Maybe just pull over there," Jeld said.

Erol nodded and veered around the grand entry, stopping before an outcropping Jeld knew to be the kitchens.

"I'll be right back with the key," Jeld said.

He met Erol's eyes and let his friend's stoicism calm his rising panic. Sucking in a breath, he turned, pulled his high servant's shoulder cord off, and marched through a small servant's door.

At once Jeld dodged a servant only to collide with another bearing a silver tray. He helped right her and scooped up another tray from a nearby table, holding it up with one hand as he'd seen so many servants do with apparent ease. When it only tottered wildly with each step, he set it upon another table, nodding confidently to a perplexed servant and snatching up a decanter of wine.

Jeld followed another servant toward a narrow passage glowing with the golden light of the ball. His racing pulse quickened further. Tensed for the buzz of the ball, a certain death one recognition away, he burst into the ballroom to find it completely still, all eyes raised to the balcony. High Priest Naelis stood at the center of the balcony, an inquisitor to his either side. Queen Darene stood with him, her eyes swimming as usual about the ballroom, only with a melancholy about her in place of the typical fanciful bliss.

"Let us remember also that we are warriors," High Priest Naelis said. "That we few are the generals in the Idols' war against Discord. We few must restore decency to the kingdom."

Jeld pressed his back to the wall and scanned the ballroom crowd as all muttered their agreement. He spotted Sir Lasken in a small group with Lady Hepsbry.

"This purge of indecency begins with us. Our drinks be benign, our wars sparing and righteous, our justice swift. We must carry forth our Idols' vision and see the kingdom and the world made good. So, be merry, for you all now bear a great burden, and your dedication to the kingdom and our Idols is to be celebrated. And may they watch over you now, and in dreams."

"In dreams," everyone echoed back.

The music and murmur of a hundred voices began anew. Jeld bowed his head and pressed toward Lasken, circling wide around Olind and Lady Edenwood. He pretended not to notice Chancellor Cerus gesturing for a refill of his goblet as he marched past and came to a stop beside Sir Lasken.

"And of *course* she did," Lady Hepsbry said before glancing to Jeld. "Oh, great. More of Naelis's juice."

Jeld eyed Lasken as he refilled Lady Hepsbry's goblet. Lasken wore a black doublet with no apparent pockets nor purses. Not uncommon for a ball goer, Jeld considered, but nonetheless his hopes sank. Lasken rubbed at his chest and Jeld noticed a leather band on the back of his neck peeking out over his collar.

A necklace. It had to be the key. When Jeld took a step toward him, Lasken moved his goblet out of reach.

"I'll see what the bar can cook up," Lasken said and started off.

Jeld waded into the crowd after him, snatching a towel from another servant and filling the occasional Topper's goblet with short pours lest he not have enough left to spill on Lasken. Eyeing Lasken at the bar as he filled another, an inquisitor appeared through the crowd. The inquisitor pressed closer, looking about like a bloodhound on a scent.

Jeld quickly looked away. Filling another goblet, he opened his mind and felt the inquisitor draw closer. He bowed his head lower and audited his character—a flexing of the nostrils, creasing of the brow, thinning of the lips. Just then he felt another pair of eyes upon him and looked up to find Lord Tydel Demerious squinting at him. As Jeld's mind's eye stared in horror at the impending recognition, he found himself weaving his illusion into the very substance dancing between them, pushing back on the aura where before he had only ever observed. *This* was the veil, he knew then. Not merely a change in himself, but a change in the very perception of his audience.

Lord Tydel blinked and turned away. Behind, the inquisitor too seemed to lose his scent, wandering aside with a puzzled look upon his face. Letting out a breath, Jeld looked to the bar but Lasken was gone. He spotted him in the crowd and wove into his path. Doubt forced Jeld to a near stop as he closed, but he bit his lip, spun, and crashed into Lasken.

Stunned, Sir Lasken gulped air like a caught fish as his doublet soaked up the contents of Jeld's decanter. At once Jeld set his decanter down and pressed his towel to Lasken's collar, a knife beneath it slicing the necklace. He patted Lasken's chest as he slipped the necklace free and wrapped it beneath the towel.

"I'm... so sorry, sir!" Jeld stammered. "So sorry. Let me get you more towels. I'll take care of it, sir!"

Jeld hurried back toward the kitchens, clenching the towel-wrapped necklace with both hands. His heart raced as he braced for a hand upon his shoulder, but none had come when at last he reached the kitchens. He pressed through, narrowly remembering to pin his high servant's shoulder cord back into place before bursting back into the cool night air.

Erol sat up straight at once before managing to look less surprised. Beside him, the corporal seemed not to notice. Jeld climbed onto the bench next to Erol.

"All set," Jeld said.

Erol flicked the reins. "Think I'd have stayed for a meal."

"Princes to execute."

The cage wagon rattled toward the jails. Jeld peeled the towel open and glanced down to find not a key, but a small silver flask within. His stomach twisted.

He leaned in to whisper to Erol. "I don't have it."

Erol did a double take. "What!" he mouthed.

"Will be good to be back to patrolling a day sooner, at least," the corporal said.

Erol grunted. "Right. Beats standin' still."

Erol shot a look at Jeld, who shrugged helplessly and gestured ahead.

The wagon rattled along and Jeld's mind rattled with it as he fruitlessly plotted. Sweat streamed down Jeld's forehead as they neared the jails. He looked to Erol, and just as he opened his mouth to call the whole thing off, his eyes suddenly widened. Jeld offered a reassuring nod to Erol, who shook his head and brought the wagon to a stop before Alal and the young guardsman.

"All set," Jeld said, climbing down from the wagon. "Sergeant, Inquisitor. Shall we?"

Erol frowned at Jeld before shaking his head again and following him into the jail, Alal at his side.

"He doesn't have the key," Erol whispered to Alal.

"What?" Alal hissed. "What are we... doing, then?"

Erol shrugged, gesturing at Jeld.

Alal rushed ahead to Jeld's side. "What are you going to do, cut him into pieces?"

"No time to explain," Jeld said. "Don't worry."

"I'm worried."

The scent of life or something like it grew stronger with each empty cell they passed, the light of the entry dimming and dimming. Suddenly someone was standing beside them beyond iron bars.

Prince Dralor was dressed in dirtied beige underclothes, his once-neat goatee surrounded by whiskers. He glared at Alal.

"Prince Dralor," Jeld whispered. "It's J—Arvin. We're getting you out."

"Arvin? What—do you have Lira?"

Jeld handed Erol the flask and dug in his collar. "No time, the guards are waiting."

Erol cleared his throat. "Jeld...."

"No key, I know."

Jeld pulled his flattened bag from his collar and unbuttoned the lining, pulling it away to reveal the black void beyond.

"What in dreams..." Alal breathed.

Jeld reached through the bars and set it on the floor.

"Get in."

Looking up from the bag, Dralor met Jeld's eyes before kneeling over the bag. He reached into it and felt about until his hand seemed to close on the rim. Dralor met Jeld's eyes again, frowned, and pulled himself into the void. The last of his bare feet disappeared inside, the black void not even so much as rippling in its wake, only erasing him with a silent and still finality.

Jeld slid the bag out from the cell and knelt over it.

"Come back," he whispered.

When nothing appeared, Jeld frowned at his wide eyed friends and reached inside.

"Come on!" Jeld hissed. "The guards are waiting!"

Jeld flinched as a hand closed upon his. Dralor pulled free of the bag, his eyes wide.

"What the..." a voice said from behind.

Jeld turned to find Bren standing just behind, his jaw hanging open. Realization crept across his face and he took a step backward, but Erol was upon him. Erol punched him in the chin and he folded to the ground.

"Alright then," Jeld said. "Alal handle the corporal?"

Alal looked up from the bag. "Why not."

Stuffing the bag into his collar, Jeld rattled the cell door then started toward the exit. Erol took a swig of Lasken's flask and followed after with Alal.

Outside, the corporal frowned. "No chains?"

Erol raised an eyebrow. "You heard of inquisitors?"

When the man turned, Alal jabbed him in the nose. The guardsman only stumbled backward and Alal swung again, then again, his hands just a blur. On the fifth hit, the corporal finally went limp, Alal catching him while he was still standing.

"Well, you're fast at least," Erol said as he and Dralor dragged the unconscious guard into the jail.

"I was trying not to hurt him."

Erol grunted. "Nicer, too."

They bound the guardsmen and returned to the wagon.

Erol turned again toward the stables. "What's the bag?"

Jeld watched the cobblestones go by before answering. "Kelthin's bag. We think."

"Traveler's bag," Erol grunted.

He asked nothing further, as if Jeld's answer was perfectly normal. Jeld smiled.

Erol pulled to a stop a short time later beneath the trees.

"Hate to leave you two."

"We'll be alright," Jeld said. "Wouldn't do well to have Krayo's man unaccounted for when the prince went missing."

"Uhng. All this scheming."

"Well," Alal said. "Can't exactly rescue a prince from the keep by bashing something with a stick, can we?"

Erol climbed down, offered a nod, and started toward the stables on foot. Jeld took the reins and soon they cleared the gate without incident. Breathing easy, they both fell silent as they pressed through the night toward their rendezvous.

Looking out at the passing buildings, Jeld loosed a humorless breath of laughter.

"What is it?" Alal asked.

"I'm driving a watchman's cage wagon through Tovar, with the prince in its back."

Alal chuckled.

Jeld looked back at Dralor, finding him gazing distantly behind. The usurped prince met Jeld's eyes, finally nodding and looking out to the stars.

How can I cast a single person to the rolling seas, even if it means keeping the raft afloat for the many? Can I not forgo logic and simply heed this feeling of rightness—reject none and sink with the masses? And to blight the very soul of my most loyal priest with this unspeakable act... to end all I love, so that love might persist at all.

Cursed logic. Cursed reason. It is for the best. It is for the best. I cast my web. Forgive me. Forgive me.

—Vincet Ellemere

Chapter Forty

⸺◆⸺

"You know, Your Grace," Hawss said from his seat near Lira, "Jeld used to play the best little girl on stage. But, he might be a bit too big now. Gained a few pounds on the hill, by the look of him."

Beside him, Cass rolled her eyes with a practiced precision. Lira laughed along with the rest of the crew in the cozy den, save Erol who frowned somehow jovially.

"That's a most impressive range," Lira said. "And please, really, just *Lira* will do."

"Jeld's always been full of surprises," Roba said.

She was seated upon a plush chair beside Fen, their hands intertwined. Shaking his head at the couple, Jeld winced as he plucked another sour note on Master Edlin's lute.

"Are you about done yet, Jeld?" Fen said.

"Sounds that bad?" Jeld asked.

"Yes, but not the noise. Your damned sideways glances."

"Er, yes. Yes. Sorry. It's just that—"

"It's weird seeing us together. Yeah, you mentioned that once or ten times already."

"Well, right, but it's even more strange seeing you both *here*. Like my two lives blended together while I was away."

"Luckily you seem to have plenty of lives to spare," Roba said.

Director Sammel cleared his throat. "Roba and Fen have brought a new life to our little troupe, and no few talents. They deserve more, but with the shows on donations only…"

"A family and a workshop. I should be paying *you*," Fen said.

"I don't think anyone here is getting paid enough to go rescuing princes and sheltering fugitive princesses," Jeld said.

"Enough of that, boy," Erol said. "Not about to dance around on stage while Naelis shits all over the city."

"Aye," Yelana whispered. "The whole kingdom, really."

"Here, here!" Onders cheered, the whole crew following suit.

Jeld handed the lute back to Master Edlin. "I just can't help but feel I've put you all in danger."

"I've spent my life impersonating heroes and staging legends," Evelyn said. "It's time I do my share, honey. Danger be damned."

Smiling broadly, Director Sammel patted Jeld's shoulder and turned to Lira. "Your Gra—ah, Liraelle. I'm sure you don't remember, but I had the privilege of meeting you long ago. You were five, if I recall, and we had the honor of performing for the king during Fallstival."

"I must confess I don't remember the meeting," Lira said. "But the show stands clear in my memory. It has never dulled. A moment of pure magic."

The old director beamed.

"You met my father too?" Lira asked.

"A most wonderful man, my dear."

"I met him as well," Evelyn said. "He was nothing but kind to us all. You should be very proud of your father."

Lira returned a sad smile. "Thank you. He was very fond of the arts."

The room grew suddenly quiet. Jeld followed the collective gaze of his companions to find Krayo standing before the hallway behind him.

"I would offer you all my thanks, but from what I gather you would not accept it," Krayo said. "Let me then just say, *welcome*. Welcome to the team. And as for pay, more risk and more responsibility warrants more compensation. You'll all be receiving raises."

The crew cheered.

Krayo nodded. "Your Grace, Jeld, would you join us upstairs?"

He turned and left without waiting for an answer. Lira stood but Jeld only looked gravely across the den from face to friendly face. At last Jeld gave the crew a firm and full nod and started down the hallway with Lira.

"Your friends are wonderful," Lira said.

"Yeah. They are."

"And it's so nice to see Roba and Fen again. Can you believe they are... together?"

"It's great. Weird, but great. Almost as weird as my working for Krayo so openly in front of the crew. And having you here! It's like I said, all these different lives are suddenly converging.

"Whole again at last."

Jeld nodded and led Lira up the steps. "Are you doing alright?"

"I don't know... as good as could be expected, I suppose."

Emerging from the stairwell, she paused at the base of the steps to the upper level, the brilliant red stage curtain behind her.

"I haven't really... I'm not sure it's all—" She looked down at the ground and took a breath before meeting his eyes again. "It's all too much, I suppose. It just doesn't feel real."

"You'll have to confront it some time, but I think our minds have a way of... ignoring our wounds until the battle's over."

Lira nodded. "I don't think it'll be over any time soon."

"One battle at a time."

Lira pursed her lips thoughtfully then nodded again. "Well, shall we?"

"After you, Your Grace," Jeld said with a bow.

Lira raised an eyebrow at him and led the way to Krayo's office. Inside, Krayo, Prince Dralor, Sir Benam, and Ement sat already in conversation.

Krayo waved them toward two empty chairs. "Welcome. Please, have a seat. Your Graces. Gentlemen. We've much to discuss. We need to get Your Graces out of the city. I know you're set on Delvarad, but that would not be wise. Delvarad can't stand against Naelis alone, and it's too close. Many lords to heed your call to arms would never make it in time. You must go farther, buy yourself more time. Perhaps Warrinton?"

The prince shook his head. "We fight from Delvarad. I don't intend to run away. Relthid will stand with me, and Delvarad is steadfast. If Naelis wants to camp outside its walls, we'll be fine to wait and watch while our allies descend upon him. We will rally the kingdom from there."

Krayo frowned. "And if Delvarad falls before they come? *If* they come at all. You risk too much. Delvarad is too close. If you bring the war there and it falls, the crown falls with it."

"No, it doesn't. Liraelle is going to Warrinton."

"What?" Lira exclaimed. "No, I'm going with you. How can I help rally the kingdom to war in Delvarad if I'm in Warrinton?"

"It's as Krayo says. If Delvarad doesn't hold it would mean the end. We are the crown. One of us must live. You must be kept safe."

"No," Lira said flatly. "Maybe Naelis started all this but we're here because of *you*. This is all *your* fault. I only survived your... *blunders* because Jeld saved me. Twice! The kingdom only survived this long because Benam and my father fought for some shred of decency. Don't presume to give me commands. I'm going to Delvarad."

The prince stared distantly before turning to Krayo. "We go to Delvarad. Both of us."

"*All* of us," Lira ordered, exchanging a nod with Benam.

"It's risky," Krayo said. "But… it's your risk to take. Very well. In two days, you'll take a wagon out the northwest lane of Kingsfinger Gap. Inquisitors have been spotted leading patrols around the gaps, and guardsmen from the palace have been posted alongside those at the gates to try to spot the prince, princess, or Arvin fleeing the city. Perhaps Benam as well. So, the back of a wagon will be safest. My man there will let you through."

"Your man," the prince said. "A bought watchman."

"I hope to abolish such practices in my new role. For everyone."

"Because you'll make more money that way."

"Because the crown and I will *both* make more money. Past sins. I trust you'll understand?"

The prince said nothing.

Krayo turned to Jeld. "Fendrith will drive the wagon, I've decided."

"Fen?" Jeld said. "Why?"

"With so many searching, having you drive is too risky. We need an unknown. Sammel has agreed to let Fendrith go."

Jeld nodded. It made sense, but that did little to diminish the guilt washing over him for pulling Fen further into danger, and farther from Roba.

"Jeld will secure more horses outside town. You will have papers for transporting a family and some medicines back to Plemenol, and another copy with a destination of Delvarad for when you are past Plemenol.

"Sir Benam, at Delvarad go to the Knight's Helm Inn, a day outside the Southern Gate. Tell the innkeeper Heshal that you're under my protection and he'll see you into the city and put the others up until you can secure an audience with your father."

"Knight's Helm. I know the place," Sir Benam said. "It pains me to leave when so many here are in need, but deposing Naelis is the only way to cure the disease. Anything less is merely fighting the symptoms."

"Are we in agreement?" Krayo stated more than asked.

Everyone nodded or murmured their agreement except Prince Dralor, whose eyes fell aside thoughtfully. When he looked back up, he frowned and gave the faintest nod.

"Thank you," the prince said.

"You're most welcome," Krayo answered, his eyes on Jeld.

***

The wagon canopy overhead glowed the crisp yellow of that wondrous and calm time just before the sun itself appeared to set the world into motion. It was a time when the first twinge of warmth gave hope to frozen bones after a cold night—that time when it seemed one could run faster, leap farther, climb higher. Like anything was possible. It was Jeld's favorite hour, but today he took no notice.

Beneath the glowing canopy, squeezed amidst crates of medicines and other wares, Jeld, Lira, Benam, and Prince Dralor swayed in unison with the rocking of the wagon. Jeld turned his thoughts from his painfully short reunion with the theater crew and looked over to Lira just beside him. Her eyes were distant, sorrow and fear in equal parts shimmering before her like a mirage. What comforting words might he offer her, Jeld wondered. Everything he considered seemed just as likely to drive her thoughts right back to what pained her. He reached to take her hand then thought better of it and disguised his intent by scratching his leg.

"It will be okay," he whispered finally, cursing himself an idiot for the lame attempt. Still, it seemed to pull her to the present and she managed a half smile before the woes of the present stole it away just as fast.

Jeld peered out through a tiny gap in the canopy. Fleeting glimpses of people and wagons passed by, the towering Kingsfinger Gap beyond them like a stage backdrop. The wagon turned toward it and came to a stop, Jeld flinching back as a figure in black suddenly blocked his view. He eased closer again to behold not a person but a scorched black obelisk etched with the symbol of the kingdom treasury, the towering walls of Havaral. Beyond it, laborers cleared rubble from the scorched husk of a building.

The wagon pressed on, the calls of the gate guards soon joining the bustle.

"On up, on up!"

"On through, on through!"

The wagon inched forward with each call, Jeld's heart beating faster as they grew louder. He looked about the cluttered hold, first to Benam who was frowning with calm but distant eyes. Prince Dralor sat erect, his eyes closed above a set jaw. Jeld looked to Lira next to find her staring back. He offered her a nod and she blew out a breath then nodded back.

"Is it just me, or do the rats get bigger every year, guardsman?" Fen's voice came.

An agonizing pause followed before another voice acknowledged the passphrase.

"Saw one carrying off a horse just the other day, friend."

Relief washed over Lira until suddenly the scream of a horn pierced through the market. When at last the screech ended, there was silence for the span of a breath before the city bells chimed in a frantic barrage. A heavy clang of iron rang out from above and the unmistakable ratcheting of a falling gate began it's terrible countdown.

"Mustn't be late," Fen said. "See us through, guardsman!"

"I—I can't. They'll kill me!"

"You might fare worse breaking deals with certain people!"

"I... I'm sorry. Don't let them pass! Stop them!"

The ruse over, Jeld darted out through the canopy and onto the bench beside Fen as two mounted guardsmen turned in from beyond the gap to block the way. Jeld turned toward a commotion from behind and spotted a mounted watch patrol cutting through the crowd toward them, an inquisitor at its rear.

Just as Jeld turned back, a blade jutted out through the center of the nearby watchman's chest. Prince Dralor pulled his sword free and the guardsman toppled to the ground.

"Go!" the prince roared as the mounted watchmen drew their swords and charged toward him through the falling gate.

Jeld's eyes flicked from the prince to the inquisitor closing in from behind. The wagon couldn't hope to outrun riders without more of a lead, and Dralor knew it.

"Go!" Jeld yelled to Fen, but the reins were already coming down hard. They cracked against the team and the wagon sprung forward.

Jeld grabbed a sword from beneath his feet and swung with all his strength as one of the charging guardsmen sped past the wagon. The startled guardsman flinched back just out of reach and the force of Jeld's missed blow sent him sliding off the edge of the bench. Fen's firm grip closed on Jeld's arm and yanked him back onto the bench just as the blunted edge of a huge sword beat into the passing guardsman's chest, sending him toppling from his mount.

Hanging out the back of the wagon, Sir Benam reeled his sword back in. Beyond him, the other rider closed on the prince as the wagon pulled through the gate. Dralor dashed across the rider's path and brought his sword down hard onto the face of the charging mount, sending it crashing to the ground. A gasp sounded beside Jeld and he turned to find Lira on the bench beside him, looking back through the gap to her uncle.

The prince swung his sword out before him and the mounts of the charging patrol reared to a stop.

"After the wagon!" the inquisitor spat as the gate fell.

The watchmen reined in their mounts and pressed ahead, but the prince was upon them. He toppled the nearest with a blow to the chest then dashed to the next, slashing across the forelegs of the mount and sending it crashing to the ground. As more dismounted guardsmen stalked toward him, he spun to find the inquisitor remounting beyond the gate. Dralor split the nearest watchman down one shoulder then blocked a blow from another and slashed his throat even as he turned and charged toward the gate.

The first teeth of the gate slipping into the ground, Dralor reached back his sword and with a roar flung it through the gate toward the fleeing inquisitor. The blade spun end over end from the gap, and just as the inquisitor looked back over his shoulder it slammed into him, sending him tumbling from his horse.

Jeld and his companions watched helplessly from their speeding wagon as watchmen encircled the prince, pressing inward until not a trace of him could be seen beyond the swarm of bodies, flashing of steel, and rising clouds of dust in the wagon's wake. Before the gap, the inquisitor struggled to his feet. Blood flowing freely from a long gash down one cheek, he stared out after them, the cold rage in his glare striking terror into their hearts even across the distance. Behind him, the gate of Tovar slammed to the ground.

Milton Keynes UK
Ingram Content Group UK Ltd.
UKHW012139010124
435322UK00011B/384/J